THE
CURSE-MAKER

ALSO BY KELLI STANLEY

City of Dragons

Nox Dormienda

THE
CURSE-MAKER

KELLI STANLEY

MINOTAUR BOOKS

A Thomas Dunne Book

New York

A THOMAS DUNNE BOOK FOR MINOTAUR BOOKS.
An imprint of St. Martin's Publishing Group.

THE CURSE-MAKER. Copyright © 2011 by Kelli Stanley. All rights reserved.
Printed in the United States of America. For information, address
St. Martin's Press, 175 Fifth Avenue, New York, N.Y. 10010.

www.thomasdunnebooks.com
www.minotaurbooks.com

ISBN 978-0-312-65419-1

First Edition: February 2011

10   9   8   7   6   5   4   3   2   1

For my family, and particularly for my father,
Van Stanley, who loves history and
is the original horse-whisperer.
Thanks, Dad, for teaching me about horses.

And for my mother, Patricia Geniusz Stanley,
whose loving spirit is brighter than the sun.
Thank you, Mom, for always nurturing my dreams,
and for giving me the strength to realize them.

And for Daisy, a stubborn gray donkey,
whose bray I still miss.

ACKNOWLEDGMENTS

Authors are rightly very grateful every time they get a chance to write acknowledgements. Book publishing—particularly fiction—not only requires the work and dedication of a great many people . . . it requires luck. Or, in Arcturus's adopted language, Fortuna.

The Curse-Maker would not be in your hands or on your e-reader without the support of my original publisher, Five Star, who brought out my debut novel, my first Roman noir, and thus introduced Arcturus and friends. Though a small-press book, *Nox Dormienda* was blessed with Fortuna and the good wishes of many readers, winning the Bruce Alexander Memorial Historical Mystery Award as best historical mystery of the year in 2008. I'd like to thank Marty and Roz Greenberg, John Helfers, my first editor, Gordon Aalborg, and most particularly the angel of Gale publishing, Tiffany Schofield, for all their support and belief in my work.

Much of the historical and archaeological background embedded in *The Curse-Maker* was inspired by research I conducted on the spot in Bath. My profound thanks to Susan Fox, Collections Manager for the Roman Bath Museum, who made it possible for me to get up close and personal with curses. This book would never have been born without your help!

I am personally blessed with an outstanding agent and wonderful friend in the person of Kimberley Cameron, of Kimberley Cameron and Associates. She is wise, dedicated, smart, talented, and simply one of the best people I've ever been privileged to know. This book—indeed no book—would be possible without her guidance, encouragement, and support, and she manages to keep me sane even at the most insane moments. She is, without a doubt, a true goddess.

Truly, my *kylix* runneth over. In a time of economic despair and publishing uncertainty, my fabulous, gracious, and supremely talented editor, Marcia Markland, believed in Arcturus and the story of a curse-maker. Thank you, Marcia, for your incredible, incredible strength, and support and faith in me!

The smart, savvy, and fantastic team at Thomas Dunne/Minotaur agreed to publish the continuing adventures of what started in a small press book, and I am overwhelmingly grateful to them for allowing me the opportunity to publish two series with Thomas Dunne/Minotaur. It is a privilege and an honor to work with them, and I'd like to thank Andy Martin, Thomas Dunne, Sally Richardson, Peter Wolverton, Amelie Littell, and Matt Baldacci for their support and encouragement.

I would be lost without Kat Brzozowski, Marcia's assistant editor, who is absolutely fantastic and a constant pleasure to work with. Likewise, the talented and delightful Sarah Melnyk is a publicist extraordinare, and Hector DeJean, Bridget Hartzler, and Jeanne-Marie Hudson are phenomenal. I'd also like to thank Talia Sherer and Ben Rubinstein for their superb library outreach.

Fortuna in the form of David Rotstein has graced *The Curse-Maker* with an incredible cover. David was the cover artist for *City of Dragons,* and his genius and versatility are simply breathtaking. Thank you, David, for your inspired and absolutely beautiful work! Thanks, too, to Michelle McMillian, who rendered interior text with sensitivity and skill.

I'd also like to thank my foreign rights team led by Whitney Lee, and my film management mavens (and fellow horse lovers) Mary Alice Kier and Anna Cottle at Cine/Lit. Thank you all for believing in me!

Special, special thanks to those who took time away from busy schedules to read and blurb *The Curse-Maker:* authors Rhys Bowen, Cara Black, Heather Graham, and David Liss, as well as Poisoned Pen publisher Barbara Peters. Your support and generosity humbles me.

Profound thanks to the stores and libraries that deliver my work to the hands of readers. Thank you for welcoming me with hosted signings and reading events for both series, and special thanks to the American Library Association, Public Library Association, the Independent Mystery Booksellers Association, independent mystery bookstores, and members of the American Booksellers Association for their hand-selling of my work—you made this book possible.

Thank you to Barnes and Noble for their dedication to and support of the written word and for making my books as widely available as an author could dream, and thanks, too, to the Book of the Month Club, the Mystery Guild, and senior editor and author Jane Dentiger for championing my work.

Writing is a solitary profession, but fortunately the crime fiction field is filled with friends, from the Mystery Writers of America to Private Eye Writers to International Thriller Writers to Sisters in Crime. I'm grateful to all my colleagues and friends and fellow group members for the honor and gift of their friendship.

No book is truly complete without readers. Thanks to all the reviewers and bloggers and fans and readers who kept asking if—and hoping that—Arcturus would be back! Thank you for following me down a dark Roman road and not giving up on Roman noir, and for taking a chance on a new subgenre and a new author. Thank you to our wonderful magazines like *Crimespree, Mystery Scene, Deadly Pleasures, RT Book Reviews, Mystery Readers International,* and all the amazing bloggers and reviewers who are key members of the extended crime fiction family, particularly the wonderful Jen Forbus and Becky LeJeune. Thank you to the reviewers who selected my work to read, whether in a newspaper or a magazine or for a blog. Special thanks to reader Patrick Thornton, whose incredibly generous gift helped me finish a deadline, and my devoted friend and reader MaryJane Smith.

Finally, let me thank some people in my personal life. My dear friend Sam "Kiyat" Siew enables me to keep writing and living in San Francisco, through his help, dedication, and accounting skills. Thank you, Kiyat!

My family enables me to keep the dream alive and to keep pursuing it. They are the real heroes, and it is to them I owe everything I do.

From my Polish mother, who is the most precious person on earth, to my father, the Kentucky coal miner's son . . . you've graced me with strength and values and I've tried to use them in a way that will make you proud. I love you both.

And for Tana . . . you are the one who knows how the pieces fit together. Thank you for keeping the key.

AUTHOR'S NOTE

How Greco-Roman cursing actually worked is still a matter of debate. No one is really sure; and curses and the kinds of curses that were the most popular varied from place to place.

With *The Curse-Maker,* I've given you as sound a reconstruction as I can, from how and why people used curses, how they may have been made, and the circumstances under which they could have been abused. The system I suggest is based on extensive research I conducted as a Classics scholar and author.

Aquae Sulis—today's Bath—was the inspiration for the book, and if you travel there, you can still see glorious Roman baths and the magic water, the Sacred Spring and the pipe where Calpurnius met his end.

As you walk through the museum, notice the glass cases. They display objects recovered from the Sacred Spring, all gifts to Sulis. You'll find a strange tin mask and a bag of gemstones, both discovered in excavations, and both still mysteries as to how and why they were dedicated . . . until now.

My goal as a writer is not only to thrill and entertain you, but to immerse you in an environment—one you can smell, hear, taste, and experience along with the characters. You'll find much to explore on my Web site at www.kellistanley.com, along with information and multimedia on the Miranda Corbie series, which began with *City of Dragons* and is set in 1940 San Francisco.

I hope you will enjoy a trip to Roman Bath and the world of Roman noir, and I would love to hear from you. It's a crowded field out there, and Arcturus and I both appreciate your support.

Thanks for reading!

DRAMATIS PERSONAE IN AQUAE SULIS

Rufus Bibax: a dead curse-writer

Sextus Papirius Super: head priest of the Temple to Sulis
Flavia: his wife

Lucius Valerius Philo: leading *medicus* in Aquae Sulis

Big Belly, a.k.a. Quintus Pompeius: a councilman
Crescentia: his wife

Spurius Octavio: *abalneator*, or bathmaster
Prunella: his wife

Julius Vitellius Scaevola: a fop
Sulpicia: a widow with a reputation

Drusius: a young stonecutter

Tiberius Natta: a *gemmarius*
Buteo: his apprentice

Grattius Tribax: *duovir* of Aquae Sulis
Vibia: his wife

Gaius Secundus: horsey *duovir* of Aquae Sulis
Materna: his wife
Secunda: his daughter

Faro Magnus: a necromancer

Marcus Mumius Modestus: a soldier

Calpurnius: a low-grade priest and drain cleaner

Senicio: another low-grade priest and drain cleaner

Aulus Marcius Memor: an ancient *haruspex*

Titus Ulpius Sestius: a wastrel
Hortensia: a farmer's daughter

Lineus: head of the household slaves at Agricola's villa

Crassa: an elderly, wealthy woman

GLOSSARY

aconitum: highly poisonous flowering plant used as a medicine, particularly in eye crèmes; also known as wolfsbane, and a common poison in Roman lore

Aesculapius: Roman version of the Greek god of healing (Asklepios)

animus: a word with profound meaning to the Romans: mind, will, character, force, spirit; the essential element of being

apodyterium: changing room at the public baths . . . where notes were left, clothes and possessions were stolen, and assignations made

as/asses: bronze coin and basic unit of the Roman monetary system for everyday transactions . . . and virtually the only coin the poorer classes would commonly see

auctoritas: a supremely important concept within the culture and difficult to define; more than authority, more than importance, *auctoritas* implied leadership, strength and trustworthiness, as well as another prized Roman characteristic: *gravitas* (significance or seriousness)

aureus/aureii: Roman gold coin at the top of the monetary hierarchy, worth approximately four hundred *asses,* one hundred *sestertii,* and twenty-five *denarii,* and—like silver *denarii*—minted based on bullion weight *balneator:* manager of the public bath—a position of great importance in a spa town

caldarium: the hot, heated pool in a Roman bath

Caledonii: Northern British tribe of Celtic origins; defeated at the battle of Mons Graupius by Agricola

canis: a canine—as in *"cave canem,"* beware of the dog

Cloaca Maxima: the largest sewer in Rome

contubernium: group of eight soldiers who shared a tent (while on campaign) or barracks quarters

cui bono: phrase popularized by Marcus Tullius Cicero (lawyer, orator, consul, and political figure of the Late Republic) which means "who profits?"—an excellent question to ask after a murder

defixio/defixiones derived from a verb meaning to tie down, bind, or fasten, *defixio* was the Latin word for a curse tablet

denarius/denarii: silver coin worth four brass *sestertii* and minted by bullion weight like the gold *aureus*

depilator: bath worker with the unfortunate job of plucking body hair; hairy bodies were considered uncouth

deus ex machina: a theatrical contraption used to suddenly lower an actor playing a god onto the stage; a sudden and improbable resolution, with the ends too neatly tied

dominus/domina: master/mistress, typical address of respect by a slave to his owner

duovir/duoviri: one of two head councilmen who sometimes managed the affairs of a *municipium*

Endovelicus: a native god of fertility and healing within the Roman province of Hispania

fibula/fibulae: large Roman safety pin, used to close cloaks and other items of clothing

Fortuna: the notoriously fickle goddess of luck

formula/formulae: a spell, incantation, or other set of ritual words used in magic or curse-making

forum: marketplace and beating heart of an ancient city—where politics, business, meetings, legal transactions, and much of daily life transpired

frigidarium: cold pool in a Roman bath

garum: a very popular condiment and spice used in many Roman dishes, made from liquefied fish guts; similar to anchovy sauce, and definitely an acquired taste

gladius: short, two-edged Roman sword

gemmarius: a jeweler, particularly a gem cutter

haruspex: a man who practiced the art of Etruscan divination by reading the livers of sacrificed animals—usually sheep

iactus: a game of throwing dice, derived from the Latin verb meaning to throw or toss

Ides: fifteenth of the month in March, May, July, or October, and the thirteenth of the month during the rest of the year—Julius Caesar did not heed the warning to "beware the Ides of March"

insula/insulae: an apartment building usually located in the middle of the block; derived from the Latin word meaning "island"

Kalends: the first day of the month

kylix: shallow Greek drinking cup with handles

lacerna: an outer cloak worn by a man, sometimes with a hood, and fastened on the right shoulder

medicus: doctor—not always intended as a compliment

municipium: in Roman Britain, was more of a ceremonial title awarding a town the status in between that of a *colonia* (usually settled by retired legionaries) and a *civitas capital* (city independently managed by the local tribe of the area); a *municipium* could enjoy some independence from Rome and was granted the right to a local government

Nones: seventh of the month in March, May, July, and October; fifth of the month in the rest of the calendar year

ordo: local town council in a *municipium*

palaestra: exercise room in the public bath where you were expected to work up a sweat

palla: a large outer wrap or mantle worn by respectable Roman women, rectangular in shape, and reaching at least to the calf

posca: diluted vinegar and herbs: the cheapest sort of alcohol

rufus: an apt name for a redhead

salve/salvete: singular and plural forms of the common Roman greeting; literally means "Be well!"

sesterius/sestertii: brass coin below the silver *denarius,* which was worth four times as much; one hundred equaled an *aureus*

stola: a somewhat dated fashion choice by the late first century CE, only Roman matrons could wear this feminine version of the toga, which featured a plunging neckline, was belted below the breast, and was worn over a tunic

strychnos: a hallucinogenic drug derived from deadly nightshade— better known as belladonna

thermae: the public baths

triclinium: the dining room

tunica: an undergarment worn by both men and women; often the only clothing of the poor

Ultor: the Avenger

veritas: the truth; "*in vino, veritas*"

vigiles: the fire/watch/police force of Rome—singular term is *vigil*

vino: wine, the gift of Bacchus

THE
CURSE-MAKER

CHAPTER ONE

The man was floating, serene, tunic swirling in the undulating waves like clouds against a blue sky. His mouth was open. He was dead.

I looked back toward Gwyna. She was kneeling in the saddle like a circus acrobat, struggling to see what was going on. At least she seemed focused. Not the aimless woman, the lost wife I'd brought here, hoping to find the woman I loved.

Voices rose from the crowd, agitated.

"Pollution! In our town! The council must—"

"Why doesn't someone do something? Where's Papirius?"

"How dare he do this to the goddess? To us?"

They shoved forward, scrambling for a closer look, taking me with them. Another voice, calmer than the rest.

"Can someone help me pull him up?"

The crowd was stiff with excitement, and I pushed my way through. I was stiff, and not so excited, but I was there, even if it was early in the morning after a long trip, and I was just trying to get some goddamn directions.

The reservoir was seven, maybe eight feet deep, filled from the famous Sacred Spring of the famous goddess Sulis. From the look of the pipes, it dispersed the famous hot water to the famous baths, just to the south. Everything in Aquae Sulis was famous.

Female faces were lining the three windows of the main bath building, staring down with horrified pleasure. The corpse bobbed against the wall, mouth still open, looking just as shocked. He danced and waved, making a low, slushing thud, held upright by a hemp rope secured under his arms and tied to a balustrade. I could see what the heat and the water had already done to his skin.

A young man with arms like Hercules was trying to unwind the rope and haul up the body. I grabbed the end of the rope.

"Go ahead and try it. I'll anchor."

He eyed me up and down with doubt. I planted my feet, and maybe something about my jaw made him start to unwind the damn rope. The mob stepped back half a foot.

Every time he pulled, I took up the slack. The dead man himself couldn't weigh too much—he was on the small side—but the water made him heavy. The sun peeked over the golden limestone of the buildings, throwing a lurid yellow light on the water.

The corpse was near the top of the reservoir, and I grabbed enough rope to get it right on the balustrade.

"Move, damn you! Give him some room!"

The crowd inched backward while the body spread out, halfway on the pavement. Magic water dripped, making small magic rivers on the smooth pavement stone. I elbowed through a fat man with a wig and a slack-jawed servant girl, joining the young man with the big arms.

Now we had to touch him, and hope his skin wouldn't flake off like cooked fish. Together we dragged him fully on the pavement, nearly intact. The herd hushed for a moment, making the squelches and squeaks of the corpse all the more audible.

Three men pushed toward the front, gawkers parting with a rustle. They all looked the same: neat, tidy, proper provincial business- and councilmen, togas too big and minds too small. A fat one in the middle seemed to be the leader.

"Yes—thank you, Drusius, thank you. How—how unfortunate." One of the others cleared his throat, staring down with eyes as watery as the corpse.

The big one continued. "Don't, er, touch him here, please. Philo is coming. Philo will, er, take it—take him—away."

I stood up straighter, surreptitiously massaging my sore hip. "I don't know who or what Philo is, but this man needs to be looked at now. And here."

A titter or two. A couple of gasps. The three glanced at each other. The one with the fish eyes was older than the rest and looked to the fat one for guidance. The middle one blended in with the pale yellow rock.

Big Belly puffed like a peacock. "Lucius Valerius Philo is the most respected *medicus* in Aquae Sulis—and a member of the council. Who are you?"

I was tired. Saddle weary. Provincial towns always make me itch, even if everything is famous and the waters can raise the dead.

"I don't give a damn if he's the doctor for Domitian's prick. I'm a *medicus,* and I'm examining this man. Now."

A murmur ran through the crowd. The rope was too wet to lynch me with, and besides—no one ever wanted to touch a dead body. Hercules—or Drusius—took a step near me. There was support in the stance. And respect.

I knelt down. The dead man was about my age, maybe a little older, thirty-five to forty. Short, fairly muscular, but getting soft even before the water. Arms and face tan, but his legs never saw the light of day. They were dotted with freckles, like some kind of exotic mushroom.

The gown was cheap linen, white when Homer was young. Imitation Egyptian that might impress old ladies who liked exotic Eastern cults, if they were half-blind and wholly gullible. Bathing sandals were still on his feet. The crowd was getting closer again. I could almost feel Big Belly breathing on me.

"Give him some room!"

Drusius was answered with a low, throaty chuckle. Not from Big Belly. Feminine. Very feminine. The crowd made room for the woman who made it. I looked up.

Riding hard on forty, red-haired, and everything she shouldn't be, but what most men would want her to be. The kind of woman who always made her own way, in life or out of bed. She reminded me of Dionysia, my youthful indiscretion.

"Well, well, Drusius. It is Drusius, isn't it? I've seen you hauling stone for your father, I believe. For dedications." She peered down at the corpse and suddenly knelt next to me, a puff of sandalwood drifting up from underneath her dress.

"I promise I won't crowd the doctor," she whispered.

A loud squawk erupted from the back of the growing mob. Big Belly and Fish Eye were whispering to each other, and finally another voice—thin, whining, male—reached the front line, audible over the rustle of sweaty bodies and hushed conversation.

"Sulpicia? Sulpicia? Ah—there you are. What—what the hell is that?"

I didn't bother to answer or look up. I'd continued, letting Sulpicia and her pet idiot distract the onlookers for me. The man had been dead anywhere from eight to twelve hours. There wasn't much water in his mouth or lungs, and the red, engorged face and the two thumb-sized bruises by his windpipe confirmed he hadn't drowned in seven feet of water.

Something glinted from the open mouth, and I noticed his cheeks were bulging. I reached in and pinched with two fingers, drawing it out while everyone looked at Sulpicia and pictured her naked. Her boyfriend suddenly realized there was a corpse dripping water on his toga hem and yelped.

"That's—isn't that the curse-writer, the scribe—"

"Rufus Bibax."

I looked at the corpse again and noticed a faint tinge of red in his hair. Not much of a *rufus*. I stood up. The voice that identified him expressed authority. I wanted to see who it belonged to.

Standing next to a coiffed Roman in a gaudy toga was a middle-aged bald man. His expensively plain tunic was made louder by a heavy gold necklace. Priest was written all over him. Big Belly and the other two crowded close, giving me baleful looks when they weren't staring at Sulpicia's nipples.

The priest plastered a tight smile on his face. "I am Sextus Papirius Super. Head priest of the Temple of Sulis Minerva. I understand you're a doctor."

I stared at him. "Julius Alpinius Classicianus Favonianus. I'm the governor's doctor, as a matter of fact."

The murmur spread, growing progressively louder, until it broke against the edges of the crowd like a ripple on the water. He raised an eyebrow. "It's very good of you to, er, help us with this unfortunate—incident. As this is holy ground—"

"Not any more, it ain't!" Rough voice, croaking from the back. Laughter. The priest continued, his color rising. "As this is holy ground, we will have to remove the body at once and clean the spring."

A tall man was making his way to the front. Almost exactly my height, handsome, distinguished. Maybe fifteen years older. The throng made way for him, some grabbing at him as though he were the featured gladiator. He exuded warmth and charisma. I didn't like him.

He stepped forward, glanced at the priest. Papirius nodded his head in my direction. "The governor's *medicus,* Philo. Julius Alpinius Classicianus Favonianus."

His strong, lean faced creased with what looked like a genuine smile of welcome. "Favonianus. Of course, I've heard of you. You're also known as Arcturus, I believe. We're very lucky you're here." He reached out and grasped my arm. "Philo—one of the many doctors in Aquae Sulis."

Modest, too. Big Belly grumbled, "We asked him to wait for you, Lucius."

Philo shook his head, the gray in his temples glistening in the sun. "You have a much better doctor here."

"Are you here on business, Favonianus?" The priest asked it as if there wasn't a corpse between us.

"Actually, no. A holiday for my wife and me."

I felt Sulpicia raise her eyebrows.

"Well, then perhaps you wouldn't mind if Philo . . ."

I looked at the dapper doctor. He seemed competent enough, if a little disgusting in his perfection. I shrugged. "Be my guest."

The young stonecutter—Drusius—stared at me, his thick eyebrows furrowed. What the hell did he want me to do? Fight over the dead body of Rufus Bibax? I'd been asked very politely to mind my own goddamn business, and I intended to do just that.

Philo smiled apologetically. "Please come by and see me. We'll talk. Where are you staying?"

"The governor's villa."

The murmur went around again. I didn't want to spoil it by asking where the hell the villa might be.

Papirius crooked a finger at two slaves, who ran up with a litter chair for the corpse, then started making priestly noises. "Please disperse, good people. The spring shall be emptied. Sulis will renew life, just as she has seen fit to take this one. Sulis will—"

I was heading out of the mob, and eyes—some friendly, some not, all curious—were following me. I turned around. "Sulis had nothing to do with it."

Papirius and Philo looked at me, the priest irritated, the doctor curious.

"What did you say?" asked Papirius.

"I said Sulis had nothing to do with it. That man was strangled and thrown in your pool. Murdered—and the murderer left behind a little note."

I held out my hand. In the palm was a small piece of lead, very thinly hammered and square cut. On it was inscribed one word: *Ultor.* The Avenger.

. . .

Gwyna looked disappointed, which dumbfounded me. I'd done what I thought would please her—avoided getting involved. I'd even avoided Sulpicia, which was no easy task because she kept getting in my way. I climbed back on Nimbus, looking around at the small-pored golden limestone of the buildings. It reminded me of Gwyna's hair, and was safer to look at than she was.

The wealthy owned long, low villas close to the temple and baths, or in the hills above, to the northwest of the town nearer the small fort. Somewhere among them was Agricola's. Gwyna asked me: "Did you find out where the villa is?"

I turned red and she gave me a pitying look. Another market square up ahead. I nudged Nimbus, who obligingly trotted forward—the one female in the family who tolerated me—and dismounted at the nearest shop, a *gemmarius* around the corner from the oversized temple area.

A tattered sign boasted that Tiberius Natta offered an assortment of carved gemstones, set and unset. He was a swarthy man with gray hair, short and stocky. Used a cane, though he couldn't have been sixty yet. An assistant, another dark man in his late thirties, came forward to answer my question.

Seems Agricola's villa was right up the street, on a little hill overlooking the temple area. I thanked them, and told Gwyna while I climbed back on Nimbus.

She nodded, avoiding my eyes. Once we could see the villa from the road, I pointed it out, and we started the climb up the path to where it perched, low and inviting, with a superb view of the temple and the river. The silence was broken by the morning song of birds and the sound of the horses' hooves stepping on the fragile rock.

We rounded a corner, and the house was in front of us. Large, with a detached stable, private bath, and a small attempt at a vineyard. The terraced gardens were full of lavender, Gwyna's favorite scent.

Suddenly, she asked: "Why didn't you stay?"

I must have looked as stupid as I felt, because she said it again.

"Why didn't you stay?"

"I don't understand. Stay where?"

"At the pool. Why didn't you stay with the body? Why did you let those other men take it away?"

I dismounted and came around and offered a hand, which she ignored, springing lightly to the ground herself.

"Gwyna, we're here to relax. And to take care of you, and—and to fix things. Why the hell should I have insisted?"

She stared at me, holding Pluto's reins as he tried to get a bite of hollyhock while Nimbus gave him a withering look.

"Because it was the right thing to do. It happened for a reason, that we came into town and you were there when that poor man was discovered. Besides, I don't need anybody to 'take care of me.'"

She flounced ahead, jerking Pluto's nose away from the flowers.

The slaves were the best kind: invisible, accommodating, unquestioning. Everything was ready for an extended holiday for the newlyweds. Except the newlyweds themselves.

Gwyna busied herself with the servants, a vast improvement from the apathy of home. I watched her moving around in her riding breeches, until she got tired of me blocking the way and ordered me into the *triclinium*. The cook served a delicious lunch of sheep's milk cheese—much creamier than we get in Londinium—figs, olives, and snails cooked in garlic.

Gwyna didn't eat, though she came in to make sure the wine was poured correctly. She said: "Why don't you bathe, Arcturus? You touched a dead man, didn't you?"

Clipped and chilly. I headed for the villa's bath and the warmth of Agricola's *caldarium*.

After a good rubdown by a strapping Pannonian named Ligur, I started to relax in spite of myself. Ligur was shaving me when Gwyna walked in. She saw me, stopped, turned to leave.

"Wait—what—where are you going?"

The shrug was elaborate. "Your face needs a shave. I see you're already taken care of."

She was dressed in a modest bathing tunic, different from the more revealing breast band and short skirt she normally wore, and left before I could say anything else. I wondered again what happened to the woman I married less than a year before.

I dressed for dinner. I could hear her in the *caldarium* and imagined the slave girl massaging her with oil. That should be my job.

Thinking about it meant either another trip to the *frigidarium* or a brisk walk, so I left for the garden, where I could breathe again. A breeze from the hills carried the sweet scent of roses, mixed with lavender, and ruffled my hair.

The governor's villa in Aquae Sulis. A goddamn beautiful spot to be miserable in.

CHAPTER TWO

The roses and the hollyhocks laughed, their petals shaking in the wind. She was right, of course. Normally I would've stayed with the murdered man, drawn by that gnawing hunger to know, the same feeling that used to earn me a few *sestertii* before I became old and complacent and the governor's *medicus*.

Goddamn hands. They got me in the goddamn business. What happened to the other doctor, the younger man who fought his own goddamn fights, who made his own goddamn way, who could, on occasion, discover the goddamn truth.

I leaned against a pear tree, staring out over the hazy yellow town, the past nine months washing over me like that foul, churning water from the not-so-Sacred Spring.

My eyes closed. Goddamn it. Thirty-four years old. I was thirty-four years old. I wasn't going to give up yet.

Nones of September. Agricola's finest hour. Last hour for thousands of *Caledonii*.

He conquered the island. Slaughtered the last army. Had gone farther than anyone ever expected—far enough to secure his fame and yet not far enough, maybe, to push the emperor to outright assassination. A delicate dance, with all the precision of a sacrifice.

A light flickered by the governor's quarters, officers darting in and out. Agricola was moving the men out this morning, heading south to establish forts. He'd work his way slowly to Londinium, where he'd wait for the inevitable order from Domitian to return to Rome. Term complete.

I squinted at the small hill squatting peacefully on the plain. I thought of the men with families, the women and children, loaded into carts and crawling like ants on the surface. Three days ago.

Their horses got tangled up in the wagon leads, the cavalry hunting down the ones who fled. Painted warriors, scars and tattoos proud on their bodies, long swords and short shields useless and clumsy, running, shouting into the path of trained soldiers. All gone, dead. Last wild men of Britannia.

I closed my eyes. I could still hear the cries of the children when the survivors killed them afterward. Better dead than slaves, they thought. For the love of their children, they murdered them. For the love of his son, Agricola slaughtered the Caledonians.

May.

I'd done everything I could to save his son, everything I'd ever learned, or felt, or knew, or guessed. Not enough.

What about the tonic? Just to make him sleep—sleep was his only chance. Too much? A little saffron, enough to make him drowsy. As drowsy as I was. Up for three days straight, tried everything else. The little boy weaker and weaker, restless, unable to sleep. He'd die without sleep. I gave him the right amount. As soon as the crying stopped, and I heard his breath, even, peaceful, I got what rest I could, so I'd be ready for when he woke up.

Except he never woke up.

Domitia's eyes, accusing, wild, asking the question, the same question I asked myself, over and over, every night. Could I have saved him if I'd been awake? My lullaby, my prayer, my reason. My excuse. Every night.

She screamed at me, beat my chest, called me a quack, a charlatan, broke down and locked herself in her room. Stayed there until the ship came.

Cleaner than the dazed look on her husband's face. Not a word against me. No questions. Focused on his strategy. Left for the North the next week. His household—his namesake and heir, the boy he'd wanted all his life—gone. Nothing to lose.

He never blamed me. He channeled his energy into his last, supreme battle as governor, his final chance for glory. Glory didn't die.

I watched the dawn shine over the plain. Four months of guilt? More like a lifetime.

It had gnawed my insides since I was ten. I thought I rid myself of it when I found Gywna. Thought I'd forgiven myself for not saving my mother. At the first real crisis, the first tragedy, I left my wife. Left her emotionally. Quit writing. Quit thinking. I withdrew from the woman I loved. My beautiful, oh, so beautiful wife. Gwyna.

I rode north with Agricola, sent a few pitiful scrawls with the governor's messenger. Her responses were full of hurt. She didn't know what the hell happened to me, what was devouring my gut every night, wanting to help and not knowing how. I didn't tell her, either—I ignored her, punishing both of us for my failure.

Her responses became spare and lean. Finally stopped altogether. I withdrew into my nightmares, familiar, safe. Watched my mother get murdered every night. I dreamed about Gwyna, too—dying in childbirth, while I stood by, unable to save her.

Bilicho kept writing, thank God. He did what he could to keep some part of me from drifting too far off the edges of the maps. I was already at the edge of them all, staring at a plain littered with corpses. I thought about my mother, and what she would have wanted. What she would have said.

She told me something that September morning, a whispered southern wind blowing clouds across the bloody sky. Forgive yourself, Arcturus. For not being able to save every life you come across. For not being able to save the child. For being alive.

Simple words. I took a breath and filled my lungs. I was done with war. As much as I was done with the guilt. Finished with stitching up butchered men who'd butchered other men who couldn't be stitched up. It was time for both of us, governor and doctor, to see what else Fortuna had in store.

Light was flooding the hills, and a fresh gust of wind blew down from the west.

I could hear Saturninus before I reached the tent. A loud roar rose from the governor's quarters, and the heavy cloth shook with the sound. The flap belched open like a fat man's mouth in a seaside bar. The tent fought to steady itself.

"Arcturus! Glad to see you're still among the living!"

Saturninus's expansive slap on my back rattled my teeth.

"I'll be feeling that welcome all the way back to Londinium."

His white teeth gleamed beneath the bushy black beard. Sometimes I thought Saturninus was part bear. Sometimes I thought he was a bear.

"You should be happy to get back home." The elbow in my ribs emphasized what he meant. He recognized the look on my face. "What's wrong? Trouble?"

"Nothing serious. I just need to get home."

"Is your wife—"

"She's fine."

He stared at me, chewing his mustache. Respectful, but with the acknowledgment that I wasn't fully Roman.

"Have all the scouts returned?"

He nodded. "No enemy movement anywhere. Everything's nice and quiet. The general's giving orders to the fleet to sail all the way around Britannia."

"How is the general?"

"He's all right, Arcturus. Knows he's on the way out. Hell, we thought he was out last winter, and he might have been, if it hadn't been for you. He hasn't forgotten."

"Neither have I."

He knew what I meant and reached a paw out to pat my shoulder. "He's in there now, with that scribe takin' down everything about the battle. It's for his son-in-law, Tacitus, fancies himself a historian."

I didn't much fancy Tacitus. Always creeping around, perpetual gloom hanging over his stooped shoulders like an undertaker at the Colosseum gates. I couldn't help it if his wife tried to seduce me.

"The Battle of Mons Graupius. Not much of a mountain."

"But a hell of a battle. Memorably fought on the day of Jupiter Stator, the *Nones* of September—"

"You mean the *Nones* of Germanicus, don't you?"

Saturninus's snort would have done credit to a three-ton bull. "That little jerk-off Domitian wouldn't know what to do with a German if one pulled off his baby pants and tugged on his—"

"Arcturus!"

It was Agricola, calling me inside, but too late to prevent Saturninus from announcing to all and sundry what a German would find upon pulling down Domitian's underwear. Someday that mouth of his would get him in serious trouble.

Soldiers scurried about with various orders. A small man with a pointed chin that matched his stylus was taking down notes in a minuscule hand. Whenever Agricola grunted, he hurriedly scrawled away. He looked like he'd be a friend of Tacitus.

"There you are. Where have you been keeping yourself?"

"Sorry to keep you waiting, sir. Saturninus was filling me in."

"On what, I wonder? So long as he wasn't filling you up."

The scribe scribbled furiously over that one.

"The scouts, the fleet. Your memorialization."

I nodded at the scribe, who was still gazing at Agricola with the ardor of a bitch in heat.

The general glanced down. "Oh, yes. My son-in-law."

When the brown eyes met mine, they were softer. "We're building a large fort south of here—by that river we passed, with the grazing land. Haven't named it yet. It will have a good-sized hospital, Arcturus."

The tent flap opened with an abrupt slap, and in walked a man I wished I could kick in the face. He was striding toward Agricola and stopped when he saw me. The governor raised his eyebrows and, after glancing my way, turned to Quatio.

"What is it? Aren't the horses ready?"

Gnaeus Quatio was a bully, a braggart, and an all-around asshole. He'd crawled into favor with the governor because he risked his life to bring back the body of Aulus Atticus, a young idiot who ignored orders, lashed his horse, and rode straight into the enemy spears.

"All except one, your governorship. A gray mare has gone missing, and that thick-skulled British idiot of a hostler won't tell me where she is." He fingered a leather crop in his hand. "Not even after he tasted this."

I was going to owe Ranor more than the *denarius* I'd slipped him. I took a step toward Quatio.

"You still beating up Brits as a pastime, Quatio? They're on your side, or are you too 'thick-skulled' to remember it?"

His face got even uglier—a trick I hadn't thought possible—and his fingers grasped the bully stick as if it were my throat. "Mind your own business—*medicus*. I'm here to see the governor."

Agricola interjected. "You are seeing him, Quatio. Find the other horse. Bring the hostler to me, if necessary."

I cleared my throat. "That won't be necessary, Governor."

Agricola turned to me, his eyes narrowed. He didn't like surprises. "What do you mean?"

"The gray mare he's talking about is Nimbus. My horse. I have her by the south gate."

Quatio looked happier than I'd ever seen him. "Deserting, are you, like the rest of those mutinous—"

"Enough!" Agricola seldom needed to raise his voice. The scribe crouched with his mouth agape, and the other officers and men stared at us, afraid to move.

"Leave us, Quatio." The general said it without taking his eyes off my face. I stared back at him. First time in months I was able to.

Quatio turned bright red. He mumbled as he headed out the tent, the words "son" and "killer" reaching our ears.

"*Quatio!*"

Jove hurling a thunderbolt. My hair stood on end.

"Come here. Now."

Quatio crawled back to the governor, his dark head hung low. Even his whip shrank.

"You're demoted. Return to your *contubernium* and send me the next officer. If you can't hold your tongue, and repeat idle gossip—especially in my presence!—you're not worthy of command."

Quatio backed his way toward the exit, in a gratifying, crablike shuffle. The scribe was still slack-jawed, drool starting to form at the corner of his mouth. When the flap finally closed with a thwack on Quatio's face, I realized I was a little slack-jawed, too.

Agricola glanced toward the scribe. "Write it down! That's part of being a general." Then he turned to me. "Come, Arcturus. Let's go outside."

We surveyed the busy camp, the men removing the pickets and temporary fortifications in the distance. He stood with his hands on his hips and took a deep breath.

"Nice country." He said it conversationally. He never liked goodbyes.

I agreed. "Beautiful."

He looked at me sideways. "Trouble at home?"

I shook my head, wondering how much to tell him. The man—my patron, my friend—carried too many burdens already.

"Some. Mostly with me."

He pulled on his lower lip, turned back toward the view, and waited.

I ventured a question. "How are your wounds?"

He'd taken some superficial cuts early in the battle. They were healing well, beyond the point of worry. Or I wouldn't be able to go.

"Keeping them clean, as you always tell me. The mallow poultice helped."

"Good. Governor—Agricola—I—"

He turned to me suddenly. I was surprised to see the moisture in his eyes. "Don't say anything, Arcturus."

He cleared his throat and faced the camp again. "I would, of course, like you to come to Rome with me. If half of what I hear about Domitian is true, I'll need someone who can prepare a good antidote."

It was my turn to react. "Do you really think—"

"No, no. I'll be fine. I think I've reached a good middle point. Too popular to kill, not popular enough to damn the popularity."

He eyed me again. "Avitus has been watching Lucullus. I don't think he'll replace me as governor." He reached out a gnarled hand and gently, for an old soldier, laid it on my shoulder. "Thanks to you."

I shook my head. This was harder than I expected. "General, if you need me—"

"Then I will call you. Have no doubt about that."

He let his hand drop easily to his side, and pointed over the hills. "This is the farthest north any Roman or Greek has gone, Arcturus. I've achieved what I wanted. I'll die a happy man, all in all."

I caught the catch in his voice. He kept his focus on the landscape.

"I expect I'll have a grandson soon, and there'll be plenty to do in Rome."

He turned to me again.

"My friend, it's time for you to get on with your life. I knew I couldn't keep you forever. I knew the army couldn't, either. You feel things too much, Arcturus, it's the native in you. I'm thankful for the years . . . you've saved me, my work, too many times to count."

I looked down at the strong, scarred hand that grasped my arm, and I took it in my own hand and brought it to my lips.

He cleared his throat again and put his hands behind his back. "So I want you to take your wife to Aquae Sulis."

That shocked me out of sentiment. "What? Why? Aquae Sulis is a—"

"Beautiful resort town, with some excellent healing baths. I purchased a small villa there, back when I took Domitia every winter. I'm sending word ahead that you're to make yourself at home for as long as you like."

For as many years as I'd known the governor, he'd taken his wife to spas and resorts, small villages with any medical or even magical repute, hoping she'd become pregnant with a boy. Finally, after Gnaeus was born, they'd stayed in Londinium for the winter. I'd forgotten he credited Aquae Sulis with the conception.

He stared straight ahead. "She's young, Arcturus. Go make some sons with her."

I swallowed hard. "And you—"

He chuckled. "I'll take my time coming back to Londinium, and take my time composing the perfect report to Domitian. He'll probably recall me sometime in midwinter, hoping my ship will capsize and spare him the annoyance of having to deal with me. You'll beat me home, no doubt. Just pick up your wife, settle your house, and go straight on to Aquae Sulis."

"But what if—"

He turned to look at me, and this time grabbed me by both shoulders, hard.

"No what-ifs. If I need you from Rome, I will get word to you. You've got a family now. As I'm still governor, consider this an order. Go to Aquae Sulis. Take some time to take care of yourself and what you have. We don't know who the emperor will be sending to this little green isle, but whoever it is, it won't be easy for you. So please—do as I say."

I stared into the wrinkled face. The eyes were human again but would soon go back to metal. They had to. Pain makes us more mortal, even with scars of iron.

Sometimes speech is the most awkward form of communication. I embraced him like a father. Then I turned toward the south, and never once looked back.

CHAPTER THREE

Ninth hour of day, and Londinium. Home.

I took Nimbus to the stables and thanked her for the ten-day journey, patting her down myself. She gave me a stern look, tucking her nose under my arm before shoving me with her head. She knew how scared I was.

The door was imposing. I took a deep breath, put in the key. Half expected Brutius to come running and fling it open. No one heard me.

A chill ran up my arm and down my neck. It was quiet, too quiet, with a thick layer of dust on the hall floor. I threw open the door to my examination room. Nothing disturbed, but again, dust.

I backed out, walking straight into the *triclinium*. Gwyna should be sitting in front of a brazier, knitting or carding wool or something, Hefin should be quietly reading Greek, and one of the dogs should be lying at their feet.

No one was there. My breath was coming fast and shallow. What about the slaves—Coir was supposed to be cleaning the house, Brutius minding the animals, Venutius cooking, and Draco standing near by, looking strong. Where the hell was everyone?

I sniffed, and caught a whiff of sauce. Venutius. I rounded the corner of the *triclinium* into the kitchen and ran smack into my cook.

He somehow managed to perform a leap and a twist in midair, which prevented the honeyed coriander sauce from spilling on the floor. He set it down carefully on the counter and allowed himself a gracious smile in my direction.

"Welcome home, *Dominus*. Dinner will be served in approximately fifteen minutes."

"Where is everyone? Where's my wife? Hefin? The other servants?"

A guarded look crept into Venutius's aristocratic face. "The mistress—I'm not sure. I expect in her bedroom. Her brother—the young master—is with *Dominus* Bilicho."

"Bilicho? Why? And why is Gwyna in her room? She's not ill—"

He shook his head. "No—no, I don't think so."

I grabbed Venutius by the shoulder, and he gave me a distasteful look.

"What do you mean you don't think so? What's wrong with her?"

He lowered his head. "I don't like to speculate, sir. For the last six weeks, she hasn't taken supper in the dining room. She won't direct the servants and has stopped telling me what to buy. Master Bilicho came over, saw the state of things, and took the little boy back with him. His woman has come by to check on the mistress. I usually see her in the morning, and if I don't, I leave the food out. Sometimes I find her in the middle of the night, in the bath chambers, or roaming the house."

My mouth was dry, and I needed to sit down. "Anything else I should know, Venutius?"

He thought for a moment, considering.

"Yes, there is, *Dominus*. Brutius has been staying outside with the animals most of the day and night, because of Coir. She's impossible, sir. Since the mistress started to—since she stopped giving orders, Coir has refused to clean the house, or do any work at all. Draco is very unhappy—he's lost weight. She seems to have him and everybody else—even the mistress, if you pardon me, sir—under her thumb. I've kept up the food accounts, and make meals at the regular times, whether

I'm told to or no. But not her, sir. That's why the house is in the state it's in."

The edge of the kitchen counter steadied me. My legs were too strong to buckle, but I felt like I was going to vomit. Venutius put down the sauce and poured me some wine.

I threw it down my throat. The ripe red taste of the Tuscan flushed some color back into my cheeks.

"Where is she?"

"The mistress? Most likely—"

"No. Coir. I want this dealt with before I see my wife."

"I believe she's out, sir, with Draco. Perhaps at the baths." He took a step backward from the look on my face.

"Are they usually home when you serve a meal?"

"For the evening meal, yes, *Dominus*."

"Very well. I'll wait."

Venutius nodded and went back to his duties as if everything were normal. I pulled myself together from the pieces lying about on the floor and walked outside into the courtyard. The kitchen and herb gardens were tended, the well covered, even the altar dusted off. I figured I'd find Brutius sleeping in the kennel.

Pyxis heard my approach before she smelled me, and came out of the little building with the hair on her neck standing up, growling.

I murmured: "Not you, too."

She sniffed and wagged, and three large dogs ran up the front of their fenced yard, barking like Cerberus with a headache. The puppies were grown up. A bushy-haired man crept out, squinted in my direction, and suddenly grinned. He ran up with a sidewise gait and grabbed the top of the fence in excitement.

"*Dominus!* You're home!"

"You've been sleeping with the dogs, Brutius?"

He turned his head away, looking down. "Coir's bad, sir," he said flatly. "I won't have nothin' to do with her. I took care of the courtyard as best I could, and me and Venutius made sure the garden was all right.

But with Coir actin' like the mistress, and the mistress not actin' like herself, beggin' your pardon, sir, I was safer out here with the animals and they was safer with me."

I rubbed my chin. "Thanks, Brutius. Get cleaned up, then come in and eat."

He grinned again. "No need, sir. I'm not hungry. I had a bit of cheese before I laid down with the dogs."

"Well, get cleaned up anyway. You'll be sleeping inside tonight."

I left, wondering if Brutius felt like he was being punished. Doubtless he enjoyed sleeping with the dogs, but I was determined to treat my slaves well even if they didn't like it. Ah, and look where that policy led . . .

Something heavy leaned against my legs. Fera purred when I bent down to pet her. Her kittens—now cats—were nowhere to be seen. Seems everything grew up while I was gone.

Voices rose from the *triclinium*. Venutius wouldn't have mentioned that I was home.

I entered the kitchen, peeking through the curtain. Coir was reclining on the couch, eating the trout and coriander sauce. Draco stood, his huge shoulders tense, his massive neck hanging low. He looked shrunken, his eyes hopeless and helpless, fixed on Coir. He kept his voice down. They were arguing.

"It's wrong, Coir. It's just wrong. I don't see how you can go on, day after day. The master will find out—"

"And what have I done wrong? Tell me that! Were I given an order by anyone? Do I disobey an order by anyone? No. If I'm not told to clean, I don't clean. It's not my fault the mistress don't care. I've not done nothing wrong."

"You should have been the slave of a lawyer, Coir. You've got a real gift for argument."

The knife in her hand fell to the floor with a loud clank, splattering some yellow-green sauce on the couch. Draco was as white as a spring lamb, if not quite as fluffy. He backed up and shrank against the wall.

Coir stared at me. Her brown skin was browner, and she'd grown her hair long. No fear in her eyes, but a kind of gloating triumph, like a general who knows he's beaten the better man.

"Leave us, Draco."

He bowed so low his head nearly scraped the floor, then retreated into the kitchen.

I walked over to her and raised my hand to strike her. I had never hit a slave. I'd slapped a woman once. She looked like she didn't give a damn whether I did or didn't. She'd already won. I lowered my arm and swallowed the bad taste in my mouth.

"You're free, Coir. I'll be going out of town again in a few days, and I'll make it official when I return. Leave tomorrow."

She'd expected—maybe even wanted—me to hit her, but this she hadn't counted on. She'd asked me to free her before I married Gwyna, and a combination of cajolery and kindness persuaded her to stay. I thought that was enough. I'd never understand women.

She looked up, eyes flat and cold.

"What about Draco?"

I stared at her for a long moment.

"Draco!"

He ran in, bowing all the way.

"I've just freed Coir. She's leaving tomorrow. You're free as well, if you want to join her."

The big man looked more shocked than he had before. His eyes darted back and forth between us.

"I—I don't want freedom, sir, but—Coir, I—"

"Well, you have it anyway. You can either go or not go. It's up to you."

I looked down at her. Her cheeks were red, her head held high.

I said softly: "You'll both have your freedom, even if I have to proclaim it to the governor himself. Now get out of my sight."

She walked, in not too great a hurry, to her room. I heard the door clack shut.

"*Dominus—I—*"

"No explanations necessary, Draco. You're welcome to stay on in the house as a freedman. If you follow her, though . . . be careful. Be very careful."

He nodded with a dim recognition.

"Go on and eat."

He nodded again and backed into the kitchen. I took a deep breath, squared my shoulders, and sucked in my gut. Time to meet my wife.

I reached my—our—bedroom door. I waited, unsure of whether to open it and fling myself at her or knock. I knocked.

A small voice said: "Come in."

My eyes traced the line of her face and body, from her blond hair to the delicately formed feet. After the initial shock I always felt on seeing her, I noticed some details: She'd lost weight. Her cheeks were pale, thinner, more drawn. Her hair was askew, not neatly tied up in back. Her face was etched with pain. God help me if I made her feel like that.

She sat up and smiled weakly. "Hello, Arcturus."

I sat down and took her hand. Clammy, cold, almost lifeless. I squeezed it. She smiled again, not unfriendly, not unwelcome, but distant, as if she and I and the room and my hand and her hand were not really there, not really connected.

"I—are you surprised?"

"No. I heard voices earlier, and saw you were talking to Coir."

"Gwyna, I'm—I'm sorry." So trite, so meaningless, so little. Some blood stirred in her hand, and she pulled it away, then very tentatively reached fingertips to brush my cheek.

"You shaved?" She was a little surprised. "You always come home in a state. I thought I'd—well, no bother."

"I stopped by the baths before I came home. I wanted to be clean—for you."

She smiled again, and the blue of her eyes was misty and covered over with something I didn't recognize. Something was very, very wrong with my wife. She saw the look on my face and changed the subject.

"How was the trip? Any rain?"

I stared at her. "No. No rain. Gwyna, what's happened? How did Coir—my God, what happened?"

For a moment I saw the old Gwyna. Then the blue was swallowed up by the same misty miasma, and she turned her face to the wall.

"Nothing, Arcturus. I'm just tired. I didn't feel like ordering anyone about. I suppose Coir just took advantage."

"Took advantage? She refused to do anything!"

She shrugged as if it took a great deal of effort.

"She's never liked me. She was always jealous of you. It was—it was easier this way."

"Was it easier to let Bilicho take care of Hefin?"

Her body jerked up as if it had been stung by a jellyfish. The eyes glinted a little, but any anger was trapped by the fog.

"No. I told you I was tired. Bilicho and Stricta did it as a favor to me."

I didn't say anything. I took her hand again and noted her pulse was faster. She was frightened of something.

I took her face and turned it to mine. "Gwyna, what is it?"

Once more, I thought I saw her. Then she put the smile back on.

"Nothing, Arcturus. I'll be fine. You won't have to divorce me."

I bent over and kissed her cheek. She let me, but that was all.

"I'm sorry. Sorry for hiding in my own world, sorry I left you, in body and spirit. Sorry for letting my weakness hurt you. I'm sorry for what I've done to you, Gwyna, and I will do everything I can to make up for it. I love you more than anything in this world or any other. Please give me a chance to show it."

I kissed her lips, gently. She lay back on the bed.

"I'm—tired, Arcturus. If you don't mind . . ."

I nodded. She avoided my eyes, turning toward the wall.

Somewhere beneath this drawn, apathetic woman was my Gwyna—and she was screaming.

Coir and Draco left before breakfast. I'd miss Draco. Hell, I'd even miss Coir. I was sorry it ended like it did. Freeing people is generally a happier event. Draco was practically in tears, but I didn't know my own way and could hardly tell him his. I told him he was welcome in my home anytime—as long as she wasn't with him.

I asked Venutius to find another house slave, preferably an old woman. That was all the thought I could give to domestic arrangements. It was time to talk to Bilicho.

Typically generous gesture of Gwyna's, to give them her father's house to live in. I stood and looked down the street where I'd walked last December, trying to find the beautiful blond woman who needed my help. The neighborhood looked the same, the house better than I remembered it.

I knocked on the door, finally getting the kind of welcome I hoped for.

"Arcturus!"

He hugged me hard enough to fuse my lungs, then held me at arm's length.

"You're thinner."

"I am not—I'm fatter."

"No, you're not. You're thin and troubled, and I know why."

We walked into the surprising center of the house: a round-house *triclinium,* the Roman exterior hiding the native interior. I smelled food in the kitchen, like the first time. Except this wasn't chickpeas and pork, it was lentils and bread.

"Stricta! Look who's back!"

A dark, wraithlike woman emerged from the kitchen, wiping her hands on a towel tied around her waist. She held out her hands toward me.

"Arcturus! It is so good of you to come by! When did you get home?"

Her Latin was stronger, less inflected with an Egyptian accent, and she'd finally gained some weight. She insisted that we all keep using her old slave name, even with the dark memories. Bilicho told me with a blush that she wouldn't change it because that's how he first knew her.

"Yesterday. Where's Hefin?"

Bilicho whistled, and a small blond missile flew out of what used to be Gwyna's room and struck him in the stomach. He started to laugh and almost fell down, as Stricta tousled the boy's hair and straightened out his tunic.

Hefin stared, then recognized me, putting on his best haughty look, so much like his father. "Hello, Arcturus."

"Hello, Hefin. How are the studies?"

He shrugged. "Stricta's teaching me some Greek. I want to learn to read the old Egyptian writing, though. She's promised to teach me that if I can get through Aeschylus."

His eyes bored into mine, trying to command me. "I don't want to go back. I want to stay here."

He was exactly like his father. A lot like his sister, too. Or like his sister when I left her in May. The words hurt more than I thought they could. Stricta noticed the look on my face.

"Go on now, Hefin, back to your room. Arcturus and Bilicho and I have to talk."

He shrugged again and walked to the corridor.

My mouth was dry, and the words felt heavy when they came out. "I'm sorry. I'm interrupting your meal."

Bilicho drew his eyebrows together. "This is me, Bilicho, your freedman and assistant. The man who helps you think. Actually, the man who does your thinking for you, as I've been telling you for years. Don't be such a goddamn stranger!"

The tension deflated. Thank God for Bilicho. He always made it easier on me than I deserved. Stricta left and came out again with a plate of soft-boiled eggs, cheese, and a lentil-chestnut stew. She joined us, and I relaxed a little. So this is what it felt like. A family.

"You get rid of Coir?" Bilicho asked.

Stricta was reproving. "Let Arcturus eat. And do not speak with your mouthful, Bil-i-cho." He swallowed and grinned at her.

"Yes. Why didn't you write me?"

They looked at each other. Bilicho gave me the worried mouth, the one I used to see every time he woke me from a nightmare. No one could shake me out of this one.

"Well, it was a gradual thing. Started back in July. Gwyna—Gwyna started acting strange. Coir did less and less. It got worse, but by then we knew you'd be home."

"What's wrong with her?"

Stricta stared at him for a few moments, then looked away. He picked at a tooth, and his eyes flickered.

"I—I don't know. Wish I did. She started to get distant, kind of lost, like, in July. Acting like she didn't care where she was. Not dressing, eating just enough to keep skin and bone together, but not . . . enjoying it. Not enjoying anything, from what I could tell. Never unkind, of course, but just—not caring. Real sad, sometimes. Hefin said he heard her crying all the time, and that's when I took him home. He's been here about a month."

He shook his head, his wrinkled face drooped in pity. "I'm sorry, Arcturus. We both are. She's just not herself." He looked over at Stricta and said, in a soft voice I'd never heard before, "Reminds me a bit of you, love, when I was first looking after you."

Stricta reddened a little, looked away, and squeezed Bilicho's hand.

"It's my fault. I left her in May. I left her when Agricola's boy died."

They both understood and were quiet. I coughed, but it sounded more like a sob, even to me. Bilicho turned his head, and Stricta hurried to the kitchen. I wiped my eyes and looked at Bilicho, who was studying a spider on the wall. I cleared my throat to let him know it was safe.

"So what are you going to do?"

I told him about leaving Agricola, the army—about what it would mean for both of us. First, there was Aquae Sulis, and a chance to help Gwyna. Maybe it would let her see again. Let her find herself again.

"Best thing for her. Don't worry about Hefin, we'll keep him for you. I'll make sure he's schooled. One thing at a time for you—Gwyna comes first."

He didn't want to let the boy go. The thought hit me like a bathhouse brick. He wanted a family. Maybe Stricta couldn't have children— not surprising, considering her background. And Bilicho, my own stubborn, protective, bashful Bilicho, wanted a family.

"There's no one I'd want to look after the boy more than you. However long I'll be—however long it takes—consider Hefin your son. I know she feels the same."

His brown, weather-beaten face flushed with purple. We looked at each other, shuffled our feet, cleared our throats. Stricta recognized male emotion and walked in from the kitchen to save us.

"Arc-tur-us. You will need another housekeeper, yes?"

"Venutius is out looking for another slave this morning."

"Sioned's husband died three months ago. She is not a slave, of course, but she would work for very little—especially for Gwyna." She smiled at me, and the smile lit the spareness of her face and made her beautiful.

"That would be perfect. Do you know where she is?"

"She lives not far from here. I will ask her to see you."

I stood up. "I'll send word when we reach Agricola's villa. Thank you both. For everything."

Bilicho slapped me on the back, and Stricta said: "I'll get my cloak and find Sioned."

We stepped outside together. Then she turned to me, urgency on her face.

"Arcturus. Please be patient with Gwyna. This is not your fault. Do not blame yourself."

I stared at her. "Do you know something? Something that would help?"

She hesitated. She came to see Gwyna, Venutius said so. What did she know?

The brown-green eyes were deep. They wouldn't lie to me, but neither would they give up their secrets. Or my wife's.

"She will let you know what will help. But give her time. Make her live again, taste life again." She squeezed my hand. "You did so for me, once."

With those words, the former slave, the woman who'd been kept as a whore in the lowest of whorehouses, moved off with the grace of a dancer in the imperial court.

I hired a gentle black gelding for Gwyna. When I came home and told her we were leaving for Aquae Sulis in the morning, she raised her eyebrows.

"You must have a positive obsession with bathing, Arcturus. First you take a bath before you come home, and now we're traveling halfway across the country to take more."

When I asked her if she felt physically able to travel, she got a little sharper: "I'm tired, not a cripple. I can keep up, if it's so important to you."

"It is important to me, Gwyna. To us. I think a change of air would do you good."

She shrugged. "Air is air. But, as I said, if it's important to you . . ." She let it trail off with the understanding that she was merely doing her duty.

When Sioned came by later in the afternoon, a look of pain—and strangely, of fear—crossed Gwyna's face. She greeted the old woman and turned to me.

"Arcturus, do you mind if I take a warm bath? I'd like one before we travel, and you can make arrangements with Sioned."

The old lady squinted hard at Gwyna, her broad, plain face severe with worry. "What's the matter with the young mistress?"

More demand than question. I gave her a truncated version of nothing. There was nothing I could tell her—she could see the obvious for herself. She agreed to stay on out of loyalty to Gwyna, and probably a desire to find out if I was beating her. I gave her Coir's old room.

The next morning Gwyna was up before I was. I dreamed she was sitting beside me, her hand stroking my face like she used to. When I opened my eyes, she was dressed in traveling clothes and heading out the door.

A sardonic smile when she saw the gelding. Nimbus didn't think much of him, either, but he was a plucky little horse, maybe down on his luck. That made him part of the family.

The trip was uneventful. We kept a steady pace through the main road, taking a less traveled path through the Great Plain. She ate the food Venutius packed without complaint, just as she ate the plainer food we found at farms and inns, too.

Pluto, the little black gelding, was steady. Nimbus gradually grew to like him. I caught her giving him a nuzzle once, when we stopped for a rest in a meadow.

Gwyna showed emotion only once. There was a place on the Great Plain I wanted her to see. Not many farms around it, though plenty ringed the downland, with wheat and barley and flax growing like the buttercups. She could see it from a distance, and I knew she was curious.

"Arcturus—what is that? Those stones—"

"No one knows, Gwyna. They are the oldest of the Old Ones."

She looked at me then, almost like herself. She was excited. "Can we see them?"

A light rain fell, and the green downland hummed with crickets. Wild hares dug in the soil, making large warrens, some of them older than the Romans in Britannia. Dark birds flew overhead, lighting on the giant rocks that rose up from the Earth like fingers, grasping at the sky.

Gwyna dismounted, walking up to one of the large blue stones, taller than any man. Silent, reverent touch. She walked the circle, in and out, laying her hand on each one in turn. There were tears in her eyes.

"Thank you, Ardur," she whispered.

When we left the Plain that evening, her mask was firmly in place. But I could see it was a mask, hiding something ugly. Something she didn't want me to know.

CHAPTER FOUR

I opened my eyes, watched the sunlight glisten on the river below. The strange sound of laughter—female laughter—was floating from Agricola's house.

I ran up the path, unceremoniously throwing open the door. She was lying on one of the governor's elegant couches, smiling . . . her hand lightly touching the arm of Lucius Valerius Philo.

There was someone else with him I couldn't see at the moment.

"Arcturus?"

She was wearing a new purple tunic with a midnight blue *palla*. Her eyes were light and quick. Was this the same woman who couldn't control Coir? Had five minutes with Philo made her laugh for the first time in weeks? He must be some doctor. I gritted my teeth.

"It's Philo, Arcturus. He's come to talk to you."

He stood up. "Favonianus—may I call you Arcturus, as your charming wife does?"

No, you may not call me Arcturus as my charming wife does. No one calls me Arcturus like that, especially you, you unctuous, wife-stealing sonofabitch.

"Yes," I said.

"This is Grattius Tribax. He's one of the *duoviri* of Aquae Sulis—we're a *municipium,* you know."

So they had some small independence and a direct relationship with Rome, while Grattius was one of the two men who thought they ran it all.

He stood up, a coarse, florid man who dressed as loudly as he talked. Clapped my shoulder as if we were old friends.

"Arcturus—so glad to have you in our little town. Philo tells me you've got quite the reputation—not that we don't get the very best people, mind, we're used to that in Aquae Sulis!" His mouth opened wide enough to show everyone in the room his gold fillings. Philo looked at him tolerantly and then spoke.

"Arcturus—we're here to ask you a favor. I know you're on leave, but your wife said you have no definite plans."

We both looked at Gwyna, who opened her eyes wide, all innocence. Philo looked a lot longer than necessary before turning to me with a frank expression.

"I'd appreciate your help on this Bibax problem. There'll be talk in the town, and it will spread. Aquae Sulis is in a delicate position right now. We can't afford the bad publicity."

I looked from my wife to Grattius to Philo. My eyes came back to Gwyna.

"What do you want me to do?" The question was aimed at her.

Grattius cleared his throat. "You have a reputation. For solving problems and making sure they stay quiet. We'd like you to take a look at our little problem, and clear it all up so's Aquae Sulis don't lose business. Couldn't be simpler, eh?"

He laughed, and I nudged a wine cup back into place. Philo looked at me earnestly.

"Anything you could do for us would help reassure the townspeople. Would you help?"

He said it to me but turned to Gwyna as well. A smart bastard,

Philo. He already knew my weak spot. I took a step closer to her without thinking.

She looked at me expectantly. I had no choice. And somehow—somewhere—I'd known this would happen.

"I'll do what I can. But as we've just arrived—"

Grattius interrupted. "That's another reason we came by. You're both invited for dinner."

I looked at the fat, red, eager face of Grattius Tribax, rich freedman. I looked at the well-bred charm of the handsome Philo. Lastly, I looked at my wife—and saw interest and even some amusement.

I said: "Be delighted."

I held out my hand to help Gwyna up, and she let me. A slave fetched our cloaks, and I bowed to the superior medical knowledge of the goddess Sulis.

There must be a special level of hell reserved for people like Grattius. Unfortunately, I was eating dinner in it. Guests included a retired *haruspex* and Philo—who, I found to my growing irritation, wasn't married.

The host's wife, Vibia, was a dull, plain, brown-haired woman, a former gymnast, so she said. She'd kept her figure, which was all she had. Her appetite reminded me of Draco's. She probably threw it all up again to keep slim. I thought about joining her.

The hors d'oeuvres were duck eggs drowned in *garum*. The main course, in addition to the roasted dormice, was some unidentifiable fish in a wine sauce, and dessert was honey cakes, figs, and dates cunningly arranged to look like a beehive with bees. God, how I missed Venutius.

I made the mistake of letting the host see my full wine cup.

"Drink up, m' boy, that's Trebellic wine, you know. Can't get any better than that!"

I smiled weakly and glanced at Philo, who was sharing a couch with his hosts. The old man who shared ours nodded off throughout the meal, emitting a loud belch every now and then to wake himself up.

The wine wasn't really Trebellium, of course—some sort of cheap wine-vinegar, not only phony, but a decade too late to be fashionable. I tried not to touch, smell, or taste the food, hiding as much as I could in a napkin. Gwyna was beside me, animatedly talking to none other than Sulpicia, who was on an adjoining couch to the left with the fop from earlier.

Julius Vitellius Scaevola was a merchant, an equestrian, and an investor in mines to the southwest of Aquae Sulis. He was absent-mindedly rubbing the back of Sulpicia's legs, drunk, and trying to make conversation.

He hiccupped. "So—Favonianus—can I call you Arcturus?"

"Everyone else does."

"Yes. Well. How about that Bibax? What about the tablet, eh? The *Ultor* and all? Whaddya think?"

I pretended not to hear, letting the rest of the conversation swirl around us. Snippets from Grattius, talking to Spurius Octavio, the bath-master of the entire complex. Octavio's wife, a silly, loud-mouthed woman with henna-dyed hair and a garish green *palla,* was discussing something with Philo. Words separated from their meaning floated by—"Roscia's new litter" and "a divine new treatment by Audax— such a masseur!" and "haunted mine."

"Haunted mine?" I couldn't pin down the source. All I could hear was Octavio's wife talking about Roscia, who wasn't a lately pregnant cat.

"I say—Arcturus! The murder, what about this murder?"

Vitellius hadn't succumbed yet, but before I could answer, the old *haruspex* growled: "Wickedness. That's what it is. Town's become wicked. Aquae Sulis is cursed."

The room was suddenly quiet. The old man glared at the assembled party.

"I know what I say. I've seen the changes come. Aquae Sulis is cursed."

Grattius leaned over to me from the right and whispered loudly: "Don't pay attention to old Marcius. He's only here because Papirius was busy tonight." He added in a louder voice: "Have some more wine, Marcius!"

The old man shook his head. "As sure as my name is Aulus Marcius Memor, there is wickedness in this town. And the goddess will make it pay. She already has."

His wrinkled mouth turned downward, as he stared at his empty wine cup. Then his eyes closed and he went to sleep.

The bathmaster's wife laughed loudly, yellow teeth bared. "Good old Marcius! Always good for a laugh."

She caught my eye. "So what about it? What about Bibax? Was he really strangled?"

Everyone looked at me with an eagerness only stories about death and sex can inspire. I took a shot of the wine, and was proud of myself for not making a face.

"Yes."

"How do you know?" the woman demanded. Octavio nudged her in the ribs.

"His body says so. And someone put the piece of lead in his mouth."

Vibia snorted. "Died how he lived, didn't he? Choked on his own curses!"

Her husband's laugh was unnecessarily loud. "Now, dear, mustn't speak ill of the dead. At least while we don't know yet who killed him." He looked at me hopefully, as if I might produce the solution then and there.

So the piece of lead was a curse tablet. I shrugged. "He didn't choke. He was strangled, by someone with large hands. Then the tablet was put into his mouth, wedged tight, and they tied him up so he wouldn't sink to the bottom of the reservoir."

Philo was quick. "Why do you think there were two people?"

"Because one person could throw him in, but it would take one very strong man or two people to lower him slowly enough to keep him in an upright position."

An "ah" sound went around the couches. Grattius was beaming. He hadn't hired musicians for the evening, and his guest was providing the entertainment for free.

"My, you're clever," Sulpicia murmured. Gwyna shot her a look I found highly gratifying.

Octavio added: "You don't become the governor's physician because you don't know a leg bone from an arm bone!"

Philo cleared his throat. "Speaking of the governor . . . any word as to whether he'll be staying, Arcturus?"

"I really don't know. You know how politics are, especially in Rome."

That made everyone nod, as if they really did know how politics were in Rome.

"Well, my boy, you're welcome in Aquae Sulis anytime. We have so many doctors now, one more can't hurt! Especially an up-and-comer like you!" Grattius laughed again.

My adopted father was a procurator under Nero, appointed to the Senate. I was the private physician of the governor of the entire province. Yet here I was in a cheap and tawdry dining room, in the small town of Aquae Sulis, being called an "up-and-comer" by a man who couldn't tell he was drinking his own piss.

Gwyna's hand touched my leg. I took a deep breath, changed the subject. "What's this I hear about a haunted mine?"

I was unprepared for the effect. Grattius turned red. Marcius woke up, and so did Vitellius. Octavio opened his mouth like a gasping fish.

Philo chuckled. "Stories always float around this town. Product of the atmosphere. Some people don't go to doctors, Arcturus. They put their trust in magicians and soothsayers—people like Bibax—instead."

Marcius growled again. "Wickedness!"

The whole party laughed. I turned my head to look at Gwyna. She was staring straight ahead, thinking.

The party broke up soon afterward, and Grattius insisted we use his litter.

"You don't want your pretty little wife to get her sandals muddy, do you, eh, Arcturus?" He elbowed me in the ribs. I thought I heard a dormouse squeal.

Philo cornered me as everyone made their good-bye. "Come see me tomorrow. We can talk more freely. I'm across the street from the east end of the temple."

He stared at Gwyna, who was saying good-bye to Sulpicia as if they were long-lost sisters. "How long has she been ill?" he murmured.

I tried to keep my face in place, but I felt it slip for a second. "Why do you say she's been ill?"

He smiled. "I am a doctor, Arcturus. The eyes. The skin. The way she carries herself. She's a beautiful woman, and I'd be protective of her, too." He patted me on the back. "The waters really will help."

I was confused. I wanted to hit him. Nobody told me what to do or how to treat or how to look at my wife. Nobody. Except maybe my wife herself. But he seemed to notice things I hadn't. Why? Was he a better doctor? Was he a better person? Was he a better man?

I stood there like a statue until Gwyna tugged my arm impatiently and whispered: "Come on. I don't want to have to go through all that again."

We clambered into the litter. Grattius and Vibia were waving madly at us, and I waved in return. Gwyna waved, too, then leaned against the cushions out of sight. Her eyes were bluer than they'd been in a long time.

She leaned forward. "Well? What did you think?"

My mind was still on Philo. "About what?"

"About those people. Are Romans usually that decadent and disgusting?"

"These were prizewinners. They'd give Trimalchio a run for his money."

She looked puzzled. "Who's Trimalchio?"

"Just a character in a book."

"Oh." She looked wistful. "I'd like to read it."

I was surprised. "Of course. I'll get you a copy."

She nodded, lost in thought. "Arcturus . . ."

"Yes, Gwyna?"

"Was I—did I do everything properly?"

I was surprised again. Gwyna had been to parties before, had experienced the Londinium social whirl when she was very young and married to her first husband.

"You were magnificent. I, er, I was surprised to see you and Sulpicia so chummy."

She opened her eyes wide. "That cow? Chummy? Ha!"

"But you—you—"

She looked at me with pity. "Of course. How else am I going to make sure she doesn't sit in your lap and play 'find the *gladius*'?"

This time I was shocked.

"But I—I'd never—"

"Yes, I know, Arcturus. But you are a man, and men are easily gulled, especially by women as inventive as Sulpicia."

"Well, Philo—"

"—thinks I'm attractive. I was only flirting with him to get information. For our case."

Now I was just dumb. "Our case?"

"I thought Grattius's reaction to the haunted mine story was odd—of course, I didn't catch the whole thing—that loud-mouthed woman was talking about it, but she garbled her Latin so much I couldn't—"

"Gwyna—"

She paused. "Yes, Ardur?"

The old name slipped out naturally. "I—are you—I—"

She folded her arms across her chest and leaned back. "Spit it out."

"We're here—we're here to make sure you're—you get better."

She looked at me hard. I noticed, finally, what Philo already had: Her skin was too pale, too translucent. The litter stopped. I opened the curtain and peeked out. Before I could turn back to Gwyna, she jumped out from the other side and ran into the house.

I tipped the bearers and followed her. Two of the slaves were up, and I told them to go to bed. No sign of Gwyna in the dining room, kitchen, or bath. I tried the courtyard.

She was standing in front of a statue of Diana, her head bowed in the moonlight. I thought her cheeks looked wet.

"Gwyna. Listen. I'm doing everything I can to take care of you, but I need you to talk to me, tell me what I'm doing wrong. I love you—I love you more than my life. You are my life."

She faced me. There was anger in her trembling voice.

"Why did you come home clean, then? Why didn't you surprise me, like you always do?" She burst into tears, and I pulled her to me. She made fists with her hands and hit me in the chest.

"Why, Arcturus? You don't act like you love me—you—you keep me at a distance—ever since you came home—ever since you left—you act like you don't need me!"

She wrenched herself away from me, pushing me with all her strength, and ran sobbing into the house. I stood outside in the cold air for a while, thinking. Then I walked into the bedroom. I didn't knock. She was sitting on the bed, huddled, facing the wall. I sat down and picked her up and held on to her.

"Gwyna, I need you. More than air, more than than anything. I wanted to run to you—tell you I needed you to manage the house, needed you to manage me. I've been stupid, and worried, and cautious, and I've just made it all worse. I'm sorry."

She looked at me, her face soft, while her hand caressed my cheek.

"Do you want me to shave you?" she asked in a small voice.

As an answer, I bent down and kissed her, gently, fully, my tongue exploring her mouth until I felt her respond. Then she pushed me away. An indescribable pain crossed her face.

"I'm—I'm sorry, Ardur. Not yet."

I looked at my wife. Then I kissed her forehead, and her hair, and I laid her back in bed, tucking the covers around her, and kissed her eyes.

"Let's get some sleep. We have a busy day tomorrow, if we're going to find out who murdered Rufus Bibax."

She looked up at me and smiled. She didn't face the wall that night.

CHAPTER FIVE

I woke up before she did. She was on her side, turned toward me. A small metal disk on a leather strap spilled out of her tunic. It was an Isis medallion, with the goddess on one side and Isis and Horus on the other. Gwyna had never shown much interest in foreign cults. Maybe Stricta gave it to her.

She stretched and groaned and opened her eyes. Then she smiled, and the sun came out. "Hurry up and get dressed. We have work to do."

"Aren't you getting up?"

She stretched again, like a temple cat on a warm stone step. "In a few minutes. You get dressed first."

Stalling so that we didn't dress together. Just like last night. I swallowed my worry and asked: "What should I wear?"

A game she enjoyed. After wrapping up in a cloak and clucking over the few clothes I'd brought, she pulled out a white undertunic, a dark brown outer tunic with gold trim, a studded military belt, and a green cloak—my only fashionable *lacerna.*

"I'll have to buy you a few more things. You didn't bring your toga, did you?"

"Why the hell would I drag that moth-eaten old—"

"It isn't moth-eaten, and you look very dignified in it." She sighed. "Well, if you didn't bring it, I'll have to buy you a new one. Although a ready-made toga with a senatorial stripe will be hard to find."

"Why do I need it? Why should I wear it?"

She looked at me as if I were a child. "Because, Arcturus. This is a society town, remember? If you're going to fit in and get people to talk to you, you need to look the part."

She glanced at her own clothes, which almost filled the chest in the corner. "I'm just glad I brought my red *palla*. I wish I'd thought to bring some more jewelry, though."

I kept forgetting that we weren't really on vacation. This was work—as foul a job as cleaning the Cloaca Maxima. Rome's biggest sewer bore a striking resemblance to Grattius's mouth. I told Gwyna I'd see her in the *triclinium*. She was busy choosing a bracelet but held her cheek up to be kissed.

The household was so efficient I thought maybe one of the slaves could figure out who murdered Bibax. They bustled around, serving a perfect breakfast of oats, figs, honey, hard-boiled eggs, and cream, all at just the right temperature.

Mine rose when Gwyna walked in. A gleaming underdress flashed from beneath a marigold tunic, fastened with a violet belt under her breasts. Her hair was piled in soft curls, and a gold bracelet of native design shone at her wrist.

"You're—you—"

She waited patiently until I regained the power of speech.

"Yes, Ardur?"

I swallowed. "You're beautiful."

The smile nearly blinded me. "Why, thank you."

She reached for an egg. To distract myself, I stood up to look at Agricola's calendar.

"*Kalends* of October already. *Fides*'s Day."

"Does that mean it's a holiday?"

"No. We're just supposed to pay honor to Fidelity." I gave her a dark look. "In that outfit, I don't think it could hurt."

She swallowed the egg she was eating and burst out laughing.

After breakfast, I found one of the slaves—how many were there?—to take messages to the fort. A military courier would deliver them to Agricola and Bilicho. I scrawled a few lines on a couple of sheets of papyrus while Gwyna told Ligur and Quilla to get our bath things ready.

If the Aquae Sulis *thermae* were like every other bath in the province, there would be separate hours for men and women to bathe— women in the morning, from daylight until the sixth or seventh hour, and men from then until sundown. I thought we'd walk down the hill into town, but Gwyna shook her head at me.

"Arcturus, think. You were invited to dinner by one of the *duoviri*. You're famous—and you're investigating a murder. You must do what is socially expected, if you want to get anywhere. We'll take the litter."

She said it so decisively I couldn't argue. "But Grattius—"

She raised her eyebrows. "Grattius? What does he have to do—oh, I see. No, silly, Agricola has a litter here, and two litter bearers. They're much bigger and better looking, too."

I knew I'd hate the goddamn thing.

I grumbled, but somehow we were able to fit bathing shoes, bathing clothes, towels, ointment boxes, strigils, an exercise ball, a perfume case, and makeup equipment. There was no room for Ligur and Quilla; there was barely room for us. They walked. I wished we could.

Gwyna planned everything. "I'll stay all morning, and catch the latest gossip. That's the best way I can help, I think." She looked at me to make sure I was listening. She smelled like lavender and sandalwood. "Then I'll do some shopping—find you a toga—and perhaps another mantle for me—and then I'll meet you at home when you're done."

"Done with what?"

"Arcturus, aren't you paying attention? The *baths*. That's where we'll find out everything. Isn't that part of your plan?"

I tried to look as though I had a plan. "Well—yes. I was going to talk to Philo first. I can do that while you're bathing. Then take a look around."

I tore my eyes from Gwyna, and felt my mind grind into gear like a millstone. "I—I mean, we—need to find out about Rufus Bibax. That *Ultor* curse was used to leave a message, for someone still in Aquae Sulis. And the spring . . . convenience? Or a warning to the temple? And what about—"

Gwyna was smiling at me. "We're here, Ardur. Now, don't forget to put some oil on your hair. I know you don't like it, but—"

"I know. It's expected."

"And watch your language. Don't use that street Latin you like so much, and not too many British words."

"Anything else?"

She reached over and squeezed my hand. "Be careful."

Then she stepped out of the litter, which had been so carefully lowered by Agricola's strapping bearers that I barely noticed it. I watched her blend into the swirl of colors of the open *forum,* heading for the entrance to the baths.

So much for a holiday. Time to work.

It wasn't the kind of town I'd want to die in.

The yellow stone was pretty, especially in a dim dawn or failing twilight, like a woman who picks up sailors at a wharf-side bar. The closer you got, the more you wanted to run for the next ship out of port.

The noise made you wish you were deaf if you weren't already, and even a morning breeze couldn't waft away the stench of decay. It lingered sensuously, the choice perfume of the marketplace.

The scent fanned from the potions hawked by a shrill old woman, who promised life just short of immortality. She didn't tell you she was twenty-six. It kissed the sweaty little men in sweaty little tents selling spells for a toothache. They'd knock it out with a hammer for only two *asses* more. It touched the bored wood-carvers, chiseling shapeless blocks into breasts or legs, whatever it was that needed a prayer. It even followed you to the spring, where you'd mumble an imprecation, and throw something in. Maybe you'd live another week. Maybe Sulis would take care of you.

A one-eyed woman could tell your future, and see if you were still in it. A pockmarked youth with a perpetual itch sold Egyptian lotions. Amulets for every disease ever known and a few that someone made up dangled from the neck of a large woman with a growth under her chin. She'd let you touch it—for a price.

Retired soldiers hobbled by, one-legged, while women with festering breasts started to cry because they couldn't nurse, their babies shrunken from illness or hunger. They bought potions made of cow piss and olive oil, and Babylonian unguent that was local beeswax dyed purple. The sellers mixed in shit from the public shithouse, of course. Everyone knew it was a phony if it didn't smell bad. But what the hell—put it on, rub it in. Sulis will take care of you.

There were other faces in the crowd, sharper and quick-eyed, recognizing opportunity and holding open the door. Old people in chairs were carted this way and that by hopeful relatives who weren't hoping for recovery. Stepmothers eyed their stepsons carefully and fingered certain concoctions with an appreciative gleam. Then there were the parents with the baby keeping them up at nights. They were looking for a potion-soaked rag, and they leaned on the counter and you could see in their eyes they weren't overly particular about what was on it.

I looked up. The sky was blue and cloudless. Maybe for the rich, the pretenders like Grattius, all this was invisible. They could drift in and out of the waters, indulge their vices, enjoy being blind. But I couldn't shut my eyes fast enough. I walked around to the east side of the temple to find Philo.

The house was about five years old and expensive. Sculptures of naked goddesses lined the way, and the floor mosaic was a sea scene, complete with frolicking nymphs. Expensive—but I expected his taste to be better.

I was shown in by a pretty young slave girl. She looked like she was on her way to the baths. Philo must be a kind master—maybe especially to the young and pretty ones. He was ushering out an old man hobbling on a stick, with an impossibly twisted and atrophied knee.

"Just keep it wrapped and soak it in the waters, Sulinus. It will feel better eventually."

The old man looked at Philo as if the town were called Aquae Philonis. Must be nice to inspire that kind of faith. I wondered if I could. I wondered if I should.

I looked around for somewhere to throw the thought, but there was nothing but pricey furniture for it to land on. A beautiful room, beautifully and expensively furnished. My half-broken basket chair with the saggy bottom and the unfinished back wall by the kitchen flashed in front of my eyes.

"Arcturus! Glad to see you—I was hoping you'd come. How do you like Aquae Sulis so far?" Philo turned the full force of his charm on me, and I felt like I was under a waterfall.

"I don't."

He raised his eyebrows. "Well, you haven't really seen the best part of it yet—"

"I think I have. I don't hold much hope for the baths."

He stared at me, then nodded.

"Ah. I see. You've come through the main marketplace, where every toenail collector in Britannia congregates to sell cure-alls. It is a bit ugly."

"A bit? It makes a battlefield look like a fresco by Fabullus."

He put his hand on my shoulder. "It's difficult, I admit. Eventually, though, you come to understand that you can't save everyone. Surely as a doctor you realize that."

I looked up sharply. A recent lesson, and still too painful to hear from Philo's mouth.

"I do realize that. But giving them false hope—"

"Any hope is better than no hope, Arcturus. People can live a few days longer on a lie. Does it matter so much who gives it to them? You, or I, or Faro Magnus, who claims to talk to the dead?"

His voice was strong, and his good-looking, aristocratic face gleamed with vitality. Or was it almond oil? Philo couldn't have lived near the marketplace for long without a little of it rubbing off. He was probably close to sixty, looked twenty years younger if you didn't look too hard. The gray temples weren't just affectation. The lines were fine and the body still lean, but the age was there.

"Who was Rufus Bibax?"

The abruptness of the question took him by surprise. Probably an affront to his gentility. His smile said he was willing to make allowances for me.

"Bibax was a scribe, one of the professional curse-writers who surround the temple area. Beyond that, I'm afraid I don't know anything else."

"You didn't know him?"

He laughed. "Heavens no, Arcturus. You saw what it's like out there. I may tolerate it, but I don't wade in it."

"Do you know how long he's been in Aquae Sulis?"

He shook his head regretfully. "I'm afraid I can't be of much assistance to you there, either. The town has grown remarkably over the last few years. I've only lived here for six years myself. The other sellers and scribes might know. I don't think he has any relatives—none have come forward, anyway."

I looked at him. "Tell me, Philo—if you don't know anything about Bibax, why the hell did you want me to talk to you?"

He laughed his easy laugh again. I couldn't see any cracks in the clay, and I was looking.

"I appreciate your directness. It's a welcome break from what I put up with on the council. First, I wanted you to come because I like you. You're a talented, intelligent man, a fellow professional. Second, I wanted you to know that we buried Bibax, and I didn't find anything else on his body. He dyed his hair, probably an effort to appear exotic. Several of the scribes claim to hail from Egypt."

Egypt. Every two-*as* hustler selling goat gonads claimed to be from Egypt. That explained Rufus's lack of red hair.

"Finally, I thought you might want to find out how things work around here, especially since Bibax's murderer sent such a vivid message."

I leaned forward. "Any guesses as to whom?"

Philo shrugged. "The temple or the priests who run it, perhaps. It's the most obvious choice. Though I can't see Papirius or anyone else strangling some poor scribe. That's how the temple collects its money."

"From the hustlers?"

"Yes, Arcturus. Every hustler—and every legitimate practioner, myself included—who has a stall or a space or a house around the center of the town, pays a tax to the temple. The temple owns the baths. Oh, I know, it's all public, but the profits go to the temple, which cycles them—or is supposed to—back to the community. They collect the paltry entrance fee—collect taxes from all the freelance bath attendants, masseuses, *depilators,* et cetera. Even the towel rental."

"Must be a complex operation. Accounting-wise, especially."

"It is. It's a separate city, really. Octavio is the head of the daily operations, but he has many centurions of a sort underneath him."

"So all the bogus ointment-makers out there—"

"Pay the temple. As did Bibax."

I shook my head. "*Ultor.* I just don't get it. If it was revenge on the temple, why choose such a minuscule player? Why him?"

"It doesn't make sense, I know. But listen. I wanted you to be aware of how important you solving this murder is to the community. We don't want the legion involved—in fact, they've just reduced the number of soldiers stationed at the fort, so I don't know that there's anyone there to help. We want to handle this independently, as a *municipium.*"

"Why? Why not involve the army?"

"Because the baths and the temple are the heart of Aquae Sulis. Look out there. People from all over the empire have heard about these waters, and they come here looking for rest, for a cure, for health."

"Go on."

"Right now we're in the middle of development plans for another complex. There are two more springs to the northwest of town, and we'd like to build a temple to Aesculapius, along with more baths. The council is hoping to make a deal with a mine consortium—you know, free baths for the miners thrown in. This sort of thing could jeopardize the entire proposal."

Not to mention tourism. Murder at a health spa is bad for business. I stood up.

"I understand, Philo. I'll do my best to find out what's wrong with Aquae Sulis." I wondered if he caught the sarcasm.

He looked at me. "You know, we help a lot of people—and not just through false hope or phony promises. These waters truly are gifts from the gods."

"I'll get a report on them later from my wife."

He smiled. "How is your wife today?" He asked it softly.

"Fine, thanks." I held his eyes a little longer than was customary. Turned to go, then turned back. "About that warning—"

"*Ultor?*"

"Yes. Maybe it's a message to the other curse-writers—to the charlatans—to the quacks." I laid particular emphasis on the last word.

He grunted. "Maybe. There are quite a few. Everyone from Tiberius Julianus and his eye cream to Faro the Great."

"The one that talks to dead people?"

Philo nodded.

"Ask him to find out from Bibax who killed him."

He laughed and clapped me on the shoulder again. "Arcturus, you're a hell of a man. I really wished you liked me more."

I didn't know what to say, so I smiled stupidly and walked out. Philo always seemed to get the last word. Damn him.

CHAPTER SIX

The vultures were still circling when I walked out of Philo's well-bred, handsome house. I started walking toward the temple, trying not to think about Quilla rubbing Gwyna down with oil. Then I banged into someone.

"Why don't you watch where the hell you're—"

"Sorry—"

It was the young stonecutter. Yellow dust covered his head and plain tunic, making him look like a statue. He glowered at me.

"Oh. It's you."

I glowered back.

"I said I was sorry, goddamn it. You should learn some manners."

"I'm not the one who walked into someone, am I?"

We both stood there, glaring at one another. It was uncanny the way he reminded me of myself.

"I'm investigating the murder."

"I hope you're better at it than walking." Then he smiled, right before I was about to punch him in the stomach. He held out his hand to grasp my arm. "My name's Drusius."

I grasped his. "Arcturus."

We stood looking at each other, a little awkwardly.

"Just install a statue or something?"

He nodded. "Anybody with money wants to put up a statue or an altar to Sulis or Minerva, or whoever the hell they think she is, and there's a lot of money floating in the water. At least these days."

He coughed and turned to spit out something on the pavement.

"Is that why you were there yesterday?"

"Yeah. Laying groundwork. Then somebody shouted, and half the population of the town poured out to take a look." He shook his head. "Poor bastard."

"Did you know Bibax at all?"

"Only to look at. Our shop"—he pointed to the southwest corner of the baths—"is over there, and I used to pass him occasionally. Didn't have a steady booth, that I could tell. Moved around a bit."

"What kind of man was he?"

Drusius shrugged. "Same as everybody else. Out for himself." He eyed me with a little suspicion. "Hear you're from Londinium? Some kind of doctor?"

"I live in Londinium, and I'm the governor's doctor. But my mother was British, if that makes you feel any better."

He shrugged again. "Don't make me feel one way or another. Just wanted to know what your business was. I was hopin' someone would show up."

Now I was curious. "Show up for what?"

He spat in the street again and looked at me steadily. "Did you have a look around? See all the sick people?"

I nodded, wondering where this was going.

"Well, a lot of them get better. They do. Something in the water, they say, or maybe just havin' a holiday. You might even say Aquae Sulis is a healthy place—plenty do."

"And?"

His brows drew together, and he gave me another long look.

"Then maybe, Doctor, you can tell me why so many people die here."

He shouldered his tools and walked away before I could ask him anything else.

I stood there with a stupid look on my face, staring after Drusius. God-damn it. He'd made sure to tell me where his shop was. Now I'd have to find it and coax the story out of him. There were a couple of hours left before the baths opened for male business, but let the bastard wait.

I faced the temple and looked around. At least it was cleaner than the main marketplace. Curse-writers and scribes lined up in neat little rows next to sellers of offerings. Coins, secondhand silver, jewelry, what-ever you had or whatever you could afford—ready-made bribes, if the goddess was willing. I give you this, you do that. Don't forget to say please. Simple. The curses, though—I wasn't sure how they worked. I'd always cursed people to their faces, and I never asked a god to do for me what I could do for myself.

I approached a small stall. A thin man in a stained blue tunic looked at me with the eyes of a malnourished rat. I expected to see a tail.

"Wanna curse? Lose a robe? Somebody steal your wife?"

I leaned over the termite-infested board he used as a counter and let him assess how much money I had. He licked his lips, as the eyes clicked over past *asses* into *sestertii* and maybe even *denarii*.

"I can write you a good one. Court case, maybe. Make sure you win, make sure they swear to pay."

I leaned a little farther in, and I started to make him nervous. "Maybe you want a boy? Can't get him interested? Got a love *defixio,* too, he'll bend over faster than a—"

"How do these work?"

That threw him off. He stared at me, at first with his mouth open. A fly flew dangerously close. Then the beady little eyes narrowed.

"Whaddya mean? These here are *defixiones.* Curses."

"I gathered that. What's the process? What do you do?"

Now the eyes were darting back and forth, trying to find an angle, or maybe find out what my angle was. Then his mouth closed up tight.

"I buy my lead fair and square. You ain't goin' t' catch me sayin' nothin'."

"I'm not saying you don't. I just want to know what it is you do."

"I keep to the rules! I pay the temple! My lead's all bought, I'm not one of these water-pipe thieves—you go down and talk to that one, he's the one you're looking for."

He started to gather up the odd pieces of roughly square or rectangular lead that were stacked on the board, then took out a tattered leaf tablet from underneath and stuck it under his tunic.

"My spells is good ones, and my writing's good, too. And my lead!" He looked at me angrily and swept the rest of the metal pieces into a worn leather pouch.

"You go down there to them others. I'm closed."

With a twitch of his mouth, he scurried off to a dark hole he'd probably watch me from. I was left standing in front of a rotted board propped on two empty barrels, with a mildewed sailcloth sheet stretched above.

Someone chuckled behind me. I turned to find another priest. This one looked a little ratlike, too, but better fed. "You can find more educated versions next to the inscription carver."

"I'm Julius Alpinius Classicianus Favonianus. I'm investigating the murder of Rufus Bibax."

He sucked his teeth thoughtfully. "Yes, I know."

I was starting to run out of patience. "Can you tell me how all this works?"

"Well, as to how it works, I leave it to the goddess, but I can tell you how they run their business. Come with me."

He walked ahead, his toga dragging the dirty pavement. It wasn't draped properly, and I noticed it was wet along the bottom. Not exactly an advertisement for clean and healthy Aquae Sulis.

We stopped at the end of a row. A man in his late forties was hammering out a sheet of lead on a board. This one wasn't rotten.

The priest jerked a thumb at me. "He wants to know what curse-writers do, Peregrinus. He's trying to find out about Bibax."

The scribe looked from the priest to me and then kept hammering.

"Don't know anything about him," he said carefully, "but I'll tell you what we do. All of us are a bit different, though we all use roughly the same curse books, and the materials are the same."

"Curse books? Are they like spell books?"

The priest folded his arms across his chest and seemed to be enjoying himself. Peregrinus answered patiently.

"They are. There are *formulae* we use that are tried and true, for all sorts of problems and situations. Oaths, court cases, love problems—you love someone, she doesn't love you—gambling and races, so your horse comes a winner—not so much of that here, as we don't have chariot racing. Not yet, anyway. Here, of course, the most common problem is health or stealing. People constantly losing clothes and goods at the baths."

He pounded the lead a few more times, then picked it up and gave it a satisfied look. Then he handed it to me.

"Some people use thicker sheets because they're in a hurry—or maybe the client's in a hurry. Or because they're too lazy or clumsy to hammer it right. But the better ones among us, when we get a commission, we take a thick piece of lead, square cut, and we hammer it out thin. It not only saves us on lead, but it shows up the writing better—don't have to press as hard."

I handed it back to him. "Do you hammer it before or after you get a commission?"

"Oh, afterwards, of course. You can see for yourself the lead's too delicate to sit around here waiting for someone. As soon as I get a client, I prepare the lead. This is for a lady who wants a ring back. I'll have it ready for her when she comes out of the baths, and then she'll throw it in the spring."

He turned to rummage in a shallow box and pulled out a very small, thin stylus. "This is my favorite stylus. Writes real fine. Writing's important, don't you believe those who tell you it isn't. They just can't do it properly. The goddess likes it done nice."

I took the stylus and looked at it carefully. I started to understand why Bibax, Rat Face, and Peregrinus were all on the small side. The tablets were tiny, and the writing could be a delicate process.

"So I take my stylus, and I write. This one'll say something like 'May the person who took my ring—be it man or woman, slave or free—be tormented with no sleep, no rest, and never be free from pain, and may their insides rot from within, until they return my ring to the temple.' She might want more detail, and more specific punishment, and she may even give me a list of suspects. We can include that, too. This lady just paid for a general."

"You pay more for more detail?"

"Of course. It's more work. For me and the goddess, eh, Calpurnius?" He laughed, and the priest joined him.

"What makes the goddess listen to you?"

He grew serious. "That I can't say. We put in a formula to get the goddess's attention, and the client promises to give her something. This lady may even give her the ring, once she gets it back."

"So she'll pay you to ask for the goddess's help, and then once Sulis finds and punishes the thief, she'll pay the goddess. Seems like they'd lose less money if they just bought another ring."

Peregrinus winked. "Well, don't be spreadin' that around. We'd be out of business. The final thing to do is fold up the curse—it's important that it be folded right, because that helps bind the spell. That's another reason for hammering it out so thin. Some of these amateurs"—he looked around and spat contemptuously—"they don't understand you can't just throw in a thick piece of lead and have the magic work."

He looked up at the sun. "I'd best be getting back to this. Hope that helped you. Terrible thing, what happened."

"Yes. Thanks. The council's asked me to find the killer."

He squinted up at me from underneath his gray-red eyebrows. "Well, if you can't, Sulis will." Then he went back to work.

Calpurnius was smiling sardonically. "Did that answer your questions?"

I looked at him. "I always have more."

He sucked his teeth again. "I have a few minutes before I'm needed at the temple."

"What do you do there?"

He laughed without mirth. "I'm a temple cleaner. Lowest of the low. A priest in training, suckling the hind tit of Sulis, and lucky to get a few drops."

"How does the temple collect its taxes? From people like Bibax, I mean."

He raised his eyebrows and said in a dry voice: "You'll have to ask Papirius about that. I don't get to touch the money."

"Did you know Bibax?"

He shrugged. "Not personally. I saw him around. He wasn't the best or the worst of his kind."

I asked slowly: "Will the lady get her ring back?"

He gave me a funny look. "Maybe. Sometimes they do. Fairly often, in fact. The curses are a way to keep order in this town. We're far away from Rome—that little fortlet doesn't give a damn about us—and we don't have *vigiles* or even a native system left to enforce the laws. And it's a small place, Aquae Sulis, for all the cosmopolitan airs it puts on. And that's only been within the last few years, anyway."

"How do curses enforce the law? I don't understand."

"Don't you? You can't keep secrets in this place. Take a look around. Between everyone going to the baths, and the sellers at the marketplace—who would sell their grandmother's teeth if they could find a buyer—everyone knows everyone else's business. If Flavia's ring gets stolen, there are a limited number of people who probably did it. If word gets around that she's had them cursed, well—why take chances? Just leave it at the temple anonymously."

"Why should a thief care?"

"Because a thief has to live here, too. And a thief depends on Sulis's waters, just like the rest of us." He shivered. "I'm getting cold. I'd better go back."

"Calpurnius—what if the thief isn't a local?"

He paused and smiled. "Ah. That would be a problem, wouldn't it? We hope fear will keep them all in line." Then he turned to leave again.

I changed tactics. "Do people die here?"

That stopped him midstep. "What did you say?"

"Do people die here?"

He laughed again, a dry wheezing sound that sounded frozen and empty.

"Have you looked around you? Of course, people die. They come here sick—wills made out—she can't save all of them, can she? Not even a precious *medicus* could do that."

He gave me a withering look and headed back to the Temple, his toga still trailing a growing collection of dirt. On an impulse, I ran after him.

"*Ultor*—the message. Was Bibax killed because he was a failure? Because his curses didn't work?"

He was only a few feet away from the temple, and there were other priests on the steps. He stood for a moment, wavering. Then he turned around and stared at me.

His voice was lowered. "Oh, no. I don't think so." He looked from left to right, then up at me, his brown eyes narrowed and penetrating. "I think Rufus Bibax was killed because his curses came true."

For the second time that day, I was left standing on the pavement, feeling like a gaping idiot.

CHAPTER SEVEN

I spent the rest of the afternoon quizzing the offering stalls and curse-writers. No one wanted to admit knowing Bibax. No one mentioned his curses as possessing an unnaturally high success rate.

The priest knew something, obviously. Something I'd undoubtedly have to pay for. I accumulated a collection of eye creams, a badly sketched picture of the temple pediment, a blank piece of lead, and some clay testicles, the purchase price of small information. I shrugged and threw them into the spring with the other offerings. Not that I needed the testicles.

The bell for the baths finally sounded, and a throng of women rushed out, hair gleaming. I looked for Gwyna, and thought I saw her arm toss something out the window into the spring, but then I couldn't see the rest of her and couldn't be sure.

I made my way to the entrance, threading past females of all ages, shapes, and income levels. It was a relief to see Ligur, who'd been waiting all morning. We waited for the last stragglers, crimping their perfumed hair with their fingers, smearing rouge on their cheeks as they walked. I still didn't see Gwyna. She'd stand out in the crowd like Venus in a roomful of gorgons.

Other men were waiting, too, trying to get an eyeful of any body part the last few women hadn't shoved back into place. I paid half an *as* to the toothy attendant and finally stepped through the archway.

Dressing room first. This one offered large shelves in the shape of open boxes for you to store your clothes, and a not-too-narrow bench for slaves to sit and watch them for you. A few freelancers stood around, for those who couldn't afford one or more slaves of their own.

The *apodyterium* was decorated with little sayings and greetings some promotionally-minded person obviously thought were clever, like GREETINGS, BATHER! THIS WAY TO HEALTH! Another small fresco illustrated a scene of two women bathing one another—a perennial favorite. Some poor bastard suffering from impotence had scratched a grafitto: I LIKE WOMEN. I LIKE SONG. I TAKE BATHS. SO WHAT IS WRONG?

I changed into a plain linen wraparound kilt. The steam from the heated pools was making it hard to breathe. I left Ligur sitting on the bench beneath my clothes and walked through another arch into the main building. The exercise room was on the right.

It was a spacious *palaestra*. Three large windows on the north, with views to the *frigidarium,* and three on the south, with unfortunate views to the market square. A few ex-gladiator types were trying to attract the attention of the women outside, flexing muscles and raising their kilts a little higher than was necessary.

Some were getting massaged, some getting their hair plucked here instead of in the baths themselves. The hell with fashion. My chest hair wasn't in anyone's way. Besides, there were too many hairy asses strutting around for anyone to pay attention to me.

I'd brought a handball, started throwing it at one of the walls. The sounds from the bath area filtered through the doorway, making it harder to concentrate.

"Sausage—fresh sausages with basil!"

"—all night long. She just wouldn't stop! I thought my back would—"

"Perfume from the East—perfume from the East! Only two *sestertii*!"

"—and watch as this amazing performer will thrill you with her ability to fold herself into this tiny little box—"

"Quit splashing, you buffoon!"

"And I said—you won't believe it—and I said—"

"Ouch! Goddamn it, that's not a hair!"

I threw the ball and caught it on the return. A throaty chuckle made me feel even less dressed.

I turned to the window. Sulpicia was leaning on it with both arms, staring at me—and my kilt. I felt myself flush.

"Hello—Doctor. How do you like the baths?"

I threw again, missing the rebound. It hit a fat man with a furry back, who shot a venomous look in my direction. I picked it up, careful not to bend over toward Sulpicia.

"I haven't been inside yet."

"The water is special. Not the building, so much. You'll see. Everything's at just the right temperature." Everything except me.

"Where's Vitellius?" I asked abruptly.

She laughed. "He's in the big bath. He never exercises."

Her eyes crawled all over me. I felt like a slave at an auction. Measured, weighed, assessed.

I retrieved the ball from where I'd dropped it yet again. "I'll go find him."

"I'm sure he's getting rubbed down. He likes his oil. I'd do it for him, but . . ." She shrugged. "Proper ladies don't bathe with men." She winked. "Unless they have private baths."

I smiled weakly, took the ball, and retreated to the dressing room. I'd had enough exercise playing with Sulpicia. I told Ligur to follow me with the oil and strigil, then beckoned to a young boy in the corner.

"I need someone to watch my belongings. What's your name?"

"Aeron, sir."

"You're hired. And Aeron . . . if you notice anything unusual that happens in this room, I'll give you two *sestertii*."

"Yes, sir!"

He reminded me of Hefin. I winced. Not here, not now. I'd gotten fat enough on the guilt diet. I tightened up my stomach muscles and moved on.

I turned left, to the artificially heated section on the west side. The water was plain, still, and cold, straight from the ground and heated by man. These pools weren't as popular as the Great Bath, since it wasn't Sulis's water, and no one knew who its mother was.

The usual assortment of flesh displayed itself. Propped against alcoves, slumbering on the paved stone, a shoal of beached tunny on a stretch of yellow sand. I poured some oil on my skin, stepped into the *tepidarium,* and did some requisite splashing while I looked around.

Public baths were always hailed as the great leveler. The rich could rub elbows with the poor, and the poor could rub something else, if you paid them well enough. Baths were cleaner than whorehouses, and there were plenty of dark corners you could get to know each other better in.

Dandies with a ring on every finger strutted by in tight, wet kilts, advertising the daily special. Middle-aged merchants entertained whores in the *caldarium,* too fat to do anything but pant over the smell and sight of wet, jiggling skin.

Then there were the artistic entertainments. A poet croaked a turgid epic in a dull monotone while a younger version in the opposite corner recited naughty lyrics, punctuated by the snores of an old man who obviously didn't find them naughty enough.

No lyre player today, but a juggler was doing tricks with a discus. When it landed on a muscular specimen in the *caldarium,* he proved his feet were faster than his hands. Various sellers of cakes, candies, sausages, and snacks wandered by, each item less appetizing than the one before it. I bought a mint breath freshener from a freckled man who obviously never tried his own product.

I climbed out of the *caldarium* disappointed. A typical day in a typical Roman bath. Nothing of particular interest.

Ligur gave me a vigorous strigiling, and I headed for the cold plunge. I was holding my breath, preparing for the shock of the water, when I recognized an eager voice behind me.

"It's Arcturus, isn't it?"

I exhaled and turned to see Octavio, who was clearly delighted to see me, because he raised his voice several levels and shouted: "Wonderful to have you, Arcturus! And how is the governor?"

"The same as he was yesterday, Octavio. Nice baths you have here."

"Oh, but you haven't seen the best of them yet. You must go to the Great Bath." His voice went up again. "A doctor of your skill will appreciate the waters."

My sarcastic smile bounced off of him and made a plunking sound in the pool. People were looking at us. So much for anonymity.

"Thanks. I will."

Before he could advertise a free corn removal by the governor's *medicus*, I jumped into the *frigidarium*. I stayed in as long as I could, which was exactly as long as Octavio lingered before someone told him something about a clog in the drain, and he went running.

Ligur met me with a soft towel while I dripped on the soft yellow stone. I looked out the *frigidarium* windows to the waters of the Sacred Spring, undulating like a Babylonian belly dancer. They were hiding something. Maybe I'd find out what in the Great Bath.

When I walked into the hall, I finally understood why so many people limped, hobbled, and crawled to Aquae Sulis. The misery outside was lessened just a little on the faces of the men waist deep in the pool.

A green-blue haze rose from the steaming water, dissipating by the time it reached the soaring yellow vaults and high windows. Statues— good ones—lined the aisles, reminding you of what you looked like when you were nineteen, and whispering words of encouragement that you could look like that again. Seats for slaves and companions lodged in commodious niches, and warm, secluded alcoves allowed for private conversations and secret assignations.

The whole room was big, even by Roman standards, and it filled itself with light and air, balancing the heat of the water. I sniffed. The smell was brisk, unmistakably of the earth, with a pleasant volcanic tang that reminded me of Baiae—but cleaner somehow, softer. The water droplets beaded like sweat on my arm hair and soothed my skin as they wetted it.

On the eastern end, more pools of the water tapered into two separate, smaller chambers, each one less warm than the previous. The entire complex was designed to give the greatest pleasure to all your senses. Even the noise was subdued, as if it melted away with the steam. I was starting to like the place when another voice I knew and didn't like reminded me why I was there.

"Arcturus! Hallo, there! Arcturus!"

Vitellius was stretched out on a stone above the middle of the pool, getting a back rub from a young boy, whom he eyed with evident interest. I wondered if Sulpicia knew—or cared.

I walked around to his side and looked down at his vacuous face. "Hello, Vitellius."

"Marvelous, isn't it? Have you been in yet?"

"No. I'm about to."

"Oh, go on. Don't let me keep you." He closed his eyes in ecstasy as the boy's short, strong fingers plied his butt cheek. I stepped down into the green water, which was a little deeper than the usual baths.

It was as hot as the hottest *caldarium,* but not harsh or jarring. I dipped my arms. The water was like a smooth, gentle hand that packed an invigorating slap. I closed my eyes and felt my muscles relax. They fought the water, but the water was winning.

I let myself be seduced for a while, and only opened my eyes and looked around when I started to feel cheap. Then I wet my hair and face and tried to wake up.

There were a lot of old men in the pool, squeezing the last drop of pleasure from a dying body. One face I recognized: the *gemmarius* who gave me directions. His swarthy son or apprentice was with him, helping him walk without a stick. Our eyes met. I was on the point of saying hello when Grattius made his entrance. Octavio was following him as if he thought gold *aureii* might drop out of his ass.

"You see, Grattius—Arcturus"—a louder voice—"the governor's doctor—is already here."

Grattius waddled his head complacently. "Good, good. Of course, I never arrive before the eighth hour. Best time, you know." That would be the Roman Book of Etiquette under Nero. Let's see—he was only six emperors behind.

He settled his freckled, hairy bulk on a chair one of his slaves carried in. Then, with an arch of his eyebrow and a crook of his finger, he summoned a depilator. That would be my cue to find a different view.

I stepped out. Ligur dried me off, and I walked over to pay my disrespects to Grattius. He was holding court next to Vitellius, who wisely kept snoring. I wanted to bring up something to irritate him, and the elusive mining conversation of the night before seemed promising.

"So, Grattius," I said in my best jovial tone, "tell me about this haunted mine?"

He raised his eyebrows and yelped. "Don't pull my goddamn ear out!"

The hair-plucker was used to both abuse and cries of pain. He changed his focus to Grattius's nose.

"Haunted mine? Nonsense. You shouldn't listen to rumors." He swiveled his neck to yell again. "Can't you see I'm talking? Do my armpits."

I stepped back quickly and walked to his other side. I was a doctor. My stomach was supposed to be strong enough for anything. Still, no sense taking chances.

He turned in the chair to look at me, a little irritated. "Don't know who started it. It's a damn mess, is what it is. Can't find people to work in it—slaves too expensive for the consortium—go through 'em too quickly in mines, you need to have a high output to pay for new ones every six months. This is just lead, a simple lead mine, and now people won't go near it. Idiots!"

"Are you one of the owners?"

He looked gratified. "Not me, my boy. I have too much to do to run the town. I represent their interests, though, if you know what I mean." He rubbed his nose knowingly. "We're trying to get it going again—always a need for lead in this town, what with the pipes and the curses—good pewterware made here, too. Opening it up can help get those other springs developed. Make a nice little profit on it."

More noise from the doorway. It was Philo, and he, too, was escorted by Octavio. Various men pressed around and mobbed him, seeking medical advice. Octavio managed to shoo most of them away. It was dangerous being a doctor in a hot room full of desperately ill people. Dangerous—and judging from Philo, profitable.

The *gemmarius* stepped out of the water and limped toward him. Their physical difference was striking—both about the same age, one feeble and shrunken, the other looking twenty years younger than he was. The smarmy bastard.

The jeweler plucked at his sleeve. "Got some help for a bad leg, Doctor? Any advice for me?"

Philo smiled down at him, and outside the clouds parted and the birds sang.

"You've done the best thing you could do for it—you came here." Then he grasped the man's arm warmly and walked toward us. The jeweler wouldn't, or couldn't, let go, and Philo graciously but firmly unbent the man's fingers from his arm, gliding away.

Between Grattius's armpits and Philo's smiling perfection, I couldn't stand the smell. Not even the water could clean it. I motioned to Ligur, and Grattius's piggish eyes didn't miss it.

"What? You're not taking the cold bath, Arcturus?"

"Already did, Grattius." Ligur ran up with more towels and some lightly scented oil. He rubbed it quickly into my back and arms while I stood waiting for the all-over scrutiny and inevitable word from the good doctor.

"Hello, Arcturus. Glad to see you here. What do you think now?"

"It's a special place."

Grattius chortled, as if I'd made a funny. "Of course it is, my boy."

Ligur rubbed some oil into my hair. When Grattius was busy arranging himself for the depilator, Philo leaned over and whispered, "Did you find out anything?"

I shook my head, partly to disperse the oil and partly to make Philo get away from me. "Not much."

"Keep me informed, if you would."

"Of course."

I crooked my finger at Ligur. That's apparently how they did it at Aquae Sulis.

"Off to dinner, eh, Arcturus?" Grattius's mouth stretched into his version of a sly smile. "And who knows what else that nice little piece of yours will have waiting?"

Vitellius woke up from his nap, and said: "Sulpicia?"

The subsequent laughter saved Grattius from needing Philo's professional attention. I gave him a stare that made him go white. Quite an accomplishment, considering he looked like a hairy boil. I turned my back and walked out.

The waters were good. Whatever was wrong here had nothing to do with the waters.

When we got back to the dressing room, I changed my clothes and gave Aeron a whole *sestertius*, more than a day's worth of tips.

"Anything happen?"

He scratched his head. "N-no. Not that I can figure." He sounded disappointed.

"Offer still stands. You see anything around here you think qualifies, you come get me. All right?"

He nodded. He was smart and poor, and therefore invisible.

The litter bearers were waiting by the door. Ligur looked appalled when I asked him if he wanted a ride. By the time the chair was lowered again, I was almost asleep. I opened my eyes and stepped out and walked into a large, chestnut brown horse.

He was a stallion—obviously. He could also smell Nimbus—obviously. She was nickering to him, and when he answered her, everyone in Aquae Sulis could hear what he said.

I strode into the house. "What the hell—"

A tall, hearty looking man of about forty was sitting down, starry-eyed, admiring my wife. Join the goddamn fraternity. Maybe I should put her in the barn with Nimbus.

"Arcturus—I'm so glad you're home. This is Gaius Secundus. The *duovir* of Aquae Sulis."

Of course. How could I forget there were two of the bastards?

I tried not to ask him what the hell he was doing with a stallion in my garden. I said: "We've already met Grattius."

A look of distaste crossed his face. At least that was something in his favor.

"Well, Grattius and I run the town together, though we don't always see eye to eye. I'd heard you were here, and thought you might want to come to dinner tomorrow."

I glanced down at Gwyna, who smiled bewitchingly. "Of course. We'd love to. Thanks for asking." Another neigh nearly shattered a glass.

"Is that your horse?"

"Noble beast, isn't he? I understand you have a mixed Libyan breed yourself, a little gray mare."

Ah. The horsey set. "Nimbus used to be a courier horse."

"Fast devils. Good endurance, too." He stood up. "Well, glad you can come. Not a lot to do in Aquae Sulis if you're not infirm. Got a theater, of course—the wife and I are avid for theatricals. No arena yet. Hopefully, that'll come. We could use a good gladiator show—liven things up a bit—but first things first. What we need is a good track. Run some fast circus breeds, have a little racing farm." He clapped me on the back. "Always glad to meet a fellow who knows horses."

I escorted him out, to make sure he left. Then made sure no one else was waiting around to make love to my wife. Then walked into the dining room.

The dinner was laid out. Gwyna dismissed the slaves so she could serve us herself. Lamb stew, peas, lettuce leaves with onions, and wine cakes. The food was almost as delectable as the sight of her pouring wine.

"Priscus was hiding this in the kitchen until Secundus left. I didn't think he ever would. He kept hinting around, hoping for an on-the-spot dinner invitation. Now, sit down, Ardur, and tell me what you found out."

Her eyes were bright. I told her about my day, and ended with what Drusius and Calpurnius had told me—and not told me.

"It doesn't make much sense. People die in Aquae Sulis, and Bibax's curses came true. What does that mean?"

Gwyna was looking at me strangely. "Ardur—"

"Yes?"

"Ardur . . . what if it's in the wrong order?"

"What do you mean?"

"What if it's 'Bibax's curses come true' . . . and *then* 'people die'?"

I stared at my wife. Why the hell hadn't I thought of that?

CHAPTER EIGHT

I leaned forward. "You mean, hire Bibax, curse someone you want to get rid of . . . let the goddess take the blame. Making Bibax and whoever he was working with murderers for hire."

She nodded, her curling blond hair falling down into soft waves, and I was struck by how young she looked. She'd been so drawn when I came home from the North, so tired.

I tried to concentrate on Bibax. "Did anyone mention him at all?"

"No one admitted knowing or ever using him, but they were willing to imply other people did. When Prunella spoke of Bibax, it was . . . well, it was when we were talking about wanting things to happen. Do you see?"

"I think so. Who's Prunella?"

"You met her last night. Octavio's wife. The one with a laugh like a donkey. She was there early—her husband runs it, after all. She checked me over, of course. So did everyone else."

"What do you mean, 'checked me over'?"

She threw me a tolerant smile. "You don't understand women, do you? They had to inspect my clothes, what sort of perfume I wore, how expensive it was. Jewelry, shoes, hair oil—everything. Find out if I was keeping my figure. Or if I had a lover on the side."

I drank my wine too quickly. Gwyna arched her eyebrows and smiled. I said: "That must be uncomfortable."

She reached around to gather her hair, twisting it at the back of her neck. "It is. But you get used to it, especially in this kind of company. The trick is to find out more about them than they find out about you."

"Like what?"

She shrugged. "Lots of things, most of them unimportant. Prunella drinks, you know. I was glad I brought wine."

"You brought wine?" I was beginning to feel stupid again.

"Of course. I saw last night she drinks too much. I thought it would be easier to get her to talk, and it was, as long as I kept her by herself."

I shook my head. "You—you're—"

Her eyes opened wide. "Yes, Ardur?"

I hadn't forgotten the remark about lovers on the side.

"Go on. What did they tell you? And who was there?"

"Grattius's wife, of course—Vibia—and Prunella, and Flavia, the priest's wife—"

"Which priest?"

"Papirius, the head of the temple. She thinks she's some kind of bath duenna, and a terrible snob. I was quizzed on all my relatives—and yours, of course. That shut her up."

She paused, and poured herself a drink, and then let it float like an afterthought. "And there was Sulpicia, of course."

"Sulpicia? She was with you? But I—"

The blue eyes narrowed into arrow slits, and the arrows were loaded and ready.

"Did you see Sulpicia today? You haven't mentioned it."

"She came by the *palaestra* while I was exercising. It wasn't impor-tant." I gulped again and spilled some on my tunic. Nonchalance is difficult with wine dribbled down your front.

"Arcturus—whenever that cow pays you a visit, you're to tell me."

"Of course. I didn't think it mattered." I was stuttering like a boy in his first toga. Squirming, too.

Her voice was dry. "It matters to me. The bitch is trying to seduce you. If you had any sense where women are concerned, you'd realize my pride's at stake."

I squinted at her. "I understand. Can we get back to Bibax?"

She bent forward and poured me more Caecuban.

"Where was I? Oh, right—Prunella. Some young tart was frisking in the pool. This was before the others arrived. Prunella got catty—said that Titus something—Sestius, I think—well, he wasn't getting his money's worth, was he? Here he fixed his aunt good and proper, inherited all her money three months ago, and now he was wasting it on this cheap little piece."

"His aunt died?"

Gywna nodded. "Her name was Rusonia Aventina. Came out for a cure, never got back home."

"Did she mention Bibax?"

"Not then, but something she said later made me think of it. It was when we were getting rubbed down—when you're with women like that, you have to do everything all at the same time. For your own protection—otherwise they'll look through your things while you're in the water. It's best to follow someone's lead. Vibia and Flavia practically wrestled over who was going to be the leader. One of them was always trying to tell us what to do."

"So what happened?"

"Prunella was drunk. The others made bitchy remarks about Materna—wife of Secundus, the *duovir* you just met. Fat, ugly, red-faced woman. Her daughter is pretty, though. Still not married. Vibia mentioned something about Secundus scaring off a young man his daughter liked. Wants her to marry rich."

She shook her head with feeling. "Always the same story."

"What about Bibax?"

"I'm getting there, Ardur. We were watching this girl and her hulking mother—I don't want to end up on a couch with her, let me put it that way—and Vibia was saying how poor little Secunda was pining for her lover. And then Prunella said something about 'losing a chance to fix it.' Flavia gave her a warning look, but Prunella was too far gone. Slurred something like 'She coulda got ol' Bibax to help. Good ol' Bibax. He was real. Not like the res'.' Then Flavia hit her in the stomach and they changed the subject."

"She said Bibax was 'real'?"

"There's more. As soon as we were done with the rubdown, the other women left for a few minutes to talk to Sulpicia." A distasteful look crossed her face. "She makes such a spectacle of herself. And her body's not that good."

She shot a glance at me. I was innocently studying my nails.

"Anyway, Sulpicia was walking around, and she looks every bit of forty and then some. They left me alone with Prunella because she was asleep, but I got out the wine cup and held it under her nose. That woke her up."

"What did she say? Did you ask her about Bibax?"

She took another drink and stared at me. "Of course I did, Ardur. I may not be Bilicho, but I'm not stupid."

I tried to wag my tail and give her my paw. It always works for dogs. "Sorry. Go on."

"Well, I asked her what she meant about Bibax. What he could have 'fixed' for Secunda. She gave me this look, and a wink, and said to ask Sulpicia."

"Sulpicia again?"

"Yes, Sulpicia. Then she said—well, she said some things about you."

"Me? What could she say about me?"

Gwyna blushed a becoming shade of pink. "Nothing that you need to know. She seems to be under the impression—how, I don't know—that you're, well—that I'd never need to—shall we say—resort to anyone—or anything—else. Unlike Sulpicia, who did—and does."

I grinned. I'd remember Prunella, and be extra nice to her next time we went to dinner. Gwyna was watching me, her lips pursed.

"She was drunk, Arcturus."

I cleared my throat. "So what's this about Sulpicia?"

"That's what I wanted to know. So when Flavia came back I asked her how long Sulpicia has been with Vitellius."

"Vitellius likes boys."

"I know. Everyone knows. That's why she roams around like a cat. She'll stick her tail in the air for any good-looking man who gives her a sniff."

"Maybe she's lonely." I withered under my wife's look.

"Sulpicia?! Ha! Flavia said the old slut's rich, ancient-as-the-hills husband fell down and died just a year and a half ago. He was about thirty-five years older than she is, which made him roughly the age of Homer. And he was the severe type, against all so-called luxuries like clothes and jewelry, and of course couldn't give her what she wanted— and wants all the time. She's about as lonely as Messalina. Don't you dare feel sorry for her."

"You think—"

"I think she hired Bibax to conveniently remove an unwanted husband who stood in the way of some fun. Though why she chose Vitellius as a lover is beyond me. Maybe he's bigger and better than he looks, if she can ever get him off a boy's back end. Oh, don't look so shocked, Arcturus. Women talk about all kinds of things—just like men."

"I'm almost afraid to ask, but . . . anything else?"

She leaned forward. "There's more about Sulpicia. I watched her after what Flavia told me. She didn't bring a slave with her, which was odd. I thought perhaps she had to sell them or something, but she was wearing a beautiful necklace—gold and amethyst, absolutely stunning—so that didn't make sense. Well, when we were dressing in the *apodyterium*, Sulpicia left for a few minutes, heading back to the *frigidarium*. I thought it might be because she saw someone she knew, but it wasn't."

Gwyna squeezed my knee. *"She threw it in."*

"Threw what in? Where?"

"Ardur, aren't you paying attention? The necklace. She walked to the *frigidarium,* to where those three big windows overlooking the spring are, and she threw it in."

"She threw the necklace into the Sacred Spring?"

Gwyna nodded triumphantly. "Yes. Don't you see?"

I scratched my ear. "I'm afraid I don't. Lots of people throw all kinds of things in there."

"But she didn't want to. I could see it in her face. What's more, she just dropped it, so it landed on the side of the reservoir, and not in the water."

"So you think—"

"I think Sulpicia is being blackmailed, and someone at the temple is involved." She leaned back and smiled at me as if I'd thought of it.

"If she's being blackmailed—"

"Other people are, too. Even though Bibax is dead—"

"He had a partner. Or partners. Maybe that's where *Ultor* comes in. Disgruntled associate not scoring enough of the take. Or maybe someone discovered the goddess's magic was just a curse-writer with a lucrative side business."

I looked at her. "Gwyna—I thought I saw you throw something in the spring."

She reddened. "I'm not being blackmailed, if that's what you're worried about. When I saw what Sulpicia was doing, I—I went to join her."

"What did you throw?"

She avoided my eyes. "It's not important."

I let it get away. "Was there anything else? This information—your ideas. They're invaluable."

Her face flushed, and she leaned forward and squeezed my knee again. "I'm glad. I want to be useful to you. Be part of what you do."

I met her eyes. She reddened, looked away.

"There was something else. What was it? Oh, yes—the mine—the haunted mine."

"You talked about it?"

"Vibia likes ghost stories, and Aquae Sulis is full of them. Someone mentioned that the baths are haunted, too."

"By whom?"

"A boy—he died about three years ago. He's supposed to haunt one of the baths on the eastern end. Flavia told the story and pointed out the boy's grandmother. Old woman, no money. Still comes every day. Her grandson was accused of stealing some bathing clothes. He was the town simpleton, I guess, and couldn't defend himself. She still swears he's innocent." Gwyna shivered. "It's a sad story—and frightening, somehow."

"Was he cursed by Bibax?"

"I was listening to Vibia talk about the mine. You think—"

"I think you need to speak to the grandmother."

She rubbed her hand thoughtfully. "I'll do it tomorrow."

"And the mine?"

"The mine. The story is that a man died in a cave-in."

"Slaves die in mines all the time without ghosts shutting them down."

"This wasn't a slave. A Roman—maybe an official, I don't know. Vibia was very vague, and Flavia was uncomfortable with the conversation."

"When did he die?"

"About two, two and a half years ago. A lot of people swear the mine is genuinely haunted—that's why it's still closed. Even an investor was scared off. He came up from Durnovaria, I think it was, and wanted to reopen it but was frightened away by the ghost."

She shivered again. "I didn't like hearing about it. There's something—*wrong*—about Aquae Sulis, Arcturus."

I grunted. "Curses. Ghosts. Murder . . . though murder's nothing new in this town, not if we're right about Bibax. Two years, three— who knows how long he could have been playing Sulis."

"What would you like me to do?"

I took her hand in mine. "I want you to be careful. Killings and blackmail and whatever the hell else are rotting this town from the inside out. No one knows it, or maybe they just don't give a good goddamn. It's going to be dangerous to ask the right questions, and even the wrong ones. I'd like to get the hell out of here, today, tonight. It's poison. A goddamn city of poison."

"I can take care of myself, Ardur. I've told you that."

"I know you can, but until Bibax turned up dead, things were running nice and smooth—and they all want to keep it that way. We don't know what we're waking up, and no one—not the innocent or the guilty—will like it. I gave my word or I'd move us back to Londinium tonight."

She nodded. Nothing I said had frightened her.

"All right. What about tomorrow?"

"Do what any well-bred woman would do. Go back to the baths. If you get a chance to talk to that old woman—"

"I will. I'll find a way, don't worry. Anything else?"

I gave her what I hoped was my disarming grin. "I don't have to tell you to keep an eye on Sulpicia."

She frowned. "Better mine than yours."

I bit my lip. "But Gwyna—I will have to talk to her tomorrow."

"What? Why should you have to see that—"

"Because I'll get better results than you will. I think a direct confrontation about the blackmail will work with her. Even if it doesn't, it will set things in motion."

Her lips stretched in a thin line. "As long as certain other things aren't set in motion."

I ignored her and poured myself another drink. I was congratulating myself on how well I'd handled it when a light flamed in Gwyna's eyes that made me suspicious.

"Maybe I should talk to Philo."

I nearly spat the wine across the room. "Philo? Why the hell should you see Philo?"

"For the same reasons you're seeing Sulpicia. The weak spot, Arcturus. He'll be less guarded, and as the leading doctor in Aquae Sulis he'll probably know about these deaths. I can at least bring up Rusonia and Sulpicia's dead husband, and find out the details."

Logically, she was right—but goddamn it, I wasn't logical. "No."

"What do you mean, no?"

"No is what I mean when I say no. I don't want you to see Philo. Besides, you'll be in the baths in the morning."

"I can go a little later. It's more fashionable anyhow. You'll have to get there midafternoon as well, if you want to catch Sulpicia somewhere other than the exercise windows. Or maybe you want to show her what big muscles you have."

We glared at each other. I was trying to treat her like a real partner, and not like a jealous husband, but partners don't look like wives. Philo would never try to seduce Bilicho.

"He's sixty."

"She looks sixty without her clothes on."

We glared again. Both of us were breathing hard.

"All right. Talk to Philo. Just don't let him get near you."

"Same to you. If I smell any of her scent on you—"

One of the slaves came in to get the dinner leftovers. Gwyna straightened her tunic, smoothing it over her legs. I got up and paced for exercise.

Later I asked her to give me a shave. We changed and strolled into Agricola's private baths. There were three small pools, with lovely mosaic work in the bottom.

I sat on a stool near the edge of the *caldarium,* and she took out some oil and one of the razors. She still wasn't wearing what she usually wore—when she wore anything at all—but that was at home, and before I'd left for the North.

She grabbed my chin and forced my face up to look at her.

"Ardur—"

"Mmm?"

"Ardur—pay attention."

My hands were crawling down her hips, and she fought not to arch her back.

"Listen to me! I—I can't do this. Not now. Not—not yet."

The blue of her eyes was too deep to see behind.

"I—when, Gwyna? What—what can I do?"

"Nothing. It's not you. Please, Ardur. Please don't be angry."

I took a deep breath. "I'm—why don't you just finish that side of my chin, and I'll take a quick plunge in the cold pool?"

She nodded, her face white in the dim light. We didn't say anything else, and after she was through, I waded in our private *frigidarium* until I was numb.

When I came to bed, she was still awake, and she took my hand. She held it to her lips and kissed it. "It won't be so very long. I just—I just need a little more time."

I held her close, and was surprised when she started to cry.

CHAPTER NINE

Breakfast was awkward. Gwyna avoided my eyes. I got up and walked behind her chair. She craned her head to look at me.

"Ardur—what—"

My hands on her shoulders silenced her. I massaged her neck and pulled her hair up. She leaned back against me, eyes closed. I kissed her neck, my lips traveling around to the front of her tunic, gently brushing her lips.

I said in a playful tone: "Just a reminder for when you see Philo today."

She relaxed and smiled—a little wickedly—looking around to make sure there were no servants lurking. "Ardur—give me your hand."

I held it out, and while I was still standing behind her, she calmly tucked it under her tunic. The breast strap she was wearing was very thin. I completely forgot why I was standing there. I also forgot my name.

She removed it—she had to be firm with it—and returned it to me, with another smile.

"Remember that when Sulpicia tries to climb in your lap."

Breakfast suddenly tasted much better.

• • •

I decided not to take the litter, since walking helped me think, and I sure as hell needed some help. The weather was gray, as unsettled as my sense of purpose.

I walked down the hill to the *gemmarius*. The little shop clung to the dilapidated corner as if it were out of breath and tired of running. Not the moneyed area of Aquae Sulis.

Dirt streets, same yellow color as the baths. A fountain with a lion's face, cracked, mended, broken nose, stood a few doors away in the center of the square, its drip unsteady. The smell of piss rose from the *insulae* above, carried on a breeze that would blow it into the marketplace, where it would disappear and be overwhelmed by worse.

The man's son was standing in front, his hands on his belt.

"Yes? You want to buy something?"

"Necklace for my wife. I was here day before yesterday—asked directions. Your father gave them to me, thought I'd return the favor."

Burly, dark complexion, wiry beard. He stared at me. Intense, but not hostile.

"Natta isn't my father."

"My mistake. I noticed you together at the baths yesterday and assumed—"

"Buteo? Are you—" The old man hobbled out from the darkness. He stopped when he saw me. "Good morning, friend. What can I do for you?"

"I'd like to buy a necklace for my wife."

"We have some beautiful things. Come inside."

An old, smooth oak plank was both work space and selling area. A draft blew up the edges of a discolored, torn curtain hanging behind the counter. I assumed it divided his living area from the shop. Buteo disappeared behind the curtain. I figured he'd watch me.

Natta pulled out some surprisingly beautiful work. Carved gemstones were his specialty—jet, onyx, amber, garnet, amethyst, carnelian, even lapis and malachite. I pointed to a pile of carved stones he'd carefully wrapped in an oiled piece of leather.

"Can I see those?"

He smiled. "I'm afraid not. I'm saving them."

Probably to sell for when he couldn't work anymore. A day fast approaching. "I see. Holding on to your best work for last?"

"It is my best work. Yes. I'm waiting."

Buteo climbed back out from behind the curtain and squeezed by, carrying a large rug that needed cleaning. He set it on his shoulder effortlessly. I noticed the size of his arms rivaled the stonecutter's.

"Do you take pieces down by the baths? You might get higher prices."

The old man shook his head violently. "No. I do not go to the marketplace. Sometimes Buteo—yes. It is a good plan. But . . ." He peered at me, his eyes rheumy. "It is a bad place, no? Not like—not like before."

Before what? The old man wasn't from here—his Latin was accented. Sounded like maybe Baetica or Mauretania.

He answered me without hearing the question. "Before. When Aquae Sulis was younger, and so was I. Now—well, you see for yourself what it has become. I saw you at the baths yesterday. You are a *medicus*. The governor's *medicus*. Yes?"

"Arcturus is my name. The town has asked me—well, the *ordo*—the council—has asked me—"

"—to find the killer. I know. The curse-writer." He shook his head. "There is much that is bad in Aquae Sulis. I wish you luck. I wish you luck in finding it and rooting it out. Then—maybe—it will be healthy again." He sounded if he were talking to himself. "And now, *Medice* . . . have you chosen? And have you any advice for me?"

I remembered what Philo said about hope. I picked up a gold and emerald necklace, let it run through my fingers. "I'll take this, and that carved gemstone—the mother-of-pearl Diana. As for advice—"

He smiled at me. "No need. You haven't examined me, but I know what you would tell me. Still, thank you, Arcturus. I shall remember your name."

A cold gust of air blew in the doorway, and it started to rain outside.

The rain came down in sudden, unexpected waves, as if someone were pouring a slop bucket out of the sky and aiming it at me. The drops hit the soft soil with a splat, churning up bile-colored mud before they gathered enough strength to form a rivulet. Just yesterday that color had been so pretty.

At least I wasn't wearing a toga.

By the time I reached the stoneyard, the storm was over and a chill had set in. Drusius was surveying the pieces of newly washed stone. He stood with his hands on his hips, waiting. He couldn't miss me—I was the tall man in a dirty wet tunic, too stupid to take a goddamn litter on a cloudy October morning in Aquae Sulis.

"Thought you'd come around."

"I don't like mysteries, Drusius. They piss me off."

He shrugged. "Then why are you here?"

"Because you know something that will help me. I want the hell out of this town, but I'd like to leave it a little healthier than it was when I walked in. Call it a gift to Sulis."

He kicked some mud away from a large rectangular slab of yellow rock. "Come inside."

We walked through a small doorway, where the smell of cabbage and mutton overwhelmed the odor of rock, dirt, and sweat. An old man was lying on a nearly flat rush bed in the corner, facing the wall and snoring loudly.

"My father," Drusius said abruptly. "Sleeping one off again. He won't wake up."

I followed him to the opposite corner, where a crooked wooden table crouched on three legs. He pulled up a clay flask from the floor underneath.

"Want some ale?"

"Yeah."

He poured some dark brown liquid into two wooden cups covered in yellow dust. We drank at the same time, while he watched me. I smacked my lips.

"Local. Nice flavor. A little on the malty side, but maybe the barley was picked too late."

His eyebrows rose in surprise, and he put down his cup. "Maybe you can do something in this town."

"If you open your goddamn mouth and tell me what you know."

He glanced over at his father. The sawing noise continued without a break. "I don't want him to hear."

"*I* can barely hear."

He looked over at the old man again, then turned to me, his face hardened by resolution. "My best friend—a farmer—was murdered."

"How do you know?"

"I knew him, I tell you! We were age-mates—grew up together—best friends. His father was an old crony of my father, same way. He was getting too old to do the work, same as mine. They said Aufidio had an accident."

He leaned back in the willow twig chair, grimacing. "Accident—load of bullshit. He knew that property, every rock and tree on it."

I poured some more ale. "When did this happen? And what was the accident?"

"About two years ago. His father found him. Looked like he'd fallen and hit his head. But goddamn it, Aufidio was more sure-footed than a goat."

Drusius shook his head darkly and threw back another shot. "No. It was the boundary. That's what killed him."

"What boundary? Between the farm and another property?"

He nodded. "Farm and a mine. The one everyone says is haunted. That's when I started to think, add things up."

He crouched forward, eyes burning. "This town has been changing. Getting mean, getting greedy. I saw things. An old lady died—nothing wrong with her but needing some attention and a holiday. I put up a big stone for her in the temple, paid for by her nephew. Inherited a hell of a lot of money. Guilt, I say. Guilt."

I said: "That would be Rusonia Aventina."

That surprised him again. "You heard about it?"

"I hear a lot of things. What about the mine and the farm? What was the boundary problem?"

"They said he couldn't keep sheep nearby. Said it wasn't Aufidio's land, but goddamn it"—he pounded his fist on the table so hard, I thought he'd wake the old man—"goddamn it, it was. Aufidio wanted to go to court. His father didn't have any fight left, but Aufidio did. Last time I saw him was here, in town—he came out to the baths, said he had trouble sleeping. He was determined to fight. Then I hear it a week later. He's dead."

Drusius stared into his cup as if the ale were talking.

"What happened with the mine afterward?"

"Nothing. His old man kept away from it, like they wanted. He went last year, and the farm sold. Lots of land sells around here."

I rubbed my neck. "What about other deaths? Like Sulpicia's husband? Did you know him?"

"Old man. Marcus Atius Vettus. Died in bed. Nothing strange about that. 'Course, his wife was happy, but I couldn't blame her much. He was a nasty old bastard and she . . . she's quite a woman."

He blushed. He was young.

"You said Aquae Sulis has changed."

"Marketplace, for one. More of these astrologers and whatnot. Curse people. Ghost stories, people say they can raise the dead. It's not right. We always got lots of tourists—it's a healthy place, good for bathing. But the *ordo* and the temple—they keep wanting more money. So they let more of these types in. Papirius didn't used to run it—he was promoted to head priest, and he likes the money."

"What about Grattius?"

He shook his head. "A fat, slobbering fool, but he's lived here his

whole life, same as me. It was his turn to be *duovir,* I guess." He coughed
and spat on the floor.

"Do you think people are being murdered?"

He looked me full in the face. "I don't know. I just know it's not
right. People are dying who shouldn't. Those mine people—they had
something to do with Aufidio, that I do know, and they're supposed to
be out-of-towners, not from around here. Plus there's the development
down the way, with the *ordo* wanting to bring more baths, more temples, more crooks."

He shook his head. "It's not right." He poured himself another drink.

I reached across the table and grabbed his arm. "Did Bibax have
anything to do with this? Was he a contact for—getting rid of people?"

He spilled the drink on the table and wiped it with the sleeve of his
tunic. "I don't know. Maybe. He didn't have nothing, though. He
wasn't rich, or at least he didn't look like it. Lived down by where the
new baths will be—not much down there but a couple of apartment
houses."

"But you suspected something."

His eyes got evasive. "Look, maybe I saw somebody see him who
shouldn't see him. And maybe somebody died. That don't mean it was
wrong, exactly."

Sulpicia.

I stood. I'd gotten as much as I could hope for.

"Thanks for the ale."

He looked up at me, spat again. "I'm not saying anything about
Bibax. But I do know Aufidio was murdered."

"Do you remember a boy dying at the baths a couple of years ago?
Sort of the town simpleton?"

"You must mean Dewi. Some out-of-towner said he stole a bath
towel. Dewi died a few days later. That—that was another one,
shouldn't have happened. Dewi was a good lad, couldn't help the way
he came out."

"Do you remember how he died?"

"You know, there was something about it—but damned if I can think of it now. If it comes to me, I can let you know."

"Thanks. And Drusius—"

He looked up from where he'd been staring at the floor.

"Stonecutting's not good for the lungs. Mix some horehound and mustard leaves with honey, and put them in some wine. Not ale. Drink it every day. And think about getting a farm. You can grow your own barley."

He looked surprised again, but didn't say anything.

I left for the temple, walking through the precinct area. Papirius made me wait. Even if he was inside playing footsie with the incense bearer, he would make me wait. He had to. He was important.

A junior-grade priest finally fluttered down the steps and pulled at my mantle. "Papirius said he will see you now."

"How accomodating of Papirius. Lead on."

We walked around the temple and into a back building that adjoined it. Papirius was lying on his side on a couch, attended by two other priests, drinking some wine. I sniffed. It smelled like Trifoline. An underappreciated variety. Papirius must be a connoisseur.

He motioned for me to join him.

"No, thanks. Just had some ale."

He raised his eyebrows as if to say he hadn't been aware he was hosting a barbarian. After a long, savoring sip, he put the silver cup down. "What do you need, Arcturus?"

"Just some information. Understanding how the temple works might help me figure out who wanted to pollute your spring with a dead body."

He said dryly, "It's not my spring. It belongs to the goddess. But yes, I see your point. What would you like to know?"

"Is the spring ever guarded? Does anyone in Aquae Sulis have access to it at any time?"

"Actually, yes. We've been thinking about building a covering over it, especially after this, but that won't be for some time. Buildings cost money."

"So if someone, say, wanted to throw in—say—a necklace in the middle of the night, they could?"

His smile was tight. "Certainly. If they wanted the goddess's favor."

"Or a dead body?"

He picked up the goblet again. "If they wanted her curse."

"I see. What about the offerings?"

He took another sip and stared at me over the edge of the cup. "What about them?"

My smile probably curled a bit on the edges.

"Forgive me if I'm wrong, Papirius, but with the amount of offerings Sulis collects, in a month her spring would look like a rubbish heap, and no one could see the goddamn water. That is, if it wasn't cleaned out, and cleaned on a regular basis."

His lips pinched together. The goddess was displeased. Or maybe just Papirius.

"That's no secret. Of course we have to clean out the spring. Mud collects in the bottom, and would eventually prevent the water from even coming in. There's a sluice in there we open, and the force of the water flushes itself and the mud down an outlet to the main drain."

"Then what happens to the gifts? The donations to the Guild for Lesser Goddesses?"

"Kindly watch your tongue. You're still on sacred ground."

"I'll watch my tongue if you watch my face. Take a look at it. It's the face of an impious, impatient man, who is trying to solve a murder for you and your claque of upstart hicks. This is a business, we both know that, and the sooner I can get it all fixed for you, the sooner I can get the hell back to where I belong."

He stared at me rigidly, the goblet midway between his lips and the table. Finally, he put it down. "Some of the offerings are collected by the drain cleaners and brought into the temple."

"Only some? Why not all?"

"You've seen the spring. Heavier objects fall in the mud, and the mud is deep. The force of the water is very strong when we clean it. They can't catch everything."

"How many cleaners are there?"

"Four. All priests. Only those dedicated to Sulis's service may touch the offerings."

"What if something particularly pleasing to the goddess—a nice piece of jewelry, for instance—doesn't hit the water?"

He shrugged. "If it lands on the reservoir wall and doesn't slide down, one of the cleaners can go along the walkway and retrieve it. There's enough room. Then they bring it to me, and it's logged and deposited in the treasury."

"What if someone else wanted to pick it up? Someone who knew it would be there?"

That surprised him. "Someone stealing from Sulis? In this town? I don't believe it."

That is, someone *else* stealing from Sulis.

"Why not? Isn't it physically possible?"

"Physically, yes—I suppose so. They'd have to do it at night, or whenever they could snatch a moment and people weren't looking. I suppose they could dress as a priest—or use some kind of rake to pick it up. But it seems like a great deal of trouble for a very undependable source of income. Of course, there's also the risk of—well, the goddess's revenge."

"If you collect it, what happens to it? Where does it go?"

He sighed. "Into the temple treasury, which is stored inside the temple. It belongs, as I've told you, to the goddess. And I fear, Arcturus, I fear very much that you've already angered her past redemption."

"I tend to do that with women. But thanks for the warning." I stood up. "Can I see the temple treasury?"

"That's highly irregular. But if you must—"

"I must. By the way, when do you empty the spring again?"

"Tomorrow. We do it at sundown, as soon as the baths are empty."

He led me in silence from the plushly decorated room and back around to the front of the temple. I felt eyes on my back and turned around to catch a glimpse of Calpurnius.

"Calpurnius is a cleaner, isn't he?"

Papirius turned to look at me. "Yes. Why? Do you know him?"

"Not really."

We continued into the temple, the other priests scurrying out of his way.

"My wife ran into yours at the baths yesterday."

He cocked an eyebrow. "Oh? She met Flavia?"

"Had a great time. You know how women are—talk, talk, talk."

By now we were in the sanctum of sanctums. Sulis was one rich lady. Gold, silver, gemstones, coins, statues—all lined the walls, covered the floor, or filled chests stacked and labeled. The dates on them went back a long time. I whistled. Hell of a business.

Papirius led me to the nearest chest. "We haven't received many large offerings lately."

I guess Bibax didn't count.

He opened it and let my eyes feast on the bangles and bracelets. It was about half full. I looked up at the priest, who stretched his mouth and nodded.

I dug my hands in and brought up handfuls of gold and silver. They must let the bronze wash away. No clay, no wood. Just liquid assets, suitable for a spring.

I stood back up and thanked Papirius. He put a strongly fingered hand on my elbow and ushered me out. I'd seen plenty of jewelry and money—but no gold and amethyst necklace.

CHAPTER TEN

I shook my elbow from Papirius's peremptory grip. A sound of wild geese flying south hit my ears, and I realized it was the baths, letting the women out. The head priest ran hurriedly back to his rooms. I was heading toward the marketplace when a thin shadow crossed my path. Calpurnius, looking more than ever like a well-fed rat.

I confronted him. "When can we talk?"

"It depends on what you want to talk about."

"You know what I want to talk about, Calpurnius. Don't play games. I just got done playing with your boss, and if I can beat him, I don't think you're much of a contest."

His tongue ran over dry lips, pulled back in a mirthless smile. "If you talked to him, you don't need me."

I grabbed his arm and started to move him toward the spring. I kept my voice low. "I need to know what you know. I'll make sure you're rewarded for it."

That lit his sallow complexion more than the trickling sunlight, and made his skin blend in with the stone. He only wanted money, which made him one of the cleaner people in Aquae Sulis.

He murmured: "Will you be in the baths today?"

I nodded. "In about an hour. Can you meet me there?"

Barely perceptible nod. He looked around quickly, scanning for ears or eyes. Some priests were cleaning off the altar, others were sweeping the pavement.

I took my hand off his arm and he melted back into the yellow. A pair of red-brown eyes fixed mine with an intense stare before he rounded the corner of the temple and vanished.

I sighed. Time for Sulpicia.

I was staring at an expensive-looking town house with an Egyptian cat statue by the doorway and an antefix that proclaimed it was a souvenir from Arabia. A sweetly pungent odor of sandalwood and myrrh sinuously wound its way under my nose and started to do a striptease. It looked like the place she'd call home.

I knocked on the heavy door. A wizened old lady answered with wine on her breath. She looked me up and down—mostly down—and then threw the door wide open. I guess I met the qualifications for admittance.

She showed me into a gaudily decorated *triclinium*. I noticed the red dining couches were a little wider and a little plusher than usual, and there was a conspicuous lack of chairs. The smell was stronger now, mixed with other spices and a bit of violet. Lightly melodic lute music started somewhere from inside. Sulpicia must keep a slave with musical talents on hand . . . just in case.

The heavy curtain was covered with an additional layer of strung blue, purple, and green beads, completing the exotic allure. It was suddenly thrown aside. I stumbled on one of the couches, nearly falling. Sulpicia stood in the doorway, one hand bracing herself against the frame, the other on her hip, a knowing smile on her face.

"Welcome, Arcturus. I was hoping you'd . . . find me."

She sauntered into the room. It took her about half an hour to lower herself on to one of the couches. Then she clapped her hands for a servant and turned to me with more than an invitation. It was an outright demand.

"Any—preferences? Falernian, perhaps? Oscan? Maybe some . . . Greek?"

I looked down and found my feet on the floor. They were trying to point to the exit.

"No—no, anything will do, Sulpicia, thank you."

She raised an eyebrow. "Certainly not anything. One must be—particular—mustn't one? Do sit down, Arcturus, you're making me nervous just standing there, like a particularly strong specimen of—oak."

I moved to the opposite couch and perched on the edge, making myself as uncomfortable as possible. Sulpicia eyed me for a moment and then burst out laughing.

"Oh, really, now, Doctor, you mustn't be so frightened. I don't bite—at least, not unless you want me to."

Another servant—this one young and handsome—brought in the wine.

"Thank you, Gaius, that will be all. Please tell Numa to keep playing." She turned to me. "I find the lute so relaxing—don't you? And they say relaxation and leisure are the ideal things in life, don't they?"

I gulped the wine. I knew it would be good, much better than anyone else's in Aquae Sulis. Sulpicia sipped hers, long nails delicately wrapped around the silver cup, her eyes making promises I was afraid she'd try to keep.

She set the wine cup down with an air of decision and rose to her feet. Her body was outlined in a diaphanous sheath, and she wasn't wearing anything underneath it. She made sure I noticed. It was hard not to.

The smile never left her face, but widened as she approached. Finally, she sat down. The heat from her body wrapped itself around me like an ivy tendril, and I shifted a few inches away.

"Come now, Arcturus. You're a hard—hardworking, I should say—man . . . you're also a man of the world. You've seen something of it, the palaces of Rome, the granaries and temples of Egypt. Let's be . . . adults, shall we?"

She was curving herself closer, her smell overwhelming me, as the lute music echoed in my head and started to make me dizzy. I leaned as far back as I could without actually lying down. That might be fatal.

"Aquae Sulis is a place for relaxation. A temple for the soul . . . and the body. I think you should relax, Doctor . . . and think about . . . think about healing yourself."

Her lips parted to reveal a small tongue, which darted over them before hiding itself, but promised to come out again if I blinked my eyes. She was leaning in, her breasts brushing my tunic, and I thought I could feel her hands start to travel up my legs. She was almost in my lap, and I thought about Gwyna, and this morning, and I jumped off the couch.

Sulpicia fell over, unprepared for the hasty exit. She glared up at me and suddenly looked a lot older.

"What the hell is wrong with you?"

"Nothing—now. I didn't come here for an easy lay, Sulpicia. That would be young Drusius, not the old doctor."

She flushed, angry, flounced back over to her couch and her cup, and threw back a shot of wine like a professional. She glared at me some more. When I met her eyes and held them, the anger started to fade. After another shot, she was able to smile, albeit a little vindictively.

"Did Drusius tell you? Maybe he mentioned how good it feels when I—"

"No. He's a stonecutter, but he's a gentleman."

She snorted. "I don't need a gentleman. Too many goddamn 'gentlemen' in this town as it is."

"You mean like Vitellius?"

"Vitellius makes himself look too much like a hairless worm. I prefer men with some—hair—on their bodies."

I felt like I was the one in the transparent sheath.

"Oh, dear. You really blush like a virgin, don't you?" Her laugh was deep and throaty. I cleared my own throat and tried not to look too much like a boy on his first trip to the whorehouse.

"No. Vitellius is all right. He keeps himself busy, but when he's mine, he's mine. And he . . . does things for me . . . he's very good at it."

She smiled lazily, like a cat about to pounce. "You should try it sometime on your wife. It might make her feel better. Poor thing. How long has it been?"

She caught the shock in my face and raised her eyebrows. "What? You mean—you don't know? You? The *medicus* of all Britannia?"

She started laughing, and it was a sad sound, even with the cruelty in it. I sank back down on the couch and wondered what the hell was wrong with my wife and why everyone knew about it except me. Sulpicia's laugh trailed off, and she stared at me for a few minutes. When she spoke, her voice was unexpectedly gentle.

"I won't tell you if she hasn't. Her secret—such as it is—is safe with me. Talk to your wife, Arcturus. And—well—depending on the outcome—the offer . . . still stands."

She got brusque, as if the seduction scene were over, and too much emotion would spoil the act. "So why did you come? Curiosity? Or was it a preview?"

I leaned forward. "Who's blackmailing you, Sulpicia?"

The wine cup dropped on the floor with a clang, spilling yellow fluid over the Gallic rug. Sulpicia's hand crept up to her throat. Her eyes were enormous and her tall, lean body rigid.

"What—what are you talk—"

A middle-aged woman of undoubted but fading charms, frightened for her life. She didn't bat a single one of her thick black eyelashes over Bibax's body, and here she was trembling beneath the thin sheath.

"Sulpicia—listen. I know you're being blackmailed. I think Bibax's murder was connected with other things in Aquae Sulis, foul things. As foul as—maybe even fouler than—putting a curse on your husband, and . . . having it come true?"

"I—I didn't know—I wasn't sure—"

"What you did or didn't know is between you and Nemesis. It's true, isn't it—you're being blackmailed."

She nodded, her face whiter than her makeup.

"And Bibax—Bibax's curses—they sometimes came true, didn't they? For a price?"

She nodded again, her eyes flickering around the room.

"Who's the blackmailer, Sulpicia? Who?"

I gripped her face by the chin and turned her head to look at me. She was still terrified, and I couldn't just slap her. My only other choice was to kiss her. So I slapped her lightly.

She put her fingers to her cheek, looking at me in surprise. "I—I don't know. I get notes—where to go, how much to leave. I'm almost—almost out of money."

"Is is always at the spring? Or the baths?"

"N-no. Sometimes I leave things in the cubicles, with no one to watch them. Sometimes it's the spring. Once it was under the statue outside my door."

"Do you have any of the notes?"

She shook her head. "I burn them. They say to burn them, and I'm afraid—"

"You're afraid if you disobey, you'll be next." I got up to go to my own seat. "You never struck me as a superstitious sort."

"You—you don't know. They—whoever it is—they have some kind of power. They'll kill me, if they know I've talked."

I thought about it for a minute. It would be hard to explain to my wife, but it could work.

"Listen—when you get the next note—how often do they come?"

"About once a month."

I grimaced. I hoped to be out of Aquae Sulis long before a month.

"If you get any communication from them at all, let me know. I'll come over immediately."

"But if someone sees you—"

This was the difficult part.

"Tell them we're having an affair."

The farce of it all overwhelmed her fear long enough for laughter.

She laughed for long minutes, drawing out each breath and shaking with it. Finally, they subsided, and she looked at me with half a smile.

"But you don't want my body. You want my information."

I grinned back at her.

"No offense. Your body is quite nice—and I've seen a lot of them. But my wife . . ."

She sighed. "She is a beautiful woman. And you love her. I hope she realizes how lucky she is. I've always wanted a man who loved me—not just who loved loving me."

I let myself feel gratified while she watched me with a wistful expression. But hope died hard in Sulpicia, and she got up from the couch with a gleam in her eyes. Suddenly I heard lute music again.

"I'd better go. I have an appointment at the baths."

She was getting uncomfortably close standing there and was somehow looking much younger than a few minutes ago. Her voice was a purr.

"I'll send you a message the second I know anything. And I'll tell you . . . whatever it is . . . you want to know."

I backed out of the room. "We'll have to talk again. Maybe tomorrow."

She leaned into me suddenly, and with such force that I had to hold her to keep her upright.

"Anytime, Arcturus. And remember what I said . . . the offer."

Her pelvis was slowly gyrating against mine. She put her lips to my ear to whisper, and I felt a nibble.

"I'm still fertile. I could give you anything. Anything, Arcturus. I know . . . all kinds of things . . . that can help you . . . relax."

I fled the house, my ears full of sandalwood and lute music in my nose.

Ligur was waiting for me. I hoped Sulis's miracle water would get the smell of sandalwood out of my hair. I was undressing when I felt a small pluck at my elbow. Aeron.

"Sir—you told me to tell you—"

"Yes?" I said encouragingly.

"There's a man been here to see you. A priest."

Calpurnius. "Where did he go?"

"He was asking around to see if anyone saw you come in. I knew he was talking about you from what he said. He went inside—the Great Bath."

I tipped the boy and walked through the arch. Everyone was already there—I'd missed the fashionable hour again. Grattius splashing on one end, Vitellius stretched out on the pavement near Papirius, Philo leaning against a side of the pool with his eyes closed. Gaius Secundus was on the opposite end from Grattius, with Big Belly and Fish Eye, the two men I'd seen when I first arrived, and a competing gaggle of others I didn't know.

I saw the *gemmarius* and Buteo among a less moneyed group, in an overcrowded part of the pool farthest away from the pipe that fed the water. No Calpurnius.

I was hoping to escape notice, but Octavio appeared out of no-where.

"Arcturus! So glad to see you again!"

He could've been heard over Hannibal's elephants. The poet trying to sing Apollonius looked over at us in irritation, and Grattius bellowed out to me.

"Arcturus! C'mere, my boy, c'mere!"

Octavio escorted me over; Secundus looked around, saw me, and decided to join us. Two *duovirs* at the same time. You're such a lucky bastard, Arcturus.

"Arcturus—Grattius. We've got to set that census date, Grattius, next session. No gettin' around it, this time."

Grattius climbed out of the water, looking like a pimple that needed to pop. "No talking shop, Secundus. You know my baths are sacred."

The other *duovir* grunted. "Bring your mare tonight, Arcturus. My stallion can cover her. She sounded like she was in heat." He nodded at me and Philo, who'd sidled up, before returning to his own territory.

Grattius looked after him with dislike. "You're having dinner with Secundus? Poor boy. You should stop by my house first so you can eat decently. Secundus thinks everyone should eat like horses. Probably shits in pellets, just like his stallion."

He guffawed, and a hammy hand slapped his freckled, quivering thigh, leaving a pink suffusion that slowly spread through the white.

"Arcturus—can I speak to you?"

Philo sniffed the air suddenly, and I wondered if I still smelled like Sulpicia. He took me by the arm and led me to the west end, in an alcove near Vitellius and away from Grattius. I could find everyone I didn't want to see, but no Calpurnius. Where the hell was he?

I was impatient. "What is it?"

Philo studied me for a moment. "It's your wife."

My eyes narrowed. "What about her, Philo?"

"She came to see me this afternoon. She asked me not to tell you."

"She did? But what—why—"

He shook his head. "She's worried, Arcturus. Overly interested in this Bibax problem, and the Aquae Sulis gossip. It's not good for her— especially in her condition."

I tried to keep from exploding and to look like I knew what he was talking about. "What do you suggest, Philo? I chain her to the kitchen stove?"

He smiled and infuriatingly patted me on the back. "Every woman likes excitement, and she's a woman of tremendous spirit. She told me what you've been doing—how you think you've stumbled on a series of murders, possibly connected to Bibax. It sounds fantastic, but I've seen enough of the world to expect the unexpected. I'll help in any way I can."

He looked into my eyes with intensity. "If it's true, she could be in danger. If it's not true, the excitement could overstimulate her. I would just—watch her. But there—I'm giving advice that isn't wanted to a better doctor—and a husband, besides."

"Thanks for the concern."

He shrugged. "Not at all. I care about your wife. And you. I'm sure you find that hard to believe, but I do care. The welfare of everyone in Aquae Sulis—visitor or resident—is important to me."

My back itched. I turned around, and a pair of rodent eyes were peering at me from the western room.

"Excuse me, Philo. Thanks again. We'll talk soon."

He stared at me and then turned back toward Vitellius, a slave trailing behind him with a bottle of scented oil.

I walked into the dimmer room with the smaller pool of magic water. Calpurnius was lurking in a niche on the end closest to the Great Bath.

"Where've you been? I've been waiting!" he hissed.

"You're early. What've you got to tell me?"

He glanced around the stone, which in the murky light looked like the color of old cream.

"I can't stay much longer. I have to empty the spring tonight."

"When?"

"Sundown. Senicio and I."

"Then talk. What did you mean about Bibax and his curses?"

He shrugged. "I think you already know."

"Maybe I guessed, but you can tell me more. Like what happens to certain offerings—the ones made by former customers."

His narrow eyes got bigger. "You—how did you—"

"It doesn't matter how. I'm after three things. One—who *Ultor* is. Someone being blackmailed? Maybe. Or someone who figured out the game and didn't like the score."

He looked increasingly nervous. The pool around us was not quite empty, and someone standing at the other end could still see us talking.

"Two. Who's behind the Bibax scam. He had a partner, or maybe more than one. The dead don't collect blackmail."

Calpurnius was breathing harder, and his knuckles were white.

"Three. I'd like to find out, before I leave, what the hell is wrong with this city. It's got too many goddamn ghosts."

He looked up from his lap, where he was holding on to his hands as if they might fall off. There was a curious light in his eyes.

He whispered: *"Cui bono?"*

I remembered my Cicero but still didn't understand the reference.

"What do you mean?"

He bit his lip and searched the room again. "I can't talk now. Meet me tonight. By the spring."

"We've got a dinner party—"

"Make it late. The fifth hour of night."

I nodded brusquely. "All right. Fifth hour. By the spring."

Calpurnius got up from the wooden bench and faded into the stone like a small patch of mildew. *Cui bono.* Who the hell profits?

CHAPTER ELEVEN

The walk home was drier but more uncomfortable. Calpurnius and his *cui* goddamn *bono*. Sulpicia, who made me feel like the new girl at the discount whorehouse. Then there was the small matter of strangers telling me what was wrong with my wife. Or, more specifically, not telling me.

I looked up and found myself at the door to the villa. I wasn't in the mood to discover anyone else fawning over Gwyna, and I banged the door extra loudly.

Well-trained slaves appeared, as they always did in this house. Ligor melted back into them while a shepherd detached himself from the flock and ushered me into the *triclinium*. Gwyna wasn't there.

"Where's my wife?"

"In the bedroom, sir. I believe she is dressing for dinner."

He gave me a look like I should be dressing for dinner, too, and wasn't I just a wee bit embarrassed to be running around Aquae Sulis with a mud-spattered tunic and my hair unpomaded?

I grinned at him. "Thanks. What's your name again?"

"Lineus, sir."

"Well, Lineus, I will now go into my bedroom, with my wife, and change for dinner. Is that right?"

He bowed stiffly. "If you are going out to dinner, *Dominus*."

I murmured, "Remind me when I don't use the right knife with the appetizer."

He raised his eyebrows, bowed, and withdrew. Damn good servant. I bet *he* knew what was wrong with Gwyna.

I walked down the corridor and softly tapped on the bedroom door. "Is it you, Ardur?"

I said yes and heard some whispers, rustling, and a drawer being shut. The kinds of noises you always hear whenever a woman is behind a locked door and wants to make an entrance.

The door opened, and one of the other slaves skittered out. She looked at me and smiled. Thin woman, carried herself with a certain Gallic fashion. Probably a dressmaker.

"Come in, Ardur. I'm ready."

No lutes, but the Muses were doing a group chorale somewhere in the garden. She was taller, wearing some sort of high-heeled cork sandals. Her hair swept up from her neck and was piled high in gently falling ringlets of golden blond.

The silk tunic showed off her collarbone and draped very low in the front. The purple glowed against her skin, and a red mantle clung tightly to her bare shoulders. Clusters of pearls were hanging at her ears. My mouth was hanging open.

She smiled at me. "I've done a bit of shopping. I hope you don't mind."

I shook my head and dug around in my tunic for the necklace I'd bought her.

"For me? Why, thank you Ardur!" She sat on the bed and started to open the small pouch. "Why don't you get dressed? I found a toga for you—nothing special. At least it's one of the shorter ones you like better—not as many folds. It's on the other side of the bed."

Still mute, I skirted around her, to where a gleaming white toga was lying on the blanket. It was stiff and uncomfortable. That made two of us.

Arms wrapped around my neck and lips showered the back of my head with kisses.

"I love it! It's beautiful—thank you, Ardur, my love, my husband, my—"

I turned around and kissed her long and hard. She ran out of breath before I did. I didn't need to breathe.

"Ar . . . dur. We—I missed you, too, and I'm glad you don't object to the shopping. I got the prices down, but it was still a little expensive."

I looked at the toga. My togas usually got dirty in proportion to how white they were when we started out together. This one was very white.

"It's nice, as togas go."

"Well, hurry and put it on. We don't have much time."

She watched as I took off my tunic and shoes. It was nice to be stared at by my own wife for a change.

"I love the emerald necklace—and the Diana. She's a special goddess to me, did you—did you know that?"

"No. I'm glad I bought the right thing."

She was quiet while I wrestled with the toga. Then her voice came out small.

"Ardur—you didn't buy this out of—of guilt, did you? You saw Sulpicia today . . ."

The toga was half on, and I had to yell through the cloth.

"Of course not! I bought it this morning, I'll have you know! What the hell does Sulpicia have to do with anything? Come here and help me with this thing, and bring some *fibulae*."

I finally got my face out of the cloth and was starting to wrap it around myself when she came over with two pins.

"Well—I want to hear everything that happened today. Especially with Sulpicia."

"I'll be happy to tell you. After the dinner party. I want to know what you did, too—Philo said you'd come by."

She nodded, a satisfied look on her face. "That was a test. I wanted to see if he'd be more loyal to you or to me."

"I'm not sure it was such a good idea to tell him about our ideas."

"Why not? If he's involved, then it might make him do something rash. If he isn't, then he can help."

She stood on tiptoe and started to pin my shoulder. I yelped.

"Sorry. I hope he's not tangled up in this. I rather like Philo."

I looked down at her darkly. "Don't."

"Now, Ardur. Don't be jealous."

"Look who's talking! When poor Sulpicia—"

"Poor Sulpicia? Poor Sulpicia?! 'Poor' Sulpicia as good as murdered her husband. Just because she makes you feel like a satyr in rut—"

"I am not a satyr in rut!" I protested.

The wicked smile came back. She raised her lips to brush my cheek.

"Yes, you are," she murmured, "but we have a murder—several murders, in fact—to bring to justice. If Sulpicia doesn't quit trying to scratch her itch on you, there'll be another—and you'll know who did it."

I was beginning to like togas. A lot.

The host greeted us with disappointment when he saw the litter bearers.

"No mare? But Arcturus—"

"She's not in heat, Secundus. If she goes into heat, we'll talk."

He grumbled a bit and led us in. His wife, a great hulking toothy woman who seemed to fill the room to capacity by herself, greeted us with a ferocious smile.

"Welcome, welcome. Glad to have you both. 'Course, I know the little wife."

She chucked Gwyna under the chin, and Gwyna flinched, her eyes narrowed. Materna cleared her throat and dragged forward a pretty young girl, obviously bored.

"Secunda. My daughter."

Her tone implied that Secundus had very little to do with it.

Secunda nodded, showing some interest in looking over Gwyna's clothes and jewelry. When the survey was over, she closed her eyelids and slumped into the dining room. The other guests were already assembled.

Secundus offered me the so-called position of honor on the couches: *imus in medio.* I was glad for once. From the position on the low corner of the traditional square *C,* I could see everyone else's reactions, the reason why this was supposed to be an honor. Maybe the bad food and worse society would be worth it.

Gwyna was below me and to the right. Below her was Big Belly, the councilman I'd met on our first day in Aquae Sulis. He was introduced as Quintus Pompeius—the town tax collector, a frequent dinner guest at every rich table in town. He nodded at us and scooted over. His wife was stuck in the bottom on the far right, in the lowest-of-the-low seat.

Above and next to me, middle on the middle couch, was a soldier, a middle-aged legionary with the unfortunate name of Marcus Mumius Modestus. He was the kind of man who never got beyond the middle, even at a dinner party.

The young Secunda was immediately above him, and mama Materna was keeping a beady eye on both of them. Her daughter might want to play "sheathe the *gladius*" out of sheer ennui.

Materna took up most of the room on the highest couch. To the right and above her, Secundus tried not to disappear. Their most interesting guest held on to the far right *summus in summus* position with his fingernails.

"Arcturus—this is Faro Magnus. You've probably heard of him."

Faro the Great. The one who could raise the dead. Sounded easier than raising any life in this place.

I nodded at Faro while Secundus talked about him like one of his horses.

"I told you the wife and I are keen on theatricals. Well, Faro has agreed to do something special for us tonight. He's quite a little find,

Faro is." He winked broadly. "Right after we eat—can't keep the cook waiting!"

The food was as stale and tasteless as the party. We gummed our way through a watery oyster and anchovy appetizer, gnawed an overcooked capon stuffed with cold chestnuts and tasteless truffles, and glued our lips together trying to eat the honeyed dates. I proceeded to ruin another set of napkins. They weren't cheap. We couldn't afford any more free dinners.

Faro, at least, was interesting. Slight man, well groomed, with black hair, thick and curly. His skin was startlingly white, his eyes an eerie, penetrating gray. He looked the part. Like the rest of us, he ate without much appetite.

Materna watched everyone, her eyes shining like a beetle's back. A frightening woman. If I looked in her hand, I'd probably find some strings tied to Secundus's back. Somehow I didn't think she liked us. Especially Gwyna.

Our eyes met, and she bared her teeth at me. I smiled and accidentally swallowed a date pit. For relief, I turned to Mumius.

"So, Mumius—what legion are you with?"

He was picking date off his teeth. "II Augusta."

"Oh—so you're at Isca Silurum?"

He nodded. "Right now I have a message for the fortlet outside Aquae Sulis, and then I'm to report for Household service in Londinium. Hurt my leg, so they transferred me."

"How'd you injure it?"

He turned red and stared at his dates. "Tripped on a picket."

I changed the subject.

"What do you do?"

"I'm a wheelwright."

I was hoping for more fascinating conversation from this unexpected new source, but Secundus made a noise in his throat, and everyone except Materna looked at him expectantly. She was gazing at Faro, with a suggestion she hoped he would raise more than the dead. Poor bastard. That would be a real miracle.

Two slaves cleared the tray in front of the necromancer, and he sat up, moving as deliberately as a tightrope walker. His eyes stared across the room, unfocused and blank.

"Well, as I say, the wife and I—we're interested in things. Entertainments, and whatnot. And, if I may speak for you, dear"—Materna nodded her massive head at him graciously—"I—that is to say, we—think there's much to be said for certain talents."

He cleared his throat again and looked around nervously, as if he were afraid we'd all take the chance to yawn and leave the party.

"Faro here, for example. Now, I'm sure you've all read about people raising ghosts, but Faro here can really do it. He can talk to the dead. Gets 'em to talk back. So I thought—that is to say, we thought—why not give him a go at the party?"

Secundus sat down and smiled at his wife like a dog waiting for instructions.

I glanced sideways at Gwyna. She'd been talking with Crescentia, Big Belly's wife, for most of the night. Now her eyes were enormous, and riveted on Faro. The black hair, the pale face, the expressive eyes—which seemed lifeless and dull, as if he had to empty his own soul to make contact with others. The mask was just about perfect. I couldn't tell if it was comic or tragic.

The Entertainment waited a decent interval for the Host to be patted on the head by the Hostess. Then he looked around the room as if he'd just noticed it. His mouth opened, and the voice was sonorous and commanding.

"Dark. We must have dark."

Secunda giggled and arched her back toward Faro as if to say, "Take me now." Big Belly and his wife squirmed a little. Gwyna's eyes were still on the necromancer. I was beginning to dislike him. He was like a smell that started out tolerable and got rank the more you inhaled. I didn't object to a con man. Just an oily, good-looking one.

Secundus clapped his hands and told the slaves to put out the lamps.

One by one, the room started to become dim, then gray, then nearly dark. It was always dull.

Magic didn't mean much to me. People like Faro had to make a living, too, and I could usually spot the tricks they pulled on rubes like Secundus. Most necromancers were small, starved-looking men, with lean eyes and furtive mouths, who looked like they not only spoke to the dead but borrowed their clothes. Their palms would be sticky with sweat and anything else that could help them deliver a trick or two. Faro's hands were dry and steady, more like a doctor's than a magician's. I couldn't see anything on them but skin. Not yet.

When all but one of the lamps were extinguished, a slave brought out a small table with three vases and set it in front of Faro. He picked up the first one and held it up so we could make out its shape in the darkened room.

"A sacrifice of milk—pure milk, mother's milk, suckled from the breast of the earth—"

Secunda stifled another giggle, choking it down when her mother turned a baleful look on her. He poured it into a shallow dish reverently, then held up another vase in the same way.

"A sacrifice of wine—pure wine, god's seed, spent from the body of Bacchus, intermediary of the dead, savior of man, intercessor with Proserpine—"

An Orphic touch. Nice work. Showed Faro was educated, maybe even a member of one of the more exclusive religious cults.

He poured the wine into the same dish, just a few drops. No one made any sound. I stifled a yawn. I hoped it wasn't the old water-to-wine trick. That was hackneyed fifty years ago.

Finally, he picked up the smallest vase. "A sacrifice of honey—pure honey, the moisture of the goddess, the life-giving Proserpine, the wife of Pluto, and mother of the dead."

The honey drizzled very slowly. Materna leaned forward, waiting for it to drop from the vase, as if she believed the royal couple of Hades would suddenly materialize in the dish. Even Secunda was awake and not picking at her fingernails.

When enough honey oozed out, Faro shook his head three times, shook the plate three times, and started to chant.

"*Amoun aunantou laimoutau riptou mantaui mantou* Apollo, hear me, Apollo, God of prophecy and oracles, *Amoun, Aunantou laimoutau riptou mantaui mantou,* hear me, oh goddess Minerva, goddess that is Sulis, send your fallen, send your secrets, *amoun aunantuou laimoutau!*"

The chant got louder and more emphatic with every name. Faro's eyes were rolled back—I could see the white catch in the dim light. A breeze wafted through the room, and the last lamp flickered and died out.

"*Amoun aunantuou laimoutau!* Sulis—your secrets—the dead—lately or past—who is here who wants to speak? Who is here who misses? Who is here that yearns? *Amoun—*"

He was yelling, building to a crescendo that was almost a scream. The hair on my arms was standing on edge. Faro was good. Too good for Aquae Sulis.

"—*aunantou—laimoutau!* Sulis—let them speak! Let them hear! Let them see!"

Silence fell like a gravestone. Ragged breathing was the only thing I could hear. Then Faro's voice . . . but it didn't sound like Faro's voice. It sounded like a child's.

"Mommy—Daddy—we—we love you."

Crescentia was sitting rigidly upright, her body trembling in the darkness. Big Belly—Pompeius—was beside her, his arm around her shoulders.

"P-Pompeia? Is—is it you?"

The voice came again. It didn't seem to be coming from Faro.

"Yes, Daddy. Sextus is here, too. We miss you, Daddy."

Crescentia turned to Pompeius. "Oh—God—"

They clung to each other. Faro's mouth was open, but I couldn't see it move.

"We—we love you, too, children. Please—please see us—come to us—if you can."

"Yes, Daddy—we will see you and Mommy soon. We will come to you."

The voice was fading. Crescentia was sobbing in Pompeius's arms, and her husband was a grayer shade of gray. My muscles were sore from tension. What the hell was going on here? Who the hell was Faro, and what was he getting out of causing people pain?

I was halfway off the couch when a different voice pierced the darkness. This one was deep and authoritative.

"Another one waits. One who cannot talk."

It was Materna, this time. She thrust her neck out like a turtle, eager for more.

"Someone else? Who?"

The voice was silent for so long I thought it was finally over and we could turn on the lights and get some answers. Mumius grumbled and said something about "not what he expected." I agreed with him. Then the voice started again.

"One is waiting. He . . . he cannot talk. He is . . . too young. He was—never born."

I heard some shuffling next to me and felt sorry for Crescentia. Would the bastard never stop?

"He—he does not blame her . . . it is not her fault—for what happened. He says . . . he says he wishes he could have been—he would have been—a good son . . . for his mother. And his father."

One of the tables crashed to the floor, and I could see a figure below me rush off the couch and out of the room, sobbing uncontrollably. Poor Crescentia. I was off the couch and standing. I'd settle the bastard. No one should have to go through something like that.

Secundus called for a light, and a slave lit a lamp to my right. The table was on the floor, and wine was spilled everywhere. Pompeius was sitting, staring down, clutching his wife in his arms. Crescentia was still on the couch. It was Gwyna who'd run out.

CHAPTER TWELVE

The shock was starting to wash over me, but I didn't have time to feel it. Much. Secundus was staring at me, slack-jawed and stupid. Pompeius tried to quiet Crescentia. Materna's eyes glittered, darting, the show better than she'd hoped. Faro lay stretched on the couch. Time to break the fucking trance.

I grabbed his tunic and lifted him off the floor. "Mumius! Hold this man. I want him in custody."

Secundus started to speak. "We—that is, I—"

I turned to him. The look on my face was enough. "Get your sword out, Mumius."

"But—I don't—I don't have author—"

I lowered Faro to the ground suddenly, hard enough to make his knees buckle. "You do now. I'm a senior officer."

His *gladius* was shaking, but he pointed it in the right direction. I stared down at Secundus.

"He'll stay here tonight. You'll all stay here tonight, except for Pompeius and Crescentia." They were still holding each other, and I nodded at them. "You've had enough. Go home."

I threw Faro back into the couch and watched it skid a few feet across the mosaic floor. Then I turned to leave. Materna rose from her seat like the Minotaur.

"Just who gave you the right to come into my home and—"

I spun around from the doorway.

"Who gave you the right to do what you've done to my wife? Or them?"

I pointed at Pompeius and Crescentia, who were gathering their cloaks, and my finger was shaking with anger. I stared at her glistening eyes, the fat, yellowed face.

"Keep your mouth shut, lady. Or I'll shut it for you."

I shoved two slaves aside on the way out, tried to find the litter bearers. They were nowhere in sight, and neither was Gwyna.

"Gwyna!" I didn't give a fuck who heard me. "Gwyna!"

Still no answer. I started walking.

I called her name intermittently, as I wound down a low hill to the outskirts of the city street. Calm night, not too cold. She'd be all right. She had to be all right. Goddamn it, Arcturus. You should have known. You're a doctor—you've seen it often enough. You should have fucking known.

"Gwyna!"

No answer. I stepped on rocks and didn't feel them, and the toga—the toga she bought me—was turning brown. She wouldn't like that. I held my breath and screwed up my face tight. No time for it. No time for panic. No goddamn time.

"Gwyna! Where are you?"

Rocking back and forth, back and forth. Keep walking. Not the goddamn time, not now. Not now. The drops fell on my hands, and I rubbed my cheeks and jaw viciously. Keep it in, goddamn it, Arcturus, find your wife. Find your wife.

"Gwyna! Gwyna! Please answer!"

I was almost at the villa. The door was there, and I pushed it in and was running into the *triclinium* when Lineus appeared.

"Where is she?"

"Your—your wife isn't here, sir. The litter bearers returned, but she wasn't with them. I assumed you both decided to walk back."

"She's not here—are you sure? She's got to be—Gwyna! Gwyna!" I ran through the house bellowing her name. Lineus and a trail of slaves followed me.

"Gwyna? Gwyna!"

They looked in every corner—outside in the garden, the barn. Lineus mobilized them like an army, staying with me while I threw open every door in the house. No Gwyna.

I turned to Lineus. "I'm going to look in town. If she comes in the meantime—"

"I'll hold her here for you, sir. Don't worry."

Aquae Sulis was a pale cream in the moonlight. The fountain by Natta's shop sputtered its uneven drops, my footsteps echoing, a hurried, urgent shuffling in the desolate market square.

What did she say about Diana? A special goddess? And the Isis—it made sense now. Diana and Isis. Both goddesses for childbirth.

Don't think, Arcturus. Don't feel. Just walk.

"Gwyna! Gwyna!"

No answer but my own voice bouncing against the yellow limestone. Maybe—maybe a goddess—it was a chance. A hope. A prayer.

I found her looking over the edge of the spring. The square was empty, and the temple was just a rectangular building, but the spring still bubbled.

She was holding the Diana stone I'd bought for her, face pale. She couldn't do it here—it's not easy in six and a half feet of water. But she was thinking about it.

Her shoulders were bare and cold to my touch, the skin flat and dead. As dead as the child we'd made together.

"I'm . . . I'm sorry I failed you. I should've known—should've realized . . . and—and I'm sorry we lost a child."

Her face was emotionless. Empty, like Faro's eyes. I shook her, her hair tumbling.

"Goddamn it, I love you! I don't care if we never have children! I love you! Do you understand? You! Not your goddamn womb!"

She looked at me. Her hand crept to my face.

"You don't want—you don't want . . ."

"Of course I'd like to make a family—with you. Because I'd like to leave the world a better place when I'm gone, and the only way I know how is to make sure there's a little bit of you still on it. But you . . . when I thought you might—please, God, please—please don't . . ."

I couldn't hold it back anymore. I clung to her, holding her so tight against my chest that I could feel her heart beat, even through the sobs that were shaking my body.

We stood like that for a long time. And the spring bubbled.

The look of relief on Lineus's face endeared him to me.

"I see you've found her, *Dominus*."

"Yes, and I'm never going to misplace her again, I promise you."

I looked down into Gwyna's eyes. "Lineus, please tell the litter bearers we won't need them tomorow. Give them the day off. Could you make sure that for the rest of the night, we are not disturbed—I mean, complete privacy. Is that clear?"

"Oh, yes, sir."

He beckoned the door slave away and handed me a lamp. By the time we reached the bath, there was no one else in the entire wing.

She told me everything.

How she kept it from me because of Gnaeus's death. She wanted to surprise me, give me life again. Give me a son.

She told me how she was doing some cleaning and bent down and started to bleed. It wouldn't stop, and the pain kept growing. All she thought of was the baby—how to save the baby. I felt like I was bleeding myself, hearing how she fled to our room, holding a pillow to her abdomen, trying not to scream. She didn't want Hefin to know.

She told me how she sent Coir for Stricta. Thank God she knew what to do. Stricta thought of Gwyna. She saved her life. The baby—the baby was four months along.

Stricta kept Gwyna's secret. Even from Bilicho—because she knew Bilicho would tell me, and Gwyna . . . Gwyna didn't want me to know.

Then she told me how Coir had seen the bloodstains, realized what happened. How she used the knowledge to keep Gwyna in the palm of her hand.

Despair gave way to anger. Anger at Coir, even a little anger at Stricta, but especially at myself. Gwyna didn't tell me she was pregnant because she wanted to surprise me, bring me out of my guilt and depression. She didn't want to interfere with my—duties. But the only goddamn duty that mattered was the one I failed her in.

She was still dressed in her purple gown, shivering. She needed the warm water. I did, too. I brought some towels and the oil and started to undress her, as carefully and gently as my shaking hands would allow.

"Ardur—what are you—"

"Shh. You did this for me once, when I came home dirty and sore and miserable. Now it's my turn."

She looked up at me, her mouth trembling. I was unpinning her tunic. When I started to unwrap her breast band, she tried to push my hands away.

"N-no, Ardur, I—I'm not—"

I held her hands in mine and raised them to my lips.

"I don't know what you see, Gwyna. I see a woman with a beautiful, miraculous body, as desirable as the day I first saw it. More so, if possible. You don't have anything to hide, and nothing—nothing—to be ashamed of."

She stared at me for what seemed like forever. I unraveled her breast band and looked at her.

Her breasts were fuller, just as lovely. But all she could remember was the milk that had started to flow in them, and the baby that would never suckle.

I held her eyes up with my own. "You take my breath away."

My hands cupped them, and she shuddered while I used my tongue.

"Ardur—Ardur, not—not now . . ."

"Now is the best time. No more waiting. No more running away. For either of us."

After a few minutes, I gave my attention to the small briefs, as my hands molded the line of her hips down to her legs. She shuddered again when I slid them off. It was the first time I'd seen her naked since I'd left home, so long ago.

Her abdomen was gently swollen, and she hadn't lost all the extra weight of the pregnancy. The telltale signs others had noticed, but not her blind husband.

I led her into the *tepidarium* and gently washed her with a sponge. I touched every part of her, made it mine again. She stopped shaking so much every time she felt my hands. Then I rubbed her back and buttocks with oil and massaged her legs, stomach, and breasts until her nipples were ready to burst.

We climbed out of the pool together, and I dried her with a towel. She reached a hand up to my face and kissed me, softly first, but with a growing need to blot out the night. While our mouths were still intertwined, I picked her up in my arms and stumbled toward the bedroom.

We kept kissing while I kicked the door and laid her gently on the bed. Then my mouth traveled lower down her breasts to below her belly, until she objected.

"Ardur—what—no—"

"Shhh. Trust me, my love. Trust me."

The happiness I felt when she gasped with pleasure, and gave herself over to it, helped cleanse some of the guilt and washed away a little of the pain. It was equaled later when we were both crying out, not with sorrow, but with a love that was our whole life. Toward morning, we fell asleep in each other's arms.

I woke up before dawn. Gwyna nestled in the crook of my arm, hair tousled and curling on my chest. She groaned and stretched and opened an eye.

"Good morning."

"Good morning to you. How do you feel?"

She blushed. "Like a loose woman."

Some anemic moonlight filtered in from the small window. She sat up and stretched again, making a shadow on the wall.

I yawned. "You feel nothing like a loose woman. I've had a few."

She threw her pillow on my face, and I reached up and pulled her down on my chest again.

"Ardur."

"Yes, love?"

"What—what do you think happened last night?"

I sat up in bed, set her in front of me. "A fraud, Gwyna. Someone put Faro up to it. Someone's trying to hurt us."

Her face held doubt as if she were reluctant to let it go. That was the problem with cons like Faro's. That's what made them so evil.

"Darling—listen to me. None of that—none—was real or true. Please believe me."

She lowered her eyes and shook her head. "All—all right, Ardur, but who—who knew about me?"

"Philo, for one. Sulpicia, for another."

"Sulpicia? Philo, I can understand—I—I asked him about it—said a friend of mine—"

"He would've guessed it was you, and Sulpicia may've had—I don't know—some similar experiences. Maybe she recognized how you felt. She seemed to—well, be sorry."

Gwyna looked over at me with a little of her normal spirit. "When I want her pity I'll ask for it."

"The point is that they knew, and maybe other people—women—could guess. Everybody except your doctor husband, of course. Too busy sticking his head up—"

Her fingers brushed my lips. "Shhh. I don't want to hear it. It's over."

"It'll be over when I'm done with Faro. I'm sorry, but I think I ruined all the rest of our social life in Aquae Sulis."

"What did you do?"

"I told Materna to shut her face before I shut it for her."

She shook her head. "We can't forsake appearances. That might be exactly what they want us to do. Give up going to the baths, give up Aquae Sulis. We can't, Ardur. Or we'll let them win."

"That's fine. We'll go to the baths. I'll wear a toga. But I'm still going to handle it in my own way."

My jaw hurt. Gwyna ran a finger down my cheek. "Ardur—don't put yourself in danger. I know you want to hurt Faro."

"I don't want to hurt him. I want to kill him."

She lay stomach down on the pillow and propped herself up with her elbows. The view of her cleavage distracted me.

"What about Bibax? Where does he fit in?"

"I don't know, and I don't—goddamn it. Shit!"

"What is it?"

"I was supposed to meet Calpurnius last night at the spring. At the fifth hour."

"You were busy at the fifth hour." She gave me a half-smile.

My tongue was slow. "We were both a little—busy—last night."

I set her in my lap. She wove her arms around my neck, and started to make a few noises when I buried my face in her breasts. Then a knock sounded at the door.

I looked at Gwyna, and she smiled. I was breathing hard.

"What?! What the hell is it?"

A thin voice came through the wood. "So sorry, sir—but there's someone here—very important—need you."

That's all I got. Lineus was too well bred to be any louder. A lesson in deportment I never quite mastered.

"Just wait a goddamn minute!"

Gwyna climbed off of me and put her feet on the floor. "Go on, Ardur. It must be something serious. We have"—she leaned over and brushed her lips against my neck—"we have the rest of our lives."

It felt almost as good to hear it as it would to prove it. I still grumbled when I threw on a dirty tunic and laced some sandals halfway on my feet. She was getting dressed more carefully.

"Go on. I'll meet you in the dining room."

I kissed her cheek, then opened the door with unnecessary violence. It made me feel better.

Lineus was hovering in the background. "Please, sir—it's very important."

"It better be. Who's here?"

"A gentleman, sir. A Philo. He said you'd know him by that name."

Philo? At my house? This early?

"What time is it?" I asked Lineus abruptly.

"Not even the first hour of morning, sir. He arrived just a few minutes ago."

I grunted and strode into the dining room. Philo was sitting in a chair, looking immaculate as ever. Did he go to sleep like that?

The expression on his face was the kind you saved for the cases you couldn't help.

"Arcturus—I'm sorry to wake you—"

"What is it?"

"It's—it's a priest."

My stomach knotted up, and I knew what he was going to say before the words started to form, and then I saw them come out with a terrible kind of slowness, as if he were speaking underwater.

"They found him—just half an hour ago—in the drain. He's been murdered."

Calpurnius. Goddamn it. *Cui* fucking *bono*.

CHAPTER THIRTEEN

Philo walked beside me, stride for stride, echoing my own anxiety. There wasn't much light to see by. Dawn was wearing black today.

The cool breeze from the western hills blew through the yellow dust and yellower leaves, sweeping them in flurries down the worn stone paths, toward the one place in Aquae Sulis everything ended up. The baths.

Bibax died next to them; Calpurnius died underneath them. Others died from deals made, curses cast, and money furtively handed over into a ready palm—all around the blue-green waters of Sulis. She must wonder why the hell she bothers.

The good doctor said little. The ragged light, playing hide-and-seek with the clouds that threatened rain, caught the fine lines in his face and dug them into crags. He looked his age today. I can't say it bothered me much.

Octavio had fetched him out of bed in a panic. Philo had in turn fetched Papirius. No one knew who to blame for bringing Grattius. The three of them were waiting for us with various degrees of impatience by the large drain, along with a smaller man in filthy robes, obviously terrified.

The drain was typical Roman engineering—efficient, well built, and designed for maximum exploitation of resources. In this case, it let Papirius and company exploit the goddess.

My eyes traced the path of the pipes. Up above, somebody opened a sluice at the top of the spring. The sacred waters—carrying sacred gold and other donations to the Sulis Mutual Benefit Society—rushed through pipes and emptied into this drain via a wide terra-cotta channel. The drain was made large enough for men to walk through and clean or repair it—or pick up anything Sulis left behind.

Other pipes ran from the baths into the same system. I expected the spring was cleaned nearly as often as the pools were. No one bathed in it, but then nobody threw gold necklaces in the *caldarium,* either.

Octavio's torch flicked orange light in everyone's faces. I brushed it away, and it bounced on the brick walls and made teasing little shadows that promised to tell me what I wanted to know.

I asked: "Where is he?"

Papirius answered, distaste on his face. He clutched his long mantle, raising it several inches off the ground. The head priest was clearly not impressed with the temple sanitary system.

"He's—he's inside."

I looked over at Philo. "Have you—"

He shook his head before I could get the question out. "No. I—I turned him over, saw that it was too late, and suggested we get you."

I grunted and headed down into the drain. Small steps were built into the rock for the cleaners, who would come along and replace missing bricks or repair leaks to the pipe whenever the sluice wasn't open. The wide, half-pipe channel carried the bulk of the water and mud through the hole. In the darkness of it, presumably in the channel, was the body of Calpurnius.

I looked up to where they were all staring down at me, and held up a hand.

"Somebody give me a goddamn lamp."

Philo handed me a two-wick portable with a sturdy handle and a picture of Apollo and Daphne carved on it. The light was flickering, and the cold, dank air from the black hole of the drain threatened to snuff it out permanently.

I shielded it with my left hand and walked in, stooping half a foot so I could fit. The acrid odor of the burning wick blended with the volcanic bite of the water and the clean smell of wet earth. The walls were still wet and slippery a couple of feet up the sides, and a fine brown and yellow silt oozed along the channel like snail slime. I got about five feet in and finally saw Calpurnius.

He was lying facedown in the channel, his legs bent behind him in an unnatural pose by the force of the water and mud that had run over him. Poor bastard. The water didn't leave him any cleaner.

His robe was caked in silt, his thin hair coated with it. His hands were bent into claws, as if he tried to scratch his way out.

I set the lamp down gingerly, and hoped like hell it wouldn't blow out. I had just discovered that I didn't like drains.

Calpurnius was heavier than he looked, and there wasn't much room to maneuver. I tried not to let his head hit the terra-cotta when I wrestled him over, but his legs and arms smacked the hard surface with a thump.

"What's going on? Are you all right, Arcturus?" Philo's voice echoed weirdly in the muddy tunnel.

"Yeah. I'll be a few minutes."

I thought for a minute the lamp was playing tricks on me. Calpurnius's face was twisted into something inhuman. The tongue extended, lips drawing over teeth in a grimace of absolute horror. Mud filled the mouth and nose and eyes, which had been open when the water came.

I felt his hands. They hung toward his side and were curved as if he tried to scratch himself. Stiffness wasn't fully formed. The drain was cold, but the water and mud were warm. That made it hard to tell.

Neck was splotchy. Ground-in dirt on the back of his head, what looked like blood. I felt the skull gingerly. The skin was broken along the back. Shit. I should've caught it earlier. I didn't want to flip him again.

I lifted his arms and took a closer look at his fingers and the heel of his palms. There—more skin torn. Both hands. Confirmation. No need to check the legs.

I stood up and nearly cracked my head. I was running out of time, and missing something. The lamp was wavering with uncertainty. So was I.

I bent down again quickly, tried to scoop water from the channel into my hand. I poured a few drops on Calpurnius's face. Not enough. Not nearly enough.

I tore a piece of his wet robe, using a jagged piece of flint that lay in the channel. His nose and his mouth disgorged finger-fulls of silt and mud. Then his mouth threw up a piece of lead.

It was wedged in, like Bibax's, but was a thick, rectangular piece that could've come straight off a pipe. I pried it out between Calpurnius's tortured lips and dunked it in the channel. Under the lamp I could just make out a thick, straight line dug in with a stylus. I tilted the lead until it caught the flame just right. It read *ULTOR* in capitals.

I tucked it into my tunic. One last place to check before we moved the body. I rubbed the mud out of Calpurnius's eyes until I could see some of the iris. The rims were red and inflamed, like they always were—one reason he looked like a rat. But underneath the mud the skin glistened faintly, as if an unguent or cream had been rubbed in. That was before he was dragged facedown into the drain. Dead.

I stood up again, slowly, looked at what had been Calpurnius, and said a small prayer for the poor bastard. I wasn't sure if anyone else would. Then I cradled the lamp and made my way back out of the hole. They were waiting for me.

"Well?"

I ignored Papirius, brushed off some mud. I wished I could brush off the image of Calpurnius's face. I turned to Philo.

"How did you know it was murder?"

He reddened slightly. "The look on his face. I turned him around to see if he was breathing at all. I assumed—well, I assumed with a look like that—"

"You assumed right. He was poisoned."

Gasps all around.

Grattius shook his fat head. "Poisoned? Somebody poisoned a drain cleaner?"

I could barely make out the small, dirty figure hiding behind Grattius's bulk. I shoved the *duovir* aside and walked over to the man shrinking in the shadows.

Papirius glided over immediately. "This is Senicio. He was the other cleaner who was supposed to work tonight. He found the body." The head priest gave me a look that was supposed to mean something. "I trust him."

That made one of us. I rarely trusted men trusted by a man I didn't. Senicio quaked in his sandals, his feet looking like the bottom of an ugly statue.

"You found the body?"

"Y-yes, sir. Calpurnius—Calpurnius never showed up."

"Were you supposed to meet him here? What time?"

Papirius intervened again. "Sixth hour of night. They empty the spring, and that gives it a few hours to get some water back. We make sure the baths are clean and full before we empty it, as it takes a full day and night to refill."

I gave Papirius a smile he tried to give back. "Thanks. Now, if you don't mind, I'd like to talk to Senicio."

Senicio shifted his small frame, picking at a wart on his left cheek.

"When was the last time you saw Calpurnius alive?"

He glanced over at Papirius as if to ask for permission, and I moved sideways to block his view.

"When?"

"Last night. Maybe—maybe the third hour, or so. He was eating at a tavern we like to go to. I stopped in for some wine, and Calpurnius was there."

"Did he act any differently? Or say anything to you?"

Senicio ran his tongue over dry lips. "Uh—no. At least, not really. Nothing specific. He—he just seemed excited, is all."

"Did you ask him why?"

He shook his head so vehemently that I thought he might make himself sick. "No. I—I just had a drink and left."

I studied him for a few minutes. The squirming started almost immediately.

"Are you sure he didn't say anything, Senicio?"

"He—he didn't say anything, but—he was eating—what he was eating cost more than—more than usual."

"He was splurging on a meal, in other words?"

"Yes—that's it. I thought it was funny, you know, why tonight, when we have to clean the drain, and it's not special, or anything. He—he just said he was celebrating."

Papirius jumped in. "He said he was celebrating?"

The smaller priest cringed. "Yes, sir. That's what he said."

I changed tactics. "When did you realize something was wrong, Senicio? That was quick thinking."

The little man expanded under the praise.

"Well, he—he never showed up. I called him, and I went into the tunnel—just a little ways—and didn't—didn't see him, and then Gregax opened the sluice, and I was busy."

I glanced over at Papirius and made my tone friendly and conversational. "Find anything good? For Sulis, I mean?"

Senicio shook his head again before the head priest could react. "Nothing much. Some gold coins I managed to catch. Heavy things stay in the channel, and that's what I was looking for when I found—when I found—"

"When you found poor Calpurnius. I see."

I paused a few moments. "Senicio—did Calpurnius have eye trouble?"

"Yes, sir. Most of us do, in fact."

"Did he take anything for it? Anyone in particular did he see?"

"Not that I know of, sir. He was the suspicious type, if you know what I mean. Liked to try things himself."

I nodded. "Thanks."

The junior priest looked like he might fall down. Papirius asked drily, "Are you done, Arcturus? May I send him away to get clean?"

"Please."

Octavio asked no one in particular, "Should I open the baths, do you think?"

The question brought Grattius to life. "Of course you must open the baths. Nothing to do with the baths, eh, Arcturus? But you never explained yourself. Why would someone want to poison this drain person?"

I brought out the piece of lead from my tunic pocket.

"*Ultor* again?" Grattius exploded. "But we've asked you to stop this *Ultor* business. Bad for the town! Now here it is again!" Grattius glared at me through his piggish little eyes.

Philo said softly: "How do you figure on poison, Arcturus?"

I stared at him. "Same way you did. His expression. He was murdered. The murderer watched him die, then dragged him into the drain. They must've arranged to meet close by."

"Do you have a guess as to what it was?"

"*Aconitum.*"

The word sent a shiver through the rest of the men, while Philo looked at me thoughtfully.

"Hecate's poison," murmured Papirius.

Philo was nodding. "The pain, the paralysis. Even the itching. It makes sense. How was it administered?"

"Probably through an eye cream."

Grattius exploded. "What about this *Ultor* business, Arcturus? Does this mean *Ultor*'s one of these eye doctors, always trying to sell—"

"Not necessarily. In fact, it's possible that this may be the last we'll hear of *Ultor*."

"What? You know who he is?"

"No. Still, I have a theory, and if Bibax and Calpurnius were killed for revenge, and I'm right about why, I don't think *Ultor* will kill anyone else."

A broad smile spread across Grattius's face. "Well, that is good news. It would be decent of you to catch 'em, of course, but as long as he stops this murder business—"

He turned to the others brusquely. "Gentlemen, I'm cold. I'm going home."

He wagged his head at Octavio. "You mind the baths—I'll be in this afternoon, and I want my massage. Nobody needs to know about this priest." He twisted his neck toward Papirius. "And you—you handle telling the ones that need to know—you know, the other cleaners. Get the body out of there and give it a simple burial. At night."

He shivered. "This air isn't good for me. See you later, gentlemen."

He waddled his bulk back up the stairs and the pathway out. Papirius made some priestly noises about taking care of the dead, grabbed Octavio by the arm, and told him to get the furnace slaves, presumably to haul out Calpurnius. They both left, Papirius majestically, Octavio scurrying to do his bidding.

Philo was watching me. "So you think Bibax and Calpurnius were partners, then? Partners in the murders you've uncovered?"

I shrugged. "Makes sense. And if they were partners, then *Ultor*— someone who is being blackmailed, probably, or someone who figured out what they were doing and lost by it—*Ultor*'s job is over."

He thought it over. "I see. You will still try to find him, of course?"

"Try is the operative word."

He patted me on the shoulder. "I'm sure you'll succeed. *Aconitum* was a brilliant deduction."

"Not really. It adds to the allure—all the associations with Hecate and the Underworld. Makes it seem like *Ultor* isn't a person."

We were walking up the ramp toward ground level. The sun finally agreed to make an appearance.

"Shall I see you later today?"

I shook my head. "I don't feel much like the baths."

Philo smiled sadly. "Death is the ugliest thing in the world, and we see too much of it."

"Especially in Aquae Sulis."

He stared at me, patted me again on my upper arm, and walked away. I wasn't sure whether he swallowed the story. The others did, without even tasting it.

The *Ultor* who killed Bibax and the *Ultor* who killed Calpurnius were two different people. That lead was written with capitals, deeply etched. This was a copy of a murder that was just three days old.

Calpurnius was killed because he made an appointment with someone—someone he thought he could shake down. He could collect from that someone to not tell me what he'd figured out, and he could collect from me to tell me a little of it. He played both sides against each other, and got the life squeezed out of him. And the poor bastard suffered. He wasn't feeling any *bono* now.

I took a deep breath and looked at the spring, filling up with the bubbling, eternal water. Time for my interview with Faro Magnus.

CHAPTER FOURTEEN

reakfast was ready by the time I got back home, something simple and quick because she knew I'd be in a hurry. She was watching me stuff my mouth with oats and honey. Our eyes met.

"I wanted to talk to you before you left. I don't want what happened—I don't want it to distract you."

I swallowed hard, reaching for a gulp of cider. "I don't trust Mumius to hold Faro for long. If I don't show up early . . ."

"I know. I found out things yesterday I haven't had a chance to tell you."

Deep circles under her eyes this morning. She reached over and put her hand on mine.

"Two people murdered. There's something evil here, and it frightens me. I can't help it. Perhaps, Ardur . . . perhaps the gods sent you here to fight it."

She took her hand back and put it away before it could distract me. Then she leaned into the basket chair, tucking her legs underneath her, and stared at her half-eaten breakfast.

I said: "I'll fight, but they—whoever the hell 'they' are—don't fight clean. They've targeted you. I don't know if it's connected to

Bibax, and I don't care. You're my priority, goddamn it. Protecting you."

She looked away, her voice low. "Of course you protect me. I can protect myself, too. I've been through the worst they can do."

I swallowed my oatmeal and stood up to hold her, but she waved me back into the chair, face intent.

"About yesterday. Prunella told me the name of the man Secunda was in love with. I didn't think it was important until now."

"Who was it?"

"Faro."

"Then why the hell—"

"Why was he at the party?" Her mouth formed a tight, bitter line. "I think Mama was saving him for herself."

"You mean Materna—"

Gwyna shuddered. "Please, Ardur. Don't mention her name. The sight of her face last night—after—"

"What makes you think Secundus would tolerate—even given the chance that Faro could make himself—"

"Secundus is totally dependent on her. He's afraid of her. Surely you saw that last night. Although I don't think it's come to anything but fantasy on Materna's part, she broke up their romance, hoping to hold on to Faro, and then threw a bone to her daughter."

"In the form of Mumius. One better left buried."

"He's not that bad."

"I'm reserving judgment until I see whether he's still holding the bastard."

"Faro is very good-looking, you know. It's understandable." She was looking at her fingernails.

I felt my lips pinch up against my teeth. "He reminds me of Philo."

She sighed. "You wouldn't say such things if you really knew him. Poor Philo."

"'Poor Philo?' Why the hell is he so poor?"

"He was worried about me yesterday, but respectful. He spoke very highly of you, and said he'd heard about curse-deaths from patients, but never really paid attention. Thought it was part of the ghost-mine non-sense."

"So why 'poor Philo'?"

"Oh, nothing important. He's from Hispania—Lusitania, I think. When he was a young man, he was a temple doctor for a healing god. Endo . . . Endovelicus or something. And he lost the only woman he ever truly loved." She looked down at the table and blushed. "He said I reminded him of her."

I looked around to see what was making the noise and realized it was my teeth grinding. So the bastard made the most out of his age. The smarmy bastard.

Gwyna looked up at me. "It's just a story. Don't be too hard on Philo."

"Did you find out anything from anyone who didn't want to sleep with you?"

The color in her cheeks increased. "Don't be vulgar. I tried to talk to that boy's grandmother—the one that died."

"His name was Dewi."

"She wouldn't tell me anything. Gave me a baleful look, and kept making the sign against the evil eye."

She shook her head, and a couple of stray blond tendrils tumbled down the side of her face. "The people . . . the women . . . they're so afraid. Something needs to be done."

I stood up, shoving the basket chair aside hard enough to make it squeak. "I'm going to do something right now."

She looked down at her shaking hands. Behind the grief, anger. The Trinovantian woman I married.

"I hope you can find out who put the son of a bitch up to it. I'd gladly slit his throat myself."

I took her by the shoulders. "Leave it to me. I'll get back as soon as I can. We can separate ourselves from the Aquae Sulis social scene for one goddamn day."

She grimaced. "I may as well let the talk spread before I start to wade in it."

I walked out, leaving her to keep busy with the servants. Action was better for Gwyna. Normal. Not like the lethargy. Fury hit me full force, and my hands—my long, nimble doctor's hands—were clenched and shaking.

My wife thought about killing herself last night. She'd been exposed and humiliated in front of people who weren't fit to look at her. Someone had done it on purpose, had set her up to suffer. Now it was his turn.

One of the slaves brought Nimbus out to me. I was in a hurry to meet Faro Magnus.

The house was shuttered. No sound, no bluster, no pestering me to breed my mare. I patted Nimbus on the neck and tied her to the branch of a nearby ash.

A slave opened the door a crack. Older woman, terrified, shrinking as if I were going to hit her.

"Where's Mumius?"

"The—the gentleman who stayed?"

I nodded. "Soldier. The only 'gentleman' in the house."

Her eyes got bigger, and she flattened herself against the wall. "I'll show you to the mistress."

I strode after the old lady, who led me into a dark room where thin gruel and gray-looking eggs lay unadorned on a table. Materna was squatting in a chair, looking like a tick torn off a particularly juicy vein.

"Oh? So you've come back, have you? Come to apologize?"

I didn't want to get too close. She smelled. The dim light highlighted the beard she was growing, reflected the shine on her beetle eyes. The kind of beetle that likes to eat dead flesh.

"Actually, no. Although maybe I should, Materna. Maybe I should."

The crack of a triumphant smile started to crease her lower lip. "Well, if you think—"

I was in a hurry. I got closer and held my nose.

"I do think. About a lot of things. Like why you like to sit back and watch other people suffer. Like why you get your kicks from pain—and watching Faro stoke it. Better get your kicks where and while you can, Materna . . . since he won't be stoking you."

The beetle eyes hid under the beetle brows. "You rude, miserable—"

"Before we start on what I am, let's start on what I'm not. I'm not sorry for what I said, what I did, what I'm saying now, or what I'm likely to say or do to you in the future. The only thing I'm sorry for is not having the time to say it well. You're a sick woman. The kind of sick no doctor could heal. I wouldn't even try."

Staring silence. Even her fingers quit tapping the chair.

"What do you want?" she said abruptly.

"Faro. Is Mumius still holding him?"

She turned her head slightly to the left, as if she couldn't bear it. "My worthless husband is with him. In the study."

"Where is it?"

"Second door on the right. Down the corridor."

I turned to go. She murmured after me: "You worried it wasn't yours?"

I breathed in, out, a little at a time. In and out. Got control of my lungs.

"See these hands, Materna? They deliver babies. They clamp arteries. They sew up the guts of men who don't know they're already dead. They're strong hands. If you were a man, and I was less of one—I'd break your fucking neck."

I don't know whether it was my shaking fingers an inch away from her face or the rasp in my voice. She pushed her square head back as far as she could.

My arms dropped, stiff and sore with tension. "I wouldn't poison myself by touching you."

I walked down the corridor, catching a glimpse of Secunda, lurking in the shadows. I threw open the door without knocking. Secundus was asleep in a chair while Mumius groggily watched Faro, who was stretched out on a couch, staring at the ceiling.

"Secundus. Mumius."

Secundus woke up with a start. "Eh? Arcturus! About time you got here. It's—what, nearly the third hour?"

"I got here as soon as I could. There's been another murder."

Secundus blanched. Mumius blinked a few times. Faro kept his eyes fixed upward, but his breaths were coming faster.

"What—who—"

"A priest. Name of Calpurnius."

The two men showed no recognition. Faro was still watching the ceiling rot.

"Secundus—whose idea was it to invite Faro last night?"

He lowered his eyes. "The wife's. He's a friend of the family. My daughter likes him a little too well, but the wife didn't want to not see him on account of it."

The necromancer was listening intently.

"When did you decide?"

"It's been planned for weeks. She's—she talked about nothing else. Not even been interested in the horses."

"And whose idea was it to invite us—me and my wife?"

He scratched his head. "You know, I can't remember. Seems like I thought it up, once I heard who you were."

Most of Secundus's ideas would seem like that, nearly all of them would come from Materna's mouth.

"I'm going to interrogate Faro. Are you staying?"

Secundus turned red. "We—that is to say, I—I think I should. It happened in—in our—in my house . . . but—but Arcturus—"

"What is it?"

"Did he—did he—break the law?"

I massaged the back of my hand. "He broke my law, Secundus. He hurt my wife. While we were guests in your home. That means he also broke the laws of hospitality." I stretched my fingers out and flexed them. "Don't worry. I'm not taking him to court."

Mumius and Secundus looked at each other. Mumius finally spoke. "I guess I'll stay, too."

"Whatever you like, but anything this maggot says about my wife doesn't leave this room."

I looked up at them and they nodded, fear twisting their faces.

"Neither does anything about the murders. If he talks, you don't. To anybody."

They nodded again, fading into the background. The room was small, on the shabby side, with a desk and some rolls of papyrus stuck in cubbyholes. I walked toward the couch, slow and deliberate.

"Faro."

He gracefully pulled himself to a sitting position in one movement.

"Yes? Oh—you."

"You know I've been here for several minutes."

He shook his head regretfully. "No, no, I didn't. I was communing with the Beyond, until it was time for you to talk to me."

Eyes large, brown, full of warmth. The easy smile of a man who'd always been able to talk his way into or out of anything. Looks helped. Small body, well shaped.

I pulled up a chair and sat in front of him. Leaned forward and stared until his phony quizzical look gave way to nervousness, then finally broke out into a sweaty question.

"What did you want to ask me?"

"How long have you been in Aquae Sulis?"

"Let me see—I've been here for a year, on this trip."

"This trip? You were here before?"

"About four years ago. I travel the different spas. Usually in Gaul or Baiae. I've been most places at least once."

"What brought you back here?"

He leaned back, started to relax a little. Thought maybe I wouldn't disfigure him after all. "The spirits, of course. There are many spirits in Aquae Sulis, many people who are haunted by them."

"And who are willing to pay you to talk to them."

He shrugged. "A man must make his living—"

I moved so quickly he didn't have time to uncross his legs. My hands were around his neck and his toes were barely brushing the floor.

"You make your living hurting people. Like you did last night."

Dangled in front of me, still calm, still confident. Didn't piss on himself. Not yet. Men like Faro thought everyone could be gotten to. Everybody nursed a weakness he could charm, hid a secret he could figure his way around. He reached up to pry my fingers off while his skin burned red and he coughed from the pressure on his windpipe.

"I wasn't told—set me down, please, so I can talk—I wasn't told you were unprepared. The world of the dead can be very disturbing."

I lowered him back to the couch. "Tell me about the world of the dead, Faro. You seem to know a lot about it for a man who gets paid in cash."

There was a jug of wine on the desk. Faro's eyes strayed toward it like iron to a magnet. Then I noticed the broken veins around his cheeks and barked out an order to our host.

"Secundus! Get Faro some wine."

He flinched. "No. No, I do not want any."

Secundus was sloshing old vinegar into a dirty wooden cup, and handed it over. I held it out in front of me and swished it around. The flat slop odor of sour wine rose, teasing the bastard. He didn't look the type. Such a pretty boy.

"You sure, Faro? You sure you don't want some?"

He drew himself up on the couch. "I'm not a lush, if that's what you're thinking. I won't drink slop."

I smiled and set the cup on the table beside me. "Well, let's just leave this here until we need it."

We stared at each other for a few minutes. His eyes drifted toward the wine again.

"You say you weren't told—that we were—what was it? 'Unprepared.'"

"That's right. I was paid, told that there would be two couples of particular interest, and—and that was all."

"Who paid you?"

He nodded his head in the direction of Secundus.

"His wife."

I smiled. "You must be nice and cozy with the family. You tried to seduce the daughter, isn't that right?"

Secundus started to sputter from somewhere in the background.

Faro said: "She has a sensitive character."

"Money under the mattress, too."

The show face was back. Concerned warmth radiated from his fingertips. He reached out with it, trying to use the charm again.

"You must shed this anger—the spirits don't like it. Let it go. I can help you."

I leaned forward. "You know what? I think you can."

The backhand took him by surprise. He fell against the couch, and I picked him up and threw him into the wall. The thud shook a dusty papyrus from one of the slots, and it rolled open, covered with mathematical figures.

Blood trickled from his lip and his nose. He raised a shaking hand to wipe it off.

I handed him the wine. "Drink it."

He grabbed it with two hands and gulped. I pulled him up by the arm.

"Who told you about my wife?"

His breath was coming out ragged. I squeezed harder on his upper arm.

"Who?"

He glanced sideways at Secundus and shook his head. He was refusing to answer me. I didn't mind.

I slapped his face hard enough to put some color into it. Twice. Back and forth. Back and forth. A large welt rose on his cheek, and the blood kept streaming from his nose.

"I'm running out of patience, Faro. I could use my fist."

"No—no more. I'll talk."

Mumius came forward with a dinner napkin from last night. Almost funny, if it weren't so fucking ugly. Faro wiped his nose, and I shoved him into the couch. To remind him who owned him.

"Who told you about my wife?"

Quiet now, furtive. He'd tell as little as he could, then run somewhere else, hide, rebuild, do it all over again. Men like Faro worked in cycles—sometimes up, sometimes down, finally sinking low enough to die in rags, wine breath, broken body, shit and piss their only embraceable warmth. Pariahs. Outcasts. Not even remembered in hell.

I almost felt sorry. For him, for the men like him. Some of them with talent, looks, brains—even connections. But they started down the road tripping people. They couldn't resist the fraud, the trick, putting one over on the gullible and stupid—or the vulnerable and hurt. It gave them a sense of power, and they needed power to keep living. Whatever it was they called life.

"Materna. Materna told me your wife—your wife had a miscarriage."

I sat back in my chair. It was part of what I wanted. "What are you doing in Aquae Sulis?"

"I told you. I—I summon ghosts. Communicate with the dead."

"I'll ask you again. What are you doing in Aquae Sulis?"

He was hiding something. I was tired of hitting him. The satisfaction wore off after the first time. I knew how he would end up.

"I don't know what you want from me!" He turned to Secundus and Mumius. "Make him stop! I don't know what he wants!"

I punched him in the stomach in the middle of a whine, and he fell to the floor, the wind knocked out of him.

Mumius stepped forward. "Is he all right?"

"He'll be fine. He's just scared of something."

I hauled him back up when he started to gasp. His nose bled some more, and I picked up the napkin from the couch and wiped his face with it.

"Faro. Tell me what you're paid to do here. Not by the regular customers. You know what I mean."

It depended on whether he was more afraid of me or whoever he was hiding. True to his kind, he tried to compromise.

"I can—I can tell you this much, and only this much—don't bother to hit me any more, because you won't get anything else. There are things—things worse than pain."

I let go of his arm, and he fell back into the couch.

"What is it?"

He wiped his mouth with the dirty, bloodstained napkin. "I want to leave here. Leave this town. That's part of the deal."

"I don't make deals, Faro. What makes you think I won't hurt you so bad you can't leave?"

He grimaced as he ran his tongue over the cut on his lip. "Because you're not the type. You don't like to hurt people. Not even when you're angry."

"I've enjoyed hurting you. I could stand a little more enjoyment."

"No—no. I'm just asking to leave. Please—I—I can't help you. I'll tell you what I can, and then—just let me go."

I stared at him and watched his eyes drift back over to the wine jug. "All right. Tell me."

Relief poured out of him like sweat. "I'm—I'm here for the mine."

I leaned forward. "The haunted mine?"

"I'm the one—the one who spread the rumors. I was here four years ago, when it—the death—happened. I make sure people still believe it."

"Who pays you?"

He shook his head. "That's all I can tell you. I mean it. Go ahead and ruin my face, if you'd like, but—but I can't tell you anymore." He tried to straighten his tunic.

"Where is it? The mine?"

"I can tell you that. Then—then you can see for yourself. It's about fifteen miles from here. Right off the Sorviodunum to Iscalis road. There are a lot of mines in those hills. This one—this one is the farthest one north, about seven miles from Iscalis."

I stood up and said softly: "Do you ever hear voices at night, Faro?"

He looked scared again. "What do you mean?"

"Not dead ones. Living voices, full of pain and misery. Pain you've put there. That's the only thing you bring to life. And sometime soon it's going to drown out the sound of anything else."

He was already looking old. I turned to Secundus and Mumius. "Don't repeat this to anyone. Especially your wife, Secundus."

He started to sputter again. "My wife—my wife—you're—you're going to believe—"

"Yes, I believe him. Your wife takes a malicious pleasure in watching other people suffer. I'd—watch what you eat, Secundus. Just watch what you eat."

Secundus and Mumius gaped at me. Faro was staring at the ground, trying to read his own future.

CHAPTER FIFTEEN

Materna wasn't anywhere to be seen or smelled. The road home was a blur, and Gwyna was reading a letter in the *triclinium* when I walked in the door.

"What happened? Are you hurt?"

"No. That's Faro's blood."

She needed to hear it, and hear it in full.

"That bitch. That unholy bitch. So we were just there for her 'amusement.' I wonder how she found out—it must have been the baths. I tried to wear loose clothes. Or maybe it was Sulpicia—"

"I don't think Sulpicia would've told her. What about Philo?"

She looked at me sideways. "Ardur—don't blame Philo for everything. It's not that hard to figure out. Everyone knows we don't have children, and I—I—"

I leaned forward to kiss her. "You're the most beautiful woman in Britannia, and people talk. Forget it."

She squeezed my hand, and changed the subject. "So Faro is connected to the mine?"

"Yes. That's where I've got to go."

"Now? But—" She thought about it and nodded her head. "You're right. I'll go with you."

"You can't. This is dangerous."

"So is Aquae Sulis," she said drily.

"Gwyna, it's a hard ride, and I don't know what I'll find when I get there. Please—for me—stay here and see what you can find out. And take two slaves with you, wherever you go."

"Well, Agricola seems to have an endless supply. But don't you— don't you want to hear the news from home first?"

She waved the tablet in her hand.

"Is it from Bilicho?"

"Yes. And Stricta."

"Are they all right? Is Hefin all right?"

"Of course. Bilicho says Hefin needs more friends his own age— you know how important age-mates are—what is it, Ardur?"

I wiped my forehead. My head hurt. "I don't know. Nothing, probably." I tried to be interested. "What else did they say?"

Gwyna stared at me and smiled as if she could see through me. Which she could.

"Your mind's not here. You can read it later. Go on and change. I'll tell the servants to pack you some food. I want to know exactly where this mine is, and what road you're taking."

She committed it to memory and sent me off to the bedroom. It took her considerably longer to do whatever she was doing than it did for me to put on my leggings, boots, and traveling cloak. I told one of the slaves to pack a club and *gladius* on Nimbus where I could get to them in a hurry. I stuck a dagger in my belt as an extra precaution. My foot hurt from tapping on the floor when she returned with a medallion.

"Wear my necklace, and think of me. It'll help protect you from whatever's there."

"I think of you constantly."

She smiled and put it around my neck. "Go on, Ardur. It's already the fifth hour of day. You want to get there before dark, and that's hill country. You'll have to go slower than you'd like."

I bent down and kissed her gently. "I miss you already."

She plucked at my sleeve. "Ardur—did Faro—did Faro say what made him choose—a boy?"

I raised her face to look at me. "The law of averages, my love. Faro is a fraud. He admitted it."

She gave a small nod. Her hand squeezed mine, and she stood on tiptoe to kiss my cheek. "Go on. Nimbus is waiting for you. And be careful!"

I smiled at her and walked outside. The air was fresh, with a threat of winter rain in it, the sun shining thin and pale through the clouds. A good day to travel—and find out who the hell was haunting the haunted mine.

The countryside around Aquae Sulis was some of the most beautiful I'd ever seen. Wooded hills filled with ash, elm, oak, and holly stood sentry over lush green meadows, bright with the boisterous colors of fall.

Nimbus and I enjoyed getting out of town. A kind of creeping melancholy unwound from around our necks. By all rights, Aquae Sulis should be a lovely place. Maybe one day it would be.

I thought I heard a horse behind me once or twice, and when I climbed a hill, I caught a glimpse of dust in the distance. Nimbus flared her nose and gave me a worried look. I patted her on the shoulder. I wasn't unprepared.

It was about two hours before sunset when I finally found the mine, but it already felt too late. Shadows from the hills were stretching toward the valleys. The peaks would keep the sunlight for a little while longer.

A small, rocky path meandered from the main road, passing by two other operations that looked closed. The trail itself was clear of debris, except for a log dragged across the road to block it. I didn't believe in trees that conveniently fell across unused paths. Especially when the dirt was tightly tamped and there weren't any weeds.

About three or four miles farther—up a steep shale-and-rock ledge the scrawny pines were barely able to cling to—I found the last stop in the trail. I was hoping it would be, in more ways than one.

Like most things the Romans get personally involved in, mining was big business, and this had been no small-time operation. A large, rectangular shaft marked the opening in the side of the hill. It was framed with wood and, from the size of it, probably led to several horizontal and deeper vertical galleries inside. That's where the Roman was supposedly killed—and where he was still supposed to walk.

I got off of Nimbus and bent down in the light dust. Somebody was walking around here, all right, but I didn't think it was a dead Roman.

Somewhere above me a kestrel shrieked, and I jumped. The wind was getting ready for the evening. Nimbus's ears pricked forward, and she nickered softly. I wondered at what.

I walked around, looking at the wood beams stretched on the ground. It was an artful arrangement. Everything looked deserted—except, like the roads, there weren't any weeds around the wood. Disturbed earth grows weeds like the Hydra grows heads, if the ground is ever let alone. This place felt about as lonely as the Circus Maximus.

My feet crunched on something as I walked toward the entrance, and I bent down to see what it was. A clay cup, exactly the kind used to extract silver from lead.

This was supposed to be a lead mine, not a silver mine. And it was supposed to be closed.

I rubbed my finger inside the bowl of the cup. Fine metallic dust covered the tip. He sure as hell was an energetic ghost. Maybe he was trying to scrape up enough cash to pay the ferryman.

I tucked the cup in my saddlebag and took out my favorite club. No metal to catch a gleam of failing light; big enough to crack a head. I just hoped it wouldn't be my own.

I walked slowly toward the mine opening, my feet crunching on bits of charred wood and broken cups. The cave loomed open like a Cyclops's mouth. Busy mine. Fire marks scarred the rock around the hole, where they'd used fire and water to crack open the mountainside, Gaia's wealth spread out for the taking. On the ground, fifty feet from the entrance, there were embers of fresher vintage. Still glowing. Someone built a fire and didn't want any smoke.

I repositioned the club in my right hand. He'd be nearby. I flattened against the side of the mountain and inched toward the entrance.

Nimbus nickered again. A sturdily built man in a thick, filthy tunic, face covered in dirt and lead dust, cautiously crept out of the opening. He was going for my horse.

I waited until he was in front of me. Before I could land a blow on his back, he heard or felt me behind him and spun. There was a long, sharp knife in his fist.

The club landed on his arm. He yelped, dropping his hand, but didn't drop the knife. Quickly it passed to his other hand. Just what I liked, after an all-day ride. An ambidextrous knife-fighter.

We stood and watched one another for a minute. No feints, no circling, no snarling. He was a professional. I was, too—but not with clubs.

I said: "Why don't you show me around?"

He looked at me, face too dirty for expression.

"Why not?" He motioned with the knife toward the cave. "After you."

I laughed. "I'm not that stupid. We go in side by side."

He shrugged. "Sure. Whatever you'd like."

We walked beside one another, keeping a distance. He was getting more confident. Maybe he'd make a mistake. Hopefully before I did.

I knew the cave would be dark, and my eyes would need time to adjust. So I started blinking them quickly, and he got a little closer. Probably figured there was dirt in my eyes. When we reached the outside of the cave, I faced him, so that I was standing sideways. I could see a little way in, and still watch him.

A shuffling noise came from inside, and the unique odor of donkey hit my nose.

"What's the donkey for?"

He spat on the ground. "Stubborn bastard. Works the screw pump, keeps the water out."

"So you're down pretty deep."

He eyed me. "Yeah. We're deep enough. Wanna see?"

I smiled. "Not tonight."

The donkey was on a short tether and started to walk toward the light. There were raised, bloody welts on its back. Hip bones stuck up where they shouldn't, ribs protruding through the scarred scruff of fur. It raised a hopeful, bleary eye toward the waning sun.

He raised his knife toward it, still watching me, and made a movement like he was going to hit it. The donkey's head flinched, and it took a step backward.

"So that's what you do for fun, all the way out here. When you're not stealing lead and silver, that is."

He spit again. "What I do—and what I do it to—is none of your goddamn business."

I was too angry to be careful. Fuck careful. I'd take this bastard, and I'd take him now. He saw it in my face.

He lunged for my side, but I swung the club low, figuring he'd think I'd go for his head—the most satisfying, but hardest target. It caught him on the side and back of his knees, and he fell backward with a yell.

He tried to grab his knees in reflex, but I already had mine pushing down on his chest. I smashed his hand against a helpful boulder and watched it crumple. It wouldn't hold a whip for a while. He couldn't breathe much, and whined between his teeth, and the knife finally came loose. I scooped it up and tucked it in my belt. I was breathing hard.

"Get—off—me!" he hissed.

I was beginning to like hitting people like him. I punched him in the face. Twice. My knuckles got scratched when the teeth broke off. Then he was out. He'd be eating a soft diet of donkey shit for a long time to come.

I climbed off and looked down at him. He obviously couldn't give me any information, but he wasn't worth carting back to town. I doubted he knew the kind I needed, anyway. The rest I could see for myself.

I walked into the cave, and the donkey shied away from me. I held my hands up to her and untied the greasy, grimy rope she was moored to.

There were niches all over the walls for lamps, and a few looked like they worked. Clay cups were stacked in the corner. Pitch-lined buckets, copper pails, and chisels and picks were strewn against the sides of the cave. It led into a back gallery that looked at least as large—probably where they kept the water pump.

I led her out. She didn't want to trust me, but she'd seen what I'd done and took a chance. I got her outside and gave her some water and most of Nimbus's oats. Nimbus gave me a dirty look and sniffed at the donkey as if she smelled bad.

I put the donkey on a long tether, securing it around a spiny dogwood branch. She was in bad shape, but I figured freedom would help her get down the mountain.

The bastard was still unconscious. I fought an urge to kick him when I walked back inside. It was getting dark, and I took some flint and lit one of the lamps along the wall. Started to walk toward the other gallery.

A crunching noise behind me made me spin. Nobody. Probably the donkey. I breathed again. When I reached the arched opening, I found the reason for the ghost.

Silver. A lot of it. Unmarked ingots, not stamped, no money going back to Rome. Rome wouldn't like that. She never liked people who cheated on their lease.

A silver mine, not a lead mine. Cousins, sure, and incestuous ones, too—you could get the silver out of the heavier metal with fire and the clay cups. But this was more than extraction. This was a good-sized vein.

I turned around to leave and the world went black. Somebody was digging for something in my own head. And he was using a pick.

Goddamn it. I screwed up. There were two of them . . .

CHAPTER SIXTEEN

I opened my eyes and saw exactly what I expected. A stubbly-faced man with worried eyes stared down at me in the dark as if he were waiting for something. The black fog around him started to clear, and I wondered why the ferryman looked so damn big. Then a pain that made my toenails quiver shot through my head. I was alive. I squinted. The ferryman looked familiar.

"Draco? What the hell—Draco?!"

He shrank back, as if I were going to jump up and chase him away.

"I—I came with a message from Bilicho, and the mistress—I mean—your wife—sent me after you. She—she said she didn't want you to know. So I followed you here."

He stood up. He was thinner than usual, and the only thing up here that looked genuinely haunted. I didn't want to be the one to tell him that Coir wasn't worth it. I rolled over on my side and groaned, then tried to push myself up.

He helped me to my feet. We were standing outside of the cave, near the fire, and the darkness did nothing to lesson my feeling that any second Cerberus would take a bite out of my ass. I rubbed my eyes. The ears still worked. I could hear the horses snatching illicit bites of thistle.

I tried to walk and wobbled instead, like a bird just out of the nest.

As soon as I could stand without his arm, I figured my head would live to be hit another day. I took a good look at my new freedman.

"I'm goddamn glad to see you. I thought I'd never get to—well, I thought I was dead, let me put it that way. What—what happened?"

He stood up straight like he used to and didn't look so much like a broken-down arena fighter.

"He hit you with a shovel."

He jerked his thumb toward the woodpile, where another man, large and bearded, lay trussed and tied to a log. Draco was never much of a storyteller.

"Where did you come in?"

"I was down the road. The mistress—your wife, that is—gave me the black horse to ride. I left him down the hill, walked up here, saw him on the ground—"

He gestured toward the bastard I'd skinned my knuckles on. He was groaning, tied up next to the other one.

"—and I thought I'd better tell you I was here. Then I saw him hit you from behind. I couldn't yell in time—and—and, well, I wrestled the shovel away and hit him with it. Then I carried you out here, and tied them both up."

I held his eyes. "You saved my life—and I'm rather attached to it, as lives go. They would've dropped me down a shaft without so much as an apology to Pluto for the intrusion. Thanks, Draco. That's not nearly enough, but it'll have to do for now."

He shuffled his feet and tried not to look embarrassed. For Draco, that was like trying not to look large. I grimly explored the back of my skull and winced. Same old bumps, but no new cracks, and no blood came off on my fingertips. I got the flat end, not the sharp end. I'd be all right. I was a little alarmed at the extra head I was growing.

"How long have I been out?"

"About—about two hours, I reckon." He looked down at the miner I fought. "You must've hit him hard. He's just now waking up."

That meant it was the second or third hour of night. We had a long, bumpy fifteen miles to travel—and me with two heads, and not much sense between them.

"Draco—you are staying, aren't you? With us?"

The shuffling noises increased, and even in the dark he was as red as the embers in the fire. Nobody mentioned Coir. "I'd—I'd like to, Master."

"You're a freedman. Call me Arcturus." I grinned and reached out a hand to grab his arm. "Welcome home."

I could see the firelight reflect in the smile on his face. It was good to have him back. And it was the last time I'd go to a goddamn resort town without a bodyguard.

"Where are the horses? And the donkey?"

"The little black one is with Nimbus. The donkey is still by the dogwood tree."

I grunted. "Nimbus smelled Pluto. That's what she was nickering at."

I looked around as far as the light would go. Draco had lit some of the lamps inside and taken a couple outside, and stoked the small fire while I'd been unconscious. I wondered if he'd mined any silver while he was at it.

"Master—I mean, Arc-Arcturus. What should we do with them?"

It hurt to think. That was nothing new.

"They'll slow us down if we take them to the fort. They'd have to walk. Or be dragged."

I stepped carefully over to where the men were tied, trying to get used to the pain. I spoke as loudly as it would let me.

"Of course, we could just throw them down one of the tunnels, tied up, and they'd starve to death. Or drown, from water coming in. Or maybe we should feed them to the rats. They're always in tunnels—big, red-eyed, hungry rats. They're not too picky about what they eat, either. Isn't that right, Draco?"

He nodded, eyes wide. I looked at him. I couldn't very well wink in the dark, even if one side of my face wasn't twitching. I hoped he understood.

"Yeah. Rats, I think. Some of 'em wouldn't turn down a meal, even of—this."

I kicked at Bushy Beard's leg. His face reflected the moon and was starting to form a scream. Not too much longer.

"It'll be slow, of course. They always start with the extremities. First the toes. Then they work their way up, until—"

Bushy Beard pissed in his pants. It trickled into the ground and ran in a little stream toward the one I'd hit. The bastard wriggled over as much as he could, trying to keep from getting wet. I leaned over him.

"Don't bother. You smell worse than piss already."

His mouth was bloody. He spit some of it at me. I was gratified to see there were some teeth chips in it. I wiped my hand off on his hair and turned to Bushy Beard.

"Who hired you?"

He was shaking, his eyes bouncing back and forth between me and Draco, as if we'd transform into rodents when the moonlight struck us. Rat stories. You can always get them with rat stories.

"I don't know—honest, I don't know him. Just a man, I met him in an inn. He was looking for—looking for workers. I used to be—used to be a soldier—I know a little about mines—"

He was too young to retire. Probably a deserter. If I turned him in, he'd be better off with the rats.

"I see. You're a deserter from the auxiliary."

He'd already pissed once but was trying again. "Oh, God, please— please don't. I got—I got a wife somewhere, probably kids—please— please—"

The other one wasn't as intimidated. He tried to talk. He'd get used to the lisp.

"Shu' your god'am mouf. Don' 'ell 'em nofin."

I turned to where his hand was still crumpled from its earlier introduction to the rock. I stepped on it. He screeched. Lucky for him he was ambidextrous.

I said softly: "Remember that next time you're around a donkey, asshole." I turned to Draco. "Any food and water in there?"

He nodded. "In a room to the left. Want it?"

"Just enough water for the trip home, and extra feed for all the animals."

Draco headed for the cave. Grotesque shadows from the flickering lamps danced and writhed against the wall, making it look like the entrance to Tartarus. When Draco came out with a couple of sacks and two water skins, I was more than ready to leave.

"Feed a little to all of them, and give what extra you can to the donkey. The journey will be hardest on her."

And not so easy on me. The pains kept stabbing at irregular intervals, and each time I felt like I was going to fall. Draco got the horses ready, and I checked the donkey's legs. She'd been beaten and battered and was unsteady on her feet, but her heart was sound. I stroked her on the neck.

The fire was dying down. The men's eyes glistened in the dark. With Draco's help, I clambered on top of Nimbus.

"All right. Cut the garbage loose. Hell doesn't want them just yet."

Draco took his knife and sliced the ropes, first on the bearded one and then on the other. They stayed on the ground until he crawled onto Pluto. Whom I'd have to call Little Pluto from now on. I'd been too damn close to the real thing.

I watched as the one I fought cradled his broken hand and ran his tongue around his mouth. Bushy Beard almost wept with relief. They hobbled toward the cave, blending into the darkness until the black maw swallowed them whole. Lamp lights jumped and danced. Now they were just two more shadows on the wall.

My head felt like a kettle drum played by a three-hundred-pound deaf-mute. But I was alive, Draco was back, we uncovered an illegal mine, and we saved a donkey. A good trip.

There's a difference between five hours in daylight and eight hours in the dark, and it's more than three hours. Particularly when you've got a skull the size of Mount Aetna. After the first hour, I was thankful for the concussion. I didn't want to know where I was.

Draco didn't say much. It took him three hours to mention Bilicho. Apparently, Gwyna wrote Stricta as soon as we arrived in Aquae Sulis. Something about "Can you find Draco and ask him to come, there's a dead body, etc." Bilicho found him living in a little shack on the south side of the river. Coir had already moved on.

I tried to console him, but it was all I could do to stay in the saddle. Besides, after my recent and most notable lapse in perception, I didn't feel qualified to give anybody advice on women. I couldn't figure out what was wrong with my own wife, and then I run straight into a shovel.

I looked behind me. The donkey and I were just keeping our heads down. All three of them. She was tied to the back of Nimbus and stumbled every now and then. At least we both had someone to catch us if we fell.

It was about three hours before dawn when we finally reached the villa. Lineus himself was manning the door duties. My wife's idea, probably.

I told him to make sure the stable slaves gave the horses plenty of feed, but go easy on the donkey and build her up slowly. She needed a bath, and medicine for the welts on her back and neck. I'd mix up an unguent for her as soon as I could think again.

"Of course, sir. Right away, sir."

Lineus acted as though the governor's guests habitually brought half-dead pack animals to stay at the villa.

I made my way into the house. Gwyna was curled up on a couch in the dining room. There was at least one benefit to my aching head. I could see two of her. She woke up as soon as I weaved gracefully into the room, knocking over one of the chairs in the process.

"My God, Ardur—you look like hell! What happened? Are you all right?"

She was up in one fluid movement, her hand on my arm, gently pulling me to the couch. I grinned on one side of my face.

"You should see the other guy."

"But—but I sent—"

The sound of large, shy feet shuffling in the back by the hallway wafted into the room.

"Draco—come in here. Gwyna wants to thank you."

I sat down on the couch. Rest. Rest was what I needed. My bodyguard was still hovering at a distance, in the rear of the *triclinium*.

"He found me, as you can see. Saved me, too. I would've gotten more than merely acquainted with a shovel." I winced. The heat in the room was making my sore muscles relax, which was making my head pulse in rhythm.

Gwyna stared at me, her eyes large and worried. "Ardur—will you—are you really all right? Should I call for Philo?"

I opened an eye and looked at her. "Philo? I don't need goddamn—goddamn it!"

I lay back on the couch, panting. I shouldn't have clenched my jaw.

"No. No Philo. Please. Just—just get me a little willow bark. There's some in my kit. And some valerian. I brought it for you—to help you sleep."

Gwyna looked me over again, debating something in her mind. She stood up and started minutely examining my scalp.

"There's nothing fractured. I've got a concussion and a large bump. Think of it as an unwanted guest. It'll go away soon enough."

She bit her lip and stared at my skull as if she could see through it. Finally, she nodded. "All right. But if you're just putting on a face so I don't call for Philo—"

"If I could put on a face would I choose this one?"

She threw me one last "or else" look, then finally noticed Draco. She handed him a smile. "Thank you, Draco. I can't say it enough. Make yourself at home."

She hurried out of the room, and we both watched her go.

"Why don't you go to bed? You probably haven't been off a horse for two days."

"Will it—will it be all right?"

"Of course. You heard Gwyna. You're at home."

A smile cracked his long face. Lineus appeared behind him and cleared his throat. He timed his appearances like a striptease artist.

"Shall I show the gentleman to his room?"

Draco turned around, looking for the gentleman. I tried to nod and thought better of it.

"Please. Good night, Draco."

Lineus put a guiding hand on Draco's elbow and escorted him to one of the bedrooms. I leaned my head back slightly and closed my eyes. When I opened them, Gwyna's hand was on my cheek, and she was washing my face with a soft, wet, warm cloth. My medical kit was on the table. I was beginning to get sleepy, even with the pain and other, more pleasant distractions.

"Thanks for sending Draco. You could've told me he was here, you know."

The ablutions stopped. "Ardur, you wouldn't have taken Draco, and you know it."

I grumbled. "How do you know?"

She started washing me again. "Because I know you. You hate to admit weakness, particularly when you're feeling threatened. I asked Draco to follow you, just in case."

She was remarkably self-disciplined. There was no sense of triumph in her voice.

"You should be pleased with yourself."

She braced herself on my chest with her arms and leaned back to look at me. "Why would I be pleased because my husband got hurt? Why would I be pleased because what I was afraid of came true? What kind of wife do you think I am?"

Her lips were trembling. I'd gotten her angry and hurt her feelings. I was a monster.

"The best. What I should say is thank you. You saved my life."

She looked at me for a long moment, then bent closer, her lips brushing mine. "Ardur—you are my life."

I was starting to throb in different places. "You'd better finish what you're doing and get me to sleep. I'm—I'm sorry, Gwyna. Sorry for everything. I'm a stubborn ass."

I laughed, then yelped with pain. She stopped again.

"What is it?"

"That just reminded me—I brought home a donkey. One of those thieving bastards was mistreating it."

She placed a hand against my cheek. "Poor thing."

"Me or the donkey?"

"Both of you. Can you tell me what happened? Or do you want to take your valerian and willow now?"

"I'll wait. I think I can sleep. As long as you're next to me."

She folded herself up in my arms and kept me warm. The pain was subsiding. Her voice, slightly muffled by my dirty tunic, said: "Aren't you going to tell me what happened?"

"There's a fully functioning silver mine that's disguised as an abandoned lead mine. That's the short version. The long version will wait. Like what Grattius knows about this consortium and who the owners are." I yawned. "I'll impress you with tales of my fighting prowess in the morning. Let's go to bed."

We walked arm in arm to the bedroom. Gwyna helped me undress. Lineus brought me extra pillows so I could elevate my head. I was as comfortable as a man with a massive concussion could be, and dreamed about Gwyna in a bathing pool.

"Ardur—Ardur!"

"Wait—wait—yes—yes—I'm—"

"Ardur!"

My eyes opened, and it was Gwyna, but she wasn't in a see-through bathing garment and we weren't waist deep in the *tepidarium*.

"What—what is it?"

Her face was pale and worried. "Ardur—it's Lineus."

I raised myself up on an elbow and squinted at her.

"You woke up a man from a concussion—who was having a very

nice dream, by the way—because of Lineus? What's wrong with him?"

"Nothing's wrong with him, but he was getting the household up this morning at dawn, and—and—"

"And what? What the hell is it?"

Her blue eyes roamed all over my face, looking for comfort I didn't know how to give her. "He went outside to check the slaves in the stable, and—and he found something. On our doorstep."

It wasn't just my head that was hurting. Gwyna's face was stretched and taut, and she clutched at my hand.

"It's Faro. And he's dead."

CHAPTER SEVENTEEN

The words echoed, pounding on my skull from the inside. I climbed out of bed. There was only one of Gwyna this morning, and that one was scared.

I said: "I didn't hurt him, Gwyna. Not enough for this."

"I know." She shivered. "Go—go see him, Ardur. And—and if you could—could tell me what I should—"

I took her by the shoulders.

"Nothing, goddamn it—you're doing nothing. Just . . . just help me get dressed."

She grabbed one of my comfortably dirty tunics and helped me get it on so that the cloth didn't touch my aching head. I sat on the bed while she dug for a mantle and laced some sandals on my feet.

I reached a hand out to touch her face. "Where is he?"

She stood up, giving me a look I remembered from childhood. "I'm coming with you. You're injured, and—and I have to see it—see it through."

I wouldn't win the argument, so I shut my mouth and followed her through the house. The slaves were huddled in the *triclinium*.

I said in an undertone: "Where's Lineus?"

She whispered: "Outside."

Lineus was clinging to the wall of the house like a man in a leaky raft. Stallions in the garden, wives missing all night, the head of the house gone on sudden trips and returning at odd hours with donkeys—nothing made him blink. Until now. He stared at me, eyes wide and unseeing.

"Lineus. Listen to me. I found an illegal mining operation yesterday. This man was part of it." I thought explaining might help. If only someone would explain it to me.

"Sir—sir—"

"Gwyna will take you inside. Wait with the others in the *triclinium*. Try to calm them down, all right?"

He swallowed, moving his mouth like an asphyxiated fish. I looked at Gwyna. "Would you mind . . ."

She was staring at Faro's body, tore herself away. "Come along, Lineus." She said to me in an undertone, "I'll be right back. I'll—I'll help you."

As soon as the door was closed I bent down, unsteady on my feet, crouching with my knees bent so that no blood would rush to my head. Pushed myself to hurry, to shove the pain aside.

His face was still bruised where I hit it. Purple, swollen, skin tight, protruding pink and gray tongue. Not so handsome anymore.

Strangled. Like Bibax, only quicker and cleaner. I moved his head out of the way to check the neck. Stiffness starting to settle in the lower jaw. I tried to close the popping eyes, staring dully into the world beyond. He'd finally arrived. I wondered if he recognized it.

Eyes wouldn't close. They needed coins to weigh them down. Appropriate for Faro. I shut his jaw, leaving enough room for a fly to escape. Not the nastiest thing that ever came out of his mouth.

His hair was plastered against his temples and matted with fluid. I risked getting dizzy again and bent closer. Flinched backward on reflex, almost falling over. There were nail holes in his skull.

Something had been attached and gently pounded in—not hard enough to crack any bone, not deep enough to drain a lot of brain. The holes hadn't bled much, so it was done after he was strangled.

I looked away for a moment. I'd seen worse things that I couldn't remember at the moment. Lying a few feet away from him was a tin mask, larger than life size. I picked it up. Two nails in the back.

I rocked a little, bracing myself on my knees, and stood up to examine it further. Ritual, of course, not theatrical—actors don't like wearing nails. Neither do priests or necromancers, for that matter. Maybe it was normally attached to some sort of wooden frame.

I flicked at the tiny bits of skin and coagulated blood that still adhered to the metal. The door creaked, and I jumped. Draco was hovering behind Gwyna.

"How's Lineus?"

"Better."

"Good."

Gwyna's eyes were drawn back toward Faro's body. "Have you . . ."

"I'm in the middle of it. He was strangled, about the same time I came home last night, or a little earlier. Then this mask was tamped on his head. Probably right before he was brought here. Draco? Can you help me?"

I crouched back down on the ground and set the mask aside, moving like an old man. Draco squatted next to me. Gwyna stood on the doorstep, watching us.

Faro was wearing traveling clothes. A heavy cape with a hood, sturdy breeches under a tunic. His arms and legs were splayed, awkward in death. Looked like he'd been dropped in a hurry.

"Flip him over, Draco."

With an easy motion, Draco turned the body over and lowered it noiselessly to the ground. The back of the cape was very dirty. Bits of grass and horse manure clung to it, and the hem was caked in damp, fresh earth.

"Go through his tunic. See if you can find anything."

Draco looked a little scared, but his big hands moved with surprising dexterity. He found a worn leather pouch tied to Faro's belt.

"Go on. Untie it and give it to me. Keep looking, particularly for papers. Check his hands, too. Don't worry—they're not stiff yet."

The pouch was heavy. All coins. I poured a few into my palm. A hell of a lot of money for a traveling necromancer. Draco came up empty, and I double-checked Faro's hands. Nothing. Not even any hair. Whoever killed him was quick and professional.

I stood up again. I wouldn't be able to do that trick too many more times today.

"Stay here. I don't want any more tracks on the path than necessary." Draco stood next to Gwyna, rubbing his hands down his tunic over and over.

The wide path up to the villa was still soft and damp. Footsteps. More footsteps. Not too large, not too small, nothing unique. All I knew was that he wasn't seven feet tall, four hundred pounds, or walking with a limp.

Small cart tracks ran about halfway up the hill, near some blackthorn trees. The wheels were uncooperative, as were the horse hooves. No missing shoe nails, no crack in the wheel, mended so that it made a distinct impression in the soft dirt. So much for goddamn footsteps and horse tracks.

The pile of horse manure showed they stayed a while. My homecoming spoiled their plans, and they had to wait until the lights were off. Careful, patient murderers.

I was out of breath when I reached Gwyna and Draco, and braced myself on the door frame. Exhaustion and concussion. No time for it. I turned back to look at the body. Faro had all the time in the world.

"He was brought here last night in a cart. They waited around because the lamps were lit."

Gwyna's hand grasped my arm. "Should we—should we bury him?"

Everything between my ears hurt like hell, but it worked well enough for me to know what was next.

"No. That's what they want. They expect us to hide it. To act guilty. Draco, get the litter. We're taking Faro the Great back where he belongs."

Lineus gave us the details before we left. He opened the door just before dawn to check the stable slaves. At first he thought it was a drunk. Then he moved closer and realized it was something worse. The mask was still on the face, and through a combination of curiosity and morbid compulsion, Lineus pulled it off. Then he threw up. One of the other slaves woke Gwyna.

She wrapped Faro in a sheet. I let her do it, but I didn't like the look on her face, a kind of tenderness mixed with revulsion. As if there had been something between them.

It was toward the end of the second hour when our little parade entered the temple precinct. Wind from the west, storm on the way. Women were streaming into the baths; the tents and stalls creaked and flapped, some empty. The spring bubbled, a smell of thunder mixing with the tang of the water, the blessed, blessed water. Bathers to baths, hopeless to health, maggots to flesh.

All the actors were in place today, but someone else would have to play the necromancer.

I parked the litter bearers in between the spring and the temple. Found a stray priest and told him to get Papirius. We waited a few moments, Gwyna staring at the waters, remembering the last time she looked at them.

Footsteps hurried along the pavement. Papirius was jogging along, not a dignified gait for a head priest. My head throbbed just from looking at him. He was followed by three underpriests. He looked from one to the other of us, his eyes lingering on Gwyna.

"Papirius."

"Arcturus. What—what's all this about? I understand it's urgent."

"You could say that. Take a look in the litter."

He drew his eyebrows together. "I don't like games. What do you want?"

I shrugged, and it was worth the jolt. "There's a hard way and an easy way for everything, Papirius. I've got a concussion, and frankly, I don't give a good goddamn which you choose. I was giving you the easy option. Since you don't want to play . . ." I nodded to the litter bearers. "Bring it out."

The tall, brawny men threw aside the drape; each grabbing an end of Faro, and lowered him like a sack of barley on the pavement. A small crowd was starting to gather. Flies already.

"What—what are you—that's—"

"That used to be Faro Magnus. The former necromancer. I don't think you can be a dead necromancer, do you? Seems like a conflict of interest."

I reached in the litter and brought out the tin mask. I laid it next to Faro. "Maybe you didn't recognize him without this."

Papirius dragged his eyes up to meet mine. Little braziers of hatred burned behind them. "Why did you bring this—defilement—to the temple? What did you do . . . kill him?"

I rubbed my chin. More onlookers were starting to buzz their way in.

"No, Papirius—but someone wants me to think I did. One of the slaves found him on my doorstep this morning, and I'm not about to defile—as you like to put it—the governor's villa with a corpse that was even more unsavory when it was alive. Your temple's a little more used to dead bodies."

Gwyna moved closer to me until she could feel my arm next to hers. Getting angry made my head feel better, and there was always plenty to get angry about around Papirius.

He stood there, robes stiff and irritable, fingers curved into a ball of frustration. "What do you want from me?"

"I want you to get Grattius down here. Secundus, too—and Octavio

and any other men on the council who know anything about the supposedly haunted mine. Faro was murdered because of it."

"Meanwhile, you're just—you're just—"

"I'm just going to stand here and wait for you. And leave Faro the
Great exactly where he is."

He snapped an order to the other priests, cast a venomous look in
my direction, and pivoted away, his robes trailing in the wind behind
him.

Mutterings were getting louder, and the bodies and wagging tongues
were making the temperature rise. A tight cluster was forming around
the corpse. I ordered the bearers not to let anyone touch the body or get
too close.

I whispered to Gwyna: "Are you all right? We'll have to wait."

She murmured: "Don't worry about me."

I squeezed her hand from beneath my tunic fold. A throaty laugh
choked off suddenly. I wasn't sure if it was because Sulpicia noticed the
corpse or Gwyna.

She threaded through the growing crowd. "Arcturus—Gwyna.
What is—what is that? My God—"

"It's Faro the Great. He was left in that condition on our threshold
this morning."

"What are you doing here?"

"Getting some answers." She raised her eyebrows, but there was
more wariness and fear in her face than surprise. Her eyes drifted over
to Gwyna and took her in like someone checking an inventory list. The
smile was a little strained.

"I'm surprised you're here. Don't you find this all—distasteful?"

So she'd heard about the dinner party. Gwyna wove her arm into
mine, smiled.

"Actually, yes—but I'm devoted to my husband. You know how
it is."

Sulpicia reddened. I changed the subject to something other than
husbands and corpses.

"Where's Vitellius?"

"I'm not sure. I was on my way to the baths when—"

"Sulpicia? Sulpicia!"

Not Vitellius. The young stonecutter shoved his way through the mob, his eyes bent on Sulpicia's red hair.

"I thought I saw—"

He suddenly realized he was in a small clearing with four people. The growing crowd was packing in closer. Drusius flushed a becoming shade of rose, and Sulpicia's mouth curled suggestively at the corners.

"*Salve*, Drusius." She could say a lot in two words.

Drusius nodded to me, bowed to Gwyna. She smiled, and Sulpicia immediately started brushing stone dust off his old tunic as if it were a candidate's toga. He turned his head, finally seeing the body.

"Goddamn—Faro Magnus. Was he killed? Here?"

"He was killed, where I'm not sure. He was left on my doorstep. Thought I'd share the news."

He stared at me. "I suppose you know what you're doing."

"Faro was murdered because of a dead lead mine haunted by live miners. Except it wasn't lead, it was silver."

Excited hum from the seventy-strong herd pressing in around us. Faro was more popular dead, but so was everybody in Aquae Sulis.

Drusius stepped forward excitedly. "Does this mean you found out something about my friend—Aufidio?"

"I think he was murdered. Because of the mine. Like Faro."

He nodded. "Let me know if I can help. Who are you waiting for?"

"Priests. Council members."

Drusius moved over to stand beside me, lowered his voice. "By the way—something I wanted to tell you. Remember I said there was something odd about Dewi—you know, the simpleton boy? When he died?"

"Yes?"

"Well, he kept saying there were ants crawling on him. Over and over. That's what he said. Thought you'd want to know."

More squeals and grunts, and an occasional thwack. Sulpicia clutched Drusius's arm. Papirius was using a willow whisk to clear his way. Following him were Octavio and Philo.

Philo's eyes were moist and concerned, mostly on Gwyna. Papirius wore his usual frown, more severe as the occasion warranted. Octavio gave Faro a quick glance and shudder, and spoke first.

"I don't understand what this is about. Papirius said something about the mine. What does that have to do with—him?"

A sound that could curdle mother's milk stabbed the humid air. An angry keening. Gloating in it, satisfied malice. A younger voice ululated in harmony.

"Mur-der-er! Mur-der-er!"

The crowd divided. She didn't need a whip.

Materna hauled her beetle-eyed bulk with surprising grace into the center of the circle. She wailed again, a long, shrill cry, and tottered over to Faro. Then she slowly knelt and laid herself on top of his body. Secunda echoed her mother. The bearers were helpless. They didn't want to touch the women.

I shoved Papirius aside. "Get up."

She lifted her yellow jowls to the sky and shrieked again. The crowd was stunned and silenced. Then she pointed a fat, shaking finger at me.

"Murderer!"

Collective gasp. Whispers rose like moths to lamplight. I was about to get my fingers dirty and pull her up by the hair when someone else pushed passed me.

"Rise, you miserable old bitch. Rise and get off him. Or I swear before Sulis and Diana—I'll rip your eyes out of your skull here and now."

Gwyna's voice didn't quaver. All sound ceased. Slowly, Materna picked herself up from Faro's dead body. Secunda was already standing by the outer fringe of the crowd.

I looked at Materna. It wasn't easy. "Where's Secundus?"

Someone shoved him forward from where he was hiding. Eager

hands joined in, pushing him sideways until he almost fell. He finally reached the circle and crawled over to stand in Materna's shadow. He couldn't look up.

"Here's your latest entertainment, Secundus." I turned to the head priest.

"Where's Grattius?"

Papirius's lips were thin. "He—he wouldn't open the door."

"What do you mean, he wouldn't open the door?"

"He won't come out. He's barricaded himself inside."

I chewed over the latest bit of information. It tasted as rotten as the town itself.

"I'll find him later. We've got one *duovir* here."

I pointed to Faro and raised my voice. "Something nasty was left at my door. Maybe it was so this—lady—could make a dramatic entrance." I pointed to Materna, who swallowed like a poisonous toad.

Secundus couldn't speak. More whispers and nervous giggles popped and gurgled like the bubbles in the spring.

"This is a sort of town meeting place, and this is a sort of town meeting. I'm here to tell you a few things. One: Faro here was a part-time necromancer and full-time fraud."

A gasp this time. Some angry hisses. Still, they were eager for more.

"He confessed to me that he'd been hired to spread gossip about a haunted mine. A mine owned by some sort of syndicate—and members of your own town council." I had to wait for the shouts to die down.

"Faro also confessed to other crimes, even more cruel and malicious." I looked at Materna. Philo and Sulpicia both glanced at Gwyna. "I traveled down to the mine itself yesterday, based on what Faro told me. When I got there . . ."

I paused, waiting for the crowd to quiet down again.

"When I got there—I was attacked. Because I found that the mine was actually working, actually running, and hauling out more silver than lead."

A few people toward the rear melted away. I wondered if it was something I said. The mob got loud again. Some refused to believe it; some said they knew it all the time.

Drusius was still standing next to me, and murmured: "So that's why they killed Aufidio." Sulpicia disappeared into the crowd, after handing the stonecutter a note. Papirius and Octavio tried to look shocked.

"That's not all." I had to shout it. "I returned home in the middle of the night. This morning, one of the slaves found the dead body of Faro Magnus—whom I'd last seen at the *duovir*'s house." I pointed to Secundus. Then I looked around the crowd and raised my voice as loud as I could.

"If anyone knows anything or saw anything to do with Faro, particularly last night—please come forward. There is a substantial reward."

Someone shouted, "How much?" above the excited cacophony.

"*Denarii*, not *sestertii*. Depends on the information."

Materna came to play a scene. She began with another inhuman shriek so shrill that the people in the front row held their ears. Words and spit flew with equal venom.

"I say it again: Murderer! You hit him! You threatened him! And he's found at your house! Murderer!"

Gwyna took a step forward. I held her back with difficulty.

"Now, Materna—Arcturus wasn't even home when this murder took place, and he's here by authority of the governor, as you know. He's helping us investigate. He didn't kill Faro."

She looked at Philo appraisingly. His voice carried weight with the crowd, but I didn't want or need his help.

"Secundus! Did you or did you not witness my interrogation of Faro Magnus?"

The genial horseman of a couple of days ago was nowhere to be seen. He cringed under the malignant *auctoritas* of his wife and stepped forward like a man at his own crucifixion.

"Yes. I did."

"Did he admit the haunted mine was a hoax?"

"Yes."

"Did you tell your wife what he said?"

"Y—I—no. No, I didn't."

His wife ignored him. She stared at me and said it softly.

"But you had all the motive. You wanted to punish him. You wanted to kill him. Because he revealed the truth about—"

Philo slapped her. She held a hand up to the red mark on her yellow cheek, her mouth open. I wasn't sure whether to shake his hand or punch him in the teeth. Defending my wife was not a job I shared with anyone. Other than my wife.

Papirius cleared his throat. "Are you through? Can we—dispose of—"

"Go ahead. Do you recognize the mask?"

Papirius eyed it as though it were a poisonous snake. "No. It isn't a temple mask."

Secunda answered, surprising everyone. She whispered: "It was the ghost-raising mask. The metal part. He—he used to wear—"

She broke down and threw herself on what begot her. Materna seized the opportunity to make motherly noises, clucking and muttering, and finally withdrew, leaving a slimy trail in her wake.

I watched her leave, then said: "Bury the bastard."

The crowd disbursed, reluctantly, Faro's magnetism still irresistible. Drusius hurried off to find Sulpicia.

"Philo—thanks."

He stopped smiling at Gwyna long enough to turn toward me. "Of course, Arcturus. Only thing to be done. What's next?"

"Rome will want to know who's been cheating her. My guess is everybody. First I'll find Grattius. Then I'll talk to Secundus. If he manages to survive tonight with his wife."

He shook his head. "What an utterly wretched, ugly woman. I had no idea."

"The goddamn town is bathed in ugly. Materna's just the prime example."

He laid a hand on my arm. "I'd like you both to come to dinner.

Not tonight, obviously, but—well—Aquae Sulis being what it is, I thought—"

"You thought it would help recuperate our ailing reputations and calm gossip. I appreciate it. Though what the crooked bastards that run this town think of me isn't the foremost thing on my mind."

He smiled. "*Valete,* Arcturus, Gwyna." He turned and left, walking quickly toward the baths.

Gwyna took my arm and stood on tiptoe to get a better look into my eyes. "Come on, Ardur. Let's go home."

I signaled the bearers. We walked alongside the empty litter, through the dusty, crowded streets, people staring at us. We passed the edge of the sacred spring, and I felt a gentle drop on my head. I looked up, said a prayer of thanks to the thick gray clouds.

The rain came down. But it couldn't wash the dirt away from Aquae Sulis.

CHAPTER EIGHTEEN

It was late afternoon before I woke up. Disoriented, alone. The impression of Gwyna's body next to me was already cold. Meager light from the window said it was probably about the tenth or eleventh hour of day—just an hour or two before sundown. I stretched and sat up. Still pain, but not the delirious kind. I threw on an old tunic and found Gwyna in the *triclinium*.

She was writing something and set it aside. Her face was a little less frail. "Come sit, Ardur. I was just writing to Bilicho and Stricta."

"Don't tell him about the shovel. I'll never hear the end of it."

Her face fell into lines of worry. "Aren't you sending a message to Agricola? About the mine?"

"I want to talk to Grattius first. Once I tell the governor, the legion moves in. We lose our chance."

She leaned forward. "Do you feel well enough to talk about it?"

"I don't feel well enough not to talk about it. Did I leave my medical kit in here?"

She nodded in the direction of one of the side tables. "On top."

"I need to make an ointment for the donkey. You go first—tell me what you did yesterday when I was getting my head bashed in."

She got the kit for me and bent down and kissed my cheek. I

reached up and kissed her, long and slow, before she pulled away reluctantly and sat across from me. I checked the box. Mortar and pestle, willow, but no sage, and no ointment base.

"Hold on a minute, I've got to go to the kitchen."

Priscus was supervising the evening meal, directing an understaff of two on the proper way to braise a rabbit. He looked surprised, then irritated. "Yes?"

"Do you have any sage?"

"Sir, the rabbit will taste much better—"

"It's not for dinner. I need it for the donkey."

He raised his eyebrows until they touched his hair. Clearly the governor's taste in houseguests had declined. He opened a wooden cabinet built into the huge kitchen wall, took down a sprig of hanging sage, and handed it to me wordlessly.

"Thanks. How about some melted meat fat?"

This drew a stare from the undercooks as well. Priscus swallowed. "Do you—do you want it flavored—"

"No. It's also for the donkey."

He clicked his mouth shut and dragged out a cheap pot with a floral pattern on it. "I keep extra meat grease in this, for the candles and soap."

I turned to go and sniffed the air appraisingly. "Priscus—"

"Yes, *Dominus*?"

"Too much savory in that seasoning. Reduce it by half."

His jaw went slack before it clenched together and ground like a pepper mill. "Yes—*Dominus*."

Gwyna was waiting. "Did you get everything you need?"

"Yes. Not without the impression that I was born with no culinary taste."

She looked amused. "That's their job. The more expensive the cook, the worse sort of snob he is."

I started grinding the willow bark into a dry pulp. "Seems like a long time since we got here."

"Doesn't it? And it's only four days before the *Nones*."

"So what happened yesterday?"

"You left for the mines—"

"—and you were heartbroken."

"Ardur, it's hard enough to talk without you—"

"All right, all right. Go on."

"I thought I should go out. Talk only gets worse if you pay attention to it. I wanted to show people that I didn't give a damn for what they said or what they thought."

I looked up from the pestle. "That's why I married you."

Her lips curved for a moment. "That's not what you told me last night."

I was grinding the willow into sawdust, so I stopped, shook it out on the table, and untied the sage. "A man can have a whole list of reasons. So who did you speak to?"

"Pompeius and Crescentia. I thought—well, since we'd both been put through it, it would be natural. So I took the litter and brought Quilla with me, and found out where they lived—"

"Where?"

"Northeast side of the city, closer to the cemeteries. A nice little villa, rather modest, really, considering he's a tax collector."

I took the yew wood box from the kit and scooped some of the meat fat into it with my fingers. "What sort of tax collector? Imperial, local . . ."

"I hope you don't intend to wipe your hands on your tunic. We have to take it to the fuller's as it is."

I'd just been on the point of smearing grease down my front. I sighed and tiptoed into the kitchen, where everyone made a point of ignoring me. Stole one of Priscus's rags and a wooden stick for stirring. Showed them to Gwyna. "Is this better?"

She gave me a mock reproving look and continued. "Pompeius is a local collector for the *municipium* of Aquae Sulis, and he collects both the land tax and poll tax, based on whenever there's a new census. There hasn't been one for two years."

I grunted. Scraped the green-brown paste from the yew box into the grease pot, and started to grind more willow. "So he's not imperial. Which means no direct information about the mine syndicate, since all mine lease fees go straight to Rome. What else?"

"A few things. They're leaving in a few days—West Country. Heard there's more sunshine farther west. For Crescentia's health."

"How long have they been here?"

"About seven years. He said it's changed. Used to be a smaller town, rather sleepy and restful, but now—well, the word he used was 'rotting.' Pompeius said the town is rotting from within."

I dumped the willow into the fat and picked up the sage. "From within, huh? Did he give you any examples?"

"He said once the baths and temple became so big—and such big business—everything else went to hell. No one pays any attention to the streets, or proper inns for the tourists—no real town planning at all. He swore that since Rome made them a *municipium,* with more civic independence, there's been less money circulating. Even the grain and sheep market is slow."

"Strange. What about the investment people keep talking about, the development of those other springs?"

"He mentioned it. He said the only person who stood to profit was Octavio."

I dropped my wooden stir-stick. "Octavio? Why the bathmaster?"

"Because he owns a lot of the land down there. According to Crescentia, though, he's absolutely drowning in debt. Cash poor and land rich."

I retrieved my stick from the floor and scraped the sage into the pot. Then I scooped a big glob of everything into the yew box, careful to wipe my hands on the rag afterward.

"Yet he presumably pays his taxes."

"In cash."

"Did they mention what sort of development it is?"

"Crescentia said something about Philo being involved. Something to do with a temple to Aesculapius and another bath complex."

She turned red and looked away for a minute. "She likes Philo. It seems most women do."

"What do you mean?"

"Several are after him, but he's never responded." Now she was definitely red. "Crescentia said she's never seen him act over anyone like he does over me."

My head gave a sudden jolt, and I realized I was about to break the pestle. "We can discuss Philo's taste in women later. What else?"

She cleared her throat. "Crescentia needed a good gossip—she's the one who told me about Octavio. She knows everyone's financial standing, and she said that Octavio gets a share of the baths' profits but is always borrowing money. She thought it might be gambling. Oh, and something else interesting: He used to be a medical orderly. That's how he talked his way into running the baths."

"An orderly? He's as useless as tits on a Vestal."

She pursed her lips at me. "What an erudite and sensitive remark."

"Who else did you talk about—other than Philo?"

"Papirius. No one seems to know much about him. He came up through the ranks, was elected head priest a few years ago. Not well liked."

"How'd he get his money?"

She shook her head. "I don't think anybody mentioned it."

I stirred the paste again. The yew box was full. Three days' worth of medicine for the donkey. "How the hell did he get the position if nobody likes him?"

She shrugged. "He brought in business."

"For himself." I wiped my hands off on the rag and settled back in the chair. "Who else?"

Her eyes got big. "Oh, of course. Grattius."

"Something to do with the mine?"

"He brags about being the contact man, but other than throwing his mouth around, he doesn't have a whole lot of money. There was something else, too. Crescentia said Octavio wanted in on the investment deal with the mine but was pushed out."

"Strange. Especially if he owns the land they're going to develop. Did they explain how everything would work, the mine and the new baths?"

"It was all about getting the mining consortium—whoever they are—to finance a building by the other springs. So in that sense, the two projects are tied together, I guess. There's a reservoir down there now, just like the main temple, but that's it."

"What would the consortium get out of it, other than free baths?"

"I don't know."

"I could make a guess. They'd need someplace to launder money—and lead and silver. What better place to wash it clean than a new bath complex?"

She nodded her head. "Makes perfect sense."

"Well, I do have my moments. Sometimes I can even string a bunch of them together and get a whole day. Now—anyone else you discussed? Vitellius?"

"Sulpicia's boyfriend?" Her voice was puzzled. "What about him?"

"I don't know, but she dropped him like last year's favorite gladiator."

"Nobody mentioned him. We talked about the other *duovir,* of course. Secundus." She shuddered.

"Ah! So what did they say?"

"He was born and raised here. Made his money on sheep and horses, and then shipping."

"Go on."

"He operated out of Dubris and came back home as soon as he made enough money to impress the people he grew up with."

"He'll never have that much. What about—"

Her lips drew together in a tight line. "Materna. According to Crescentia, she's become worse as Secunda's grown up, and grown up to be pretty. She's the only surviving child. Materna's obsession with Faro is common talk. So is her resentment of attractive women—Sulpicia for one. She helped spread the rumors about Sulpicia's husband."

"Which turned out to be more than rumors."

"That's not why she told them."

"Anything else?"

"They've never had a problem with their taxes."

I rubbed my chin. I needed a shave again. "What about Philo, other than his infatuation with a certain married woman?"

"I've done nothing to encourage him."

"You don't have to."

We stared at one another. The corners of her mouth curled up and stretched a little, like a cat in the sun. "I admit I enjoy it when you get jealous. But Ardur . . . you know I love you, and I think you know how much."

We stared some more until the hair on my arms stood up and my throat made a frog noise. "Tell me what you heard."

"Crescentia said he came from Hispania several years ago. He's grown in status ever since. Pompeius repeated what she'd said about Philo and that proposed temple to Aesculapius near the other spring."

"Does he pay his taxes?"

"Oh, yes. Cash."

"He's about sixty, you know."

Her eyes enjoyed a small chuckle at my expense. "I know." Then she leaned forward and spoke with some seriousness. "Why does he bother you so much? Philo's been nothing but a friend to us since we've arrived. Look what he did this morning."

I still wasn't sure about this morning. Slapping Materna to keep her mouth shut about Gwyna was my job. Philo stepped in as my surrogate. A position he no doubt enjoyed.

Gwyna was still leaning toward me, her clasped hands encircling her knees, her eyes trying to read my face. The penmanship was messy. I was confused about the good doctor. Somehow he made me not feel—not feel like either the governor's *medicus* or the man who married my wife. That wasn't Philo's fault, though. That was mine.

I smoothed out a wrinkle in my forehead and wished what was inside of me would straighten as easily. Maybe it would, if I could just catch my breath. I looked up at Gwyna, who was still watching me, worry nipping at the edges of her face.

"All right. Let's go over the dangers of living in Aquae Sulis. Do you have any blank spots on that papyrus?"

"No, but I brought a wax tablet."

"Can I have it?"

She handed it over, and I scribbled with the stylus and handed it back. "Read it out loud, if you would."

She squinted at it. "Is that in Greek?"

"Very funny."

"Let's see—it says 'Murders.' Underneath, the first word is 'Bibax.'"

"Underneath 'Bibax,' write 'blackmail.'"

She wrote it down in an elegant hand and asked: "Are you listing motives?"

So much for the mystery of my methods. "Well—yes."

She tapped the stylus on her lips and thought a minute. "Under 'blackmail' we can list Sulpicia, of course. And Titus Ulpius Sestius."

"The nephew of the old lady? Rusonia what's-her-name?"

"Rusonia Aventina. I think he's being blackmailed."

"Why?"

"From something Crescentia mentioned I forgot to tell you. Sestius is running through his money too quickly."

"From spending it on some dancing girl."

"Not just that. He's wildly overindulgent, owes everyone in town—and he's always nervous, looking over his shoulder. He's scared of something, Ardur."

"He should be, if he killed his aunt."

"So we're not done with the Bibax business?"

"We never finished it. The mine and Faro interrupted us."

"Do you think they might be connected? Bibax and what we think his scheme was—and the mine?"

I shrugged. "Certainly the mine seems connected to this new development project. And that friend of Drusius—the farmer who died? Killed because of the mine. Was he cursed by Bibax? I don't know. Finding how everything fits together is a goddamn Gordian knot. Anyone else under 'blackmail'?"

"Not that I can think of. But what about revenge? The note said *'Ultor,'* after all. Someone like a relative of that young man—the one you just mentioned—"

"Aufidio."

She wrote it down excitedly. "Yes—a relative would want revenge on Bibax."

"Only if he knew Bibax was responsible, and right now it looks like the mine people were. The two I met would've slit their mother's throat for a bottle of *posca.*"

"I don't care, I'm writing it down."

"All right. Let's move on to Calpurnius."

"But Ardur—you haven't listed the other motive."

"What other motive?"

She drew her knees up to her chest and laced her fingers around them. "The 'unknown.' Perhaps Bibax's accomplice became tired of sharing the profits. I suppose that would make greed the motive. But maybe it was someone we don't even know—for reasons we haven't discovered yet. It's important to list, I think."

"Go ahead. It's a good idea."

"Calpurnius. 'Blackmail,' of course."

"And we don't know who."

"Any ideas?"

I said slowly: "At first I thought there were two different murderers, and that the *'Ultor'* note was faked—planted on Calpurnius to confuse us. Now I'm not so sure. Maybe I was supposed to think that. Maybe I was supposed to notice the difference in the writing."

"Maybe you're overthinking it?" It was a tentative suggestion, and I grinned at her.

"Probably. Because I can't figure out why someone would want revenge against Calpurnius. *'Ultor'* doesn't make sense, unless Papirius got really pissed off about a drain. No, I figure he was killed because someone saw him talking to me, and that person thought he knew enough to be a danger. But Calpurnius wanted money. He wouldn't talk for free. Maybe he even tried to blackmail the murderer—and get paid twice for the same information. All I got out of it was *'cui bono.'* We know what he got."

"*Cui bono.* You know, Ardur—that reminds me of the mine, and the development by the spring."

"Now you know why my head hurts."

"Poor baby. Let's get back to categories. Calpurnius was probably killed for knowledge—that works, doesn't it?"

"Yes. We should list that under Faro, as well."

Her hand shook a little when she wrote the name down. I said: "Before I forget—that boy—Dewi. You can put him under your 'unknown' category."

Gwyna looked up, pleased. Then she realized what I meant. "You mean he really was murdered?"

"Drusius said he was talking about 'ants crawling' before he died. I think he was killed, and with the same poison as Calpurnius."

"But why? Why would anyone kill him for stealing a bath robe?"

I shook my head. "I don't know, Gwyna. I don't even know how much I don't know."

She was silent as she wrote everything down.

"All right. The mine. Pure greed. But the syndicate would need a contact or two in town, especially if they were planning to dump the metal in Aquae Sulis."

"What about Grattius?"

"He's involved, or he wouldn't be hiding. But he can't be the only connection. No, Grattius is altogether too conspicuous, and maybe that's his role. To shield the real link—and the real murderer."

"You mean of Faro?"

"I mean of Faro. Someone other than Grattius must be connected with the mine—Faro was murdered too quickly. Unless, of course, Grattius killed him, but I don't think so. One set of footsteps led away from the cart, but I'd be willing to bet there were two people in it."

"How do you know?"

"Too much chance in leaving a cart and horses unsupervised while you unloaded a body, even if you were strong enough to do it yourself. Faro was small, but dead bodies always weigh more than you think they will. And the mine is guilty of more than just Faro. There's Aufidio."

"What about the ghost? Or was he real?"

"Once. Probably found the vein of silver, and got a pick in the face for his trouble."

She shuddered. "How horrible. And you—it could've been—"

"No. It could not have been me, because I have a very clever wife."

Her smile was tender. "Thank you, Ardur."

"They would've attacked anybody. Not like here. Not like Materna."

Her eyes were the hard blue of the standing stones on the Great Plain. "You can talk about it. I'm not going to break."

"Someone's been using us for javelin practice—and as tired as I am of acting like a straw dummy, I'm at least used to it. But not you. Not my wife."

My muscles tensed and a jolt slid down from my neck to my right leg. She was beside me before I could rearrange my face.

"It's my fault. I should have told you. Then those bastards couldn't have used it against us. At least not—not with such a terrible shock."

I took her hand from my forehead, where her fingertips were smoothing out the creases.

"You didn't tell me because I was too blind, stupid, and self-absorbed to see for myself. And I left you—left you before I left for the North. I'm sorry, Gwyna. I don't know why you married me. I'm a stubborn, moody fool, slow with my head and too quick with my tongue. I'm—"

I paused in the litany of my many flaws, watching her lips curve in an unmistakable fashion. She was kneeling on the couch, and she bent over me, lips to my ear. She whispered: "You're not at all too quick with your tongue."

I stared at Gywna in a cloudy haze. Then she looked over my shoulder and straightened her tunic and stood up.

"What is it, Lineus? Are you—"

Lineus was quivering in the entrance. "I'm fine, *Domina*. It's—it was just a knock on the door, and—and no one was there—"

I stood up too quickly and grabbed the arm of the couch to steady myself. "No one was there?"

"At least I couldn't see anyone, sir. I—I didn't explore, because I found this on the threshold." He held out a scrap of torn papyrus, his hand shaking.

I took it from him. "It's all right, Lineus. Tell one of the other slaves to watch the door."

He stood up straighter. "They all refused, sir. I apologize for their behavior."

Still scared from the corpse. "I'll speak to them tomorrow."

"Very good, *Dominus*."

I smiled at him. He finally got the idea and bowed himself out of the room. I'm not comfortable around body servants. There are certain functions I prefer to do in private. I made my peculiarity known on arrival, when I realized I might trip over somebody on the way to take a piss.

The paper was dirty, and the writing on the back looked like an inventory list. Tallied results of a dice game, with amounts owed. I sniffed. Smelled like wine. Definitely a tavern.

Gwyna was already standing next to me, trying to read it. " 'If you' . . . I think that's what it says—dreadful Latin—"

" 'If you want information and you're willing to pay for it, come to the Bud of the Nymph at the second hour of night.' " I looked up at her. "If I leave now, I'll be on time."

She stood with her hands on her hips. "Not without me."

"It's no kind of place for a lady, you can see that from the—"

"Yet I managed to walk into Lupo's by myself." She held her head high in that proud way of her father's. I grabbed her shoulders.

"Please, Gwyna—let me protect you from what I can. That's not a whole hell of a lot."

She stopped tapping her foot and made a noise of reluctant concession. "Arcturus—I won't let you leave this house without Draco, am I understood? I'll stay at home like the proper wife, but you've got a concussion, and I'm damned if I let you walk into another trap!"

"I'll take every precaution—including him."

Her face softened, and she took me by the arm. "You'll be late. I'll help you get dressed."

So my gambit at the spring worked. Someone swallowed the bait.

I wondered if I had, too.

CHAPTER NINETEEN

The Bud of the Nymph made Lupo's whorehouse—where Gwyna had once journeyed and where Stricta once worked—seem palatial. I contrasted the memory of last December with what was in front of me. Draco's nostrils wrinkled at the odors from the side of the building. A shed out back left nothing to the imagination. My imagination wasn't that good.

We sipped vinegar for an hour, watching the blue-bodied flies buzz around the matted hair of various drunks. The Nymph was tucked around the corner and down a block from the main marketplace, in a low wooden building with a tattered roof. It squatted in the street and clung to the adjoining apartment house like a old woman taking a piss at the public latrine. The latrine smelled cleaner.

No one who came to the Nymph had heard there were baths in town. And no one who visited the shed cubicles stayed for long. The whores were professionals. They ran it like a three-minute legion drill.

The barman was grumpy until I overpaid him. I could always buy nice. After that he got out his better bottles of vinegar and found a piece of cheese with no maggots. He watched us, though, and he was curious. No one with money ever came into the Nymph. At least not anymore. Now it was about as exclusive as the Cloaca Maxima.

Draco's eyes were swimming with the gnats in his cup of *posca*. I raised my lips to the wooden cup and pretended to sip. The door opened, and a small man in dirty leather walked into the room. His eyes were sharp.

I made a noise to Draco. He quit thinking about Coir and looked up. The man was at the bar, having a word with the black-toothed barkeep. I reached under the table for my pouch and untied it without bringing it out into the open. Then I took four small dice out of it and whispered to Draco.

"What's he doing?"

"Ordering something. Looks like soup."

"Is he watching us?"

"I think so."

I straightened up, rolled a die, and said loudly: "A six. That means I get first toss."

Draco looked at me, nodded, and dug out some coins from his pocket. I threw the four dice, and one of them came up six. I plucked out a *sestertius* and threw it in the middle of the table. "All right. Your turn."

Draco glanced around nervously, and the four dice slipped through his fingers. Two sixes tumbled out. I laughed obnoxiously and slapped the table. "That's two more you owe the pot. Pay up."

I wasn't watching Leather Man, but his eyes were cold. He'd wait some more. I sped things up a little.

"Mine again. How about we play for real money? A *denarius* for your sixes, my friend. Now that's a gentleman's wager."

Draco's eyes flitted nervously back and forth, but he remembered his part. "All right. I—I just got paid, anyway."

I showed everybody my teeth and tossed the dice. Four ones—the Dog. "Shit. You got the luck. Four *denarii* to the pot for throwing the goddamn *canis*. Go on. See if you can win it."

Draco took the dice in his large hands and cupped and shook them so they'd rattle around. Some of the drunks raised bleary eyes, awakened by the sound of chance. He threw. Two sixes.

"Well, that's half my own back, anyway." This was getting expensive.

I'd better set a limit. With a sideways glance toward Leather Man, who was leaning against the counter and watching us in the open, I said: "I've only got three more *denarii*. What've you got?"

His mouth opened slightly while he thought about it, and I stared into his eyes, willing him to keep the number low. "I—I've got five more. That's all."

Eight *denarii*, plus the six already in was fourteen. I wouldn't go higher until I knew what it was I was buying.

"Not any longer, friend. Kiss 'em good-bye—you just lost your chance to kiss anything else!" I jerked my head toward the headquarters of the three-minute special with a knowing leer and tossed the dice. Two more sixes. Almost there.

"Goddamn it! Where the hell's Fortuna? Banging some son of a bitch in the shed?" I shoved the dice toward Draco and put two more *denarii* on the table.

"Go on. See if you can roll it." I was using loaded dice, of course, but I'd also told Draco about how to roll them so the number would come up. He tucked his thumb into the cup he'd made of his hands. Three sixes leered at us. I leaned forward. Time to get on with it.

"You're down to two. I'm down to one. Whaddya say we put it all in and throw one more time?"

A calloused and filthy hand plonked down on the table. Rheumy brown eyes stared hungrily at the pile of coins. The man stank of shit, piss, and salt, and it wasn't because he was at the Nymph. It oozed from his pores like sweat. Probably a tanner.

The voice was raspy. "I want in on that game."

I eyed him, keeping up appearances. "You didn't build it. You don't build, you don't play for the win."

He untied a thick leather bag from his belt and tossed it on the table. "This'll cover the bet."

I said softly: "How do I know you're good for it?"

He looked over at Draco. "You got a big friend. And you're not so small yourself. How do I know you won't jump me to get it back?"

Now for the real gamble. He wasn't stupid. Either the information would be good or I'd need Draco for more than a game of *iactus*.

"All right." I said it grudgingly. "But let's do it right. Let's use a cup. You got one?"

"Flaccus does." He walked to the bar and came back with a worn and dented leather cup. I gave him the loaded die.

"See who rolls first. First winning roll takes it."

He rolled, and a six came up. I groaned. "Goddamn it."

Draco took the die. He rolled a three. I rolled a four. I handed it back to Leather Man. I took out my supposedly last *denarius* and Draco took out his, and we threw them on top of the mound of coins.

The tanner put the dice in the beat-up cup and shook them just right. He rolled, and they came out spinning. Draco and I—and Flaccus, who wandered over—watched them drop.

"A one—a two—a five—and a three! *Iactus Veneris!* A Venus Toss! Goddamn it, but you're a lucky bastard!"

He was fingering the *denarii* and quickly stuffed them in his pouch. Draco scooted his chair back a few inches and let his arms dangle to the side. I threw a nasty smile at the tanner.

"Least you could do is buy us some wine, seeing as you won all the money. I figure you owe us that much."

He glanced back over to where Flaccus was behind the counter and said nervously, "Yeah. I'll join you."

We watched as he went back to the counter where the barkeep was busy serving leftover vomit. They whispered to each other for a few minutes, and I gave Draco a few looks that were supposed to mean something.

He came back with a jug of wine. I kept an eye on Flaccus while the tanner crouched on a stool. We all three leaned in close.

"I got the note," I murmured. "You got the money. What do you know?"

He swished his wine around the leather cup. It was the same one he'd tossed from. "Not so fast. How do I know you won't—"

"You don't. Just like I don't know that Flaccus over there doesn't have a large club or a small knife for when we walk out of here. But you've got the money, and if it means anything, I'm a man of my word. If it doesn't mean anything, there's not a goddamn thing I can do for you."

He stared at each of us in turn. "Drusius said you're all right, and I guess that's good enough for me." He took a swig of wine. "I hope I ain't sold too cheap."

"Not unless you can tell me who killed Faro and everyone else in this goddamn town. Now talk."

He leaned forward. "All right. Faro was in here last night."

"This place? Not the type."

"Yeah. That's why I spotted him. Lot of money, too, bought the best Flaccus got. But he don't get drunk or laid. It was like he was waitin' for something."

"Did he talk?"

Leather Man shook his head. "No. Nice-lookin' horse outside, though, and a kit packed. Has this ugly wooden thing tied to the saddle, and I ask him about it. He says it's a ghost-raisin' mask." He shivered. "I'm gonna have bad dreams thinkin' about it."

"Dream about all those *denarii*. What else?"

"Well, long about the fourth or fifth hour of the night, I look around from the dice game—I'm not winnin' that one so easy—and I see this young girl come in here. Now, we don't usually get young ones at the Nymph—them whores out there are all old enough to jerk you off before you knew you was hard, and this one was young and pretty."

"What about Faro?"

"That's it. She came for him. That's who he was waitin' for, because he follows her outside like a dog. I want to see if she's goin' up against the wall, but it ain't like that. When I get outside, she's gone, and he's holdin' a note, starin' at it. So I say, 'Where you goin' so late?' thinkin' he'll never answer me, but he just looks at me funny and says, 'Where we'll meet again.' Then he climbs on the horse and rides off."

He gave me a look that was supposed to tell me something. "I guess you know what that means."

"Yeah. Is that it?"

He swigged the wine again. "Ain't it enough?"

"Yeah." I stood up, and Draco echoed me. "Thanks for the game."

He grinned. "Glad you thought of it."

I lowered my voice. "Be careful. Funny things happen in Aquae Sulis, especially to people who talk to me."

His nut-brown skin paled a little, but he shrugged and drank some more wine. "I can take care of myself. Be seein' you."

Draco and I walked out into the night. It was cold. The moon was playing hide-and-seek with some clouds. I turned to him. "You up for a long hike?"

His brow wrinkled. "Where are we going?"

"To the place where Faro was murdered. To where we all meet again."

He still looked puzzled.

"The cemetery, Draco. We're going to the cemetery."

The walk was long, and my head still hurt. A seabird lost in a cloud somewhere shrieked, and Draco jumped. His eyes were whiter than the pale shadows he halfway expected to see.

Romans have an uneasy relationship with dead people. On one hand, they like to dress up in death masks once a year and imitate their famous relatives. On the other hand, they make signs and throw beans around the house during the *Lemuria* in order to keep dead family members—the ghosts of all those mothers-in-law—out of the house. Some people say ghosts are black, some people say they're white. Some say bad luck, some say good luck. Only, nobody—and that means nobody—wants to meet up with one of them.

Unless you're a necromancer. Then you've got a temporary address in the city of the dead—and it wasn't a ghost that made it permanent for Faro.

The cemetery was to the northwest, up a long hill with a low incline. Whenever the moon came out enough, I could see Draco clutching the handle of his old *gladius* as if it were his mother's hand.

A path large enough for carts led through the graves and monuments. I paused on the road, directly across from a marble tomb. I wasn't sure what I was looking for. Faro was told to meet someone here. Most likely to raise a ghost. Either he was very stupid or he trusted the lure. A woman—a young, pretty woman.

"Draco—let's split up."

I could hear the gulp. "All—all right. What do you want me to look for?"

"Horse tracks. A horse. Anything that might have anything to do with Faro. Let's light the lamps."

I pulled the corks out of the holes in the lamps and lit them with some flint. It took a few tries. The wind was kicking up. Dark tree branches bent closer to see what we were doing.

The lamps were small enough to fit in our tunics, so they didn't give out much light, but it was something. "If you find anything, yell. Don't go too far—this place is huge. Just keep your eyes on the lights."

I was turning down one of the larger paths when I heard Draco make a small sound.

"What is it?"

"The—the lamp. Is it—I've heard ghosts—ghosts follow lights. Is it true?"

I rubbed my face with my free hand. "Draco—ghosts can't hurt you. They're dead, remember?"

"But—but they can curse—and haunt you—and your dreams—"

"We'll be lucky to get any sleep at all tonight, so don't worry about your dreams. Worry about some bastard knifing you from behind."

He took a deep breath, then walked off in the opposite direction. I crouched down to examine the ground in front of me. Horse hooves, and recent. I kept to the path and found a pile of horse manure. Bent down and rubbed some in my fingers. Dry, but still clumpy. Could be a day or two. Could be Faro's horse.

I walked some more, noticed the graves were getting poorer. The largest monuments were always along the road, so anyone who walked by could see how prestigious you'd been, and might forget you were dead. Too bad you couldn't.

I wondered where Draco was. Ghosts never bothered me. Mainly because I figure we make them up. Probably because we need something more frightening than daily life.

Smaller path to the left. Small wooden markers. A few offerings of broken dishes and bread crumbs advertising the thin, flimsy lives of the poor.

I shook my head to clear it, which was a mistake. Stood for a while, listening to the wind. No trees in this section. Faro wasn't gullible enough to believe anyone would pay him to raise anything here but dirt and tears. Both of those you can get for free.

I walked back down the road, this time along the right, the graves on this side not quite as desperate. Up in the distance, I could make out Draco's small light. I looked down and noticed fresh dirt. Followed fifty paces ahead to a newly dug mound. Next to it, on the ground, was a wooden frame with a canvas covering, head shaped. Faro's last stand.

I stooped over the grave with the lamp to see who he'd been planning to raise. I should've known. Calpurnius.

No horse hooves in the fresh soil. Probably tied up at a small tree in the distance, closer to the main road. I turned to face the light and shouted. A breeze came out of nowhere and seemed to swallow my words. I shouted again. "Draco! Over here!"

The light was getting dimmer, and heading in the wrong direction. A cold, clammy hand grabbed my shoulder, and the hair on my neck stood up and immediately fainted.

"Mast—Arcturus. It's me. Draco."

When my heart climbed back down my throat, I said: "How the hell did you get here so quickly?"

"What do you mean?"

I stared at him. "Draco—weren't you . . ."

I pivoted, and looked toward where I saw the light. Nothing there.

Fear and puzzlement spread over his face. "I was behind you, in that section."

He pointed to an area immediately to my left. The hair on my neck started to rise again, until I slapped it down with my hand. The concussion. The goddamn concussion.

"Well, you're here now. This is where Faro was headed—where he met someone. Any sign of the horse?"

He shook his head. "No, but I found some tracks on the road, going back to town."

I rubbed my chin. "The tanner said it was a nice horse. I've got an idea where we might find it." I stared at Calpurnius's grave. "Let's go. Bring the frame. It's what the mask was nailed on before someone pulled it off and nailed it on Faro."

Draco picked it up and tucked it under his arm. Neither one of us said a word until we were out walking on the road again, the lamps out and the gibbous moon leering at us from behind a wad of cloud.

"Mas—I mean, Arcturus. Did you—did you see something?"

"Holes in the ground with dead people in them."

"No. I mean—when you thought you saw—"

"Forget about it, Draco. I've got a concussion. I get confused easily."

He was quiet for a minute and then spoke again. "Are we going home now?"

I didn't want to think about the cemetery. What I needed what a good solid meeting with some flesh and blood. A quivering mass of flesh that avoided me this morning.

"No. We're going to pay a late visit to a *duovir*. Let's go see what Grattius is hiding."

The thought of scaring the hell out of him cheered our footsteps back to town.

CHAPTER TWENTY

It was a long walk to Grattius's house. I used the time to lecture Draco on the evils of bad women. I told him about Dionysia and my misspent youth. I told him about how desirable she was, and how she seduced me. I told him about how she could use her body in ways that—and then I realized we were in another conversation. So I told him how ugly it got. I made some of it up.

When we finally got to Grattius's door, I told Draco to bang on it. His massive fist hammered the wood five times before a slave opened it a crack, a bleary eye peering through the darkness.

"What do you want? Don't come any closer, or we'll—"

"Take us off the guest list? Go get Grattius. Tell him it's Arcturus, and it's about Faro, and he'd better get his fat ass out of bed."

The eye withdrew with a terrified look. I jammed my foot in the door and nodded to Draco. He shoved against the oak, and whoever was holding it on the other side fell down. I extended a hand to the two slaves who'd been bracing it and were now on the floor.

"Sorry." I turned to the eye, which belonged to a middle-aged man I'd seen on my first visit. He was shaking. "Where is he?"

The slave was loyal, but his eyes betrayed him and darted down a corridor on the right.

"Let's go, Draco."

Draco brought up the rear, keeping an eye on the slaves, who were both armed. Vibia wandered out of a room behind us, clutching a long robe. She looked disappointed when she realized Draco wasn't there to give her a good time. When we told her what we wanted, she turned around and went back to her own bedroom. So much for wifely devotion.

The room was dark and full of raspy sawing. Draco stood by the door, to make sure no one got too courageous. Grattius was lying on his back, his mouth open, an obscene noise erupting from his nose like a lava flow. I leaned in close and made it loud.

"Grattius! Get the hell up!"

The eruption choked itself and sputtered ash into the air. He did a sit-up, his jellied belly heaving with fear. "Wha—what—who—"

"Open the door wider, Draco, and let some light in."

I took out my little lamp and lit it again. Sat it on a table beside his bed, and sat myself on the corner of the mattress.

"Wake up and talk. This isn't a social call."

He scooted back in bed and braced himself against the wall, covering up with a purple blanket. "How—how dare you—"

"Quit with the leaderly noises, Grattius. You're one step away from court, prison, and maybe slavery. Rome doesn't like it when her mines are trifled with. She likes to be awake and paid off when she's getting screwed."

His eyes darted, landing on Draco. They bounced off Draco's chin and took in the stubble on my own. Then they narrowed and started to think.

"I don't know what you're talking about."

I was tired. I didn't want to dance with Grattius. He'd step on my feet.

"Look, you stupid bastard. All I have to do is tell the governor about the silver mine that wasn't supposed to be a silver mine, that wasn't even supposed to be open—the one you've been bragging about—and it's over. Your house, your wife, your slaves—all gone. Like that."

I snapped my fingers under his nose, and he jerked his head back. He swallowed and thought it over. It took him about five seconds. Then he whined.

"I—I didn't kill Faro. You can't pin it on me. I didn't know anything about it."

"I believe you. What do you know?"

His breath was coming out in hysterical little gulps. "I—I knew it was silver. And I paid Faro. To keep—keep talking about the ghost."

"How did you pay him?"

"The—the baths. Left money in a cubicle."

"Your money?"

He nodded. "I got—got paid back. Same way. Through the baths. They—they told me what to do—left instructions."

"Who's in the syndicate?"

"Don't—don't know. A man—not from town. I meet him sometimes near Iscalis."

"Who else?"

He shook his head. "I—don't—know. Someone—someone from town. I—I know that much. Someone. Not me." He raised his piggish, bloodshot eyes to mine. "I'm not taking the blame. I'm not taking the blame!" His voice was a shrill whistle of hysteria.

I grabbed his wrist. "Talk, Grattius, and I'll see you don't lose everything. Talk."

His voice quavered. "I told you! I—I just followed orders. I don't know!"

I stared at him for a few seconds while his tongue came out from behind his teeth and he opened his mouth to gasp like a beached tunny. Maybe a change in direction.

"Did you curse Aufidio? The farmer's son? Did you? Answer me, goddamn it."

He shrank against the wall. The pallor of his skin was frightening. I slapped him lightly on the face.

"Grattius—tell me. Did you pay Bibax to curse Aufidio?"

The covers knotted in his hands, and he held them up to his mouth, exposing his white, bony knees, swimming in a sea of flesh.

I slapped him harder, and he gulped air. Let the blanket down a little.

"Did you curse Aufidio?"

He looked at me, and then Draco, and back to me, and all around the room. Finally, he came back to my face and held my eyes and nodded. Slowly.

I said it softly: "Was it an order?"

He nodded again. I took a deep breath. That made it simpler—and more complex.

"Grattius—listen to me. Have you been blackmailed over this? Has anyone threatened you?"

His wispy eyebrows huddled together for comfort, and he lowered the blanket again. "N-no. No one."

"Are you sure? You're telling me the truth?"

"Yes—yes, of course."

I stood up. It was probably the seventh or eighth hour of night by now, and my legs felt as wobbly as Grattius's stomach.

"Set up a meeting. With your contact. He's got three days to see me before I tell the governor. I'll do what I can for you."

He whistled like a boiling lobster. "You—you promised! I told you everything! I didn't kill Faro—don't let them—don't let them—"

I pried the mitt of flesh off my arm. "I said I'll do what I can, Grattius."

He was already preparing a speech for the defense. "Remember—I didn't know, Arcturus. When you tell—"

"Yeah, Grattius. I know."

We left him clutching his purple blanket and whatever hopes he could cling to and ran like hell out of the room.

I wandered through a burned-out plain, wheat stalks and vines still smoking. The acrid fumes filled my mouth and nose until I retched into an open grave. They gaped between the scorched piles of the harvest. My footsteps led me to one in particular.

The earth was damp and dark and smelled clean. Then I looked again, and Grattius was in it, his body swollen with rot, the sweet odor rising like the smoke from the field. I watched as his body writhed, the maggots and the flies thick and hungry.

I turned my head and fell and kept falling, in one headlong flight that didn't stop until I found myself lying in another grave, staring at the blue sky. Agricola was above me, and Gwyna, and Bilicho, and so were Philo and Octavio and Papirius. Drusius was carving the stone. Papirius bent over and looked at me, then threw in a clod of dirt that hit my head and made me scream. The dirt was coming thickly now, and everyone was helping. I covered my face with my arms and turned over, my fingers grasping toward the dark for a way out.

They touched something soft and warm that liquified in my hands. I opened my eyes. It was Faro, and the flesh was falling off his face.

"Ardur—Ardur!! Wake up, Ardur!"

My heart echoed in my ears. It was a good sound. "Gwyna—I'm sorry—bad dream—"

I was out of breath, as if I'd been running. Which, in a way, I had been. She repositioned herself to sit next to me on the bed and stroked my hair.

"Shh. Take your time. Do you want to go back to sleep?"

I tried to focus on the window. The light told me it was the first hour of morning. I'd been in bed for four hours. "I couldn't, anyway. Best thing for me is work."

I stood up and held out my hands to her. "Come on. Eat breakfast with me, and I'll tell you all about the Bud of the Nymph."

She let the worry go when I pulled her toward me and followed that with a hard caress.

"Stop it. I'm barely awake, and the first thing you think about—"

"—is you. See how much better I feel?"

She leaned her head back, eyes closed, and smiled. "That's not the end I'm worried about."

I took my hands off the small of her back and reached for a tunic. "I can't wait to get back home and have a real vacation. Meet me in the dining room."

"In a few minutes. It takes me more than one drip on a water clock to dress."

I arched my eyebrows at her. "Are you accusing me of sartorial neglect? I'll have you know this tunic—"

"Smells like a dead fish. Here. Wear this one. And put on some trousers, Ardur. You never know when you're going to run into Sulpicia."

"I don't—"

"Yes, I know. I'm the only one you want to—run into. But you won't let me wear my blue linen tunic to Philo's for dinner—and I won't let you go out without protection. Wear some leather underneath. That woman's eyes can see right through cloth."

I was climbing into the trousers, wondering what sort of conversations women had when they were alone. Then I realized what she'd said. "Philo's? Are we going to Philo's for dinner?"

"I think we should. He invited us in order to help us, didn't he?"

I made a noise in the back of my throat that I hoped sounded noncommittal. "You'll have to send a messenger and let him know."

She cocked her head. "Ardur. Considering the slaves in this place, that's hardly an objection. Unless, of course, something you found out last night would affect the decision. Did you?"

"Did I what?"

"Discover something that would keep us from seeing Philo on a social basis?"

I laced up my sandals and turned to leave. "No. Actually—I think it's a good idea. But he's not sitting next to you."

She looked at me solemnly. "I promise, darling. If anybody gropes me, it will be you."

I froze in the doorway. Then I saw she was laughing at me, and I drew my cloak and my tattered pride around my shoulders and marched off with whatever dignity I could.

Goddamn Philo.

Breakfast was a subtle affair. Priscus cooked pheasant's eggs (I preferred chicken) and small rolls with figs and currants (I preferred plain brown bread). The porridge was Egyptian wheat with Cypriot honey (I like British oats and honey from Camulodunum). I was telling Gwyna what happened when I heard huge feet creeping along the hallway.

"Draco! Come in and eat with us!"

Lineus fluttered in from a faraway corner at the same time Draco shuffled toward us. "Have some breakfast. I'm sorry if we woke you."

"No, sir. I mean Arcturus. I was awake."

"Did you go to sleep at all?"

"A little."

He sat in a basket chair as if he were afraid he'd break it and reached for an egg. Lineus was still waiting.

"Everything all right, Lineus?"

"Perfectly, *Dominus*. The slaves are willing to watch the door again."

I smiled through a fig. "What did you do?"

"I? Nothing, sir. It was you."

"I didn't do anything. What did I do?"

"You came home, sir."

I looked at Gwyna and Draco, but neither of them could translate. I spoke slowly. "I—came home. I usually come home, Lineus. What—"

"Excuse me for interrupting, sir, I'm not explaining it well. After the note we received last night, most of the slaves—not I, sir, but many others—thought you'd be killed. The woman who cleans the bath— she's an old woman, sir, a—a northener." His nose wrinkled as if someone had farted. "She said that if you could survive last night, the curse would be broken."

I exploded. "Curse?! What curse?"

Gwyna interrupted me. "Thank you, Lineus. That will be all for now."

He bowed without another word and showed himself out of the room.

"What the hell—"

"Darling—don't mind the servants—it's flattering, in a way."

"It is a compliment." Draco's brown eyes were earnest.

"Why is it a compliment?"

He reddened as we both looked at him. "Because if they thought there was a curse—nothing, not even fear of death, would convince them, and they—they can—servants, I mean—cause trouble. They can look like they're working but get nothing done. And gossip."

"So why is that flattering?"

"Because they think your power is greater than the curse—and it was. So now everything is all right."

I shook my head. "Poor bastards."

Gwyna knew what I meant and reached over and took my hand. "They are right to have faith in you, Ardur."

I changed the subject. "Where was I?"

"Grattius. How he received orders from someone to have Aufidio cursed. That connects Bibax with the mine—if only as a murder weapon. I think that was all. You were starting to describe how Faro was killed."

"All right. So Faro's paid off with a large sum of money. He leaves with a nice horse for another provincial town but is hired—by someone he knows or trusts—to perform one last bit of ghost-raising. And the ghost is Calpurnius."

"Who would hire him to raise Calpurnius?"

I leaned forward. "That's just it. Only someone who pretended an interest in his murder. That was the most interesting thing about Calpurnius—that and whatever he knew that caused it."

Gwyna said slowly: "So you think someone—someone close to a young, pretty girl—unless she was specially hired for this—"

"I don't think so. The tanner said Faro seemed to recognize her."

"Well, whoever it was baited Faro into going to the cemetery. Someone sent a note, and probably money, and asked him to stop on his way out of town. He was waiting for the note, wasn't he? Why else would he be in that horrid bar?"

"It must've been someone Faro wasn't afraid of. Or at least who he thought wouldn't kill him. Someone with a logical interest in Calpurnius's murder."

Gwyna's hand was reaching for a fig when she sank back against the couch, her fingers curling into a fist. The knuckles were as white as her face. "Ardur—have you thought—I mean—the most logical person to be interested in Calpurnius's death is you."

"'Mur-der-er.' Yeah. I thought of it. I'm waiting for a note to be conveniently discovered."

Draco was looking back and forth between us, his forehead creased with confusion. "What note? I thought—"

I turned to him. "I didn't write a note, Draco. I was on my way to the mine. Its just that Faro's murder looks as phony as the smile on an undertaker. Except he really was killed, and by someone who would like it better if everyone thinks I did it. I wouldn't be surprised if someone finds a message to Faro with my name on it, suggesting we meet at the cemetery and play *iactus* with Calpurnius."

"Ardur—what about Materna? Secunda is a pretty girl."

I leaned back in the chair. I couldn't talk about Materna and eat at the same time. "Materna seemed to truly care for Faro. As much as a twisted, cankered mass of hatred can care for anything."

Gwyna's face was as hard as Egyptian granite. "Hate and love can be exactly the same thing."

I scratched my ear. "Yeah—but we need proof. I'm trying to stay one step ahead, and I don't even know where I'm going."

"You're going to Philo's for dinner. If someone is setting us up, we should take advantage of his social position. Not act guilty."

"Which is why we made that trip down to the spring."

Gwyna started to rise. "I'll send a message."

Draco spoke up. "I'll go."

"Draco—you're a freedman—"

He nodded. "I know. But—but I'd like to help."

It would give him something to do. Maybe even get him clean. He needed a bath almost as much as the tanner. "Thanks. Why don't you take a look in the baths, too—see if you overhear something useful?"

"That would be fine—I'd—I'd like to go." The big man seemed glad of an excuse to get up. He stuffed another egg into his mouth, smiled at us, and left for his room.

Gwyna turned and scrutinized me. "Are you sure you'll be all right without Draco? How's your head?"

"I won't be standing on it anytime soon, but I'm all right. I'll be back by the late afternoon."

"Where are you going? What's the plan?"

"To see Sestius for a little blackmail talk. You said we need to be social—so I'll be social."

"Wear your nice cloak. The blue one."

"Men don't think about—"

"Yes they do, Ardur. At least men like Sestius." She mulled for a minute. "I should chat up his girlfriend. She'll let me know if he's not spending money on her, and she's young and pretty—though we don't know of any link between Sestius and Faro."

I grunted. "I keep running into cobwebs."

"Well, I'm going to the baths to talk to people. Flavia, too—she's probably squirming in her bathing suit to hear about—about my miscarriage."

It was the first time she'd said it out loud. "Will you be all right? I don't want—"

"I'll be fine. Don't worry. I want to do this. It's important."

I reached across and took her hand. "Be careful."

"You, too. Where else are you going?"

"On a hunt for Faro's missing horse. I've got some ideas about it."

"Be back in time to dress."

"I hope to be back in time to undress."

She leaned forward and took her hand from mine and put a finger to my lips.

"Shh. Focus on the case, Ardur. There are good people here, but the town—the ghosts—the—the soul of the place—it's been infected. Corrupted. The slaves are right, you know. You can lift the curse."

Her eyes were enormous and earnest. I bent forward and kissed her cheek. I didn't want to disappoint my wife, but I was afraid that whatever was wrong in Aquae Sulis would prove to be too heavy for me.

CHAPTER TWENTY-ONE

I stopped at Natta's shop at the foot of the hill. It would be a hard day for Gwyna, and I was under the impression that jewelry usually helps. Buteo was outside. He stood with his hands on his belt, staring off toward the town. He jumped when he saw me, coughing, a dry, rasping wheeze that the coming rain wouldn't make any better. I wasn't sure if much would.

"Good morning. I'd like to buy something. Is your—is Natta here?"

I almost said "your father" but remembered in time. They looked enough alike. He gestured with his head toward the small, dark shop while his heavy shoulders shook with the force of the cough.

More dust on the wooden counter. Natta crept out of the back, pushing aside the tattered drape and holding on to it for support.

"Yes? You want—ah, it's the young doctor. Come in, come in. Your wife—she liked the necklace?"

"Very much. I want to buy her a ring."

He smiled at me indulgently, until memory overtook his features and made them look younger and less ill. "She is—she is a beautiful woman."

That surprised me. "You've seen her?"

He nodded, still in a trance of remembrance. "On her way to the baths, I think. Yes. She is very beautiful. She reminds me of—of my wife. Yes—my wife."

He stared into the damp walls. Nothing else seemed to be coming. I didn't have a lot of time, but maybe the old man needed to talk. If I didn't have time for that, I wasn't much of a doctor. Or a man.

"You were married?"

I asked it softly. I could almost see him thirty-odd years ago. Never good-looking, but love can make the ugliest man seem like Adonis. The sounds of coughing from outside finally stopped, but Buteo didn't come in.

"A long time ago. More than thirty years ago. When I lived in Hispania. She was beautiful—like yours. Blond, slim. Greek, she was."

"What happened?"

Darkness passed in front of his face. It settled in the crevices and was comfortable there.

"She—she died. A god—a god took her away from me. She died. Before she could give me children."

Common enough tragedy. I knew how lucky I'd been that Gwyna— it didn't bear thinking about. Most people blamed the gods. Natta's pain focused on one. Maybe that made it easier. I doubted it.

"I'm sorry."

Either my sympathy or Buteo's heavy footsteps in the doorway shook him back to the present. He turned to Buteo. His voice was sharp. "Have you seen Philo?"

"No. He is busy."

"You must, Buteo. You must get some medicine for the cough."

Buteo had heard this before. "I will keep trying, Natta. He is a busy man."

I cleared my throat. "As you know, I am a doctor, and if you wish—"

The *gemmarius* smiled at me, while Buteo lowered his brows into a frown.

"It is not necessary, my friend. You are here for other things. Buteo will see Philo. His cough comes and goes, like the rain in October. Now, what would you like? I have an onyx cameo—or this green glass from Egypt—"

I tried not to act like I'd been given the professional brush-off, and I tried not to let it make me hate Philo. I kept reminding myself he'd been good to us. Friends weren't so easy to come by that I could afford to throw one away.

The ring I chose came with a necklace. A pale green glass Natta said came from Egypt, supposedly with special properties of protection. They were set in gold. Gwyna would like them. Besides, we needed all the protection we could find. I left the *gemmarius* and Buteo outside, the younger man watching me walk down the hill, Natta leaning on him for support.

The smell of rain made the crowd swarm like ants before a storm. I wandered among the curse-writers, some hawking their wares with extra-loud voices, some ignoring the passers-by while scrawling a name on a piece of lead. I was looking for one in particular.

He knew me when he saw me. He told the fat woman in front of his tent that he was closed.

"What do you mean—you just told me—"

"Sorry, lady. Rain."

She threw her purple mantle around her ample shoulders and marched off in a huff to his nearest competitor. I leaned on the counter and smiled.

"Remember me?"

The rat eyes darted, looking for the nearest hole. He couldn't find one and turned around, determined to outrun me. I reached across the rotten wood and grabbed his filthy tunic. It started to rip.

"Unless you like to run naked in thunderstorms, you should talk to me. I won't bite."

His shoulders shook. "I tol' you the first time. I ain't got no bad lead. That other one—down there. You talk to him."

"No. I want you. And I'm willing to pay."

His eyes made little slits of suspicion. "You're willin' to pay—for what?"

"For you answering one question."

His pink tongue slid out between his lips. "Yeah? How much? An' what kind of question?"

"Five *sestertii,* and no one will know the answer you give. Except us."

I kept a tight hold of his wrist and dug out my pouch. I laid it on the board in front of us. There was obviously more than five *sestertii* in it.

He weighed his greed against his fear, but the scale was rigged. His shoulders hunched over and he leaned on the board. "What's the question?"

"Somebody's dumping cheap—maybe even free—lead in Aquae Sulis. Who is it?"

The eyes got big and round again, and his voice climbed to a piercing whine. "I don't know nothin'! I tell you my—"

"Keep your voice down. Tell me what you do know."

He quieted and looked at the pouch. He said flatly: "It'll cost you more than five *sestertii.*"

"Make it a *denarius.*"

He tried to see through the leather, but the pouch wasn't giving up my secrets. Finally, he nodded. "All right. Here's what I know—but you didn't hear it from me! My lead's good! My lead—"

"I know all about your lead. Talk."

He licked his lips again and lowered his voice. "Every so often there's a pile left. Down by the other spring. Good lead, too. I ain't never seen nobody leave it—we don't ask no questions, know what I mean? Why muck up a good thing?"

"What happens to it?"

"Whaddya think happens to it? We take it! That's why we can make curses so cheap. Lead's got a price—it's mined by Rome, ain't it? They fix it all. But this lead—we don't ask no questions. It's good lead, too. Not too much tin in it, like some people's."

"How long has this been going on?"

He shrugged. "I don' know. I guess two, three years tops. One reason there's so many of us. Easy start-up business, know what I mean?"

"Yeah, I get it. Not much overhead. When was the last shipment?"

He thought for a minute. "Probably about a month, month and a half ago. I missed my share. By the time I got down there it was gone."

"Who told you about it?"

He looked around his stall, craning his head in both directions. Then he lowered his voice to a whisper. "Bibax. That's worth your *denarius,* and maybe more, ain't it? Bibax always knew ahead of time."

I looked at his thin face, animated by avarice. I let go of his wrist. He wouldn't run now.

"So where's my money? I told you—"

I opened the pouch and took out two *denarii.* "Here. You deserve a tip. But don't talk about lead so much around strangers. It might give people ideas."

His eyes opened, and so did his mouth. I plonked the coins on the table and walked away.

Grattius and the mine. Faro and the mine. Now Bibax and the mine. Another web—and it stretched across the town.

Thunder drowned out the pounding on the door. I tried again. Sestius lived in a quiet town house, not too far from the baths. Convenient when you wanted to roll out of bed for a massage and some wine, and then roll back in it for a three-way poke.

Even the doorknob smelled like sex. Large and small pricks made of terra-cotta hung from strings in the entranceway, either as good luck or an advertisement. Or maybe a want ad.

I knocked again. Eventually feet answered on the other side, and it opened. The face was middle-aged and sullen, and beyond that I couldn't tell.

"Yes? What do you want?"

"Sestius. Is he at home?"

It looked at me again and squinted, and then a flash of lightning made it squeal, and it tried to shut the door on my foot.

"Julius Alpinius Classicianus Favonianus. I'm here on the governor's authority."

My Roman name was long enough to frighten everyone but the bureaucrats. The face looked up to see if it could see rain. Maybe it hoped I'd melt.

I wedged my knee against the thick oak. "I said the governor's—"

The door flung open suddenly. The face belonged to a small man with sallow skin and an equally bilious expression. He was holding on to his stomach as if he were afraid it might run away. "Wait here. I'll announce you."

I smiled nastily at him to prove how important I was. He clutched his midsection harder and scurried down a dark corridor to the right.

The foyer was covered with sea paintings and various naked sea nymphs, who had somehow lured five satyrs underwater without drowning them or diminishing their erections. A chair and table were new, expensive, and poorly made, the cheapest kind of the latest fashion. An empty pedestal stood against the wall, missing its god.

I was trying to figure out what one of the satyrs was doing to one of the nymphs when Stomach Ache walked back in. "This way. The master will be a few minutes."

He showed me into an inner room, furnished with the same kind of material. Lots of reds and browns, with garish highlights to make the paintings look more "real." There were gaps in the arrangement: empty display shelves, a missing dining couch. Sestius was running out of money. He would never run out of bad taste.

I sat on one of the couches and felt something hard. Reached underneath the cushion and pulled out a leather dildo. I decided to stand up. I walked around the circumference of the room a few times until I got bored. Then I got angry.

I headed down the corridor the servant came from. I figured the bedroom would be at the end; they usually were. And I figured the bastard would be in bed.

Stern portraits and busts sculpted in a severe style lined the passage, wrinkling noses at their wastrel heir. I reached the end of the hall and looked at the door. To knock or not to knock? I decided to kick it open.

A huge round bed filled the room. On top of it was a man about twenty-five, flabby in the middle with a jiggly ass, sleeping heavily on a woman with enormous tits. He was using them as pillows. She was awake and still, staring at the ceiling, an expression of profound disinterest on her face. Until I walked in.

She prodded Sestius with her knee and tried to cover herself, though I wasn't sure there was anything in the room big enough. She hissed at him. "Sestius! Wake up! Wake up, goddamn you!"

Footsteps outside. More servants. I slammed the door behind me. The woman succeeded in rolling him off of her and onto his back. He was naked, and the reason for her ennui was obvious.

She swung her legs over the side of the mattress, clutching a small blanket. "Who are you?" She said it as if she didn't expect much.

"My name's Arcturus."

The eyes got interested. "The one who found the dead guy?"

I wondered which one she meant. "Yeah. I've got some questions for your boyfriend."

She looked bored again. "He's not my boyfriend." She saw my raised eyebrows. "I mean, not regular. Once in a while—when he buys me something . . ."

She left it in the air as if I might make an offer.

"What does he buy you?"

"Dresses. Jewelry. He bought a cow for my father once. He's a cheesemaker."

With a prizewinning milker for a daughter. "He still buying?"

She shrugged, and the blanket slipped. She let it dangle a little more than necessary before pulling it up again.

"Not so much. Shoes and perfume. Says there's no more money."

"Did he say why?"

Her forehead wrinkled. "He said somethin'—somethin' in his sleep. Somethin' about a payment. Owes people."

"Who?"

"I don't know. Don't ask. I just let him do what he wants, and he takes care of me." She gave me a quick appraisal and a longer preview of the merchandise. "You got money?"

"Not enough for you, honey. And I'm not in the market to buy. No offense, of course."

She shrugged again and this time stayed covered. "None taken. You mind if I get up and get dressed?"

"You mind if I walk to the other side and slap that bastard awake?"

She giggled and stuck her hand underneath the covers looking for something to wear. She pulled out a transparent sheath, then took it and herself to the corner of the room. I took myself to the other side of the bed, where Sestius was lying spread-eagled and snoring.

On a small table beside him was a jug. I looked inside. Still some wine left. The girl turned around to watch me.

It rained and spattered all over the pillows and into Sestius's open mouth. He started to choke and sat straight up. He wasn't used to the exercise.

I slapped him in the face. I was getting tired of slapping people. He rubbed his eyes, coughed some more, shook his head like a wet dog. Groped for a blanket or sheet and whimpered. The girl was laughing. I was still standing. I wasn't going to sit on the bed.

He stank. Rich food, rich wine, rich sex, night after night. It oozed from his pores like sweat. His eyes were as small, soft, and red-rimmed as the rest of him. "Wh-who're you? Whaddya want?"

"To talk to you. Your slave left me in the dining room too long."

He pulled the brown blanket up to his chest. Even his breasts sagged. "Whaddya wanna talk to me for? I don' know you."

I glanced over at the Farmer's Daughter. "Honey, why don't you go on outside? He'll need you again when we're through."

She looked disappointed, and the bored expression came back. Her shoulders slumped underneath the tight tunic. "He needs something, but it ain't me. Be seein' you. 'Bye, Titus. Don't forget to send the cloth you promised."

Panic over losing his pacifier. "Wait—Hortensia—"

She slammed the door on her way out.

He stared at it for a few seconds, then turned to me, fully awake. "Who the hell do you th—"

I slapped him again, a little harder. "Call me a friend of your aunt's."

His pale flesh froze like a fat cut of meat on a slab of ice. "M-my aunt? W-what about my aunt?"

"Maybe you have more than one. I mean the one you had murdered."

He stopped breathing for a few seconds, and I was worried that I'd accidentally killed the bastard. A few brisk thumps on the back and another light slap on the face brought him back. He started to cry.

"S-she was gonna die—I swear on Jupiter—she was gonna die anyway, and I—I didn't want her to suffer—"

"So you figured why prolong the inevitable, why drag it out, why wait for your money. Is that it?"

"Yeah—I mean, no. I—I didn't care about the money—"

"Don't try, Sestius. You're too soft and stupid to make a good liar. As it is, you make only a half-assed degenerate. You're a stupid, greedy, indolent bastard, who figured the only thing in between you and a good time was your aunt's life, and that was hanging on by a thread. So you found someone to cut it. Bibax. I know all this, and it doesn't impress me. What I want to know from you is how the blackmail works."

The tears choked off like a pipe valve. He reached for a sheet and blew his nose on it. Looked at me with what he thought was cunning. "You comin' in for a share? Is that it?"

"Just answer the goddamn questions. How does it work, and when was the last time you were contacted?"

Fear rose in waves from his body and overwhelmed the other smells.

The bravado hadn't lasted long. He shrank against the wall. "A-are you going to h-hurt me? I promised I'd pay—"

"For the last goddamn time, Sestius, I want information. Keep your filthy money. The town likes to watch it run through your fingers."

He whimpered some more and looked at me with doubt in his dull eyes. "Y-you just want me to t-tell you—"

"That's right. That's all I want. Then I'll leave you, and you can go back to sleep."

The whimper got louder. "You made Hortensia—Hortensia left—"

"She'll come back. Sell another statue."

He stared at me for a few seconds, and his tongue came out and licked some crust off his upper lip.

"All right. I—I get notes. In the baths. In the cubicle."

Just like Sulpicia. "Go on."

"Then—then I leave money—or jewelry—the next day."

"Where do you leave it?"

"Sometimes in the cubicle. Sometimes—sometimes I have to pretend it's for the temple, and throw it in the spring."

"When was the last time?"

He fidgeted in bed, scratched the hair on his belly. "I don' know. Last month, I think. Notes come about every month."

"None since the *Kalends*? Since Bibax was killed?"

He wrinkled his brow with the effort. Not used to that kind of exercise, either. "No. I don't think so. I—I owe a lot of people."

I studied him for a few seconds. "Do you remember who told you about Bibax?"

The answer came surprisingly without effort. "Yeah. Vitellius. He told me. Said Bibax's curses come true. Any curse. On anybody. No questions."

"Vitellius Scaevola? Sulpicia's—"

"Yeah. Him. He wasn't with Sulpicia then."

"So he told you, and then you paid Bibax a large sum up front—and then you put a curse on your aunt."

His eyes welled up again. "I—I just asked for her suffering to be over. It—it wasn't a curse, not really—a p-prayer—prayer to Sulis—"

"For your aunt to die sooner than later."

He pulled the covers up to his chin and tried to curl into a fetal position against the wall. The eyes were far away. The voice was a whisper.

"S-sometimes I see her. In the dining room. In the hallway. Even by the s-spring. I hide. In here. She never liked—never liked it when I had girls. So she stays away."

He looked up at me like a child asking for a sweet. "Would you tell Hortensia to come back?"

"Yeah, Sestius. I'll tell her."

I turned around to look before I went through the door. He was curled up still, pinned to the bed like a worm on a hook, staring at the ceiling. The slaves would bring more wine, and more women. I left him alone. With his ghosts.

CHAPTER TWENTY-TWO

A bath would be nice after Sestius. I rubbed my hands down my mantle and looked up. A few drops were falling, large and loud enough to make a satisfying splat on the golden stone. I didn't have time for a bath. I needed to find a horse.

Thunder shook the town as I walked through the temple precinct. The cheap cloth covering the stalls flapped and snapped in the wind. Even here, the streets emptied except for a few souls so lost they couldn't feel the rain. They wandered to the spring and watched the sky reach out a finger to touch the bubbling surface. I wrapped my mantle around me. At least the smell of Sestius would be washed away.

The rain emptied itself in small fits, drops hammering the soft clay soil, moving on to the next block, the next hill. I reached Secundus's house undrowned. If Materna was home, I wouldn't be let in. I had to mind the legalities around the cancerous bitch.

I knocked again. I told myself it was possible no one could hear me. So I tried the door. Not locked. I pushed it open and entered. An old slave woman, half asleep and all blind, was sitting in a chair, snoring like the thunder. A fire was dying in the main room. Looked around. Nobody but the old lady. So I started down one of the corridors.

Rain pounded against the thatched roof. A placid drip started in the entranceway, forming a puddle underneath the door slave. No sound inside except the ruminating snore of the old and tired. Until I passed a door at the end.

Loud grunt, and rhythmic squeaking. The rhythm was getting louder and quicker, and so was the grunting. It built to a small crescendo much too quickly, and a feminine voice giggled. I guess fucking on a rainy day was the thing to do in Aquae Sulis. I kicked a door open for the second time.

Secunda was still squatting on top of Mumius. They turned toward me, faces shocked and stupid. I grinned. "Don't mind me. I'll be in the barn."

I left them stuck together and whistled a tune down the hallway. A servant ran out of the kitchen, saw me, ran back. The old lady at the door was still sleeping. I stepped over the puddle and saw myself out.

The barn was warm with hay and horses and smelled even better than the rain. A few slaves were sitting on stacks of straw and oats, one whittling something out of a stick. They quit talking when I walked in, and the biggest one got up to meet me.

"You want something?"

I looked him over. Burly fellow, with short grizzled hair and leathery skin. I didn't want to get him in trouble. Although life in the mines might be preferable to living in the same house as Materna.

I took out a couple of *denarii* from a fold in my tunic.

"Tell you what, boys. I'm not here. You didn't see me, and we didn't talk." I dropped the coins on the straw-strewn floor. "You found these in the street."

The others watched the big one. He watched me. He spoke slowly.

"Seems a shame. Too easy, like. I like to earn my money. One way"—he looked toward a pitchfork propped against the barn wall—"or another."

The others took the hint and got up to stand behind him.

"I work for the governor. I'm trying to figure out why people die in Aquae Sulis."

One of the other slaves snorted out a laugh. The big one smiled gently. "They die 'cause they're sick."

"Or murdered."

That shut them up.

"I was a guest here a few days ago. So was a small, dark man. He was killed—strangled. Out in the cemetery. He was leaving town, and he was riding a good black horse—small and fast."

The one that snorted made another noise, nudging an old man with a beard. They huddled together behind the spokesman. His face was hard, not giving anything away.

"So why are you here?"

"Because I think he borrowed that horse from your master. Or mistress. I think the horse, being a hell of a lot smarter than the man who rode it, came back home by itself."

The burly slave spoke to the others in whispers. I heard footsteps behind me. It was Secunda. The slaves scattered, some climbing the ladder to the upper floor. The big one bowed. "Beggin' your pardon, miss, but this man—"

"I'll take care of it, Grithol."

He said nothing, just started mucking out a stall, every now and then looking at the *denarii* still on the floor.

She was out of breath, and her tunic was crooked. She'd worn a mantle over her head against the rain, and her face was flushed from the exercise. All of it. She said abruptly: "What do you want?"

"To find out who killed Faro. Don't you?"

She was a stupid girl. She tried to give me a withering look but only succeeded in making herself look cross-eyed. "Mama says—"

"I don't give a rat's ass what your mama says. Your mama feeds off hate and throws it back up on everyone she meets. And I suspect—I suspect very much, Secunda—you know it."

Her eyes took on a kind of animal gleam. "She wouldn't like you poking around."

"She wouldn't like you getting poked."

One of the slaves stifled a guffaw. Some straw from the loft fell through a crack and rocked in the air until it landed. Secunda swallowed a couple of times. She was pretty, if you liked them dumb. "You—you—"

"Don't worry. I won't write about it on the temple wall. All I want to know is if you have a black horse that came home riderless the other night."

She stared at me, her face red. Then she decided to pretend I didn't exist and turned around and marched out the other end. The slaves trickled back to the main room. The big one cleared his throat.

"I—I think you might like the third stall on the right. Nice stall, isn't it, Hamus?"

"Yeah. Damn nice stall."

They all looked at me expectantly. I walked to the third stall.

Inside was a small black horse with a fine-boned, intelligent head. I climbed in with him, calming him down because he didn't recognize me.

"'S'all right, boy. Easy."

I stroked his neck while his nose took in my equine history. He decided I was all right. I rubbed him under the heavy part of the jaw and scratched a spot on his right front flank. He extended his neck for me. Now he knew I knew the secret spots of horses, so he let me pick up his hooves.

They'd been cleaned, but he was the one. I explored his haunches, found a minor scrape. Probably went through a bramble on his way home. I scratched between his ears, while he rubbed his head on my chest. I murmured: "I wish you could tell me what you saw."

A sharp whistle from one of the slaves brought me out of the stall in a hurry. Hustling down the barn to meet me was Mumius, still hiking his belt into place. His face looked dipped in beet juice.

"Arcturus. You should know—Secundus left for Londinium. Yesterday. I wouldn't—Secunda said—"

"I don't care who you fuck, Mumius. I'm just here to do a job."

He drew himself up, which was difficult considering his belt was still falling down. "I—I just want you to know—I didn't talk. You know—about Faro. I didn't."

"You want a prize for valor?"

He kicked at a clump of horse manure and didn't say anything. I studied him for a few minutes. He was still staring at the floor when he muttered: "I'm going back to camp." His voice held disgust. "I'm through with that family."

"Well, at least you got something out of it."

He shrugged and grinned. "Any port in a storm."

Then he laughed and held out his hand. Considering where it had been, I didn't want to grasp it, but I figured the rain would clean me off again.

He turned around and disappeared back inside the house. I gave the black gelding one more pat over the stall door. The slaves were nowhere to be seen. I stared up at the loft. More straw was falling like snow. Time to get home.

The rain didn't touch me. All I could see was Faro, and somebody nailing that mask on his face. Not sure why it bothered me so much. Maybe because I wanted to hurt him, and finding his dead body on my doorstep made me feel guilty. Because despite what he did to my wife, I felt—pity. Pity for him, and this whole goddamn town.

That old bastard *haruspex* at dinner, the first night. He was right. The place was rotten. Maybe not once, when it was younger and not so famous, but now it was as soft and swollen and stinking as a dead man in the summer sun. I wondered if the mine poisoned Aquae Sulis or whether the venom was old and always there, waiting to be dug up like silver.

Grattius was just a stooge, a nobody who could be pushed and pulled and led around. Someone else in town was doing the leading. I wondered who.

A lot of people seemed to know about Bibax. Vitellius. Grattius.

Sestius and Sulpicia. Whoever told Grattius to arrange Aufidio's death. Calpurnius knew, and knew enough to die for it. And wherever you turned in Aquae Sulis, whatever mean, crooked street you walked down, you always came back to the temple. The temple where the goddess collected her blackmail payments to the tune of bubbling water. Where the head priest drank Caecuban wine.

And there were the baths, of course. Notes left in cubicles, notes directing murder, and payoffs, and other business not clean enough to be done in the water. Octavio was always ready to bow and scrape at the important ones, patching a pipe here and picking up a note or two there, running errands like a rat in a sewer. I wondered about Octavio.

I wondered, too, about Bibax. Was he, after all, a murderer for hire, the netherworld's assassin? Or was he a tool, like Grattius, who was paid to curse certain people, and maybe started to believe in his own powers—until the belief got in the way? Bibax. He was the root of what was growing in Aquae Sulis.

The rain stopped, and the world was at that silent point between storms, when the wind isn't blowing anymore but the birds are still afraid to sing. I took the mantle off my head and smelled the air. The earth was cleaner—the town still filthy.

Faro was paid off. By Materna or Secundus. Who was now on a suddenly convenient trip to Londinium, out of reach from suddenly inconvenient questions.

I scratched my chin. The night he was killed, Faro was given a horse—a good horse, from their precious stable. It was as if—as if someone knew they'd be getting it back.

I swallowed the bile that crept up my throat when I thought about her. There was no one in this place, no one I had ever seen, who was more eaten away by hatred than Materna. It was her lover, her bed partner, her constant companion.

And she sat in her house, and brooded, and squatted in the bath, and brooded, and threw her parties, and played the social scene, and all the time she plotted and planned and desired, her thoughts and wants stretching to Faro, to other men and women she could trap and snare and jerk like pet birds on a string.

My doorway was solid and warm, and it comforted me when I shivered. I'd been looking for cobwebs. Maybe it was time to look for the spider.

I dreamed of horses. Manes danced in the wind, the ripples on their flanks shimmering with the pulse and throb of their hooves. Black and chestnut brown, dark gray and cream, they outran the sun, and their shadows fell on the wheat field like the passing clouds.

They were running too fast. The leader, a strong black horse with fine bones, was galloping toward a cliff that stretched to the sea. Nimbus was beside him, and all the horses were mad and joyful, even the donkey, twitching her ears and cantering at the back of the herd.

The wheat gave way to gorse and shrub. Dust rose like smoke, and still they wouldn't stop. I was running, too, trying to get in front, trying to keep them from falling, but they were too fast, and too glad, and they didn't see me. I was shouting, but my mouth was full of dirt, and still the horses kept on running.

I woke up to a hand on my forehead. My chest hurt.

"Ardur—are you—are you all right? You were turning back and forth in bed and breathing hard and—and whimpering. My poor darling—I wish I could keep the bad dreams away—"

I took her hand off my forehead and kissed the fingers while I caught my breath. "What time is it?"

"Almost the tenth hour. We should be getting ready."

"When did you get home?"

"Not too much later after you arrived. I bought you another tunic for tonight."

I grinned at her. "If it doesn't smell like dead fish, I don't want it. I like my clothes to be lived in."

"You've been living a little too much. Ardur—stop it. We don't have time. We have to talk about the mmmff—"

She was sitting next to me on the bed, so I just reached over and pulled her on top of me and covered her mouth with my own. After a while, she was out of breath, too.

"Ardur—we don't have time—"

"We would if you quit telling me we didn't."

"But—but the case—"

"We'll talk about it. Afterward. Besides—it's raining. And in Aquae Sulis—"

"Oh. Oh, yes, Ardur—"

"—the thing to do when it rains—"

"Don't—don't stop—right there—"

"Is this."

I liked rain. I sat against the wall of the bedroom and thought about it while Gwyna nestled on my chest. I looked down and stroked her hair while she stretched an arm out over the side of the bed and made a sleepy, satisfied noise.

"Now we really need to get ready."

"We have been. When we get to Philo's, I want my smell all over you."

She turned red and tried not to smile. "You're such a beast."

"It's why you love me."

This time she gave me a sideways look. "One of the reasons."

"So tell me what happened at the baths."

"I always go first. You tell me what you found out from Sestius."

While I put on the new blue tunic she bought me, and she started putting on powders and fixing her hair, I told Gwyna about my day.

She made noises of disgust at Sestius, and incredulous ones at my description of Hortensia. Her eyes got big over Mumius and Secunda, and finally narrowed when I told her my suspicions. Then she nodded and put down the mirror.

"Ardur—Ardur, it makes sense. Prunella told me this morning—Materna is the one whose cloak was stolen. You know, the theft that boy Dewi was blamed for. She bought a generic thief curse—'whoever

stole my robe, slave or free, male or female,' et cetera. Prunella didn't
know whether Bibax wrote it or not. That's not the kind of thing anyone remembers, especially anyone like Prunella. Bibax was too low for
her to notice—until he was murdered, anyway. She knows Dewi's grandmother, and she said there was a rumor the thief was Dewi, and then—
then he just died. You said he was killed. So there must be a connection.
Materna must be guilty of something!"

"Other than a capital case of the mean and uglies. I think so, too."

"What do we do now?"

"What we've been doing. We need proof. And remember, whatever
she's done, she didn't do it alone."

Gwyna thought for a few minutes while she rubbed some rouge on
her cheekbones. "Ardur—I didn't learn much today—"

"That was enough!"

"No, I mean the women weren't so gossipy around me—they didn't
want to talk. Sestius's girlfriend was complaining about how he wouldn't
take her anywhere, or buy her presents—"

"That reminds me, I've got something for you."

"You're sweet. Thank you. But let me finish."

"Go on."

"Well, I did find out from Prunella—after bringing her another
bottle from the cellar—"

"Agricola will think I'm a lush."

"Will you quit interrupting? Anyway, she said Octavio hasn't been
sleeping well—"

I started to say something, and she shut me up with a glance.
"And—it's true—he gambles. He's in debt."

"She told you that?"

Gwyna shrugged her shoulders elegantly. "In so many words. She'll
talk to herself. If you get her drunk enough."

I smoothed the nap on the tunic down. "Will I do?"

"Brush your hair, and put some oil on it. You look like a wild man
from the hill country."

I uncorked a flask and started to pour a liberal amount onto my palm, then Gwyna made a horrified noise and got up from her chair.

"What are you doing, Ardur?"

"Putting oil on my hair, like you said."

"Not that much!"

She shook her head and took the flask away from me. "How you were able to look as good as you did before we were married—"

I grinned. "Did I look good?"

She answered my vanity by scraping the oil from my hand into hers. My palm had already absorbed some of it.

"You're too dry all over."

"Not all over."

"Will you stop it? Now, hold still."

She pushed me toward the bed and made me sit while she rubbed my scalp and hair, then stepped back to look at me. "Go comb it—and use the mirror."

I fished out a comb. My hair was wavy and thick, but Gwyna had gotten the oil all through it, so I didn't pull out too much. She was pinning her own hair up, and I came over to nibble on her neck.

"Is this better?"

"Yes, but use the mirror and straighten out that lock on your forehead. You look like Pan."

I looked in the mirror and wiped the leer off my face—and fixed the horns.

"We need to find out as much as we can about Octavio. See how well he knows Materna."

"We have a chance to tonight. They've been invited to Philo's."

I was frowning. "That's convenient."

"Not really. This is a small town, after all. Grattius is shut in his house, waiting for Rome to call, and Secundus is tainted by association and has run away, and Philo knows you don't like Papirius. That left Octavio."

"How come Philo knows I don't like Papirius? I never—"

"Darling, it's obvious when you don't like someone."

"Is it obvious when I do?"

"Ardur—get your hand off my—"

"Oh—your present."

I took the small package out of my old tunic. It was still damp from the rain. "Open it."

She unwrapped the twine, gasping when she saw the green glass against the dark brown piece of scrap leather he'd wrapped it in. "It's lovely."

"Let me put it on you."

I draped the necklace around her neck and fastened it. She was holding up the mirror and studying the effect. "Who made it? The one that—"

"Yeah. The *gemmarius* at the foot of the hill. Nice old man. Good work, too."

"It certainly is."

She turned the mirror back and forth to catch the waning light better and wrinkled her brow.

"What is it? Don't you like it?"

"Of course I do. It's just—it makes me sad for some reason."

"Sad? Sad!? I'll have you know I paid—"

"Hold me, Ardur. I love the necklace, I just got melancholy for a moment."

She settled herself in my arms. I held her and tried not to wonder about women too much. Then she took a deep breath and seemed to be herself again.

"See? Just a passing fancy. Don't pay attention. It was so thoughtful of you—and I truly love the piece—"

"Hmm. Me, too."

She pushed away, pretending to scold me. "How can I get dressed if you keep—"

"Am I presentable now?"

She looked me up and down. "Yes. You are. If you put on a ring."

I stuck an onyx signet on my finger. "If I stay in the room with you we'll be late. I'll wait for you outside."

She smiled at me. "Thank you, Ardur. Don't you dare smell like the barn when I come out."

I turned around to look at her from the doorway.

"How did you know—"

"You were talking about that donkey in your sleep. Go on."

She closed the door on me gently. I thought I'd better check on Draco and take him to the barn with me—and tell him to forget I ever said I could teach him about women.

CHAPTER TWENTY-THREE

S he's built well."

"Yes—a little thick in the hind end, but that's to be expected."

The donkey was looking over her shoulder at us while I checked the welts on her back. My ointment had helped, but she still wasn't out of danger. I turned to the slave I'd appointed her chief caretaker.

"How much ointment is left, Marchoc?"

He shook his head. "Not so much. After tonight, we will need more."

"I'll make some. Meanwhile, tell Priscus to give you some cooking wine—like *posca*—and keep pouring it over the cuts here, and here, three times a day. No—make it four times. Once in the morning, once before bed, and twice during the day. And keep her stall mucked out and dry."

"Yes, *Dominus*."

He was a native, a small, wiry man with an instinct for horses. Looked as though he'd taken his share of falls in more than his share of races. The donkey pushed at his side with her nose.

"She'll be all right, won't she?"

Draco was stroking her neck, an unusually thoughtful expression on his face. More than dirt rubbed off at the baths. There was more energy to his step, maybe some life after Coir.

"If she doesn't get a fever from those sores. We have to dry them out—can't let them make pus."

Marchoc nodded his head in agreement, a smile cracking his face like old parchment. "She's a good beast, she is. Brave, too. Never complains. Only bit me once."

I grinned. "So far. Give her time."

We all shared a good laugh at the temperment of female animals, until I could feel Nimbus glaring at me from her stall. I patted the donkey's behind and walked over to see her. I opened my palm and gave her a turnip green I'd swiped from the kitchen.

"See? I saved this for you."

She wasn't impressed but allowed me to scratch her neck while she ate it. The lamplight fell on her gray coat, made it glisten in the dark. It was getting late. I was surprised Gwyna hadn't come out to yell at me yet.

There was a sudden increase in the amount of noise by the donkey's stall, where I'd left Draco and Marchoc. I took the lamp and gave Nimbus an absentminded pat good-bye. When I reached the others, I was surprised to see Lineus. He didn't care for the barn.

"Tell the mistress I'm coming."

"No, sir, it's not the mistress."

His voice was squeaky, his eyes too wide, and he looked back and forth between Draco and me as if he wondered if we were enough.

"What is it then?"

He bit his lip. It was almost completely dark outside, and the shadows from the barn lantern made even Lineus look faintly sinister. I grabbed him by the shoulder.

"Talk, man! What is it?"

"Someone—someone to see you, sir."

"Who?"

Marchoc was watching us with his mouth open, and now Lineus

frowned at him. The stableman retreated back into the stall with the
donkey. The head slave turned to me and lowered his voice.

"He refuses, sir, to say who he is. He refused to take off his mantle,
too. He keeps it wrapped around his face. He won't even come in the
house. He—he stays in the shadows, sir. He says he won't leave until
he talks to you."

I could feel Draco move to my side. "Where is he? And the door—my
wife—"

"She knows, sir, and the door is bolted, and the largest slaves are
behind it."

"Where is he?"

"By the hawthorn tree, sir. On the right side of the house. He
said—he said he'd be waiting there."

A covered face meant he was afraid of being caught. That meant
he'd done something worth catching him for. "Tell him it'll be a few
minutes. Did he say anything else?"

Lineus paused while his face fell on the ground and didn't get back
up. "Only that you're to come alone, sir."

Draco opened his mouth to speak, but I brushed him quiet with a
gesture. It wasn't my game, but I had to play anyway. Fortunately I
owned more than one pair of loaded dice.

"Lineus—does the governor keep any weapons around here? Jave-
lins, swords—"

"There are a few swords we keep locked in the tack shed—for emer-
gencies, sir—we're alone here much of the time, and—"

"What else? Any bows?"

"I—I think there might be four or five, sir."

"Find them. You've got five minutes. And listen—give Draco the best
sword here. Arm your strongest slaves with the rest. Then send them
to Draco. The bows give to anyone who can shoot. Position the men—"

I couldn't see the front of the house from where I was standing, even
if it hadn't been well into the first hour of night. I closed my eyes and
tried to remember.

"Position the men behind the big rock, the one slightly uphill from the hawthorn tree. One there—and one from any window in the house that would give a good shot. Make sure they stay out of sight. Five minutes. Move."

He blended into the darkness without more than a small squeal under his breath.

Draco was plucking my sleeve. "Where do you want us?"

"You, down the hill. If he doesn't already have someone waiting with him. If he does, same place, just stay out of sight. The other men, too. And Draco . . ."

His eyes glinted in the yellow light. "Yes, Arcturus?"

"Don't jump him unless he kills me. Is that clear?"

"But what if—"

"No. Do nothing, unless he kills me. Then take him alive."

His hand gripped mine, and my arm was starting to hurt. Then he melted away in the shadows, as silent and still as the cloud that cut the face of the moon.

I knelt down and picked up some dirt. Always cheap and effective, and it felt comforting in my hand. I poured it inside a fold of my tunic, together with a couple of small rocks. I still felt naked. Looked around the barn. Pitchfork—too big. Shovel—likewise. The donkey was staring at me as if she were trying to tell me something. Of course.

I walked around behind the stalls to the tack room. Lineus had it open and was distributing yew bows to a few of the slaves. Draco and his men were already on their way down the hill.

I squeezed in beside one of the gardeners and rummaged on a shelf until I found it. A hoof pick. Hand-sized, with a curved, sharp end that could dig out mud—or a man's throat. The donkey gave me a satisfied look when I came back to the barn.

I kept it in my hand on the way to meet him. Gwyna was in the house somewhere, watching me as I walked in front, angling slowly toward the dark mass that looked vaguely like an outline of a man on horseback.

An owl flew off a nearby branch and hooted. I jumped. Maybe this was only what it seemed to be. Just a meeting. With a man who kept his face covered. My footsteps on the stones were loud. He'd know I was coming before he saw me. He knew I was alone. I figured he had men with bows and swords, too.

His horse snorted and stamped, and now I could see it was fast-built and dark. Chestnut, maybe, or gray. A small man. I breathed a little. I lifted my right hand, palm up. The pick was in my left. My voice came out as if a fat lady were sitting on it.

"I'm here. Climb off and tell me what you want."

He was wrapped up in several mantles, but he uncovered his mouth. The voice was middle-aged, smooth, educated. A Roman voice. "I wanted to meet you, and I believe you wanted to meet me."

"Who the hell are you?"

The voice laughed. "A direct question—but not a direct hit. Let's just say I own the shovel."

So the syndicate had come out to play. I got a little closer to the horse. "It wasn't hard enough. What makes you think you are?"

He pushed some more cloth off of his face, probably trying to see me better, but he left enough to keep him completely in shadow. His voice not quite so amused. "We're not wrestlers. You're a doctor and I'm a businessman. I'm not looking for your soft spot. If I were . . ."

He lifted himself up in the saddle slightly and turned to look at the house. My hands were slippery around the pick. I tried to control my voice. He couldn't see my face, either, not clearly.

"What is it you want?"

"I told you. To meet you. Weren't you looking for me?"

"No. I don't give a fuck about you. You're legion bait. I suppose you mean I made enough noise, you heard from Grathus—and came to find me. Is that what you wanted to hear?"

"Well, it gives us an understanding. So now that I have found you—"

"You're trying to decide what to do with me."

The figure was silent for a moment, as if it were throwing a die and waiting to see what turned up. "The governor is leaving. But you knew that."

"So?"

"So you'll need new friends. People who can protect you. You've angered a good many people. The procurator—"

"The ex-procurator. Is that how you got your mining contract?"

He sat up stiffly. "I thought you might be intelligent enough to—"

"You thought I might be bought—but I don't worship money. I also don't work with men who won't show their faces and hire killers and rot out towns like the plague."

Outrage poured through the layers of clothing, his gloved hand a tight fist on the reins. His voice was soft. "You could afford that pose— once. But now . . . now, Arcturus—you've got a wife. Maybe a family coming. Will you spit on money then? Or will you run to the governor—who won't be in a position to help you?"

"Say what you came to say and get the hell out of here."

He watched me for a long minute. It came out abruptly. "We're leaving town. Pulling out. The mine is closed."

"What do you mean, leaving town?"

"I mean no investment. No temple, no bath. Our dealings with Aquae Sulis are through. Our local representative—"

"Grattius?"

A derisive rasp. "Grattius is a buffoon. Our representative got a little out of hand. Aquae Sulis isn't a good place for business anymore. So I came by—as a courtesy—to let you know you can call the legion in whenever you want. They won't find anything. The silver's all gone."

"You underestimate the legion."

"You overestimate the governor. He'll be in Rome soon, and no one will give a good goddamn about a little mine in a little corner of Britannia."

"You seem to know Agricola. Or maybe think that you do."

I could see his teeth in the dark. "I know enough."

"Who's the local representative?"

The teeth got bigger. "You're the clever doctor. You figure it out."

We stared at each other for a few seconds. Finally, I said: "Is that all?"

"For now. I'll be going. Don't try to stop me—there are seven men in various locations around the villa, all skilled mercenaries and very well armed."

I'd moved closer to his horse a few inches at a time. I looked up at him. "I don't want to stop you. I want you to get the hell off this property."

"You made your noise, native. It was loud enough for us to pay you a call. If I hear you again, you won't be shouting." He paused for a minute, then added softly: "You've got a weak spot now, hard man."

He tried to rein in the horse, but I grabbed the bridle. "Let me give you some information, since you've been so helpful. If you fucking bastards ever even look at my wife, you'll be begging me. And it won't be to go on living."

The raspy chuckle bit my ears. "But you would never know, Arcturus. You wouldn't be there—and she wouldn't tell you."

I buried the hook in his leg. The leather shin wraps ripped, and I felt the flesh quiver. Then I yanked the hook forward, dragging it around the circumference of his calf, until I was in danger of hitting the horse.

He screamed and clutched at it, and by instinct I ducked. An arrow whizzed by and stuck in the hawthorn tree. Another one flew from the rock where my men were but missed. Down on the path, I heard shouts and a clank of metal.

He was holding on to his leg, galloping down the hill. Footsteps ran by chasing him. I shouted for the servants to grab what they could and follow me. Somebody lit a torch, and we ran down the pathway until we could see a group of men in a circle. Draco and the slaves. They were holding four mercenaries at sword point.

Draco's face lit like a torch when he saw me. He'd spotted their men and circled behind them. Then he found their horses and figured capturing the mounts wasn't the same thing as an outright attack. When he heard the shouts, he tried to avenge my death. Fortunately, I was around to appreciate the effort.

The walk back up the hill felt like a triumph. The slaves started to sing, the burliest ones nudging the mercenaries forward with sword points. I sent one of the others to the legion outpost. Soldiers would pick up the men in a few hours, but meanwhile they'd be bound and gagged and harassed by the servants.

When the procession reached the front of the house again, I saw Gwyna standing in the door. She was holding a knife. "Ardur—I was so worried. My God—you're wounded—"

Everyone was quiet while I looked down in the torchlight at my new tunic. There was a bloodstain on the right side.

I reached in and pulled out the hoof pick. A chunk of leg was still attached.

"Not mine, sweetheart. Just a souvenir from our visitor."

The slaves shouted, some waving swords in the air. I heard "curse" several times, and someone was earnestly explaining to one of the women that I had magical powers and couldn't be killed.

I handed the pick back to Lineus, who gave it to Marchoc. Draco was explaining to Ligur where to keep the prisoners—the woodshed—and how far apart they should be and how often they should be given water.

I wasn't going to bother with questioning them. Too many questions tonight. Besides, they were mercenaries. They wouldn't know the Aquae Sulis contact. They could help the legion track down the syndicate—maybe. If anybody cared to find it. The bastard was right about that.

Gwyna was grabbing my arm and leading me inside. "Sit down—let me—"

"What are you doing?"

"Taking care of you. I thought I'd give you a bath, and then—"

"Just get me my old tunic. We've got a dinner appointment."

She stared at me, her mouth open, until I closed it with a kiss. She kissed me back, and I didn't care if the servants saw. Another faint shout rose from outside.

God, I was hungry.

CHAPTER TWENTY-FOUR

We were about an hour overdue. I leaned against the cushions. The litter swayed to the steady footfalls of the bearers, but I wasn't in the mood for a lullaby. I'd come close to killing a man. I was hungry for food, still hungry for blood. Always hungry for my wife. I watched Gwyna as she gazed out at the soft rain.

She was wrapped in a shiny golden tunic that glittered when she moved. A twilight-colored mantle draped her shoulders. She wasn't hiding anything in that outfit.

While Philo's pretty serving girl escorted us to the *triclinium,* I put on my party face. I was even more of an outsider tonight. Maybe it was the excitement of wanting to kill and knowing I could. Maybe I was always like this.

My stomach felt as flat and empty as the grapes in a winepress. Rich pork odor—maybe suckling pig—tinged with a hint of fig teased my nostrils, and peas—with bacon and caraway—stewed chestnuts and lentils—honey cakes. A real goddamn dinner in Aquae Sulis.

The room was warm—but not too much. The furniture was good—but not too expensive. Nothing in excess—unless it was the fat old dowager stuffed into a *stola* that was too tight twenty-five years ago.

Philo rose with an easy grace. Libations had been poured; some of

the guests were already on the road to Olympus. Even the large goblet
on Philo's table was almost empty. The good doctor was still drowning
his sorrows by drinking in my wife. I smiled and bowed and stood in
front of her.

"Arcturus. Gwyna. Thank you for sending back the message. I understand you were detained?" The always smooth delivery was for the
guests: His eyes were worried.

"An unexpected visitor."

He looked his age tonight. Anxiety dug out the fine lines around his
eyes and mouth. He absentmindedly reached a hand to brush Gwyna's
arm and spoke in an undertone. "Are you—are you both—all right?"

I grinned again and gave him a playful punch on the shoulder.
"Never better—but hungry."

He dropped his hand from her elbow, and I let the wry expression
he threw me bounce off my teeth. Message understood. "Of course.
I'm sorry—let me introduce you to the guests. You know Octavio and
Prunella—"

The *balneator* nodded and looked away, a scowl compressing his face
into that of an ill-tempered dwarf. Animosity all aimed at me. Prunella
was busy figuring out how Gwyna was keeping her tunic up—and
wondering if she could get away with wearing a copy. She couldn't.
She'd been swapping intimate secrets with the wine jug again.

"—and of course Sulpicia and Vitellius."

The smile that Gwyna turned toward Sulpicia held a certain self-
conscious sense of triumph. Sulpicia's face froze, her mouth wavering
between a teeth-clenching grimace and a snarl. Vitellius dropped his
spoon, which he'd been idiotically tapping on the palm of his hand. His
mouth was open. The round was Gwyna's.

"And may I present Marcus Tiberius Simio—and his charming
wife, Regilla. Julius Alpinius Classicianus Favonianus—and his wife,
Gwyna. Simio and Regilla are traveling through, on their way to
Londinium."

The hairy little man with red-rimmed eyes didn't give a rat's ass who I was. He went back to looking toward the kitchen. His wife was the sort of vacuuosly pretty woman you usually run into at dinner parties. About twenty years younger than her husband. The only thing that interested him was dinner. She stared at me, her eyes as round as the cheap white glass on her ears.

Philo cleared his throat. "Simio is a friend of an old client of mine. He thought he'd look me up, after all these years."

Freeloaders. Explained his sudden lack of taste in guests.

"Finally"—he was guiding me by the arm back to the middle of the couches—"I don't believe you've met Crassa. Related to the Vespasiani. Distantly," he added under his breath.

Crassa smiled graciously at Gwyna. She was covered in ancient baubles, and the diadem on her wig was crooked. She turned her attention to me, unrolling me like a scroll. I suddenly remembered the time my Aunt Pervinca slapped my hands for stealing food from the kitchen.

"Arcturus, Gwyna—you're here. In the place of honor."

The couch was plush. I tried not to sink. Philo had the taste—and self-control—not to seat himself next to Gwyna. Or maybe that punch was a little harder than I thought. Crassa was next to her, and they were already deep in conversation.

The host placed himself on the next couch, with Octavio beside him. Prunella was calling the wine boy for more. To her right was Vitellius, who also noticed the wine boy but wasn't drinking.

My eyes met Sulpicia's. All offers were still open. I grinned at her. Must be the hair oil Gwyna put on me. She was finally forced to turn toward Regilla, who kept plucking her arm. Regilla's husband was waiting for the food to come out as if it might escape.

Gwyna craned her head to whisper to me. "Is that cow still trying to seduce you with her eyes?"

"I hope you mean Sulpicia."

She shook with repressed laughter, giving my leg a vicious pinch. I leaned forward to breathe in her ear. "You can't see where you're pinching, so be careful."

"You be careful with Sulpicia, or I'll know exactly where to pinch."

The wine boy came by with wet towels for our hands and finally poured the drinks. I looked up to find Philo watching me. "Do you like the wine, Arcturus?" he said softly.

"Thurine, isn't it?"

"Yes. Last of the vintage."

There was something melancholy about Philo tonight, something out of reach. And I wondered. I wondered who Philo really was. He stood up to make the traditional speech, his eyes still haunted.

"Friends and guests. Welcome to my home. What is mine is yours."

Sorry I can't say the same, old boy. I took another sip of Thurine.

"Relax—enjoy the food and the company. As our Horace said, 'Carpe diem.' So please—carpe vinum."

Everyone clapped their right hands at his wit, and he sat down amid the applause. His face was red. He was certainly following his own advice.

Three slaves came out of the kitchen bearing simple black platters of lentils and chestnuts. My mouth was too full and my stomach too empty to think any more about Philo or anything else.

The suckling pig was tender and exquisitely cooked. When we were finished with the honeyed millet cakes, I wiped my hands for the third time on my new napkin, unrooted a piece of meat with my tongue, and finally gave my attention to the party. I felt someone staring at me. Gwyna was talking to Crassa and fortunately couldn't see that Sulpicia was using more than her eyes.

"Hello."

"Hello."

Vitellius was nearly asleep. I lowered my voice. "You managed to pry him away from the bath boy? What's wrong, is Drusius not—"

The almond eyes narrowed into slits. "Kindly keep your mouth shut."

I feigned surprise. "But I have a question for your boyfriend—Vitellius—hey, Vitellius!"

He looked around, taking a few minutes to find me. "Oh—hello, Arcturus."

"Hello. I wanted to ask you something."

"Me? You wanted to ask me something?"

There was an echo in the room, and I was looking at it. "Yes. How long have you known Titus Ulpius Sestius?"

His expression got a little less bored and a lot less stupid. "Let me see—about two years or so. Why do you ask?"

"Because he claims you're the one who gave him some information. Information that—well, let's say it helped make him the man he is to-day."

Sulpicia's skin was now a pale shade of green. She whispered some-thing to him through her teeth. When he looked back up at me, he wasn't alone. Octavio was staring at me, his face twisted with hate. God, I was good at parties.

Crassa's voice trailed off. One of those unexpected silences stood in the middle of the room and screamed. I took a drink. "Sad thing—about his aunt dying. Especially since she came out here for a cure."

Prunella hiccupped. "Lo's of people come here f'r a cure—an' they never leave."

She started laughing, out of control, and Octavio shook her. Regilla never met a pause she liked. Her chatter helped cover for Prunella.

"You never know, do you? You just never know. Why, we met a soldier who told us the governor himself lost his only son. So sad, don't you think? I mean, his wife's not getting any younger." She giggled and held her hands up to her face—"well, none of us are—and I'm sure she won't be able to have any more children, and the soldier told me it was just a cold, and it just took him like that."

She snapped her fingers and then lowered her voice. Gwyna put a hand on my leg I could barely feel.

"The soldier said it was the doctor's fault. The governor has some expensive doctor, you know, they all do, and he said that doctor just let the little boy die, same as if he upped and killed him. I always say, you can never . . ."

Gwyna made a noise in the back of her throat. Philo reacted first. He almost shouted.

"Doctors—are human—why people—why they want to talk, to gossip . . ." He shook his head in disgust.

The eyes changed direction, from Regilla—and me—back to him. My stomach was desperately hanging on to the food while the rest of me wanted to throw it back up. Somebody, somewhere—maybe Quatio—maybe someone just like him. I took another drink.

Regilla gaped at Philo, the kind of fish you threw back. Flushed up to her mouse-brown eyebrows. "Oh . . . oh—you—you're a doctor, aren't you—I . . . I didn't mean—"

"Your mouth outran the rest of you. Like always." Simio still looked bored and even a trifle hungry. He scratched the thick hair on his hand. "Always happens."

She covered her face with her napkin in embarrassment. Unfortunately, she'd forgotten there was pork sauce on it. Philo spoke again.

His voice was in a dream, his eyes unfocused. Sadness was there, too, a pain so sharp I could reach out and prick my finger on it. I recognized it. Guilt was an old friend of mine.

"You can't save all of them, you know. Come to you with hope in their faces, wanting another day—even another hour. Unfinished business. It's all unfinished." He took a long draft of wine. Everybody knew there was more.

"What did Ovid write? 'The wave, once gone, can never be called back—nor can the hour ever return.' Something like that. But you want it back. You call it, cry for it, over and over again. What if I'd done something else—would she be alive? Could I have saved her? Could I?" He looked around, his face impassioned. Nobody answered. Nobody could.

He shook his head. "It doesn't matter, in the end. You can't. I know. I tried." Philo was staring at something none of us could see. "And still—the guilt will grow in a man's soul like weeds in a garden." He jerked his wineglass up and drained it. His eyes landed on Gwyna and his voice bcame tender. "She looked like you. So very much like you."

Everyone was holding their breath, wondering how the story would end. Except me. I knew the outcome. Philo's guilt was an old habit, a way to warm his cheeks with tears when they felt the winter chill. Remorse and a jug of wine, an old doctor's best friends. After a few years, even they weren't real anymore. Oh, yes—I understood Philo now. I was watching what I could've become in another twenty years.

I looked down at my wife. Her eyes were full of tears. She murmured: "Who was she?"

He turned around to face her, cradling his wine cup against his chest. "Long time ago. In Hispania. I was a temple doctor—the Temple of Endovelicus. Native Aesculapius, but a—a god for fertility. Women spend the night at the temple trying to become pregnant."

He stared into the cup and was still for so long that Simio was able to find another millet cake. I'd seen those temples—it didn't matter what they called the god. Women, desperate for children, sometimes desperate for other things, came for help. The priest gave them a drug to eat—*strychnos,* maybe, or a mushroom. Then they'd see the god, and sometimes even feel him. It depended, often, on what the women looked like—and who was playing the god that night.

"They believed—believed that the god would come—make love to them—give them children." He shook the wine around and suddenly shuddered. Then he drained it in a gulp, and his eyes, when he opened them, were sober again.

"She stayed at the temple. Became pregnant. And—and died in childbirth. I couldn't—I couldn't save her."

He looked back at Regilla. She'd taken off the napkin, but not the scrape of fig on her chin. His voice came out as a harsh croak. "Don't abuse my hospitality."

He stood up abruptly and walked into another room. Gwyna and I both followed him. He was staring at a painting on the wall. A little too much *veritas* with his *vino* tonight.

He glanced up when we came in, his voice still sharp. "I'm all right. Go back to dinner."

"Philo—that's twice you've stepped in front of us."

He averted his eyes. "Gossip is a terrible thing. Can hound you like the Furies."

We watched his hand shake while he poured himself more wine. I owed him something.

"I want to tell you what happened tonight—why were were late."

Little by little, he rebuilt his face. Shocked by the visit, angered by the threat to Gwyna. And afraid. Maybe because he should've known about the mine all along. Maybe because he had. Disappointment settled in and stayed around longer than anything else.

"It's—it's too bad, in a way. Truly. The temple—it could've helped people. More and more come each season, and a temple to Aesculapius . . ." He threw a final drink down his throat. "Well—no matter. Maybe we can find someone else."

"Someone cleaner, I hope."

"Of course—someone legal, too."

Gwyna's voice was gentle. "You own a lot of the property down there, don't you?"

Not his evening for surprises. He set the wine jug down. His charm was reaching out to us—palpable—pleading.

"Yes—I do. It's not common knowledge, though. I've purchased land from Octavio. My—my plan, as you know, was to build a temple and then turn it over to the city. The best way to do it is to get control of the property and build—we can't really 'buy' the land, you know, because we're a province of Rome, but it amounts to the same thing. Otherwise, nothing will ever get done. Too much bureaucracy."

Too much explanation. Wrapped up in honey so it was easy to swallow. I still wasn't sure. About Philo, or anything else. He wasn't exactly himself tonight. Or was he?

He was smiling at Gwyna. I wondered who he saw. His eyes drew downward to her necklace, and he held out a finger to touch it. "This is beautiful. Is it from Baetica?"

"It's not from Hispania at all. It's Egyptian. Ardur bought me a ring to match, see?"

She extended her hand and he took it in his own and admired it, while pretending to admire the ring. He was shaking again. I put my arm around my wife. "I think it's time the host and the guests of honor attended the party, don't you think?"

He bowed at me, a dash of sarcasm peppering the motion. "At once, Arcturus. Lead on."

When we walked back into the dining room, the slaves were eating our leftovers, Sulpicia was studying her fingernails, and Crassa was lecturing Octavio. She'd taken it upon herself to rule in Philo's absence. He'd have a hard time getting the crown back.

"Good for you, Philo, never let one mistake ruin a good dinner. As for you, young man"—I looked around, but she was addressing me—"I hope you've thanked him properly. Exposing himself like that to help you. Not that anyone should ever listen to what comes out of *their* mouths." She gave a withering look in the direction of Simio and Regilla and pulled Gwyna back down on the couch.

Philo was still standing. "Why don't we play a game? How about *kottabos*?" He looked down at Gwyna's puzzled face. "A Greek game. We set up a target—something like this little saucer. Then we stand it up, and we aim the last bit of our wine at it—we throw our cups so the wine hits it, and it falls over. If you make it fall, you win a prize."

"What kind of prize?" Simio was all business. He'd been fed, and his time was valuable.

Philo shrugged. "Raisins. Dates. Sometimes women offer kisses." His eyes almost reluctantly fell on my wife, who was smiling at me. The throaty voice of experience answered the challenge.

"I'll give one—to the first man who knocks it over." What you'd have to knock over was left open to interpretation. From the look on her face she was betting on me. I guess there were no hard feelings between us. Much to Sulpicia's regret.

Octavio nearly drooled on his tunic, but not over her offer. "Can we play for money?" His small eyes were darting back and forth, trying to figure the odds.

Philo shrugged again. "Why not?"

Crassa sat upright to announce that protocol was being deflowered under protest. "Philo—are you sure—"

"Quite, Crassa."

While the slaves set the game up, I coaxed the conversation back to my own corner. "So, Octavio—I understand you're a medical man."

"Who told you?"

"I really don't remem—"

"Never mind. Doesn't matter." He brooded over something other than a gambler's luck. "I understood what Philo was talking about. Even with my own small experience. Makes me a more effective bathmaster. I have an instinct for when someone comes in who shouldn't take a chance—and they always want to."

Prunella was snoring, and she woke up with a start. "They wan' what?"

He turned to her patiently. Whatever he was, he loved his wife. "A bath, dear. Even if they're the kind of sick where it won't be good for them."

"Los' 'em like tha'. Put 'em out of their mis'ry, I say. Why let 'em suffer?"

"I agree, Prunella." Philo the philosopher again, this time not so sloppy. "I'm thinking of the lepers I met in Hispania. Poor, poor people."

Regilla forgot her embarrassment and shrieked. "Lepers? You met lepers?"

"A healing god turns away no one. Not even the hopeless. Because even they—especially they—have a right to peace."

"The peace of death?"

I liked arguments—and there was something about the way he said "healing god." I wasn't sure if he was talking about Endovelicus or himself.

The eyes that met mine were moist and tender, full of a noble hurt. "For some, it's the only kind they'll know. We have a gift, Arcturus. A gift from the gods. And it is our duty—our absolute and final duty to—"

"Act like gods?"

I had a definite talent for quieting a room. Philo wriggled his goblet between his fingers. "We are gods to some people. When we save them. Sometimes the only way to save them, to help them—is to give them peace. Peace without suffering."

The argument smelled bad. It carried the faint odor of delusion, with maybe a hint of rot. I rubbed my nose. I wasn't against helping people. I could understand holding the sword, meeting the shades with Roman honor. I wasn't even sure why I was arguing.

Octavio leaned forward. "No suffering. That's what I say. If people want to die, let them. Give them the right—the control. Give them—"

"A little help?"

His chin jutted forward. "If that's what they want, yes."

I looked back at him and smiled. "I don't mean to play Socrates. I only speak for myself, of course. But that's a hell of a responsibility. Life and death. I try to pick only one, and even then I lose sometimes. Like Philo said. I'm not saying I couldn't kill. I'm not even saying I couldn't help someone who wanted to die. I'm just saying I wouldn't want to make a living out of it."

Another pause walked in and poured itself a drink. Sulpicia's observation was as dry as her lips weren't. "Well, for one thing it would be hell to collect your fee."

It was one of those extra-riotous laughs, the kind when something unpleasant is finally over, and everyone's relieved it hadn't been worse. The game began, and Octavio calmed down and aimed at the target instead of me. He didn't hit either of us.

Philo made the second toss and missed. His hands were still shaking.

My head hurt. I wanted to go home. Octavio—Philo—Grattius, Secundus—Papirius—Vitellius—Sestius. The list of tainted men, men with secrets to hide, seemed endless. Add Bibax to that list. Good old dead Bibax.

I sipped my wine. I could even add Arcturus. I enjoyed ripping that leg open tonight. If he ever threatened Gwyna again, I'd enjoy killing him. That's your nasty little secret, Arcturus. Keep it buried. Keep it deep. I drank again and wondered if we were any closer to leaving Aquae Sulis.

Vitellius was taking his turn and splashed Crassa instead. While everyone fussed over the old lady, a slave with a worried look came to get Philo. The good doctor reappeared in the doorway, mouth grim. He crooked his finger at me. I excused myself while Sulpicia bumped into Simio to make him miss.

"What is it?"

"Papirius. Here to see you."

I was tired of unexpected visitors. Philo and I walked to the front of the house. Papirius was wrapped in a thick mantle, his body spelling impatience. There were three other priests with him.

"Papirius."

"Favonianus."

"How'd you know I was here?"

"Philo told me you were coming to dinner."

"And?"

He pinched his mouth. "We've had our differences, but you represent the governor. I'm here as a courtesy—to warn you."

"Warn me? What do you mean, warn—"

"This is what I mean."

He shoved a small leaf of thin bark at me—with writing on it. I knew what it was before I looked at it.

"It was found under the temple door. One of the priests brought it to me. I—I don't have the authority to arrest you—"

"You're goddamn right you don't. This isn't proof, Papirius—this is a setup. I was at the mines when Faro was killed. I've got four mercenaries who worked for the syndicate at my house right now—the legion will be picking them up tonight or early tomorrow morning. Or did you already know?"

His robes switched in a puff of night air like a cat's tail. "I came here—purely as a favor—"

"You came because you can't wait for me to get the hell out of town. But I've got news for you. I want out. Out of this foul little shithole you've made, you and Octavio and Grattius and your cozy little mining operation."

His face stood out pinched and drained and white, shining dully in the dark.

"You're all corrupt. All of you. You knew what was going on, free lead, free development—and you didn't give a damn. But now it's out of control. Murders, left and right. The legion involved." Contempt bit into him and stuck, like ice on a wet palm. "Silver tarnishes so goddamn easily, doesn't it?"

He took a step backward. Fear and guilt were everywhere tonight. Even in a priest's robe.

"What—what are you going to do, Arcturus? This could be dangerous to you." Philo kept his hand on my shoulder. It was heavy. I was staring at Papirius.

"I'm going to do what you asked me to do. What I've been doing all along. Find out who killed Bibax. And Faro. And Calpurnius. And others, too—people you didn't even notice were gone."

I crumpled up the note asking Faro to meet me at the cemetery and threw it at Papirius's feet.

"Say a prayer to Sulis. Maybe she can clean up your fucking sty."

Philo and I left him standing there, his mantle trailing in the dark wind and rain.

CHAPTER TWENTY-FIVE

I don't remember how I got home. I squeezed her arm, made sure she
was still there. "You all right?"

"I'm not the one who talked to Papirius. Ardur—there's nothing
they can—"

"I'm tired. Particularly of threats. We're close, Gwyna. Otherwise
they wouldn't give a shit." I fell on the couch. "Lovely little town,
Aquae Sulis. With just a touch of leprosy."

She sat beside me. "It's late. I think we should go to sleep."

My muscles uncoiled and stretched, agreeing with her. I overruled
them. "You go. I should check on Draco."

She stood up. "Are you sure? Can't it wait until—"

I held my hand out to her, and she pretended to pull me up. "Until
I can eat a leisurely breakfast, and take a leisurely stroll to survey the
estate, and stop by the flower beds to gather some petals, and—"

"Go on, Ardur." She held her face up for me to kiss, and I started
with it and ended elsewhere. She smoothed my hair off my forehead
and traced a finger down my cheek.

"Don't be too long," she whispered. And walked out of the room
like an invitation.

Several of the servants were guarding the door. They saluted me as

I walked by. Arcturus. General of slaves and breaker of curses. A man who was tired of running, and tired of wondering, and just plain god-damn tired.

The hired thugs were sleeping. They snored and smacked, stretch-ing their legs in the cramped room, curled on the floor as if it were a featherbed. A gift, the last sleep. Draco was still awake, though there were three slaves standing watch.

"Anything?"

He shook his head. "They're from out of town. Near Iscalis. Some worked the mine, some he just picked up."

"Did they give a description?"

"Small man, Roman, educated. Not from Britannia. That's all they knew." He looked embarrassed, as if he should've found out where their second cousins were born.

"Thanks, Draco. One thing—ask if they heard about our visit to the mine. If they did, make sure they make a statement of that fact to the soldiers."

His eyebrows wrinkled in puzzlement. "Yes—but—"

"Someone's trying to set me up—like I thought they would."

Bewilderment deepened the lines in his forehead and made him look sinister in the flickering orange light. I patted him on the arm. "Don't worry, Draco. You've been magnificent. There's no one I'd rather have with me in a fight."

His smile lit the room better than the lamp, and I turned to leave. "Send someone to wake me when the soldiers arrive."

I stood outside the villa, looking at the violet-black sky. The air was fresh and clean, like the magical water. I should break the pipes, flood the town, let the waters wash away the evil.

The faint whirr of bat wings came to rest in a tree somewhere. I felt old. I liked my wounds clean and my crooks obvious. I liked murderers who looked like monsters, and decay and corruption to stink as it oozed. But nothing in this yellow-gray town was what it seemed, noth-ing was straight, nothing was clear. Except for the water.

I held out a palm to catch the soft rain. It's why I was here, why everyone was here; it was the alpha and omega of this place. The waters of Sulis. I had to go back to the beginning. Back to Bibax.

She was already asleep and didn't wake up when Lineus came to get me before dawn. The legionaries wanted to know exactly what happened, and they wanted to hear it from someone other than a recent freedman.

I yawned my way through the story, making it sound less dramatic. I told them about the leg wound in case it made identification easier, though from the condition of their uniforms, these men weren't exactly *vigiles* caliber. Small detachment, filling time before retirement. Nothing much happens around here, they told me. Especially if you don't look.

They took the mercenaries away. The bright spot for them was that maybe the soldiers would be too lazy and out of shape to torture them properly. One of them remembered my visit. His friend—the one who hit me—quit for parts unknown. The soldiers listened, writing it all down on a bark book.

The legionaries hauled them into a wagon, and they cried and pleaded, the leather thongs cutting into their wrists until they bled. Desperation is always pathetic. But the same men would've been happy to kill me, loot the villa, and rape my wife. They were lucky. They'd get what they deserved. So few people do.

I went back to bed, the squeaking sound of the wagon wheels revolving in my head. I kissed Gwyna, and she turned to nestle against me, still asleep.

It was well past the first hour when we woke. We yawned at each other while we dressed, then stumbled into the *triclinium* for breakfast. The cook was all smiles this morning. He even boiled chicken eggs and made the oats just the way I like them. We were enjoying an illusion of normality when Lineus appeared.

I groaned, and Gwyna's egg froze on its way to her mouth. "Who is it? Philo? Papirius? Why can't they just let me—"

"I beg your pardon, *Dominus,* but the visitor has never been here before. He needs your help."

I looked at Gwyna. "That's what they all say. And before you can—"

"He's a little boy, sir."

The only little boy I knew was Gywna's brother, but he was safely in Londinium with Bilicho. She'd reached over to grip my arm. Her face was pale. "Show him in, Lineus—immediately."

I took her hand. "It's not Hefin. It can't be."

A ragged boy about eleven years old was pushed into the room by one of the slaves. He was staring at the ceiling with his mouth open, his feet filthy. The side of his face was red and swollen.

"Aeron?"

My voice made him jump. He started to back out of the room into the ample stomach of Lineus, who propelled him forward again. I stood up. So did Gwyna.

"Aeron—let me take a look at you."

His eyes wavered from one to the other of us, and he swallowed. Then they fell on the food and lit up with the fever of the hungry. Gwyna brushed his hair from his forehead. He flinched, then looked at her with a shy smile, and went back to gazing at the food.

She said: "Sit down, Aeron. Eat breakfast first, and then tell Arcturus what happened."

She coaxed him to a chair, and while he ate I gently felt along his cheekbone. He'd been hit. Hit hard.

He wasn't shy about devouring eggs, and we called Priscus for more. He couldn't chew so well on the left side. Gwyna watched him, a fond look on her face. We met each other's eyes over his head.

I went to get my tools and a basin of water from the kitchen. I ran a sponge down his cheek, pulling his hair to the side. His ear had been clubbed. He was quiet.

"This might hurt, son. I've got to check for broken bones."

Gwyna gave him an encouraging smile and held his hands tightly while I felt all over the left side of his face. Nothing broken.

I took out some valerian root. Not as fresh as I'd like, but it would have to do. I cut off a section and wrapped it up in a chamomile leaf and gave it to him.

"This is medicine to help with the pain. You cut this root into five slices—about this thick. Then take it and this leaf, and put it in some wine—not too much—mixed with hot water. Then drink it before bed. Can you remember that?"

He nodded. "Thank you."

"You're welcome. Now tell me who hit you."

He flinched again. "That's not really why I came."

"It's reason enough. Who did this to you?"

He looked at the floor. It wasn't in the boy to whine or complain, and he didn't want to seem less tough than he was. I knew the type.

"Does it have something to do with what I asked you? About keeping your eyes open around the cubicles?"

He looked up and his eyes answered for him.

Gwyna leaned forward, her voice tender but urgent. "Won't you tell us, Aeron? It will help Ardur."

He bit his lip, then blurted it out. "It was her. The big woman, the ugly one with the daughter."

Could only be Materna. She'd be ugly to a blind man. "Why did she hit you?"

"Because—because I found something. A note. She left it in the cubicle, and I thought it was an accident. Then when I ran after her with it, she—she took it from me and kn-knocked me down and told me—told me not to tell anyone." His eyes roamed back and forth between us. "Then I thought of you, and what you said—and I thought—"

"You thought right. You're a good lad. Now—what did it say?"

He wrinkled his brow. "I don't read so good, but I wrote down the letters. Here."

He dug around in a fold of the tunic that didn't have a hole and pulled out a scrap of tattered bark with writing on the back. He grinned, lopsided. "Somebody left it. One of the depilators told me it was a love letter. I wrote what her note said over it."

It was hard to make out, and Gwyna sat next to me so we could both try.

"This looks like—*finis* maybe?"

"Yeah—*Finis est*. Then—*illos*—or maybe *istos*—and I think it says—*caede*.

We looked at each other. Aeron's face was eager. "It is important? I know what '*finis*' means—the end—but what about—"

I looked at him. The boy was old enough and poor enough to understand evil. "It says—'It's over. Kill them.'"

We had one of the slaves walk him home with ten *denarii* and two bottles of the best healing wine in Agricola's cellar. It was enough money to quit working at the baths for a while, provided his mother and father didn't drink it away.

Gwyna said: "Materna. I felt it. All along I felt it. But the proof, Ardur—how will we get the proof?"

"Without getting killed? I don't know. The mine man is gone—he won't be back—and he's the only one who could identify her as the Aquae Sulis connection. I figure he sent word to Materna they were closing down. Maybe for her to handle any residual problems—like us. He wasn't here to kill us that night. Just scare the hell out of us. He knew his bull mastiff was on the case."

"Then why did they fire at you? And the mercenaries—"

"Because I stabbed him. I made the first move. I didn't like the words in his mouth."

She leaned forward. "I can take care of myself. I want you to know that."

"I do know it. That's not the point."

We studied each other for a few moments. "All right," she said grudgingly. "So then what?"

"That's just it. The missing piece. Materna was leaving that note for someone else. A man."

"Why a man?"

"Because only a man could've strangled Bibax and Faro."

"But she's big—and I'm sure she's strong—"

"Materna is guilty of ordering murder, I'm sure, but she's not physically capable of carrying it out—at least not that kind. Faro was quick, and muscled for his size. There's no way she could've strangled him."

"So she was leaving the note for a man. He'd know to go to a particular cubicle—"

"She always uses the same one, that's what Aeron said—"

"—and he'd be in line—one of the early crowd. Unless he had a slave he could send in to reserve it for him—"

"—which is probably the case—"

"—and then he'd read it, and then . . ."

I let it dangle. "Then he'd do something about it. Exactly."

We looked at each other again.

She took a deep breath. "Well, let's go to town and see who tries to murder us."

It took a couple of hours to prepare. We couldn't trust any food or drinks not from our kitchen. Thank God the slaves were loyal.

Draco woke up late, and I told him what happened and asked him to go with Gwyna. She protested, not too much. She was scared. She'd been the focus of Materna's bile, and she'd be in the same building, at the same time. If I knew Materna—she would want to watch Gwyna die.

I threw the thought against a wall. It made a small red splat of fear and slowly oozed down to the floor.

Materna, queen of the maggots, empress of the spiders. She'd leave a

trail of slime and putrescence in her wake. All we had to do was follow
it. Without getting killed.

I kept to my original plan. Start with Bibax. Go to where he lived.
On the way, ask a few questions at the temple.

Gwyna and Draco left before I did. We kissed each other with a bit
of desperation. I could feel her heart beating.

Trust wasn't in my upbringing. I didn't watch comedies, and I didn't
believe in happy endings. Watching your mother die can do that to
you. So I figured I'd walk along the cruel streets of Aquae Sulis, my
hands ready and my mouth mumbling a few prayers to the goddess.

I took Ligur with me. When we reached the foot of the hill, I sent
him on ahead. Heavy footsteps always choked ideas. Gwyna would be
mad at me, but that wasn't exactly a new sensation.

Natta was standing outside his shop. He was leaning on a cane,
stooped over more than usual. He didn't see me at first; then a smile
cracked his leathery face.

"Hello, my friend. More jewelry today?"

"Not today. How's Buteo? His cough better?"

He was staring down the hill toward the town and spoke as though
he couldn't hear me.

"He will never be better." His tone was final, and almost without
pity.

"It didn't sound that—listen, I know he wants to see Philo, but—"

Awareness flooded his face, and he smiled again. "Do not pay attention to an old man and his rambles. Buteo and I—we had a small dis-
agreement. That is all. Some things—some things are best left wrapped.
Hidden. Hidden and forgotten, even when you do not think you can
forget. But he is a young man—like you—and disagrees."

My mouth was a little dry. Maybe Buteo and I were alike in more
than age. I put my hand on Natta's arm.

"Listen—I'm not sure how to say this—but I think you'll understand. There's evil in Aquae Sulis, and it's getting worse. There have
been threats. Threats against me—and my wife."

His eyes narrowed until the thick puffs of skin were all I could see. "Someone—someone has threatened your beautiful lady? No. No. That is wrong. It cannot be permitted."

"Look, if Buteo knows anything—anything that could help—"

"I will tell him, Arcturus. I will tell him. Now, go—go help your lady. Protect her. Leave an old man to his thoughts."

He hobbled back to the shadows, his stick dragging against the yellow stone. I stared after him, and waited, but all I heard was the wind, and the skittering of a dry oak leaf as it was blown along the path.

The rain cleaned the surface scum from the marketplace, not its foulest residue. Desperation called itself hope and tarted itself up in bottles of piss and vinegar, still hawking, still promising. Youth, beauty, health, love—sorry, can't promise money, unless you use this to kill your aunt.

I looked around. I felt like I'd lived here all my life.

On the way to the temple, I checked the stalls selling eye ointments. Most of them would only blind you temporarily. All of them stank, and any of them could've been used to kill Calpurnius.

A few booths, far in the back and huddled in the shadow of the temple, offered dried *aconitum* root, if you knew the right way to ask. I did. Tell them you're going away. To a place with a lot of scorpions, and you need something for the sting. Then when they show it to you, under the plank of mildewed wood, you pay them, and pay them well. Then they forget your face, and you forget you just bought deadly poison. Forget, that is, until you need it.

So anybody in Aquae Sulis—anybody at all, with the cash—could buy *aconitum*. Bibax and his partner—probably ordered by Materna, for reasons I couldn't figure out yet—killed Dewi with it. *Ultor*—or a phony *Ultor*—killed Calpurnius.

I was staring at the sickly yellow of the sunshine on the temple wall when I heard the whoosh of a long, old-fashioned robe and looked up to see old Memor walk by. I hadn't seen him since the first dinner with Grattius. I was glad he wasn't dead.

"Memor—Memor, wait." I ran to catch up to him. For an old man, he could move fast.

"Can I help you with something?" His pale blue-white eyes peered closer.

"It's Arcturus, Memor. The doctor. The one who's trying to solve the murders."

"What? You're still here, young man? Why haven't you gone home—can't you find the villain, and have done with it?"

"There are too many. That's one problem."

He looked as though he could suddenly see me. "Yes—I told you so once. The curse. The curse on Aquae Sulis."

He made a sign against the evil eye and turned to leave in a hurry.

"Wait—I want to ask you something."

He paused, his back still to me, his creaky voice wary. "What do you want? I've told you what you need to know."

I put my hands on his shoulders and turned him around to face me. "You're a *haruspex*. Probably one of the few in Britannia—we don't get much call for your gift in the North."

"That is true."

"In your professional opinion . . . is the source of the evil here—in the temple?"

His shrunken body seemed to grow in height. Or maybe I'd bent too close to the oculist creams. "You know your stories, boy. Think of the Hydra."

"You mean all the different—"

"I mean one body. Many heads, heads that grow back, but with one body. It makes the curse grow. It is the curse."

He held out a withered arm and lightly brushed my shoulder. "Memory lives longer than men do, and it feeds both love and hate. Until sometimes—sometimes—they become one."

He hobbled away quickly, leaving me with a headache. Never ask a *haruspex* a direct question. All you get is lines lifted from the Sibylline books, and no smoking tripod to help you figure out what the hell they mean.

I rubbed my forehead. Love and hate. Memory. Feeding on a nice diet of bile mixed with greed and apathy. The mine was crooked. So what? The mine was money. Bring it into Aquae Sulis, build another bath, take some free lead. Turn a blind eye. They're easy to come by— just buy some of this ointment.

I shook my head and walked on. I wasn't there yet.

CHAPTER TWENTY-SIX

Senicio came out from below the Sacred Spring, smelling like wet earth. He heard my foot fidgeting on the stone before he saw me. He looked up, turning white beneath the layer of pipe sludge he was wearing as a cloak.

I tried to smile. "Senicio. *Salve.* They told me you were cleaning the pipes. I thought I'd wait."

He scratched his hair, spreading some of the slimy green algae through it. Picked at the wart on his left cheek. "I—I told you every-thing that morning—"

"I know. You were very helpful."

He looked at me doubtfully, as if no one had ever said that before, and he didn't quite believe it, either. "So—so what do you want? Why'dya want to see me?"

I leaned back and held up the wall.

"Because I figured a man like you—a man serving the goddess—a man with—uh—powers, powers of observation—a man like you prob-ably saw more than he realized at first. You're important, Senicio."

His mouth turned downward, and he looked around nervously. That line should've had him puffing and preening by now. Something smelled funny. Something more than him.

I backed off a little. Time to try another tactic.

"I need your help. I'm—this close."

I should've known altruism wouldn't work in Aquae Sulis. He looked away, picking his nose. I was running out of patience, so I got tough.

"Look, goddamn it, answer some questions and I'm through. I'll give you money for a decent meal—like your old friend Calpurnius."

The name of the dead man scared him. He looked around, making sure no one could hear. "All—all right. What do you—whaddya want to know?"

The curse was a tendril, reaching out to dark corners and unlikely throats, strangling any goodness out of them. It was green and rank, and sticky to the touch—and it was all over Senicio.

"The night you saw Calpurnius—you said he was celebrating. Why?"

His neck started to itch. "Because—because he was drinking—eating—spending money—"

"So? Maybe he felt like it. Sometimes men will do that even when they're miserable. He said something to you, didn't he? What was it?"

The itched moved to his collarbone. "Uh—I can't really remem—"

"You remember. Tell me, goddamn it, or—"

A small squeal whistled between his teeth. I didn't have to touch him—luckily for me. He looked both ways down the path and spoke in a whisper.

"I-I don't know how you knew, but—but he did say something. Said he'd moved up in the world, and was celebrating—celebrating a new—a new business."

"Did he say what kind?"

Senicio shook his head, and some mud splattered on my tunic.

"N-no. At least—"

"What? What else?"

"He said—he said something funny. That's why—that's why I remembered it. He said it was the oldest business in the world—and he was taking it over."

He looked behind me toward the temple. "Can I go now?" he whined.

I dug for my pouch and gave him a few *sestertii*.

I had a lot to think about on the way to Bibax's place. I tried to shove it aside, but it kept coming up in my mouth like vomit.

So Calpurnius turned nasty. Maybe he always was. He was greedy and smart and poor—and the Aquae Sulis curse whispered a lot of promises.

There were at least three possibilities about what he meant. Which one made all the difference in the world. But I didn't want to think about Calpurnius—not right now. It was time to focus on the man who dragged me into this.

Bibax always knew about the lead. Easy enough to figure—Materna got word to him, or his confederate, as partial payment for services rendered. A couple of years ago she pulled a string and left a message for Grattius. Grattius gave the order to Bibax, and Bibax made sure Aufidio would never be back in town to ask any more questions about boundaries.

The other crimes—Sulpicia's husband, Sestius's aunt, and maybe more—had nothing to do with the mine. They seemed like a private arrangement, a kind of retirement benefit for murderers. Kill a relative, blackmail the survivors. Forever. I wiped my forehead. Maybe it was getting warm.

Grattius never got touched for money. Because Bibax—and maybe his unknown helper—knew Materna was behind it all.

Materna knew who the partner was. That's who she left the note for.

I nodded to myself, my feet in a hurry to get to his *insula*. Bibax and partner were in business for themselves. Then Materna—always hungry for pain—Materna figured out the scam. She twitched her web, and the other little spiders came running. She liked it like that.

She used Bibax and the other killer to help her keep the mine under control. Just like she used Faro. Just like she used poor, foolish, overblown Grattius. She rooted out every crooked scheme, every twisted motive, every tainted man in Aquae Sulis. So she could own them. Own their souls. If they had any left.

The bad taste in my mouth wouldn't go away. I was staring at a dingy *insula,* the yellow stone native to the town looking like the too-thin skin of a too-thin man with liver problems.

I started on the ground floor, but the only person home was a woman busy with a colicky baby. Her eyes kept straying back toward the crib. No, I don't remember. Probably the upper floor. The door slammed.

I tried the second floor, found more success. An old man, his skin falling off in flakes, slept on a cot in the corner while his son—unemployed, just temporary—drank cheap wine, and hit his wife for spilling the chamber pot on the way out the door. No, can't say I remember him. Try the third. The door slammed again.

I walked the narrow stairs, which groaned and creaked like an aging whore going for one last throw. My foot nearly poked through the fifth step, where the wood was black. A door was facing me, and I could hear snoring behind it. Someone was home.

I knocked, and a raspy voice with years of coughing answered me.

"Who is it?"

"A man with money."

The answer was enough to get him out of bed. He was a paunchy man, past middle age, wearing a towel around his waist and nothing else. The room smelled like sweat and cabbage.

He looked me up and down. I tried not to look at him. His chest and back were furry with matted hair, and he stank. I held out three *sestertii* in my palm.

"You know Bibax?"

"He ain't here no more. He's dead."

He reached under the towel to scratch himself. I'd try one more time, so no one could ever call me a coward.

"I know he's dead. I know he lived in this building. I'd like to see where."

He looked at me thoughtfully. "Add two more, an' I'll tell you."

I'd pay five times the amount if he backed away. I reached in and pulled out the pouch again. I added two more *sestertii*. He licked his lips at the money and then belched.

"Who tol' you he lived here?"

"One of the market sellers."

"Well, they was wrong." He said it with a triumphant leer, as if he'd just scored a point. "He useta live here—still kept a room down the hall, but he moved into a—a"—he belched again—"a bigger place, small house, down by the new spring. Go there, if you wanna see."

He snatched up the money, and I felt his fingernails scratch my palm. I rubbed my hand down my tunic.

"Anyone in his old room up here?"

"No. Nobody. Three down, on the left." He turned to shut the door.

"One more thing—"

"Yeah?"

"Who owns this building? Who do you pay rent to?"

He shrugged. "Bibax always collected it for everybody. Still did, even when he moved. I never seen the guy."

"How do you pay it now?"

"I ain't paid it." His smile showed three teeth that were yellow and black. "If I did—Bibax said pay at the baths, if he ain't here. And he ain't."

The door slammed this time and shook the walls. The baths again. Everything wound up at the baths. Except Furry Back.

I walked down the hall and opened the door. The room was small, empty, and clean. Someone had cleaned it. Not even a smell of Bibax remained.

I left the *insula,* careful to avoid the fifth step on the upper stairs. No one seemed to know Bibax, and no one seemed to care. I needed to find someone. Anyone. Someone to help me see.

I caught a glimpse of the other reservoir, even from here, and hurried to it. There was urgency in the sun, urgency in getting back to the main square so I could find Gwyna, make sure she was all right. Urgency in getting out of Aquae Sulis alive.

The spring was softer, less dramatic than the other one. But the same water. It danced and trembled, holding out the promise of something. I could see why Philo wanted to put another bath down here. It was a little bit of peace in a little corner of Aquae Sulis.

An old woman was limping down a dirt path from some woods up the small hill. She stopped at the spring and looked at me. Her eyes were sharp.

"Nothing here. It's the other one, where you'll find it."

"How do you know what I'm looking for?"

She leaned on her stick, and set down the mushrooms she'd been picking.

"You're not from here. Must be looking for the temple. That's where they all go."

In more ways than one.

I stared at her. "I'm looking for answers."

Her cackly laugh braced me. "Everyone wants answers, boy. You need questions."

"I've got those, too. I'm—I'm trying to help the goddess. Help the town."

She tilted her head to the side, looking like an old thrush, and sighed, a deep sigh from the bottom of her wrinkled feet. Her blue eyes glinted.

"Help the goddess? What makes you think she needs help?"

"Maybe she doesn't. I don't know. There's something wrong with this town. I'm trying to fix it."

Her eyes pored over me. "So what are your questions?"

I stared at her. She was the first person to offer some help who didn't have a motive for it. "They're about Rufus Bibax. He used to—"

She spat on the ground. "I knew him. Knew all about him."

I reached out a hand to her elbow and asked as humbly as I knew how.

"Could you—could you talk to me?"

We sat on the bank by the spring and watched the water bubble. Her eye and memory for detail amazed me. I felt like I'd met Bibax. Like I'd seen through him to the rot inside.

He knocked around the empire, traveling from Mauretania through Baetica in Hispania and past the Alps into Gaul. From there he'd crossed over into Britannia at some point, and, like the dead leaves and garbage from the marketplace, settled in a little corner called Aquae Sulis.

Bibax had a special gift. A memory. A memory so sharp, he could remember a face after years of wine or women or poverty or money corroded it into an unrecognizable mask. He'd play games with his memory for the people who lived here, recall a series of numbers or recite poetry he just heard. Bibax had a gift—and he used it.

Blackmail was part of how he traveled, part of how he thought. More profitable still when you could manufacture the crime. Supply death for a price—cover it up for a price. Everything, for Bibax, had a price.

Healing town to healing town, curing frustrated wives and wastrel nephews, freeing them, then holding them prisoner. Curse recoiled, mirrored back. Someone to help him—someone weak or desperate or greedy or wicked, someone who was all and more. Who it was she couldn't say, but I knew Bibax now. He and Materna sharing one soul between them, *animus maledictus.*

Materna tried to use him, but nobody could use Bibax in the end. The Hydra heads sprouted wherever he traveled, and Bibax anchored them, kept them alive.

I was past ready to go. I thanked the old woman, tried to give her money, which insulted her, so I apologized, and thanked her again.

She stared at me. "So you have been given aid. You know the questions, and you will find the answers."

I felt a strange sort of confidence, but looked at the sun and saw it was past the midpoint. The baths. "I will. But now—"

"Now you must hurry to your woman."

I took her hand in mine and held it to my lips as if she were a sena-tor's wife. She picked up the mushrooms, watched me. I rushed up the path to the center of town.

About halfway up I realized I'd never mentioned Gwyna. I turned around.

"How did you—"

No one there. She moved quickly for an old lady. I shrugged and kept walking.

CHAPTER TWENTY-SEVEN

A strange dry wind blew warmth from the hills, kicking the brown-green leaves until they broke against a stone wall, spines cracked and flight ended. It was the kind of wind that made shopkeepers close early and children pay attention to their grammar lessons. There was force and threat and promise behind it, and no guarantees.

It suited Aquae Sulis.

A shrill murmur floated on the wind like everything else, held aloft until it sank in the dirt, perforated with shrieks. The baths.

I ran up the hill. Passersby that weren't staring at me were looking toward the baths. Women poured out, helter-skelter. Some running, some clustered in tight little knots around the entrance.

Men stood around, aimless, unsettled. Priests scurried back and forth like ants without a trail. I ran faster, my feet hitting the pavement hard and kicking up the yellow dust into miniature whirwinds.

I was looking for Gwyna. I couldn't find her.

My breath was coming out ragged now. I couldn't feel my heart beating, or the pain when a sharp rock bruised my foot. All I could think about was Gwyna, and why I let her walk into a room where someone wanted her dead.

"Gwyna! Gwyna!"

My voice echoed and re-echoed, bouncing off the wall of the baths and the temple, and every godforsaken roof in a godforsaken town. She couldn't—she couldn't—

"Ardur!"

Breath left my lungs. I was staring at my wife, who was in front of me, pale, nervous, excited—and very, very, very alive.

I held her. Something happened at the baths. I didn't give a good goddamn.

She said: "Are you all right?" Maybe I was fading in and out, one of Faro's ghosts. I tried to smile.

"Now. What's going on?"

She pulled me toward the side of the entrance. No one was going in. "Ardur—they're looking for you."

"Who's looking for me?"

"The priests. Octavio. I'm glad I found you before they did. Materna . . ."

Her eyes flickered. I waited for it.

"Materna is unconscious. I think she's dying. You need to—need to see what you can do."

I stared at her. "What about Philo?"

"He's examining her right now."

She was looking at something in the distance, something I couldn't see. I had to ask it. I remembered the Syrian.

"Gwyna—Gwyna, you—"

She squeezed my arm. "No, Ardur. If I had to—yes. For you—for—for our baby, when it comes. I'm not sorry she's suffering, but I—I trust the goddess. And you." Her eyes were huge, the blue hot enough to burn.

A voice hit me between the shoulders.

"Arcturus? We've been looking everywhere—" Octavio's hands were sweaty, and he rubbed them up, down, up, down over his tunic.

I murmured to Gwyna: "Stay here and wait for me."

The *balneator* grabbed my arm and tried to pull me toward the entrance. "Materna's had an attack of some kind. Philo's with her, but he wants your help. I know you two weren't friendly—"

"She tortured my wife and accused me of murder, Octavio. But maybe I'm just antisocial."

He tugged my arm again, and I refused to move.

"She won't want me—"

"She won't know, Arcturus. She's almost dead. You don't have much time." He wiped his brow with the back of his hand, let the sweat make a puddle on the pavement. "Just go, see what Philo wants. We can't let anyone in until we get her out, and he won't move her until he sees you."

I shrugged, then followed him past the eyes of the curious, who huddled near the entrance walls and made book on why they were closed.

Sulpicia was sitting on a bench just outside the door. Vitellius held her close. I nodded, and he plucked at me, agitated.

"Arcturus—give Sulpicia something for her nerves, will you? She hasn't stopped shaking."

Didn't sound like the Sulpicia every man in Aquae Sulis knew. Her face burned a bright red beneath the makeup. A mask, and not one of the happy ones. Her entire body was shaking and twitching hard enough to make her blurry. She wasn't watching me. She wasn't watching anybody.

I put up a hand to her forehead. It was on fire. "Sulpicia—can you talk?"

Her eyes roved over mine, huge and black. I bent her head back and forced open her mouth. Octavio watched me, impatient, knowing enough to keep his own mouth shut.

No saliva. Her fingers fluttered near her face like baby sparrows, making an intricate pattern of nothing. She fell forward suddenly, hands to stomach.

I shoved her head back against the wall. Vitellius yelped. No goddamn time, and not much hope.

I jammed my fingers down her throat and counted to five. Tried again. This time the reflex kicked in. She started retching, couldn't feel it. I forced her head down between her knees. C'mon, Sulpicia. Your stomach muscles are tight enough.

It came up a gush, and Vitellius jumped back. Measure of his devotion. I repeated the process until her stomach was empty and my hands and tunic were stained with rust-colored vomit.

The boyfriend was squealing. I checked her pulse. Slowing. Normal color coming back. She probably wouldn't die today.

His squeal got louder. "She drank poison. Give her simple broth and wine with a lot of water." A fly buzzed dangerously close to his open mouth. "Go. Get her out of here."

She was starting to moan a little. At least she'd had practice. He made her lean on him, and they half fell, half dragged their way to the square. The gaggle of onlookers waddled out of their way.

Octavio's face corroded around the edges like a rusty pipe. "You know, Arcturus—you may have just killed Materna. Philo needed you right away. Sulpicia was probably just drunk or someth—"

"Either you're a fraud or an idiot. If Materna's unconscious, she's gone. You said so yourself. I can't raise the dead. That was Faro's job, remember?"

I took a step toward him. His fingers curled into tight little red balls at his sides.

"Sulpicia was poisoned—probably by the same stuff that's killing Materna—and I don't make decisions about who lives and dies around here. Do you?"

We glared at each other, his chest puffing with exertion, the sweat still dripping on the pavement. Materna was dying. They were already lining up the evidence.

The baths were loud in desertion, like an empty theater. I washed my hands in the overflow pipe while Octavio breathed on my elbow. He belonged here, like mildew, and was just as hard to get rid of.

He motioned with his head toward the *apodyterium*. Materna was on the floor, her body oozing over the stone as if it were already dead. Maybe it always was.

Philo was bent over her mouth, listening to her breathe. "Arcturus—thank God you're here. I don't have much experience with this sort of thing. I think she's been poisoned. It's not *aconitum*."

His handsome face was flushed and worried. I looked down at the woman who wanted to kill my wife and me.

"How long has she been unconscious?"

"About half an hour, I think. They sent for me as soon as she collapsed."

"Did you make her vomit?"

"I tried. She couldn't do it. She's in very deep."

I stared at Materna's pulpy body, her massive chest climbing like a weary traveler, then descending slowly, waiting for the trip to end. Her body was heavy and fat, but not with food or wine. She fed off a diet of power, spiced with the occasional life.

A small breeze from the exercise yard nudged me in the back, and I knelt down next to Philo. Pulled open her eyes. The pupils swallowed everything. Humanity had been devoured a long time ago. The darkness was still hungry, and it was waiting for Materna.

Her lips were dry, pressed in a skeleton's smile against yellow teeth. Skin the color of parchment, and as hot as a blister full of pus.

I looked up at Philo. "She's not going to make it."

A sob swelled from the corner. Secunda was slumped on the stone bench, blending in with the rock. Philo stood up, his knees creaking. He wavered there, not sure if he should try to comfort Secunda or wait for a more specific diagnosis.

Octavio crawled back into the room, wanting to make sure we knew he was still in charge. He flicked a glance at Philo and let the weight of his authority drop on me.

"What is it?"

I waited to hear what Philo would say. He looked at me with a dog's eyes, and when I stared blandly back, my eyebrows raised, he made it sound like a suggestion.

"I think—*strychnos*?"

He whispered it, but it was loud enough to solicit another sob from the corner. I ignored Secunda. She could trot out the devoted daughter act on someone else's time. I didn't bother to keep my voice down.

"More than a maybe. And yes, Octavio, to your next question. It was murder. Sometimes people eat a few berries so they can have visions, but Materna would never do that. She'd be too afraid of what she might see."

The gasp in the corner was hard to ignore. Secunda stood up, her hand to her throat. "She saw Faro—before—before . . ."

"Before she fell asleep." Trust Philo to make it sound like a goddamn bedtime story.

Secunda nodded, her eyes swelling with tears. I walked over to her.

"What did she see?"

She stared ahead of us and through the archway, where the shadows from the *palaestra* drew shapes on the floor. "She saw him—talked to him—"

"What did she say?"

"Arcturus, do you think you should . . ." Philo, always so protective of women.

"What did she say?"

"She said—she said—'Faro—I'm sorry. Forgive me, my love.'"

Secunda had read one too many cheap Greek novels.

"What did your mother really say, Secunda?"

She broke off her trance, looked at me for the first time. Recognition, and a little of the old family spite. "You. How do you know? You probably killed her. I heard—I heard you tell her how you would, that morning when you—when you hit poor Faro."

She crowed it like a wedding announcement. Octavio's footsteps made a happy sound when they trotted up to me.

"Arcturus—" He was using his formal voice.

"Not just yet, Octavio. Why isn't Papirius here? He likes to be present whenever I'm accused of something."

He drew his robes together, pretending they weren't too damp and dirty and cheap to make an impression. "He's coming. He knows you're here."

"What a relief. I wouldn't want him to miss the show."

I turned back to Secunda, her eyes little slits of suspicion and malice. "Let's have the truth. From the beginning."

"I've told you—and you—you're a—"

"I'm lots of things. Murderer isn't one of them. Besides, neither you nor anyone else will shed any tears for Materna. If you're not careful, Secunda—very careful—you'll wind up just like her."

Her pink lips drew back in a snarl. Any prettiness she owned because of youth was rapidly aging. She turned to Octavio. "You let him stand there and threaten me? You heard him—he threatened to kill me, just like—"

Before I could tell her to shut her goddamn mouth, Philo put his hands on her shoulders. Maybe I wasn't the best person to get it out of her. He made soothing noises. She looked at him like most women did.

An officious throat clearing announced Papirius, followed by one of his ubiquitous slaves. He avoided looking at me. Octavio bent low, spine surprisingly mobile. But then maybe he didn't have one.

"Papirius. They say it's murder. Poison again. *Strychnos*."

"Before you hear it secondhand, Materna's daughter already accused me. Sorry you missed the first act."

His cheeks stood out like jutting rocks. He pursed his lips together, pretended I wasn't there. He said to Octavio: "What are we waiting for?"

I answered him. "For Secunda to tell us what happened this morning. Materna wasn't the only one poisoned."

Philo's eyes took in the vomit on the hem of my tunic. Octavio asked before he could. "You mean Sulpicia—"

"Was poisoned, too. With the same thing—and we don't want the fine people of Aquae Sulis to think there's *strychnos* in the water, now, do we?"

Papirius's slave whisked a fly away from his master, who made a dismissive gesture at him.

"Do we, Papirius?" I said softly.

He looked over to where Secunda and Philo were standing. "Make her talk."

She clutched Philo's arm. "Don't let them—"

"For all we know, she did it." The priest's voice was a trifle bored. "Make her talk, and get the body out of here."

"She's still alive."

"Well, for God's sake, Philo, take her to your house, then, but get her out of here. We need to reopen."

Octavio pulled at Papirius's sleeve. "What about Secundus? We should send someone to Londinium—"

"He's not in Londinium." Secunda's nose was red from blowing it on a tunic fold. She looked up at Philo and gave him the big eyes. "He's on one of our farms. The northern one."

Papirius shook his arm away from Octavio's fingers. "Handle it, then." The *balneator* bowed, more stiffly this time, and scurried away.

Philo looked down into Secunda's face. "Can you talk now?"

She leaned against him, but he drew away. She glanced at Papirius. No soft place to hide. She knew better than to look at me for it.

"All—all right. Is Mama—is Mama really going to—"

"In about an hour, more or less. So save the shock and surprise for when you'll need it."

I was tired of Philo treating her like a little girl who was losing her beloved mother. She wasn't little, she wasn't lost, and only the Furies knew what Materna was.

She blew her nose again while Papirius tapped his foot and his slave looked for more flies. Octavio ran back into the room, looking around as if he'd forgotten something.

Philo nudged her. "Go on."

"When we got here this morning—she always uses the same storage shelf, you know, our slave reserves it for her—well, there was—there was a cask of wine in it, and a note."

"Did she buy the wine herself?"

"I—I don't know."

"What about the note? Was she holding something, Philo?"

He turned to me. "I didn't see—"

Secunda interrupted him. If she was going to talk, she wanted all the lines.

"She tore it up after she read it. Laughed, chucked me under the chin, like she—like she . . ." Artistic sob on her sleeve. No one said anything, so she managed to regain her strength. "She tore it up—threw it in the spring. Said it was a dedication to Sulis."

"What kind of wine was it?"

"How should I know? Something sweet. She said it was foreign—and that she wanted to—to celebrate, so she drank it."

"How soon afterward did she not feel well?" Philo had a way of making poison sound about as harmful as a fart.

"I guess—I guess an hour or two. We could hear—hear her heart beating, and she said her chest hurt. Crassa told her to get you, Philo, but she got mad—really mad all of a sudden. Then she turned red, and her mouth got dry, and she was thirsty—and she started shaking."

"Anger is a symptom." Or maybe Materna was still thinking about the slap he gave her.

Secunda stared at me, some spittle on her lips. "If you know so much, why don't you tell it?"

"I'm not a trustworthy source."

Papirius interrupted us. "Octavio—go get the servants that were watching the cubicles this morning."

The bathmaster didn't like to be reminded that he wasn't. He faded back into the vapor.

The priest asked: "Is that all?" It wasn't a question.

"Not quite. After anger and the shakes, there's delirium. She saw Faro. What did she say, Secunda?"

I'm not sure why I wanted to know so much. The girl's eyes bounced off all of us, then settled on Philo, until they lowered at what used to be her mother stretched out on the floor.

"She said—she said—'Faro. Nail it. Nail it, or it's over.' "

A shudder twisted Papirius's straight back. "Anything else?"

She shook her head.

Philo said: "After that—she must've lost consciousness."

She nodded again. None of us said anything for a long minute, while Materna's slow breath made the room a little colder. A broken-down chorus of three little boys and two old men followed behind Octavio and trooped in the room.

He lined them up in front of Papirius. One of the old men scratched himself. Bath servants were more cheap and plentiful than the cubicles themselves.

I held up a coin. "A *denarius* for anyone who saw who put wine in the fat woman's shelf this morning. No other questions asked."

They licked their lips and stared at the money. I twisted it around, the shiny silver promising life to the old, experience to the young.

"You won't lose your place here, or be punished in any way. Right?"

I shot it at Papirius, and he flinched when it hit him, but he nodded.

An old man smacked his lips, this time getting out more than spit. "It were a woman."

"What kind of woman? Young, old, ugly, pretty—"

"Don't know. Saw her from behind. Looked young from there."

I rubbed my nose and took a deep breath. Without looking at him, I said: "Philo, ask Secunda to turn around."

"What? What are you—I can't believe—I won't stand—"

Papirius said: "Just turn her."

A combination of cajoling and physical force resulted in a good view of Secunda's best side. I looked at the old man. "Is that the one?"

He squinted and craned his neck, then looked at me. "Will I get the money—no matter what I say?"

"No matter what."

He drew up some phlegm from his lungs, spat on the floor. "Don't think it were her."

Secunda's shoulders slumped with relief. "You cheap quack—I still think you killed—"

"Not so nice to be the one accused, is it, Secunda?"

It drew a little blood and shut her up for once, and she went back to cringing against Philo, as helpless as a viper in a basket.

I knelt down by Materna and straightened her *stola,* her legs sticking out like stems on a toadstool.

Papirius asked: "Any change?"

"There won't be any. Until she dies."

"Can we move her and open the baths?"

"Sure. If anyone still thinks he can get clean in Aquae Sulis."

Papirius's mouth turned down until it met the wrinkles in his skinny neck. He directed his irritation at Octavio. "Don't stand there like a gaping fish—get rid of the slaves, bring a stretcher! Philo—you don't mind . . ."

He looked like he did, but shook his head.

"Have them carry her to Philo's house—by the back way, in a litter. Use one from the temple. And get the baths open!"

Octavio flushed, but he wasn't the kind that bites. Papirius drew himself up, nodded at Philo, and flounced out the doors. His robes trickled through the opening like a puddle of blood.

Secunda slumped on the bench, staring at Materna. Philo's eyes met mine. Octavio skittered in with some muscular slaves and a wide stretcher.

He barked at the slaves. "Get her on there. Be careful—she's not—"

"Dead yet?"

I thought I'd prod him a little, maybe get him to spill out what was eating his guts, and tell me what part of his miserable little life was my fault. He breathed hard through his nose.

"I wouldn't joke, if I were you. You were hired to make sure—"

"I wasn't hired, Octavio. I was asked. By a lot of nice people, who now all seem to want me out of town. At least as far away as, say, the cemetery."

"Arcturus—I—"

"It doesn't matter, Philo. Octavio here doesn't like the color of my eyes, or the sound of my voice, or maybe the fact that I've found out some things about mines and money and property and murder that make his tunic a little too tight. Don't worry, gentlemen. I'm almost done."

Tired anger stretched my voice and made it sharp. "Take her home, Philo. With the girl. Secunda could use a little comforting. She's been—comforted—before. And you, Octavio—you can start making odds on the time."

I squeezed through the outer doors, pushed my way through the throng. The wind wasn't blowing anymore. No birds were singing.

CHAPTER TWENTY-EIGHT

Gwyna was where I'd left her, with Ligur and Quilla. We walked home. She told me what happened.

Materna died as she lived—without a gentle thought, without mercy, pain her only companion. Except this time it was her own.

Her heart beat fast enough to echo against the stone. She burned but couldn't sweat, opened eyes that couldn't see. Lost the power of voice, her massive body helpless, limbs convulsed and thrashing. Unconsciousness a gift she probably didn't deserve. Materna wasn't merely murdered. She was tortured along the way.

"What about Sulpicia? Did she—"

"Sulpicia snuck a taste of Materna's wine, but only a drink. Said it was too sweet."

The light was weak and pale. Natta's shop was closed. Silence followed us home. She sent the servants ahead of us and turned to me, her eyes roaming my face.

"Ardur—I'm glad she's dead. She was an evil thing. Not even human."

I took a deep breath, couldn't find any air. "As human as evil always is. Human and living. Inside all of us." I put a hand on her shoulder.

"The curse on Aquae Sulis is still alive, Gwyna. It won't be buried with Materna."

She stared at me. "You know something."

I looked past her. "Let's just say I've figured out a few things."

Her voice was the first soft thing I'd felt since morning. "Do you—do you need time by yourself?"

I held her fingers to my lips to kiss them. "I'll be in as soon as I can."

She stood on tiptoe to kiss my cheek, then hurried up the hill. I watched until she was a small white speck, opening a door, disappearing inside to safety.

I looked around. I was standing near a blackthorn tree—the same tree where a wagon, two people, and a dead man waited one night. I put my hand on the gnarled trunk. The bark was rough and harsh, like it needed to be. Like I needed to be. I closed my eyes.

Strychnos killed Materna, almost killed Sulpicia. In her dreams, Materna saw Faro. She was ordering a mask to be nailed into his skull.

Poison killed Calpurnius, too: *aconitum*. He thought he'd joined the oldest business in the world, but he couldn't afford the buy-in price.

Aconitum could be bought for a whisper and a wink if you had enough money, and it was offered for sale with the bottles of piss and oil and the rough-cut wooden breasts. Everything was for sale in Aquae Sulis.

Poison killed Dewi, too. A simpleton everyone tolerated, and most liked, and somebody murdered.

I leaned away from the tree trunk and walked around it, careful not to step on the grasping, gnarled roots.

Dewi reminded me of Aeron, and how much he was like Hefin. Age-mates. Age-mates and their special bond. A bond of memory.

The crickets were starting, a comforting sound. The wind gusted through, cool against my face, while a knot of birds expanded and contracted, black against the darkening sky, until they chose a tree for the evening and alighted, taking shelter from the dark.

Memory. Memory played the starring role, in this and every act.

The food of love and the goad of hate, and in Aquae Sulis it played both parts.

I wondered who would remember Sestius's aunt, or Sulpicia's husband. Old and querulous and sick, hard to live with, too harsh and stern to understand the pleasures of the young, dying slowly, hurried along, no prosperity in their deaths. Too many ghosts, too much memory. Blackmail made them live again. Bibax, the only one to profit. *Cui bono, cui bono* . . .

Everyone made something from the mines. Octavio, Philo, Grattius, Vitellius, Papirius, Secundus. The mine promised them all what they wanted: money, power, a temple, another bath. All of them lost, some more than they could bear.

But this was more than the bankruptcy of dreams. I was looking for curses, the cursed and the curser, the cursed man, a *homo maledictus*. A human being, full of desperation and hope, greed and desire, love and hate. Above all, love and hate.

No, Calpurnius, may the earth rest lightly upon you, in your foolishness and your greed. You were wrong. And you paid for it.

The wind blew harder, and dry leaves once more tumbled down the path into town. They would blow past the temple, where the face of the goddess gazed down from the pediment and waited for the final cleansing to begin.

It would be difficult. I needed a confession. A lot of the story was still guesswork. But I was a good storyteller.

I felt the tree trunk again, my fingers tracing the dry, harsh ridges. Time for another town meeting.

The stone was golden now, bouncing off the orange torchlight. Flickers fell on the water, looking like fires on the sea. The gift of the goddess was patient. It lapped against the sides of the pools, the rhythm of forever.

Grattius hunched in a corner. He'd lost weight, strictly from nerves. His eyes roamed, and his legs twitched at every shuffling footstep.

His matching *duovir,* Secundus, drooped against a wall. We were standing near the first healing pool, next to the room overlooking the spring. Moonlight splayed shadows on the floor, dancing and twisting with the torchlight. Secundus stood with his hands in his battered toga, staring at nothing. His daughter stared at me.

Papirius's eyes flickered over the scene, lingering on no one, while the garnet robe he was wearing drank the light the way Prunella drank everything else. She was sitting on a stool her husband brought out for her. He stood in Papirius's shadow, as he always did.

Sestius couldn't quite figure out how he got there. His eyebrows formed a permanent tattoo of surprise against his white skin.

Vitellius stood with an arm around Sulpicia, who sat on another stool. She'd insisted on coming. Her eyes were a little dimmer, and the smile even lazier, and I had no doubt what she'd do as soon as she felt better. Drusius stood on her other side, an awkward third but maybe not so awkward, judging from what Sulpicia was smiling at.

Philo was looking at me, his face gray and suddenly old. Ligur and Draco stood between the rooms, closing off the circle.

It took all day, several meetings, and a lot of explanation—some real, some imagined—to set it up. I hoped it would work. I disliked the melodrama; the assembled cast of players was too Aeschylean, too *deus ex machina.* It wasn't my style. But Aquae Sulis liked its theatricals.

"Not so long ago—less than nine days, in fact—I rode into this town and expected to find a quiet health resort. What I found was a dead man. Murdered, strangled, and propped in the spring."

Grattius shuddered. No one else moved.

"You all played a part in why it happened, why other crimes happened before and after. Along with other people who can't be here tonight—at least not physically."

A small gust blew through the window. Prunella stifled a whimper.

"There was Calpurnius—junior priest, chief drain cleaner, and all-around greedy bastard. Poisoned with *aconitum,* if you remember—and even if you don't. Of course, anybody with a little money and the right smile can buy *aconitum* outside this window. But you live here. You know the secrets of the marketplace. They're about as secret as the graffiti in the public latrine."

Octavio stepped forward, his eyes like two bright coals. "Can you get on with this? You ask us to come in the middle of the night—"

"There are a lot of dead people in this story. I figured we should talk at a time when they could hear us. They might say something useful."

He mumbled something under his breath. Shrank into his tunic, shuffled closer to his wife.

"Where was I? Oh, yes—Faro. We could've used Faro Magnus tonight, but he only performs for Pluto these days."

Secunda sputtered, and her father put a hand on her arm.

"He was strangled—like Bibax—but not by a self-styled *'Ultor.'* Though somebody hated him enough to nail a mask into his skull. That brings me to Materna. Hate always does. It killed her, finally, master instead of servant."

Secundus stared at me, said nothing. His daughter held her arms across her chest and looked away.

"In between I was attacked, my wife was humiliated—shamed and threatened—I was accused of murder, set up with so-called evidence, and finally . . . finally I became a target, too."

"Gwyna—is she all right? Is she not coming?" Philo spoke softly, as he always did when repeating my wife's name.

"Doesn't feel up to it. She's a little sick of Aquae Sulis. That's the problem. It's a health spa, a resort town. Only instead of feeling better you fall down and die."

I looked around, holding their eyes when I could. "You see, there were other murders. A young man who fought a boundary line. An old woman with a profligate nephew. An old man with a short leash on a younger wife."

Sulpicia turned white and shook off Vitellius's hand. Sestius was trembling and leaned against the wall to support himself.

"Maybe the most tragic one—the one that seemed to start it all—was a boy. After he was killed—cursed, by Materna, for allegedly stealing a bath robe—the mine—the mine that would put Aquae Sulis on every map, the mine that would make everyone rich and everyone happy, give everyone what they wanted as long as they promised not to look—the mine found a ghost. Well, actually it didn't find a ghost. It made one."

The spring gurgled and lapped in the cold stillness. Their breaths made little puffs of smoke.

"The story begins with Bibax. He had a gift—the gift of memory. He remembered things, especially if they could make him money. He sniffed out the sickly odor of health spas, traveling from health resort to health resort, a funeral procession of murder for hire and blackmail right behind him."

Another puff of wind blew in from the spring, making one of the torches sputter and spit. Prunella gasped, and Octavio put a hand on her shoulder.

"In Aquae Sulis, Bibax met somebody he remembered. Somebody he pushed and threatened, somebody who could help him. Curse-writers are cheaper than the whores down the street from your temple, Papirius—but Bibax was expensive. He'd give you what you wanted, what you dreamed about. Best of all, you could blame it on the goddess."

Sestius crumbled to the floor. No one helped him up. The groups drew together in little clusters.

"So the murders started. And around the same time, a mine syndicate formed. Crime follows crime like flies follow shit. I happen to know the former procurator of Britannia, the man who awards mine contracts, and he was the biggest pile of shit of them all.

"You see, a lead mine turned into a silver mine, and when the vein was found, the miner wasn't. He became the ghost. The syndicate wanted to make sure Rome wouldn't hold her hand out and ask for more, and they needed a place to dump the lead and hide the silver and wash it until it was good and clean. They chose Aquae Sulis.

"They planted a figurehead on the council. That would be you, Grattius. Yet their real representative would stay behind the scenes, directing the drama. That would be Materna."

Secundus was chewing something, his eyes glossy, not really looking ahead. His daughter's face was red and sullen.

"Everybody agreed to play blind. The lead was dumped over by the other spring, and the curse-writers picked it clean like so many vultures. The silver passed through hands and workshops, and some of it fell into your pockets. The syndicate promised to build a temple, for you, Philo"—he nodded, his face pale—"and build a bath, for you, Papirius."

The priest turned his cold eyes in my direction, looking at me as though everything I said were supremely unimportant.

"You're the leaders of the town, one and all. You closed your eyes, and opened your palms, and you let it happen. In that sense, ladies and gentlemen . . . you're all guilty."

"We didn't all kill Bibax, Favonianus." The priest's voice was icy. "I was under the impression that we were here to find out who did—not to be lectured like a pack of naughty schoolboys." He looked around the room to the accompaniment of several murmurs.

My smile was enough to shut them up. "Very true, Papirius. You didn't all kill him. One of you did. I'll sort out the crimes for you, since some of you may not be able to count that high. One—the crimes of murder and blackmail. Committed by Bibax and an unknown partner."

Vitellius leaned forward and licked his lips, his balding head glistening with sweat.

"Crime two. Bibax and his partner were employed by Materna—to get rid of Aufidio, and any other minor problems for the mine. Materna knew every dirty secret in Aquae Sulis and made them all that much dirtier. She used people, that's how she got her kicks. She used Faro, who helped spread rumors about the haunted mine.

"Dewi was probably a test case. She suspected how it worked but wanted to make sure. So she cursed the boy, and when Bibax tried to blackmail her, he finally found something more foul and rotten than himself. Materna was a hulking mass of envy and hate. Power was her desire, and cruelty was her lover, and Aquae Sulis gave her both. For a time."

I stared at Secundus. "I don't think there's a person in this room who isn't glad she's dead."

He held his daughter and looked through the wall. I wondered what he saw.

"Materna was at the crux of every crime in this city—until *Ultor*. He's crime three. Somebody killed Bibax. Was it his partner? Or someone else? Someone they were blackmailing, perhaps?"

My eyes lingered on Sestius. His mouth was open, froth on his lips.

"I was asked to solve Bibax's murder, and do it in a hurry. Then Calpurnius was killed. He tried to join the murder team, the oldest business in the world. Still killed by *Ultor*—still crime three.

"Faro was next. Materna ordered him murdered. Seems her cock wouldn't crow for her. She ate him instead."

Secunda began to make noise. Her father hushed her, held her tight. She struggled. It was too late for that.

"The person who helped her was Bibax's old partner. Remember him? Doomed to be used, to be blackmailed?

"She tried to frame me for Faro's murder, stupidly, in a hurry. Then the mine pulled out, and we were next on the murder list. My wife and I. Instead of killing us, though, Bibax's partner decided to get rid of Materna. To free himself. From a long history of bowing and scraping, always playing the master but living the life of a slave. First to Bibax, then to Materna, but always—always to . . . Papirius."

I looked at him. "Isn't that right, Octavio?" I asked. My voice was gentle.

Prunella needed a drink. Badly. Her hands shook as she held on to his arm. "What—what does he mean?"

"You needed money. You're a gambler. It's a disease with you, and it's eaten away your life like a leper's face. You sold land to Philo—for cheap, because you needed the money. But he won't buy more. The mine's gone. You were an orderly and knew enough about medicine and drugs to help Bibax. Above all, you had access. Access to the baths."

He took a step toward me, but Ligur and Draco blocked his way. He looked from side to side, trapped.

"You could blackmail people here. Leave notes. Listen to conversations while you scurried through the walls like a rat. I don't know what Bibax remembered about you—maybe you embezzled some money, maybe you murdered a man—but he used you, didn't he? Used you to murder."

Prunella collapsed in a heap on the floor, crying and hanging on to his legs. He stared at me, looking straight ahead. Papirius drew away from him.

I said softly: "You killed them all, Octavio. You and your greed, your hate, your desire for power. Materna recognized it. She smelled it, rooted it out. She used it—and you—like everybody did. So you killed her."

Ligur and Draco stepped behind and around Prunella and held his arms. Papirius looked at me. I nodded. He motioned with his hand, and slaves appeared from the other room. They took Octavio from my men. Still he said nothing.

"Arcturus—Arcturus—are you sure . . ." Philo sounded worried.

"Yeah, Philo. I'm sure."

Papirius led Octavio away. Prunella screamed, throwing herself in front of them, and Draco helped pick her up. We all watched as if it were a play. Which, in a sense, it was.

Footsteps echoed on the stone, and we could hear the creak of the big door shut behind them. Voices erupted, and some—like Grattius and Sestius—took the opportunity to drift away.

Secundus and Secunda sniped and quarreled, voices filled with bitterness. They finally left, the daughter casting one more baleful look over her shoulder at me, before she gathered her mantle around her and glided out of the room.

It was about the sixth hour of night. The warm human bodies left the bath, and cold took their place, curling up against the yellow stone. I listened again to the lap of the water.

Sulpicia and Vitellius walked ahead slowly. Drusius kept behind them, sulking. As they crossed the opening—the window where she'd thrown her bracelet—she looked up. Her voice rose, panic in it, filling the room.

"What—what's that—do you see it, Vitellius? That white thing . . ."

Drusius and Philo rushed to the window. The figure of a woman hovered over the spring. As white and cold as a good death. The mouth opened, and a sound came out.

"Philo . . . Philo . . ."

His hand crept up to his face. "Oh—my—God—"

"Philo—why? Why did you—did you make me—"

Tears welled and ran down his fine-boned face. He leaned as far as he could through the window, the others backing away. Stretched his long, dexterous fingers toward the vision.

"It was for you, Fulviana—the temple—don't you see—it was for you—"

His back arched suddenly, as stiff as if he were already dead. He turned around, light burning behind his eyes.

"You see her—don't you? You see her, Arcturus? You understand. The temple. I could make it up to her. I—I waited, all these years, until I could start over, and I found Aquae Sulis, and I was happy. Until . . . until Bibax came."

He turned his head to look again, to make sure she was still there. She said nothing to him, but her gown was still billowing on the wind. A gust blew in from the spring where she hovered, floating.

He looked again at me, excitement contorting his face. "But I found a way to make it better. He remembered me—from Hispania. But the money—I could get money, and build the temple—for her. I only agreed on sick people. Or old people. The boy—he was better off. And I could build it, Arcturus, and she would come to me—and she has—don't you see? Don't you understand?"

He turned back to the vision, but it wasn't there anymore. He swung his head in a panic.

"I understand, Philo."

"But where is she—she isn't there—where . . ."

Then the horror of it hit him, and hit him hard enough to make him crumple, and his long, lean body folded like a lady's fan. There was nothing left in Philo. The delusion, the hope, the guilt, the love, the hate. All gone.

Papirius came out of one of the other rooms with Octavio. They looked at him. He was still kneeling on the floor.

He raised his face to mine. "Where's Gwyna?" He asked it with tenderness.

"She was—she was outside, Philo."

He nodded, his fingers playing with a ring he always wore. Papirius and Octavio didn't know what to do. I heard light steps and looked up to see my wife, a gray mantle covering the filmy white gown. She was staring at Philo, her eyes full of tears.

He sensed her before he heard her. A smile lit his features again.

"Fulviana," he said softly.

She held a hand out to him. He took it and stood up.

"You have to go with Papirius and Octavio, Philo."

"Yes, my love. You'll be with me?"

She looked at me. I nodded. Then she stared into Philo's eyes. "I'll be with you, Philo."

He nodded, and almost looked like himself—but the eyes weren't the same.

For a moment, he seemed to see Gwyna as she really was. He looked at Papirius, whose face was longer and graver than usual. Draco and Ligur were waiting in the background, but he wouldn't run. Not Philo. Not even this Philo.

Then he looked at me, and his forehead creased with recognition. He reached out a hand, touching her green necklace. He gave Gwyna a smile—a smile of triumph, even of happiness. A smile of love.

Then he twisted the top of his ring and shoved it in his mouth. He was dead in less than half an hour.

CHAPTER TWENTY-NINE

Even in death the bastard craved drama. Trust Philo. Always playing god, down to the end.

"He justified everything in order to build that temple. He bought most of the property down there to make it happen. That's what made me suspect him. He'd lied about not knowing where Bibax lived, because he owned the property."

"Did he really—really kill everyone?"

We were at home, no sleep possible.

"Bibax probably killed Aufidio by himself. Philo—at first, anyway—only agreed to kill people who were already sick or old or infirm. You remember what he said at dinner? He told himself they were better off—that he was helping them."

"You mean like Sestius's aunt?"

"Exactly. No one thought she was sick. Sestius made a comment about it—said she was more ill than anyone knew. A woman like that would always go to the top doctor in town. Who was Philo."

She folded her hands in her lap and stared at them. "Ardur—do you think Philo wanted you to find out?"

I shrugged. "Maybe. He lied about the *strychnos*, pretended not to be sure about Materna's symptoms. He knew the drug—it's used in temples like his Endovelicus all the time. The worshipper eats a little and thinks she sees the god. Maybe he wanted to be caught, wanted it to be over. I know he didn't want to kill us. Or at least you."

"So he killed Materna instead." She shivered. "How he must have hated her."

"The slap that day was real. She took over Bibax's role—and made him pound nails into Faro's skull. And he was protective of you. Wanted you."

"Because I looked like Fulviana."

"Not only that, Gwyna. I think Philo loved you for yourself." She leaned over and kissed my lips. It had been difficult to say. "He could never kill you. Or see you suffer. I think that's why he tried to help me. If he had more time, of course, he might've convinced himself you'd be happier with him. Then he could've gotten me out of the way. Materna hated you, and was cruel to you, and that made him hate her all the more. That's why he made her suffer."

"What did Bibax remember, to get him involved in the first place? He must have blackmailed Philo with something."

I hesitated. "I think something to do with Fulviana."

"But he loved her!"

"And was responsible for her death."

She shook her head. "I don't understand it. What about the young girl? The one that met Faro?"

I scratched my chin. "I'm glad you were the only one who remembered that. I left it out with Octavio. Philo's servant girl."

"I remember. Were they lovers?"

"Probably. He was a man, after all."

She squeezed my hand. "So the girl picked up and delivered things—"

"When he needed her to. She doesn't know anything. I'm sure he never confided in anyone—he was too smart—and what I said about the baths, when Octavio was playing his part—that could really apply to anyone in town. Everyone goes there, every day. Access wasn't a problem."

Her brow wrinkled. "Ardur—"

"Yes, my love?"

"I don't understand why he signed those sheets *'Ultor.'* Because he hated Bibax? It doesn't make sense."

It was almost the first hour of morning. I said it slowly.

"Because he didn't kill Bibax. Or Calpurnius."

"What? Who—"

"Fulviana—the woman he loved—the woman he said he couldn't save, when she became pregnant—"

"What about her?"

"She was another man's wife."

The light was rising over the hills, casting a pale pink light on the yellow soil. The shop was closed. Dust covered the counter.

I tapped on the door; nobody answered. I thought we'd try the spring.

We found him there, leaning against the side of a rail, using it to support his frail body. He was holding a pouch of cut and inscribed gemstones, pouring them one at a time into his hand. I recognized them. His best work, the ones he was saving for the future.

I asked him: "Where's Buteo?"

He turned away from the water. Aquae Sulis was beginning to wake, the sounds of roosters cackling and open doors banging, echoing through the streets. We didn't have much time.

Natta kept his back to the railing, his hand, misshapen from years of work, clutching the pouch. He didn't answer. He looked at Gwyna.

"You brought your beautiful lady, Arcturus? So beautiful. You like the necklace? And the ring?"

She was still wearing them from last night, and her hands drew up to feel the glass between her fingers. He smiled.

"They were hers. Now they are yours. You look—you look very much like her."

"Natta . . . where's Buteo?"

The gems rattled in the pouch as his hands shook. "Where you cannot touch him. Where no one can touch him. It was time."

"But Philo is dead! I told you yesterday I would—I would take care of everything. Why did you—"

"Because it is my right . . . and because—because, my young friend—it is difficult to stop. Once you have tasted it—tasted the power—it is hard to end it, and Buteo became a part of it. Part of the curse, the *homo maledictus* you have been looking for. So I gave him something—something to help him sleep."

He looked at Gwyna. "But your lady does not understand us. Let me try."

I nodded. He fixed his brown eyes on hers.

"Once, lady—a long time ago—there was a woman. A woman who looked—who looked much like you. Her family married her to a man, not so poor, not so rich—but . . . ambitious. Yes. He was ambitious, once.

"The lady desired children. But after one year, she was not with child. And she grew impatient, and thought perhaps a god could help her.

"So she went to the temple. The god there promised many things and many children. But the priest—the priest told her she must stay the night, and the god will come to her. If she prays hard enough, the god will give her a child himself."

He lowered his head and plucked at the pouch in his hand. "The priest was an age-mate of her husband's. A man who saw her once, and—and fell in love. That night—only Endovelicus knows who came to her. The god—or the priest—or both."

He brooded for a moment, his mind a thousand miles away and forty years in the past. Then he looked at Gwyna again. And smiled.

"They did not lie. The woman became pregnant. And—and visited the temple often. But there were problems. It was not easy for her. And when it was time for the birth, her husband was away. So she went to the priest, who was a doctor, too, as all priests of Endovelicus are. He tried to save her and the baby. He could not."

Tears rolled down Gwyna's cheek. Natta looked away from her and turned to face the waters again.

"Some said it was the priest's child in the woman, and he was shamed. And when she died . . . some said he killed her, before the truth could come out, a baby born who looked like him. He was thrown out from the temple, left Hispania in disgrace.

"He thought the baby died with its mother. But the midwife delivered it, slapped it harder, and it began to breathe. A baby boy. The midwife gave it to the woman's husband and helped him raise the child, until she, too, passed away."

He brought the pouch out and held it in front of him, staring past it to the bubbling water.

"The boy learned the story from his father when he was old enough. They left Hispania and traveled, moving from one town to the next, and one day they came to a certain place. There, in the town, was the priest—the priest who long ago had loved the boy's mother and left the child to die. And the boy—who was now a man—became enraged.

"The priest was now a doctor. And the man wanted revenge on this priest who had wronged his father, who had killed his mother. So he followed him—watched him—saw what he did. Sometimes in the name of mercy, sometimes for money. Always for reputation. A temple, the priest wanted. Another temple.

"The man saw the evil and thought he could rid the town of it. First one, then the other. Ending with the priest. Hydra heads, he called them. Hydra heads. But they poisoned him. Poisoned my Buteo."

Gwyna took a step closer to him. The pouch made a small splash, the brown leather bobbing against the blue and green, drawing the sacred water in like breath. Becoming sodden and heavy and finally drifting, waving, falling to the bottom.

Natta whispered, facing the spring.

"These stones—our future—belong to the goddess. I will follow Buteo. But do not weep, lady. I will see her again. I have waited long enough."

The spring churned and made little waves against the stone. A few people stood, some staring at the water. Some threw in a wooden carving or a small silver piece. I held on to Gwyna. Natta drew himself up from the rail and limped away, his faded robe trailing in the pale dust.

It was difficult to say good-bye after all. The slaves were still talking about the curse and how I broke it, and about the night we formed a small army and defeated Hannibal at the gates. Draco was coming back with us, a free man in more ways than one.

The donkey was healing well but couldn't work anymore, and no one else was willing to pay for her feed. I'd board her out with Nimbus and Pluto. Maybe it was time to start thinking about that farm I always wanted.

We looked around the villa again, thanked it for making us welcome, a safe house in an unsafe town. That was changing.

The market square was cleaner. You couldn't get *aconitum* quite as easily anymore, though the bottles of piss would always be big sellers. Grattius and Secundus disappeared, Grattius running from the legion, Secundus from ghosts more terrible than Rome. Papirius was still chief priest, but he would keep his nose cleaner and his hands out of the spring. Natta's jewels would go to the goddess, disappearing in the water and mud, waiting for a future he'd never see.

Gwyna fingered the necklace she was wearing when we rode by the closed *gemmarius* shop, the horses' hooves clomping on the paving stone.

A breeze blew against our backs, a warm spell that came out of nowhere, but maybe down from the green hills that ringed Aquae Sulis like a crown. It was dawn, the first hour of day, and the spring, as it had been when we met the old man, was empty. Draco waited for us up the hill.

She took the mask Papirius had given her and held it between her fingers. The splash of water rose like a little fountain. Together we watched the tin sink, the water washing over the face like a drowning man's. When it was gone, she shuddered. I held her.

We climbed out of the valley until we were on the hill. Draco was ahead, holding the donkey. A pale sun shone on Aquae Sulis, and the stone was cleaner than it had been in a long time.

We reined in the horses and looked back. By the spring, facing us, was a group of people. I couldn't make out their faces—one of them looked like the old lady who told me about Bibax. There was another old woman, a younger man, and a boy. Other figures crowded behind them. To the side of the water, by himself, was another man—dressed in the garb of a priest.

The old lady saw us, raised a hand. I looked at Gwyna. She was staring straight ahead, rigid. I raised my hand above my head. One by one, they seemed to dissolve in the dawn and the mist from the spring, until only a flicker of sun on yellow stone was shining from the waters of Sulis.

It was time to go home.